GOOD VIBRATIONS

I looked up at Brig in the dim light of the tunnel-like entrance. "How are we supposed to hide down here? Won't he see us in about ten seconds?"

Brig motioned toward the couples leaning up against every available space of the walls in this hallway. Every one of them was busily engaged in what I'd term serious making out.

Brig pulled me close. He found the darkest part of the entranceway. He leaned down and hid me from the opening with his whole body. A body that now pressed against mine with a firmness sending vibrations far different than fear throughout my whole being.

The man could kiss.

BOOK YOUR PLACE ON OUR WEBSITE AND MAKE THE READING CONNECTION!

We've created a customized website just for our very special readers, where you can get the inside scoop on everything that's going on with Zebra, Pinnacle and Kensington books.

When you come online, you'll have the exciting opportunity to:

- View covers of upcoming books
- Read sample chapters
- Learn about our future publishing schedule (listed by publication month *and author*)
- Find out when your favorite authors will be visiting a city near you
- Search for and order backlist books from our online catalog
- Check out author bios and background information
- Send e-mail to your favorite authors
- Meet the Kensington staff online
- Join us in weekly chats with authors, readers and other guests
- Get writing guidelines
- AND MUCH MORE!

**Visit our website at
http://www.kensingtonbooks.com**

Hot Stuff

Flo Fitzpatrick

ZEBRA BOOKS
Kensington Publishing Corp.
www.kensingtonbooks.com

ZEBRA BOOKS are published by

Kensington Publishing Corp.
850 Third Avenue
New York, NY 10022

All Kensington titles, imprints and distributed lines are available at special quantity discounts for bulk purchases for sales promotion, premiums, fund-raising, educational or institutional use.

Special book excerpts or customized printings can also be created to fit specific needs. For details, write or phone the office of the Kensington Special Sales Manager: Kensington Publishing Corp., 850 Third Avenue, New York, NY 10022. Attn. Special Sales Department. Phone: 1-800-221-2647.

Zebra and the Z logo Reg. U.S. Pat. & TM Off.

First Printing: April 2005
10 9 8 7 6 5 4 3 2 1

Printed in the United States of America

In loving memory of Karl Fischer Wendorf,
July 21, 1984–July 17, 2004.

Chapter 1

"Your pineapple soda, miss. Would you be wanting ice? Americans visiting Bombay seem to like ice."

I barely heard him. My focus was on the far corner of Hot Harry's Saloon and the man whose presence filled that spot. "Thanks. Um, say, do you know the Strider wannabe in the back? In the hood. Sitting under the poster for *Pirate Princess*. He's staring at us."

The waiter squinted. He seemed puzzled. "Stri-der? I do not know this word. Like stride, yes? A person who walks very fast?"

I smiled. "I'm sorry. I've seen *Lord of the Rings* a few too many times. I forget that not everyone is a film buff. Strider's one of the main characters."

"Oh. Yes. Of course." He smiled. "But I do not think this striding man is staring at me wanting a refill. I think it is *you*. Most understandable." His smile grew wider. "Striders in movies. I love Americans. Cinema junkies. But we also have much this interest in Bombay. We are home to Bollywood. *Pirate Princess* was a Bollywood film. I have seen it one hundred times. You will visit?"

I nodded. I'd already jotted that particular site down on my to-do list.

The waiter had pegged it. Cinema junkie. I spent my childhood attending Broadway shows and cinematic extravaganzas when I wasn't taking acting, dance, gymnastic, or voice lessons. Mom dreamed that she'd see my name, Tempe Walsh, above a marquee one day. Theater or film—she didn't really care which.

By age three I was reciting Bogart's "hill of beans" speech from *Casablanca* and organizing my preschool classmates into Sharks and Jets for the opening dance in *West Side Story*.

It seems logical then, given my upbringing, to assume I was currently soaking up the ambience of this bar in Bombay waiting to shoot a film. Doubtless one in which I played a starring role. Logical? Yes. But wrong.

Ironically, I was in India this week because many years ago, on the day I turned four, if one wants to be precise, my father found me reciting Bogart's "beans" speech in Russian to the doorman. My father declared that he had sired a linguistic genius, then decreed I would earn a real living in a career far removed from theater.

I became an interpreter. An occupation that consisted primarily of translating whatever to English, and English to whatever for whomevers like my current boss, Ray Decore, the man sitting opposite me.

"Tempe? What's with cozying up to the waiter? Trying to make me jealous?"

I frowned, then shoved the bourbon and Coke that Ray Decore had ordered for me back across the table for the third time in less than two minutes.

"Cozy? Discussing movies? Mr. Decore, let's get something straight here. You hired me to translate Hindi to English so that you don't get swindled in the middle of buying some crazy statue. Might I remind you that this job does *not* include extracurricular activities with the interpreter."

"Damn! Lighten up, Tempe. We're in Bombay for an entire week. This transaction shouldn't take more than thirty minutes, after which we can leave this stinking cesspool of a bar and head over to a nightclub that caters to tourists who believe in clean. Now, tomorrow night, and subsequent nights, I'd prefer spending with you alone."

"Forget it. Not interested. I'm here to complete this deal for you, although I still don't understand why you need a linguist. Most folks in India speak English quite well."

"But Himali Khan does not, and since he's selling and I'm buying, I'd like to be in a position where I'm not swindled."

"Fine. So you've stated. I'm not sure I believe it, but I'm getting a free trip to Bombay, so I'm not going to argue the point. But once the negotiations are complete? Well, I have places to see. Alone."

I took a sip of my pineapple soda.

"Wanna hear my plans?"

I did not wait for a response. "Good. First, no matter what, I'm going to the Ganesh festival. Do you know, on the last day of the festival, they throw the elephants into the bay? Well, not the real elephants; I mean, that would be cruel."

Ray opened his mouth to interrupt.

I chattered on. "Then again, maybe the elephants wouldn't mind. After all, it would cool them off. Where was I? Oh. I'm talking about the statues of the elephants. Big ones, little ones, plaster of paris, bronze, recyclable, not. You name it, they're dunked in the drink."

Rays eyes glazed over.

"Tempe? Watching a bunch of fake elephants getting tipped into water is not my idea of entertainment. Yeah, right, we're here to clinch a very big deal, but why not have some real fun while we're at it? We're thousands of miles from New York. Who's to know? Who's to care?"

He leered at me. I rebuttoned the top button of my suit before responding.

"*I* care. And believe me, I'm planning lots of fun stuff. Like hitting Kemps Corner and spending next month's rent in a mad shopping spree buying trendy, outrageous clothes."

Ray started to say something. I ignored him, lost in my dream itinerary.

"I'm gonna take snapshots of the Flora Fountain, which is a starting point for protest marches and great speechifying. Then I'm trotting by the National Park and communing with tigers and llamas and cobras and whatever other cute little pets wander around unattended."

"Spare me. Fountains? Cute little pets?"

I held up my hand. "Wait, wait! My big dream is to visit Film City, also know as the famous Bollywood, and watch a Masala movie being shot. And I'm serious about seeing the Ganesh parade. I want to get my picture taken standing next to a real live elephant. I love elephants. The first movie I ever saw was *Dumbo*. Anyway, I'm going to be the ultimate tourist and do ultimate touristy things."

Ray lifted his bottle of Rajit beer, took a swig, swallowed, then scowled. "I don't give a damn about tourist spots. I was thinking more of the one-on-one kind of attractions. Perhaps back at the Taj Hotel where my suite has the most marvelous jet bath. And the minibar is well stocked. If you get my drift."

"Guess what? My room has a Jacuzzi, too. I have plans for a good soak. Alone. And it seems obvious to me, sir, that you do *indeed* require a translator, because you damn sure have problems in communicating."

I sat back and watched as three men approached the tiny table where I continued my attempts to keep Ray's knees from pressing mine and ignore his less-than-subtle attempts at flirtation.

I'd met one of these men about twenty minutes ago. Mr. Himali Khan was a buyer and seller of precious objects. He was also the reason Ray Decore needed an interpreter. Khan now took a seat opposite me and stared at the top button of my suit for a moment. Then he gestured to a man wearing a crisp, starched white shirt and tailored black slacks who bowed, kissed my hand, then murmured something in a language I identified as Gujarati.

Mr. Starched Shirt offered me a cigarette.

I said, "No, thank you" in Gujarati.

The man's eyebrows lifted a hair as he responded, "You have a decent accent, miss. Where did you learn both Hindi and Gujarati?"

"Louie's Lingo. It's linguistics software. Um. A computer program. You load in the language of choice and a day later you're fluent." I smiled. "Assuming you have an aptitude for the subject, which I do. I'd heard Gujarati was still used for business dealings here in Mumbai—or do you prefer Bombay?"

He shrugged. "Either is fine."

"Well, anyway, I learned as much Gujarati as I could, along with Hindi. So, do you work with Mr. Kahn?"

His eyebrow lifted. The short, scarred, bald man behind him snorted, pulled out a cigar, tossed it onto the table, muttered something in a dialect unknown to me and not covered in Louie's Lingo, then whirled around and headed back to his own table. I shivered.

"Did I just witness a new Indian rite of welcoming Americans?" I asked, this time in English.

A slight flush added a hint of red to the light brown skin. He answered in precise, clean, unaccented English.

"I apologize. Mr. Patel is a rude man. He is showing his displeasure at having a woman here in the saloon and at your assumption that we work with Mr. Khan. We do not. Mr. Patel commented on your red hair. It was not a nice remark. He should not be allowed in the company of polite society."

He bowed again, then walked in silence back to a table several feet away from this Mr. Patel. I tapped Mr. Khan's shoulder, then asked, in Hindi, how he knew the men who'd just greeted Ray and me in diverse fashions.

He grinned, showing several gaps where teeth should have been placed. "Buyers. Rich buyers for my collection. You do not want to be talking to them. And you don't need to be speaking to them since you are here to be talking to me."

Khan stood, nodded to Ray, who looked upset that Khan and I were conversing in Hindi, then walked over to the bar counter.

I'm not a big drinker, but I've been in more than one pub in Manhattan since I hit legal age eight years ago. Hot Harry's Saloon seemed no different than most of the bars that line Eighth Avenue near the Theater District. Smaller and a bit dirtier, perhaps, with posters featuring Masala movies tacked on the walls and foreign-sounding names advertising various liquors, but when one came right down to it, it was a bar.

I blinked, then blushed, when I saw the ancient, lopsided poster of Miss April 1982 taped onto the broken mirror. I'd never seen a picture like *that* on Eighth Avenue or anywhere else in the city. I quickly averted my gaze from the negligently clad model.

Next up in my viewing area was the countertop that held bottles of beer, hard liquor, and wine. To the right of the bar stood vending machines. Two of them catered to nicotine addicts and did not interest me, but the tiny machine between them must have been designed for carboholics. I spotted assorted American brands of chocolate bars and pretzels and potato chips. Plus those little sandwiches with the cheese crackers filled with peanut butter.

I had no idea when this transaction would be finished, and I hadn't had much lunch. I brightened and started to rise to check out the selections. The fact that the dark-hooded Strider sat at a table only about three feet from the vending machines did not enter into my decision. Or so I told myself.

Ray grabbed my arm. His tone shifted to all business. "Not the time to go wandering, Tempe. You're on in about two seconds. Now listen well, neogiate better, and earn your pay."

Khan had returned from the bar with two bottles of beer. I guess since soda, not booze, was my drink of choice, I didn't rate a refill. Khan set the bottles on the table, popped the tops, then pushed one toward Ray. It appeared he was ready to begin final negotiations.

Khan set a price in rupees.

I turned to Ray. "If the rate of exchange is what it was this morning, Mr. Khan has just asked for a million five." My eyes opened wider. "Wow! That's one damn high price."

"It's fair, Tempe. Don't worry about it. But tell Khan I do need to see the statue."

I shrugged. It was Ray's money to spend as he wished. I turned back to Khan and asked, in Hindi, if he could show Ray the piece. Khan flashed his semitoothless grin at me, then reached into the filthy backpack he'd set next to his chair. He rummaged for about four seconds, then lifted out something wrapped in a dirty T-shirt that had what appeared to be Miss April's younger sister silk-screened on the front. Miss June? Who was definitely busting out all over.

Khan brushed the half-filled bottles off the table onto the floor, dropped Miss June over them, then set a small ivory figurine on the table. I stood and leaned in to get a better look.

"Wow! Is that it? The statue? That is so cool. But why is the lute upside down? That seems odd. Hey, Ray, is this a fake?"

I heard a scream come from the middle table of Hot Harry's. Mr. Patel. The door to the bar burst open, and at least a dozen men ran inside hollering epithets in languages I did not understand. My employer also began to spit out epithets—in a language I *did* know quite well and with words I hear far too often on the subway in Manhattan.

"You bastard! You stinkin' lousy (bleep, bleep) cheat!" yelled Ray.

"*Su-ar!*" yelled the snorting man.

Starched Shirt yelled something in Gujarati.

"*Cluipear!*" yelled the dark-haired Strider sitting in a shadowed corner by the vending machines.

Wait. Back it up just a minute there. I'd heard Ray call Himali Khan a "lousy cheat," plus a few other choice words less polite. Fine. Got it. Then the bald-headed Indian with the cigars had spat out "pig" in Hindi.

But *Cluipear*? It's Gaelic. It took me a second or two, but then I remembered it meant "deceiver." Mr. Tall Dark Striding Stranger was shouting in the language of ancient Ireland in Hot Harry's Saloon in Bombay, India. But I had no time to ponder this paradox because the bar now resembled one of the more violent scenes from *Gunfight at the O.K. Corral*.

Chapter 2

The first bullet decapitated the silver sail from my boat-shaped earring. A second or third could capsize the entire craft. I screamed, leapt up, then dove for the closest empty area of floor. Which landed me next to the vending machine. I heard a ripping sound and glanced down at what had been my skirt.

My left leg was now exposed to midthigh. I ignored it in favor of eyeing the goodies above me. I could see Butterfingers and Baby Ruths. Snickers. Snyder's pretzels. A bag of peanuts was stuck in the drop slot. I paused for one insane second and wondered if I could ooch it out. A knife shattered the glass over the Milky Ways. So much for my snack. And my hiding place.

I rolled myself into a tight ball and somersaulted away from a smashed bag of Skittles, then executed a damn near perfect front handspring to propel myself onto the purple bar counter-top. Miss April 1982 smiled at me. I shuddered.

A low-hanging chandelier beckoned. I grabbed it and swung myself toward the red and gold beaded curtain in the back of the tavern. I crashed through, rolled, then ended up behind several barrels of Rajit beer. There was a crack between two of the barrels. I wedged myself inside, then cautiously began patting various body parts to make sure none were missing.

Instead of losing a limb, I seemed to have gained one. An extra arm extended from my right side. I opened my mouth to scream and a hand clamped over my lips.

"*Éist do bhéal!*"

"*Éist do bhéal?*"

That first bullet must have killed me after all. I lay crouched behind barrels in a saloon in Bombay, yet I'd just heard someone say "shut up"—in Gaelic. I'd been right about hearing the word "deceiver" shouted only moments ago.

I was dead. Hungry and dead and bruised, and I'd landed in St. Patrick's Gift Shop in heaven where the stock boys spoke Gaelic.

The soft voice whispered again. "Quiet, lass! The hooligans are as yet unaware that we've chosen this as our small hidey-hole. 'Tis a nice idea to keep our presence a bit of a secret for a while. I'm not ready for one or both of us to be takin' part in their riot."

Enough light seeped through a crack in the closed window to allow me a glimpse of the bright blue eyes staring at me. A scent of curry mixed with chocolate filled my nostrils. It emanated from at least two of the fingers resting over my mouth.

I yanked the hand away and spat, "Don't tell me what to do, laddie! I have no intention of yelling. Not yet anyway. Give me a moment to catch my breath, and I'm sure I can add to the general noise by screaming my lungs out."

I took that breath, then added, "By the way, what's with the brogue? And the Gaelic?"

I could see a head bobbing. Just a shadow in the dim light.

"Good. That's good. You're reasonin' and not reactin'. Very good. Because if you were shriekin' like a normal lass, there's a bit of a possibility two young lives would be cut short very soon. The tall one in the overly starched shirt would feel no pain if he was arrangin' funeral pyres for other than grievin' widows. And the ugly bald one with the scars makes t'other look like a choirmaster. No ethics a'tall, that one. Murder. It's in his blood."

The hand left my face and rested on my middle. I removed it none too gently.

"Who the hell are you? And who are those guys?" I groaned, then buried my face in my hands. "I can't believe I just said that. *Butch Cassidy* was on a cable channel two nights ago. Obviously I followed the dialogue too closely when Butch and Sundance kept asking that question."

Teeth flashed in the dark.

" 'Tis all right. You're not expected to be brilliant in near-death situations."

"Oh geez. This qualifies as one, doesn't it?" I took a quick breath. "Wait. I can't think about that or I *will* start howling. So instead, I repeat. Who are those guys?"

A cheerful voice responded. "Didden ya get introductions from yer man in there?"

"Yes and no. I got a name or two, but I wasn't really paying attention."

"No? We'el, lass. Those guys could be Mahindra's thugs. Or Rashee's boys. Could be Himali Khan, the slimy seller. Where was I? Ah. Patel's goons. Take your pick. A bunch of evil-minded miscreants who are all equal-opportunity felons and all equally eager to make off with Shiva's Diva. As are we, now, right? I've been about includin' ya in the bidders, although now that I'm chattin' with ya, I'm not so sure you're part of this auction of thieves."

I couldn't speak. I wasn't certain I wanted to. Or would get a chance to, the way the garrulous Irishman kept rattling on.

The top portion of the crop of curly black hair across the forehead nodded again, then a soft finger fell across my lips. A scent of curry filled my nostrils. His rich voice softened and the heavy brogue dropped to nearly nonexistent.

"Why don't we find safer climes and discuss this without fear of bullets ripping into delicate areas of our respective anatomies?" He grinned. "I'd like to keep my own delicate areas for more pleasurable pursuits. I'm sure ya feel the same?"

My voice came back. I aimed for defiant. What croaked out sounded scared.

"I'm in favor of keeping my anatomy and my pleasurable pursuits private, thank you. But I agree. I want out of here. Now."

He nodded. " 'Tis not a night for floatin' down the Back Bay of Bombay with holes in either of our delicate anatomical parts. Now then. I've a bit of a plan on exactly where and how we can make a discreet exit. Take a look."

He pointed to the window across the room. I nodded. I helped him roll an unbroken barrel under that window, then set it upright. Within thirty seconds, we had a leverage toward the filthy glass above. He sat, then stood on the barrel, testing its ability to hold his weight.

This gave me a better chance to look at my fellow escapee from the thugs and miscreants, be they Mahindra's, Khan's, or Patel's, all of whom just shot the fool out of Hot Harry's Saloon.

That dark hair topped a wiry body dressed in a garish Hawaiian-print shirt, blue jeans, and cowboy boots. The hooded sweatshirt was draped over one arm. He pushed back a shredded curtain and his face became visible in the moonlight shining through the window. A handsome face. Pointed nose, pouty mouth, blue eyes that matched his jeans. He looked about as dangerous as a sheepdog on the hunt for a chew toy.

I took the hand he extended to help me up onto the barrel and sent up more than one prayer that he had no connection to any of the shooters. Together we edged the window open. He raised his eyebrows to me in a silent question and I nodded. I put my hands on the sill and prepared to go through. I felt hands propel my bottom the rest of the way.

When we were well away from zinging bullets and the men shooting them, I planned to give this Irish charmer a few choice words about what body parts were off limits, even during escapes. But for now, I slid down to the ground, found a sturdy-looking pallet in the alleyway, shoved it under the window, grabbed his hand, and muttered, "Push through!"

"Ow!"

"Hush! I'm not pulling you that hard."

"It's not that. I just scraped my hand over a nasty nail on this dratted sill. My fingers are bleedin'. I haven't had shots for years. I'll probably be endin' up with lockjaw by the time this night is through. Have to stay silent the rest of my days."

He paused for a millisecond. "Hold on there while I'm thinkin' this over. Now, then. Did I get a tetanus vaccination along with the smallpox and the others? I wonder if that's on my passport. I'll be lookin' first thing when I'm in the light. Although I'm also rememberin' that particular document might not be on my person just now. No. 'Tis. I'm sure I brought it. I think it's in my sock."

The thought passed through my head that a dozen rusty nails couldn't keep him quiet, but I resisted voicing the opinion. I grabbed his wrists, then pulled so the talker could be through the window and out of the club before any thugs not otherwise engaged in shooting one another noticed our absence.

A few more muttered Gaelic curses accompanied the Irishman's descent. I won't repeat these particular gems in case my mother ever reads this, but I added them to my vast repertoire of colorful swear words spoken in obscure dialects. Although, the last one confused me. It sounded like "*máthair shúigh*," which means "squid." A Gaelic curse for turning killers into calamari?

We stared at each other. He was even better looking in the dim light of the alleyway. Not the hooded, cloaked Strider from *Lord of the Rings*. More like a matinee idol, circa 1940s. Errol Flynn in *Robin Hood*.

I, on the other hand, was no Maid Marian after whirling around on the floor of Hot Harry's Saloon. I was certain I more closely resembled one of the Merry Men's horses after a foray through Sherwood Forest. My nose dripped from inhaling then sneezing out the dust from Harry's floor. My hair had turned from cinnamon to salt with dashes of chili powder peeking through the dirt. My makeup did not exist anymore. Doubtless it now decorated the bottom of a Rajit beer barrel.

Robin Hood beamed at me.

" 'Twas a nice bit of flyin' and tossin' ya performed back there, lass. I counted two somersaults and at least one backflip. Are you a gymnast? You're rather tall for one if ya don't mind me sayin' so."

"College team. Four years running. Would have made the Olympic squad except for the height thing you so politely mentioned. And I don't seem to remember dodging bullets while performing balance beam routines any of those four years." I paused. "Or even when I did the tricks you love so well. Damn. This is not how I usually spend an evening."

"No? What do you do with your nights, lass?"

"I don't think that's really any of your business, now, is it?" Another smile blinded me.

"Perhaps not, but there's a wee bit of curiosity to be satisfied, nonetheless. 'Twould be sad to be thinkin' you're wastin' your nights with someone less charmin' than I."

I can translate words in more than ten languages. However, the ability to string together a sentence that might be keen enough to respond with some intelligence to this man had vanished. Even in English.

His smile changed to a frown. He leaned down and lightly touched my ear. I shivered. Not from cold.

He stated quietly and without the brogue, "You've been bleeding."

"What? Where?"

"All over. You've spatters on your collar. You may have been hit when that blighted excuse for a human being shot off your earbob."

I hadn't noticed any pain. I reached up and patted my ear. I didn't feel any holes. No earrings left, but no holes.

And then I knew. Raymond Decore, the man who'd hired me back in New York to handle what should have been a simple job of translations, hadn't been as lucky as his employee. The blood was his.

Chapter 3

"I need to sit down."

"Not now. Just listen. You've been doin' such a fine job of being stalwart and hardy and all that. Don't go faintin' on me before we're safe."

I glared at him. "I'm not going to faint. In case you haven't noticed, I'm lopsided. That is, I'm walking lopsided. The heel of my right shoe seems to be missing. So, sitting and hacking off the left heel should balance me. I need balance just now. And I promise I won't pass out on you until I'm far, far away from this alley, and you, and this whole dreadful place."

For once in our brief acquaintance, he stayed silent. He helped me to a stair stoop in the alley and even offered to help with the hacking process. He snapped the heel off with a quick twist of his wrist, then handed my shoe back to me.

I nodded. "Thanks."

He smiled. "Not a problem. Um, I do hate to be bringin' this up, but you're covered in blood, and I don't think we're in the safest spot in Bombay, so perhaps we need to, if you'll excuse the saying, haul butt?"

"I don't believe I've ever actually voiced those two words, but I agree with the sentiment. I want to be as far from Hot Harry's as possible. By the way"—my voice caught—"this isn't my blood. It's, it's . . ."

A gentle hand took mine. "I know. The man you came in with."

I nodded. "My boss. Sort of. I mean he hired me because my real boss recommended me as an interpreter. Raymond

Decore. That's the man in the bar. Not my real boss. His name is Jeremy Tucker. He's not going to believe Ray got shot."

I took a breath. "Slow down. Okay. Damn. This was supposed to be a simple transaction. No biggie. Go to this bar, finish up the deal to buy some stupid statue, wrap it up in a nice neat little box, and leave. What happened? Why did this turn into the St. Valentine's Day massacre?"

I turned to him and glared into his eyes. "And, no offense, but who the hell are you and how are you involved? I did meet a couple of those hooligans as you call them, but I thought they were just being friendly, coming over to welcome the Americans. I had no idea they'd be shooting at me, or I might have remembered their names."

A lilting laugh followed my questions.

"With any luck you'll not need to be facin' 'em again, so you needn't be carin' who they are. On the other hand, as to names you'll be wantin' to remember? Try mine. Briggan O'Brien, the smartest, handsomest, and most talented of the entire O'Brien clan. The other things you're asking are a mite more complicated to explain. I'll be glad to try, but let's see if we can find a better spot for exchanging confidences. Where's your hotel? And what's your name, lass?"

"Since you asked so nicely, it's Tempe."

He smiled. "Pretty, but a bit odd. What kind of a name is that? Like *tempus fugit?* Time and all that? Is it some kind of diminutive version? And why would your mother name you Time?"

I growled at him. "Tempe is a city in Arizona. Happens to be where I was born. If you don't like it, I'm sorry, but my mother didn't name me to please you. At least it wasn't in Snakeville or Hogpit or something equally classy in the Wild West."

Briggan held up his hands in mock terror. "I do like it. It's charming. Just unusual. So you're from Arizona?"

"No. I am from New York. My grandparents live in Arizona where my mom delightedly gave birth to me. I say, and emphasize, delighted because during that particular January, the city of Manhattan delivered nonstop blizzards as well as one Tempe Walsh. So I've heard. Satisfied?"

He nodded.

I sighed. "Can we try and leave this area now? Mr. O'Brien, my hotel is the Taj Mahal, and it's not exactly walking distance. Do you suppose a cab will pick up a couple of disreputable looking wrecks?"

He eyed me with a thoroughness that made me blush.

"Any cabby in the city would fair be givin' up a good tip just for the privilege of havin' such a lovely lass as yerself sittin' in his car. But . . ."

He seemed focused on my chest. I considered swatting him until he asked, "Are you wearing a blouse under that jacket? The collar and the top seem to be where most of the blood has, well, spattered. If you wouldn't mind tossing the jacket, I think we'd be a mite less noticeable."

I took off the navy blue jacket with more than some measure of relief. India. Ninety-plus degrees at night and humidity. I hadn't been comfortable in the suit even before the fireworks erupted. Now that it was drenched with the blood of my employer, I had no desire to keep it on. Or even keep it. I handed it to Mr. O'Brien, who stuffed it in the nearest trash can.

I glanced up at him. "Mind if I ask why we don't just head for a police station? Those guys were not out for a fun night. They need to be behind bars. And not the kind that sell booze."

Briggan shook his head.

"Not a wise move, darlin'. There's a foul stench of corruption from many of the officials here. I don't know who we can trust and who we can't."

And what makes me think I can trust you? Had I said it aloud? He stared at me with a coldness not yet exhibited throughout our escape from the storeroom.

But with his next words I realized he'd entered a world I had no knowledge of. A world thousands of miles away and a world that had seen more violence than Hot Harry's bar would ever play host to.

"Back in Dublin, the *garde* can be a force for real good or real evil. Some of the cops are ardent IRA supporters even now. And it's the same situation here. I suppose it's the same all over the world. But till we have certainty as to the separation of good from bad, we'd best stay on our own."

"And so your plan is?"

"To head to my hotel. The hoodlums don't know where I'm staying. I imagine they are aware of the place you've tossed your suitcases. Because of your boss, ya know. We'll be safer away from a place they can track."

"But Mr. O'Brien—"

"Brig. Please. Make it Brig. I don't think we should stand on ceremony after a life-threatening experience, do you? And don't be worryin' that I'll take advantage of you at the hotel. You've been through enough tonight. Me mum brought her boy up to be a gentleman."

He smiled. It was a very charming smile. He glanced at my leg, which was now exposed up to my thigh by the ripped skirt. He leaned a bit closer and whispered, "Which isn't to say, mind you, I won't be attemptin' a bit of he-in' and she-in' on some other, finer, occasion. With your permission, of course."

I had no words for any of this. I'd dived into a situation better suited for a live CIA operative, a Lara Croft or a leather-clad heroine from *The Matrix*. I make my living translating words. Most of the time I'm stationed behind a desk in an office. Leaping over, under, and through beer barrels while listening to the sound of gunfire over my head, then ending up with a man whose first language must be romance, hadn't been listed in my daily planner under "Jobs for Month of September."

Which reminded me.

"Mr. O'Brien. Brig. Stop. I think before either of us go anywhere else, somebody needs to sneak back into Hot Harry's and see if Ray is okay. I mean, I just left the man there facedown on the table. Bleeding. He could be badly hurt. Even dying."

Brig shot me a look. One of those are-you-daft looks. He then asked, "Are you daft?"

"Probably. Especially after tonight. I feel my brainpower seeping out of my head. But why do you ask?"

"Because Mahindra's thugs are doubtless still shootin' up the place. If Patel's goons haven't joined in and started shootin' back at him. Or knifing. Patel's fond of the blades. I don't think it's the safest place to be strollin' in askin' for the tab now, do you?"

I scowled. "And you think it's any safer for Ray Decore, who wasn't fast or agile enough to do the gymnastic routine I executed to end up in the storeroom with you? Or are you afraid I'll discover you're connected by your Gaelic lip and hip to one or more of those creeps?"

He bit his lip. Whether in shame or in laughter I wasn't sure.

"All right then, Miss Tempe Walsh. We'll head in by way of the side door leading directly to the bar counter. We can creep low, then stay underneath Miss April and peer through the holes the bullets made in the bar."

I might have known he'd noticed Miss April. I almost missed his next words, thinking that Miss April, plastered lifeless on paper, doubtless had noticed him too. "But I'm telling you, Tempe, if I hear so much as a mouse moving inside, we're gone. Understood?"

I nodded, pleased that Brig O'Brien had enough kindness in him to help a man he didn't know because a lady he'd just met had asked for his aid.

We walked in silence back to Hot Harry's. All quiet on the saloon front. All quiet on the saloon back. Not a twitter from the saloon side door. Brig opened it about two inches, then peeked inside.

"Looks deserted. This is strange. Your boss is nowhere to be found. But the good news is I don't see anyone else around either, including Hot Harry, if such a man exists."

He inhaled then blew out his breath with a whoosh. "Wait! Oh heavenly Saint Bridget!"

"What? What's wrong?"

"It's still there! Under the table where you were sitting. Just a bare glimpse peeking out from underneath a bag. Must be yours? The bag."

"It's mine, unless you're talking about that filthy backpack thing Khan had. I know Ray carries a briefcase. I have this cool tote I got in Mexico City. Wait. What's under my bag? Ray?"

"They didn't find it! Saint Cecilia be praised."

"What? Briggan! Will you just shut up and tell me?"

He winked at me. "I can't be doin' both, darlin'. What's inside there is the why of that shoot-out. She's the reason you're in India in the first place. The statue. Shiva's Diva. Quick, now. Inside and let's grab her and run before the thugs discover she's still here."

I looked for the nearest heavy object to throw at the man. Since that appeared to be the statue of interest, the one he called Shiva's Diva, I decided it would not be prudent to toss her around like a volleyball.

So I yelled instead. "You *spadal teanga léitheid seo*! You didn't care whether we found Ray dead or alive. You just wanted to see if that stinking piece of ivory was still hidden in my bag—where Ray himself put it not two seconds before all hell broke loose in there."

Brig had made it behind the bar by this time. I followed close behind him. Since I couldn't reach the statue before he did, I debated whether to grab one of the few intact bottles of booze that stood on the counter and conk him over his thick Irish head.

He put his finger to his lips. "Shh! Lass. Calm down. Let's not be alertin' the neighborhood to our presence. And did ya know ya just called me a tongue-depressing so-and-so?"

"I don't give a rodent's behind whether every bum in the vicinity pops in, and I intended to call you just that."

That was a lie. The epithet I was going for was more interesting and a lot more obscene, but I screwed up my translations. A mistake I had no intention of revealing.

"I want to find out what happened to Ray. And I want out of here!"

Brig swung my gorgeous Mexican tote over his shoulder. I started to grab it. He lifted it up and out of my reach. I'm five eight, but the man topped me by a good seven inches.

"That's mine, O'Brien. Give it to me."

"Ah. We've progressed to last-name familiarity, have we now? A name yelled at a male by a female who knows she's about to lose the game."

"Duck!"

"What? Is that the best you can do for profanity?"

"Duck! Drop! Floor! Somebody's out there! Get down!"

We dove for the disgusting, greasy, boozy, filthy floor. A few candy wrappers lay next to the table. They smelled like Rajit beer. A few broken bottles had rolled under that table. Bourbon. Gin. Tequila. Each liquor reeking with an odor of its own.

For a moment I didn't care whether Brig, Mahindra, Patel, and Saints Cecilia and Bridget took off with my bag and the statue. I wanted a bath. A bubble bath filled with the most chichi fragrances I could find to disguise the fact that my body exuded scents like a sailor after six days of shore leave with the same, uh, lady.

The urge to be clean vanished faster than a soap bubble could pop. It was replaced with a different urge. Survival. That flash I'd seen in the window was gliding through the door.

It was the cigarette-smoking, Gujarati-speaking gentleman wearing the crisp white shirt. Which was still crisp and still white. He was flanked by what seemed like a battalion of hooligans. All carried weaponry straight out of *The Mummy*. And all weapons were trained dead straight at me, Tempe Walsh, linguist. Alone.

Briggan O'Brien had disappeared. I didn't know how a six-foot-four-inch Irishman gifted with the ability to talk nonstop at high volume had managed to make himself invisible in a bar decorated with only a few tables, but he had.

He'd yelled "Trap!" at me before he vanished. Duh. Kind of him to mention it. I knew it was a trap. I now faced this man and his multitude of minions all by myself.

I exaggerated about the actual number of minions. Three stood without speaking behind their boss. But they had the look of invading Mongol hordes, which made three appear more like fifty-three. Especially when those hordes are facing one female who is holding a tote bag heavy with the weight of a priceless statue.

Mr. Starched Shirt smiled at me. Cool. We were going to be civilized.

He spoke in English. "Miss Walsh. Thank you for rescuing Saraswati from the filth of the floor. Now please hand it over and you will not be hurt. This I promise."

It was a line straight out of a clichéd action flick. Nonetheless, that statement penetrated the air with all the force that three evil-looking miscreants holding cutlery and revolvers behind the leading man could produce.

I decided to bluff him out.

"This bag? Oh, really, Mr., uh, Mahindra. You think I would have been so blasé, so cavalier, as to leave this behind if it contained Shiva's Diva?"

His eyebrows shot into the middle of his forehead.

"Shiva's Diva? Where did you hear that term used? I did not call her that. And how do you know my name?"

To hell with Brig. He'd left me here to play poker with a group of killers.

"Briggan O'Brien, with whom I unfortunately shared an intimate moment-in-hiding earlier while your thugs were shooting up the place. That's what he called this statue of Saraswati everyone seems so eager to acquire. At any cost, I might add. And I figured *you* had to be Mahindra since Patel is a pig, and I remember he was the one who threw the cigar at the gentleman I came in with. The gentleman your bullet hit. The gentleman who seems to have vanished. Any idea where?"

Mahindra laughed. It was not a nice laugh. He ignored my

last question. "O'Brien? I should have known he would be in the middle of this fiasco." He stopped laughing. "I trust the moment did not become too intimate, Miss Walsh. Briggan O'Brien is not a fit companion for a lady such as yourself."

Aha! A statement Mr. Mahindra and I agreed on. I wanted to continue the topic of the fascinating life of Brig O'Brien—and divert Mahindra from such topics as statues and tote bags—when one of the minions grunted. Or perhaps it was a growl.

Grunt or growl. Neither fashioned a pretty sound.

I pointed. "I believe one of your posse wants you."

"Posse?"

"Your buddies. The thugs. Hooligans."

He shook his head. "Business associates, please. You offend them and me with such vile terms. Although I like this word 'posse.' It is very American."

Out of date as slang by at least fifteen years or so, but he was right. Very American. Maybe Mahindra liked Americans. Maybe I could smooth talk him with the latest chitchat from the Big Apple long enough to allow me to saunter out into the night with the Diva in hand.

He stared at me. All thoughts of gossip fled. Sweat dripped down my forehead. I'm sure he saw it. Sensed the fear causing it.

He nodded, checked his watch, then stated, "I have other plans for this evening. So, kindly give me the statue or forfeit your life. Avi is quite handy with knives. As for myself, I prefer guns. I find them to be much cleaner. But Avi is a friend. He must be allowed a little leeway in such matters. I would hate to damage that pretty face or even cut a lock of your auburn hair. Enough delay. Please. The statue."

Uh oh. Tempe, the lady with the auburn hair, had degenerated to what was now Tempe the dartboard. "Enough delay" sounded serious. I smiled at Mahindra, then swung the bag at Avi and his collection of sharp silverware. Shiva's Diva must have connected with something precious on the man, because his grunts changed to definite howls.

I then turned and swung my right leg in a brilliant fan kick toward the chin of minion number two. I finished with a basic punch to the nose of minion three as I silently thanked my martial arts instructor in Manhattan. But I soon realized that all offensive mutilate-the-minion moves were useless when Mahindra reached into his coat pocket and pulled out a gun.

Suddenly he and the gun sprawled on the floor. In their place, dark hair still perfectly groomed and white teeth still flashing a piratical grin, stood Briggan O'Brien.

He closed the trapdoor that had been the means for this dramatic entrance. He shoved me away from the hand reaching up from the floor to grab my ankle. Brig scowled, kicked at the offender's shoulder, and followed that with a gentler push to the man's head, shouting, "Don't you be touchin' her, you lousy squid!"

"Squid." Ha! I'd been right. He *had* said squid earlier, in Gaelic and now in English. The why eluded me but I felt better knowing my translations were spot-on.

Mahindra glared up at us both, then growled and reached for my foot. Brig lifted me away from the fallen, angry man, then took my hand in his.

Brig yelled, "Nice fightin', lass! We'll be off, then. Got our girl in the bag?"

I did. I threw the tote over my shoulder and nodded at him.

Bullets, knives, bottles, and one set of keys flew past our heads. We did the only thing we could. We ran.

Chapter 4

"Stop! Please. I can't do this."

I grabbed at Brig's outrageous Hawaiian shirt and tugged hard. He turned. As far as I could tell, he hadn't even broken a sweat. And he smelled nice. A faint trace of curry did not hide the scent of the man himself. Masculine. Heady. Yes, nice. But I needed to avoid sniffing him—at least for the moment.

I had no idea where we were. Brig had taken my hand in his and we'd been running for at least fifteen minutes. He'd transferred the tote bag to his shoulder rather than mine, which made me somewhat suspicious. The reason for the switch must have had less to do with simple courtesy and more to do with the fact that he wanted to stay in close proximity to the ivory Indian goddess.

"Brig. I'm serious. Stop. Please. I just need to rest for a second before starting the marathon again."

He smiled. "I think I can do better than a tiny respite for you. Let's pop into this club, get a drink or two, and sit for a time. How does that sound?"

I didn't even quibble. "Delicious."

The awning over the doorway read C.C. Curry's. I hoped it lived up to the name. A few spicy veggies mixed with those wonderful bean pastries called samosas would be my reward for not socking Brig in the teeth with the tote bag after we first took off from Hot Harry's.

I sank into a comfortable chair. Sitar and tabla music jangled around me. It sounded terrific, even to ears accustomed to classic rock and Broadway musicals.

I sat up. I looked around C.C. Curry's and realized there were no other women seated in the room. Either we'd wandered into a gay bar or an exclusive gentlemen-only lounge. I hissed at Brig, "What's this place?"

"C.C. Curry's. Ladies club."

"That makes no sense. I thought ladies clubs were where females go to play bridge and avoid guys. Other than me, I do not see any ladies. With or without cards."

Brig turned bright red. "You will."

He was right. The music cranked up a notch. Heavy bass and funky drums replaced the sitar. I glanced up. An Indian beauty wearing a berry-colored sari and more beads than a rosary stand began writhing and wriggling above Brig and me on a platform.

I groaned, "Oh no. This I do not need tonight. I'm in a strip joint? Thank you so much. A wonderful spot to hide in."

"They don't call them strip joints here. And they don't strip. Not like those places in Manhattan on Eighth Avenue that bare it all. Not that I ever darkened a door of one in the city, mind you." He winked. "No, luv. This really is called a ladies club. The ladies dance for the gentlemen. That's it. Very sedate, comparatively. Mind you, what they do with the gents on their own time after hours might be *arranged* in here, but the stripping then is private."

By this time, Brig had given me more information than I desired. I didn't care if the ladies were stark naked and painted blue. I just wanted to rest and get a little food in my stomach. Running for one's life tends to make a person hungry.

I glared at Brig. "Do you mind telling me why you left me to face Mahindra and his thugs—oh, excuse me—*business associates*, by my little lonesome? Aside from being damn dangerous, I found it extremely rude."

Brig's lashes fluttered. He affected the expression of a

choirboy entering the pearly gates with a signed pass from St. Peter.

"I did not leave you. Believe me. Didn't you hear me yelling about the trapdoor?"

I blew out a whoosh of air. "That's what 'Trap! Trap!' was all about? I thought you were telling me we were trapped. Which I kind of already knew before I chatted with Mahindra and his close circle of friends."

He sighed, "Sorry, Tempe. I knew about the hidden door and ducked down the instant I saw trouble. But you did a superb job of handling Mister Kirk Mahindra and his boys. I watched it all from a large hole downstairs. Your skill at punching? Impressive. And can you tell me the name of that swishy over-the-top-kick thing you did? I don't remember seein' that one even in my jujitsu classes."

"Gotta be the fan kick. It's very theatrical," I answered. "Thanks for the compliment, I think."

He winked. "More than welcome. It was a treat watchin' those legs in action. Near made me forget how to open the damn trap. With your body distractin' me so much, I'm amazed we escaped with the statue intact."

I glared at him. "Which, I notice, you seem to be hugging to your person. May I remind you that Ray was in the process of buying the damn thing? If he's still alive, it's his. I don't think he'd given Khan the money, but he had a verbal contract. So is it still Khan's? I gather since everyone seems to want this statue that I was wrong about it being a fake."

"No. It's definitely real. Well, we'll need to check and see where Ray is holed up now. Assuming he's not lying in a ditch guarded by Patel or Mahindra's goons. But in the meantime we need to be about keepin' the little beauty safe. The bad guys won't be restin' till they find her. And us. That's fer sartin, 'tis."

I bit my lip. His fine Irish brogue seemed to rise or fall as each subject warranted.

"And I can just see you handing it to its rightful owner as

soon as we find either Decore or some authority we can trust, Mr. O'Brien."

Brig slapped his hand over his heart. "You wound me. Have ye not heard of trust? Have I, in our brief but enjoyable relationship of this last hour, ever let you down?"

The man was impossible. And too darned handsome for anyone's good, including his own. I sighed.

"Where is that waiter? I could use that drink now. And some food."

I stood, glanced around, then sat again. "I don't see him. Well, while he's off trying to translate Sangria cooler into Hindi for the bartender, would you please tell me just what is the big deal with this statue? Other than price. I'm well aware of price. A damn big one. That's why Ray Decore hired me. He wanted to be sure when Mr. Khan rattled off the rate of rupees that I'd be able to translate correctly. Of course, neither Ray nor I knew that every goon in Bombay wanted Miss Saraswati. No offense."

"None taken."

The waiter brought my wine and an order of a dozen samosas. I tried not to chug the entire glass down in one gulp, but I did devour four of the spicy vegetable pastries in less than thirty seconds. Brig's eyes popped open.

"Do you realize you just ate four of those things?"

I scowled at him. "Yes. Excuse me. I am a stress eater. Sitting behind a desk translating contracts is generally not stressful. This night has been nothing *but*. And some clown shot up the vending machine at Hot Harry's before I could partake of the varied candy bars. So get over it."

He inclined his head, not bothering to hide his smile.

"We'el then, with a full stomach, are you ready for the story of Saraswati the goddess? There's a foin tale here, Miss Walsh. Sit back and I'll be tellin' it."

I settled into that comfortable chair with my glass in one hand and a fifth samosa in the other. Brig had the look of a medieval storyteller about to regale an eager audience of peasants with the latest news of the knights and dragons.

"Saraswati. Goddess of culture, literary achievements, speech, rituals, and fertility."

"Also my yoga instructor back in Manhattan."

Brig's face brightened. "Hatha or power?"

"Power."

He shook his head. "You should try hatha instead. It's far more spiritual. Truly a healing technique. Lovely. There are wonderful instructors here in Bombay. You and I will drop in on one while we're in the city. There's a fella over in Malabar Hills who can near get one into a state of nirvana within five minutes of entering his class. Where do you take your power classes?"

"At a studio in Greenwich Village. So I suppose that means I'm not healed and will never attain that nirvanic high. Brig? Could you go on? About Shiva's Diva. I'm sorry I ever interrupted. You and I obviously are easily distracted with trivia. So, please. Culture, fertility, all that jazz."

"Yes. To begin with, Saraswati is in attendance whenever and wherever speech is present, so to speak. She arrives with newborn babes and gifts them with, um, the gift of speech. Which is important. I'll come to it presently."

"One would only hope so," I mumbled, shoving a sixth samosa into my mouth.

"What?"

"Nothing. Please, continue."

He threw me a suspicious look but started his lecture again. "Saraswati is most always depicted holding a lute, a rosary, and a water pot. Sometimes she's sitting on a swan. Very pretty. Dresses in white. Pure. No gaudy jewelry for our goddess either. I'll get back to that."

I smiled. "Brig. I can't tell you how enchanted and intrigued I am by the story so far, but will you get to the point? Assuming there is one? As to why Saraswati is more pursued than a basketball star after an arrest?"

He frowned at me. "You have to understand the goddess to understand what's going on with this statue. Let me get on to the good parts. She has a curse. And a blessing."

"Oh crap. I might have known there'd be a curse."

"And a blessing."

"Yeah, well, whatever." I signaled to the waiter to bring another Sangria cooler, then asked if he could throw in another dozen of the veggie samosas. My favorites. He could. And would. Brig didn't even blink.

I turned back to him and smiled.

"All right. Saraswati loves musicians and artists and all those creative types. And since Shiva is the creator of all, he believed that Saraswati was one of his creations, even though her real daddy was Brahma, who also happened to become her husband—which is damn kinky, but we won't go into that—and Shiva loved Saraswati's music."

"Which is why you call her Shiva's Diva. Yes?"

Brig groaned. "If you knew all about her, why didn't you say so?"

"Because I still don't know about the curse, the blessing, or why everybody and their so-called business associates are willing to kill to possess this particular statue. Care to enlighten me on those points?"

Brig paused. A tiny beauty in an orange sari had begun a cha-cha around our table. I'm sure it was meant to convey a fertility dance from the fifth century BC or so, but it more closely resembled a certain cat trotting around his dish from an old TV commercial. Brig seemed bewitched. He thrust a fistful of rupee notes totaling about forty dollars into the girl's eager hands.

I scowled at both of them.

"Brig. Curse? Blessing? Hello?"

"Sorry, luv. Got to help out the working class, you know."

"Right."

The girl writhed away, then headed for a table near the back of Curry's where a new group of eager patrons had just been seated. I watched her progress, then gasped like a sappy heroine from a sappy melodrama. I slid under the table, then thumped hard on Brig's knee.

"Brig! Over there! It's Patel and his crew! Oh hell."

Brig did not waste time asking questions. He joined me on the floor. We covered ourselves with the red-checkered table-cloth as best we could, then darted glances at this second, nastier member of the Shiva's-Diva-is-mine buyers. Or thieves.

"Damn. Do you think he spotted us? How did they know we were here? Is he working with Kirk Mahindra or on his own? Ouch. I think that's the guy who threw the knife at me. No, wait, this guy's thinner."

"Shh! Tempe, can you keep your voice down? You have a pronounced American accent. Not to mention you're the only female not on stage. We don't need Patel to recognize those sweet-soundin' tones of yours. Which reminds me, you'll have to sing me a wee lullaby soon. A fine *seoithín* to soothe me to sleep. 'Twould fair be enchantin'."

I ignored the lullaby comments and lowered my volume a good two notches. "Brig? What are we going to do?"

"I'm thinking. And, for your edification about the thugs, darlin', Patel is on his own. He and Mahindra have the same mindset of evil intentions, but they don't cross paths 'less they have to. And on those occasions, they just try to kill each other."

Orange Sari wriggled away from Patel's table with a pleased look on her face. It was evident the gentlemen enjoying her performance had rewarded her quite well. Brig's eyes were shining. The twinkle worried me.

"Tempe. Can you stay scrunched down and head for the door over there to the left?"

"Why? Where's it go?"

I squinted. A small sign on the door said *"Nartaki KapRepahannaa."* Hindi. The first word meant dancer. The second word's literal translation was dressing. I opened my eyes wide at Brig. He nodded.

"I assume, having seen Mr. Curry himself dart back there a few times tonight, that it leads to a backstage arena for the ladies. Which in turn leads to the stage. Which is where you're going to end up."

"Are you nuts? Aside from the fact that I'm at least five inches taller than most of those girls, have flaming red hair and blue eyes, haven't seen the sun all winter and don't tan anyway, and all these girls have exquisite brown skin, what makes you think Mr. Curry is going to allow me into a costume and send me out to entice the customers? And even if he does, how does that get me past Patel? And what will you be doing, pray tell, while I'm bumping and grinding up there?"

"And you say I rattle on? Hush, now. Follow me. All will be well."

In the shoot-out at Hot Harry's, Patel and his goons had been recklessly quick on the trigger. Or, more precisely, the blade. Those knives had zinged past me, piercing vending machines, beer bottles, and the right eyebrow of Miss April. So, although creeping after Briggan O'Brien may have seemed a stupid thing to do, and indeed, *was* a stupid thing to do, it also seemed far better than the alternative, which was popping up and waving at Patel and company while pointing to myself and yelling, "Yoo hoo! Target! Over here!"

No one noticed the two of us crawling on the floor between tables on our way to the backstage entrance. This might have been because the entertainment had clicked into a higher gear. The music had changed from Indian raga to dance music from the seventies. God bless America. We gave the world jeans, burgers with fries, and more than twenty years after its inception—disco. Gloria Gaynor sang out the classic "I Will Survive." I was in complete agreement with the sentiment.

Backstage at C.C. Curry's was like backstage anywhere in the world. Tiny dressing areas with poorly lit mirrors. Performers chattering nonstop while applying copious amounts of rouge, mascara, and liner.

A rack of saris had been placed in the center of the dressing room. I grabbed the one that looked the longest. It happened to be in a shade of red that clashed with my hair. I didn't worry too much about choosing the best costume for my first time out as a would-be stripper. I scanned the room to see if any of the girls were about to yell "sari stealer!" at me.

Brig, after leading me back here, had disappeared. No surprise.

I removed what was left of my filthy, torn suit, then kicked it under a table. I squeezed into the little blouse, called a *choli,* that's worn under a sari. I wrapped the piece of red silk around me, then wandered over to the table farthest from any living being and began to apply the darkest shade of foundation available. Many of the ladies kept their faces hidden behind veils. Whether this was for religious reasons or to add to the mystique of the dancing girl, I silently thanked whomever had kept this custom. It meant I could drape folds of silk over my hair, nose, and mouth. A pot of midnight blue kohl paint lay next to the foundation and black eyeliner. I slathered it on.

By the time the cosmetics and I bonded, I looked like a drag queen in the Village preparing for a Halloween on the town as a belly dancer. Any resemblance to Tempe Walsh, American linguist, last seen in a business suit with hair pulled into a bun at the neck and with makeup consisting of blush, lip gloss, and a smidgen of mascara, had been extinguished.

C.C. Curry arrived at my makeup table. He snarled at me in a Marathi dialect. Thanks to Louie's Lingo, I was able to interpret most of his words.

"You! New girl! You are next onstage. We are short two girls tonight. Hurry!"

C.C. adhered to a free-and-easy hiring policy. You're in the dressing room. You're female. You're in costume. You're on.

I began striding to the entrance to the stage, then realized that the other girls minced. I had to slow down and take much shorter steps and try to remember I wasn't hauling down West End Avenue in Reeboks on my way to work.

The beaded curtain parted and I stepped onstage. I glanced around the club. Fifty tables, each holding at least four men. Four hundred eyes staring at me.

I closed my eyes. If I ever saw Brig again, I was going to

kill him. No, scratch that idea. I should simply hand him the tote bag and yell "Shiva's Diva—here!" in the vicinity of the Chor Bazaar—Thieves Market—only blocks away from C.C. Curry's. Every faction interested in the goddess statue, and it appeared there were many, would be on the man like ants on crackers.

Tote bag. I hit what I hoped was a seductive pose and realized I couldn't toss that denim carryall at Brig in any bazaar anywhere. He still had it.

The music for my improvised routine began as the riff for Donna Summer's "Hot Stuff" sailed out across C.C. Curry's sound system and around the club. My mother loves this song. Mom brought me up on disco. When I was a toddler, she taught me the Latin Hustle, the American Hustle, and the Harlem Hustle. Any hustle she knew. We'd dance around the kitchen to songs from Donna, Gloria, K.C., and the rest of the stars from the era. Doubtless Mom would be delighted to know her daughter was getting ready to do shimmies and rib-cage isolations for a crowd of eager gents while the queen of disco sang above.

The speakers were situated in the ceiling next to the booth where the CDs and equipment were stored. I squinted to see who'd picked this number. Briggan sat beside a turban-crowned teenage boy. Both gentlemen were grinning at me.

Brig wanted me to give a show? He'd get a show. My major in college had been linguistics, thanks to my father, Mr. Practicality, who'd been grimly determined that I'd learn a skill that could earn a living. My minor had been dance. I'd been captain of the gymnastics team and had performed with the dance team too. The summer between my junior and senior years of college, I played the lead in *Sweet Charity* at a small professional theater in Syracuse. The choreographer had danced with Bob Fosse. She knew all the original moves from *Charity*. She taught them all to me, and I learned them well.

I shrugged my shoulders up and down in time to the music. I did hip grinds and pelvic thrusts and head rolls and even got down on the floor and writhed a bit. That was a mistake. C.C. Curry's floor made the dressing area look immaculate. But rupee notes were being tossed at me from all sides of the room.

This had not been a fun night. Shots had been fired at me in Hot Harry's around nine P.M. An upsetting experience. Make that damn terrifying. Yet, at eleven-thirty when the rupee notes started flying and the cheering swelled, I began to enjoy being onstage at C.C. Curry's. I even tossed the veil and let my hair fly around me so I could do a few head rolls during the "hot, hot, hot, hot stu-ff" chorus.

Patel stood and scraped his chair away from his table. His eyes narrowed. He leaned over and whispered something to one of the men with him. I recognized that face. He'd aimed a gun at me at Hot Harry's. He'd been a lousy shot. Perhaps because knives were more his thing.

Mr. Crummy Aim stood. He and Patel tried to storm the stage. They were hampered by a throng of drunken French sailors who'd decided to deliver rupees to me in person. I knew this would not deter Patel and his friends for long.

I jumped off the stage and rolled under a table. A ridiculous amount of my time this evening had been spent hiding under tables, and I wasn't pleased. I sneezed when I got a whiff of the odor from a pool of wine stinking up my latest hiding place. I then got to my feet and headed for the nearest exit that was also the farthest from my pursuers.

Once again, I ran. Without clothes, other than a now wet sari. Without the rest of my samosas. Without my tote bag. Without Shiva's Diva. Without Briggan O'Brien.

Chapter 5

I ended up outside C.C. Curry's scanning the area that comprised Grant Road. To the west I could almost see the Opera House and a rail station. To the east lay the Chor Bazaar. In the middle stood the red-light district—and me. At least I was dressed appropriately. If one considered an ill-fitting bright red sari that stank of booze and sweat to be the correct attire for the area.

The good news was that as a smart New Yorker I never went anywhere without mad money and keys hidden in my tiny belly bag, which in turn was hidden under wads of wet sari. And I could communicate to some degree in one of at least four different Indian languages. The bad news was that there was now a whole lot more of me than I felt comfortable showing. I was wearing more makeup than is displayed at the Macy's cosmetics counters at Christmas, and I was disinclined to talk to anyone in any language.

Oh yes. Add to the above that my feet were bare. My ruined pumps had been discarded in the dressing room of C.C. Curry's, along with my suit and my sanity.

The train station seemed my best bet. I began to walk. It was September, but in Bombay the temperature was still in the upper nineties even at this late hour. An enchanting time to take a stroll through this 'hood. Homeless beggars eyed me with interest. Had they never seen a redheaded American in a wet sari reeking of alcohol before?

A late-night food vendor waved at me. Good idea. I changed course and began trotting toward his stand.

"Tempe! Damnation! Where do you think you're headin'?"

I turned. "Brig! Well. My, what a surprise. I assumed you'd still be at Curry's waiting out the enemy so you could retrieve my tips from the stage."

He smiled. When he smiled with all the charm of a thousand years of Irish pirates behind him, I melted. Anything could be believed of that smile.

"Ah, darlin', I wouldn't leave you to fend for yourself here in the street. It's not a safe place for a lady, you know."

He had that right. He gently wrapped his lightweight sweatshirt around my shoulders, then led me over to a bench on the side of the road. The pair of us shooed off at least twenty teenagers who were begging for anything we could give them. Brig handed them a fistful of rupees and the rest of the samosas he'd managed to sneak out of the club in my tote bag along with Shiva's Diva. Very resourceful of him. I just wish he'd saved a bite for me.

"Can I go back to that vendor before we talk? I really need something to eat."

"No, Tempe. You'd be sick in twenty seconds from the junk he's selling. You ate at Curry's. You should be fine."

"In your opinion. I'm famished." I sighed. "Well, I'll hold on for a while. What's the latest plan? Do we have a latest plan?"

"I'm hailing the next taxi I see. The train station is a terrible place this time of night. Full of felons and muggers. You're lucky you got only a block or two before I caught up with you. What were you thinking? Standin' here in that sari in the red-light district. You look like a treat waiting to be devoured. Damn, woman, you could have been snatched up by far worse than Patel."

"Excuse me! May I point out I'm standing out here in this damn sari in this stinking district because you had me bumping and grinding on stage only a few minutes ago?" I shook my head. "Oh, just forget it. How did you manage to leave Curry's without Patel on your tail?"

He leaned against the bench and smiled at me.

"The sound booth has a back stair that leads directly to the alley behind the club. As soon as I saw that spectacular leap you took off the stage—one worthy of a Kirov ballerina I must say—I made my farewell to the child running the stereo system and dashed out. Patel never knew he'd been outfoxed. If he even knew the fox had been there to start with."

"So why isn't he running down Grant Road looking for me, while I sit here on a bench with you, with the two of us planted here like pigeons at the shooting gallery?"

Brig stretched out his long legs, then yawned.

"I neglected to mention that while I searched through the pile of CDs for music that would inspire you to dance, I called Mr. Curry on the in-house phone from the booth. Told him Patel was the husband of one of his girls and that the man had riot and mayhem on his mind right there in Curry's club. Said if Patel wasn't hustled out immediately, there'd be a heap of trouble. I described Patel down to his ugly little scarred chin and bald head while you were in the middle of that marvelous hootchy-bumpy movement."

"Which one? The shoulder pulse or the pelvic 'round the world? Wait. What am I saying? It doesn't matter which one. Thanks for getting rid of Patel, although I imagine that's a temporary status."

He inclined his head. "You're most welcome. And it was the pelvic rotation. Very nice. Fair distracted me so much I nearly forgot why I was after callin' Mr. Curry in the first place. Ah. I see a taxi."

He stood. He didn't bother to wave. The cab screeched beside us, scattering the remaining beggars back to the other side of the road.

"Sea Harbor Hotel, please."

"Hold it. We're going to your place?"

"Remember I told you that no one knows where I'm staying? Since you walked into Hot Harry's with your boss and it appears everyone knows where he was staying, as well as why the pair of you were in Bombay, and probably what you ate on the flight here, it's a safe bet they now know where your hotel is too."

He was right. I knew he was right. Knowing did not make it more palatable.

"Okay. We'll go to your hotel. Where, if you don't mind, I will take a shower while you go to my hotel and get my clothes. Or skip the hotel and hit any store still open and find me something other than a red sari and this damned tight *choli* thing. Jeez. No wonder the women of India stay thin. Who can eat while wearing this?"

Brig gave me a long perusal, from face to toes.

"You fit quite nicely into that. I do have to admire the way a sari hugs a lady's curves. And you have them, luv. In all the right places, let me be addin'."

"Don't start with the flattery, Mr. O'Brien. This is neither the time nor place for it. With as much trouble as you've gotten me in tonight, I'm not sure there'll ever be a time or place."

He fluttered his long lashes. "Trouble? I got you into trouble? And just whom, might I ask, were Mahindra and Patel shootin' at this evening? 'Twasn't me, lass. I was an innocent bystander till you thrust your pretty face into mine in the storeroom at Hot Harry's Saloon. Which became the first pleasant sight of the night."

I tried to focus on something other than the equally pleasant sight of him smiling at me in the back seat of this cab. I stared at the tote bag, then pointed to what appeared to be part of Saraswati's lute. "Hey. You didn't get to finish your story about Shiva's Diva. Do we have time before we get to the hotel? Because, I swear, once we're there and once I'm clean, I'm conking out for the night. Statue be damned."

"Which it is, you know, dependin' on who's got it."

I sat upright. "What do you mean? We've got it right now. Are we cursed?"

He put his hand over mine and squeezed with a gentle pressure. I did not remove it.

"We're fine. There's a whole set of rules behind all this. Where did I leave off?"

"I don't remember. I got all the stuff about Saraswati being pure and being the patron saint of music and speech and arts and all. Also understood that this particular statue is cursed and blessed. We never got to the why or the how."

"Ah. Well, then. A Portuguese sculptor from the seaport of Chaul carved Shiva's Diva sometime in the seventeenth century. It was supposed to be placed in Parvati's Temple. Parvati was Shiva's main wife. Since Shiva the creator god liked Saraswati's music, the idea was that Parvati would be kind to the lesser goddess, Saraswati, and treat her as though she were her own daughter."

"Plus there'd be the perk of having monks look after her all the time," I interjected.

"Exactly. A sweet deal all around. But something changed at the last minute. The monks pulled a fast one and wouldn't meet the sculptor's price. So our girl didn't end up as the typical depiction of Saraswati. Normally, the goddess carries a lute and boasts no weaponry of any kind."

"The lute I saw was upside down."

Brig nodded. "For good reason. Braganza, the sculptor, had a wicked sense of humor. The rumor is that he agreed to the crummy price, but before he delivered the piece to the monks, he added a bow and arrow to Saraswati, then turned the lute upside down and placed several rubies on that lute. At his own expense, mind. Plus there's the little matter of the snake head popping out of one arm."

"Hmmm. So the goddess was pissed? Hence the curse?"

Brig laughed. "Actually, it was the other way around. Remember now, Saraswati is a goddess to artists. The lovely lady sided with the man who'd carved the piece, and she laid out the blessing and the curse."

He paused dramatically and waited. I did not disappoint him.

"Okay. I admit. I'm hooked. I'm dying to know and you've stalled enough. What are they?"

"The blessing is quite nice. If a person of artistic talent and temperament comes into possession of Shiva's Diva for any length of time, he or she will be gifted with more talent and also be rewarded with great wealth and intellect. And this is marvelous. The mute will speak."

"I like it. 'Bout damn time creative people got a break. Had I known this, I might have gone after the statue years ago, followed my mother's advice, and become a big star on Broadway or in Hollywood."

Brig glanced at me and smiled. "I doubt you'd need Saraswati's blessing for that. I think you would've, and still could, make it on your own talent."

"Well. I try not to think about it. Besides, my father, Mr. Securely Pragmatic, would have shot me. So? What's the curse?"

Brig lowered his volume to almost a whisper. "If the lady falls into the hands of avaricious souls, woe to them all."

"Ah, the old doom-and-gloom routine. Typical. Any specifics?"

"They're struck mute. The goddess of speech uses her power to end communication. And they are felled by misfortune. Poverty. Violent ends."

I lapsed into silence. Not as a result of the curse, just thinking about Brig's words about the avaricious.

"I wonder where Raymond Decore falls in those descriptions. He's quite an art collector. Doesn't possess the talent himself but is a definite patron of the arts."

Brig smiled. "I suppose your boss would have been all right. As long as he didn't try and sell off the rubies or hide the Diva in a private room somewhere."

"And me? If I'd grabbed her? I mean, heck. I dance. I sing. And talk about speech? I've earned my living translating others' words for seven years now. Think Shiva's Diva would bless me?"

"Most certainly. Of course, you're fine on your own without a blessing. But since you're not keeping her, I suppose you'll have to make do with the gifts you have. Which are many, in case I haven't told you. Starting with the prettiest shade of hair I've seen since the Riverdance Company hit Radio City Music Hall a few years back with that sweet little girl leadin' 'em around the stage."

"You saw them? You were in New York?"

"Darlin', 'tis true I was born in Dublin. Raised there until I was ten. But I'm pretty much in Manhattan now. Or in London. I saw *Riverdance* there as well. With Colin Dunne that time."

"Oh, good grief. I'm surprised I haven't run into you lurking around museums and bars throughout New York. What do you do? I mean, for a living?"

Brakes squealed as the taxi stopped. I winced. Next came the request from our driver for what sounded like a suspiciously high fare. Brig handed him the rupee notes without even asking to see the sheet with the mileage. I was glad. I had no desire to stay in the cab and listen to men fight over money. I'd seen too much of that at Hot Harry's.

I did not make a graceful exit from the cab. In fact, had it not been for Brig's hand on my arm, I would have fallen on my face. My night had been spent dodging bullets, dodging knives, dodging thugs, then dodging coins dancing onstage at C.C. Curry's strip club. I'd witnessed my boss getting shot, and I'd narrowly escaped injury myself. I'd passed exhaustion an hour ago. If Brig chose to toss Shiva's Diva into Back Bay along with my tote bag and the remaining samosa, I wouldn't argue. I'd help with the toss as long as I first had a bath and a nap.

Brig's room faced the harbor and had the added benefit of a balcony overlooking same. Doubtless it would prove to be a spectacular view in the morning; and by then my eyes might even be open enough to notice.

Once inside, I headed straight to the bathroom, then stripped and showered and soaked until I felt every piece of dirt and slime had been scrubbed away. Then I remembered I had no other clothes. A walk naked back through the red-light district sounded more appealing than putting the filthy silk sari back on. I wrapped a huge towel around my body and knocked on the door leading to the bedroom.

"Brig? You awake?"

"Haven't gone to sleep. I thought I'd be a gentleman and give you a crack at that tub, but when you're finished, I could use a good scrubbing myself."

"I appreciate the first dibs. Um. Do you have an old T-shirt or something long enough that I can wear until the shops open tomorrow?"

His response came fast. Brig rapped on the door; I opened it a wedge and took a T-shirt bearing the logo of the Broadway hit *The Producers*. Apropos. A man who was doubtless a con artist in possession of souvenir clothing from a show about two con artists. I almost smiled. I didn't know Brig's motives in acquiring Shiva's Diva, but I supposed an artist is an artist, even if the art is one of sweet deception.

I pulled the shirt on over my head, then stepped into the bedroom as casually as I could manage.

Brig's eyes lit up. "That looks far better on you than me. It's near a perfect fit."

I believe the word "mini" might have been a good description for the garment. It covered my bottom. Barely.

"I appreciate the compliment and the shirt, but I'm now ready to crash. The bathroom is yours. The water is hot and wonderful and I'm clean and tired and . . ."

Tears were sliding down my cheeks. I shook and cried, helpless to stop either activity.

Brig leapt up from the bed where he'd been reclining and admiring my latest getup. He ran to my side and held me.

"It's all right, darlin'. You go ahead and let it all out now. You've done an amazing job of not falling apart this whole nasty night. You'd be more ivory than the statue if the stress and the panic hadn't finally caught up with you. There's just so much being tough one woman can handle."

He lifted up my chin and lightly kissed my cheek. "We've been through death's own door and come back t'other side, we have. If you'd've continued this pose of calm much longer, I would've considered poking you with pins to see if you were human."

I cried for about a minute. Then I drew back. I couldn't afford to be weak. Not yet. Brig felt me step back but didn't feel my spine stiffen. He leaned down and kissed me. His lips tasted of a mixture of curry and peppermint. Nice. Too nice. The kiss became more intense. And hands that felt even more intense were leaving my back and sliding down to the bottom of that very short shirt. My body had gone limp.

I pulled away.

"Too much too soon?" he queried in a polite tone.

"In a word, yes."

He nodded, smiled, then gestured to the bed.

"I'll let you get some rest now. Don't worry. I'll not bother you while you sleep." He winked. "Not this night, anyway. Now, once you're up and back to your old self? Well, I make no promises, luv. No promises at all. I'm pretty certain I'll be interested in much more."

"Well, don't be believin' you'll be gettin' it, Mr. O'Brien," I said with a brogue to match the one he so easily assumed. "Tomorra I'll just be headin' over to the Taj Mahal Hotel, retrieve my passport, and make reservations for the next flight from Bombay to Manhattan. With or without Shiva's Diva. And now it appears without Ray Decore. But either way, I'm going home."

Brig bent down and kissed me on my forehead. "Then you get some rest, Tempe Walsh. And may the goddess herself guide your dreams."

"Thank you. Oh, Brig? Is there a vending machine or anything near your room? A candy bar or some chips might just get me back to normal."

He bit his lip, but his laughter could not be contained.

"I don't think so. I seem to remember sodas but no real food. Sorry. I promise, you'll get a nice big breakfast or brunch tomorrow. Now get some sleep, luv."

I snuggled under the light blanket and remembered one tiny thing just before I conked. Other than a T-shirt that was barely beach decent, I had no clothes.

Chapter 6

Manhindra, Patel, Khan, Ray, C.C. Curry, and a cast of a thousand chorus girls in red saris could have sculpted a dozen Saraswati statues in the room and I wouldn't have noticed. I slept. If Briggan O'Brien had made an inventory of every one of my features down to the scar on my big toe, I wouldn't have noticed, nor cared. I slept.

I did care when I finally woke up. I'd spent the night sleeping next to a strange man. A man who embodied charm, wit, stunning looks, and extreme virility. A man I knew nothing about. A man who probably put the N in "nefarious," as well as in "knockout." Wait. That was a K. Terrific. We hadn't even engaged in any activity I could call illicit, but a few kisses from Briggan O'Brien and my linguistic skill had deteriorated to the level of kindergartner—with a definite K.

I glanced at the bedside clock. Ten A.M. No nefarious knockout lay beside me in the queen-size bed. I heard no water running in the bathroom. I saw no sign of Brig nor of the tote bag holding Shiva's Diva.

I did notice another bag propped up in the chair tucked under what passed for a desk in the room. This bag displayed the name of a trendy boutique located at Kemps Corner, a spot known even by new tourists for hip designs at decent prices. The bag itself was a duffel, suitable in a pinch as luggage for a girl on the run. A sticky note had been neatly placed over the *K* in Kemps.

Tempe. Hope these are the right size. See? No reds!

*Please meet me at the entrance to Vivek Productions
Studios at what's known as Film City at two this afternoon. Have much to tell you.*

Love, Brig.

P.S. Diva is safe. Don't worry.
P.S. 2. Bring this bag.
P.S. 3. Do NOT *go to your motel.* DANGER. *Got that,
luv?*

I barely read the note. I nearly dove inside the bag to bring
out goodies. Lots of goodies. Three pairs of stretch jeans.
Black, black, and black. I love black. One pair of black leather
pants. Six pairs of black lace undies. Five tops: three in jersey knit, two in silk. Yep. Silk. Brig O'Brien had taste. I could
learn to like this man. Or worse. At the bottom of the bag
were two pairs of athletic sneakers, one pair of black spiked
heels with zippers down the center, and one pair of sandals.

A small purse embroidered with the image of Saraswati lay
beneath the sandals. I opened it. The equivalent of five hundred
dollars bound up in rupee notes had been squeezed into a
pocket of the purse. There was another note giving me directions to Film City and the name of the person in charge of this
find-a-safe-house operation. Jake Roshan at Vivek Studios.

I almost missed the one last item. Make that "items,"
plural, since they come in pairs. Earrings. Two delightful dan-
gling bobs shaped like sailboats. Brig had done more than
notice that mine had been shot up last night. He'd replaced
them—with upgrades. I'm no expert but I can tell a rhine-
stone from a diamond. I stared at the latter. Tiny sparks
nestled in the side of each boat.

I dressed, exuding yips of glee, in a pair of the new, clean,
black jeans and a T-shirt. Then I opened the top drawer of the
dresser near the desk to place Brig's *Producers* shirt inside.
About four other tees were folded in a neat pile next to boxers
and socks. I couldn't help myself. I took out one of the cotton-
knit boxers. Wile E. Coyote and Road Runner stared up at me.

The second pair featured two white mice. Pinky and The Brain. I giggled. Talk about a new technique to practice safe sex. One's lover would be laughing too much to participate.

I set the underwear back down, then noticed a picture lying between the shirts and the socks. Admittedly, this is not a kosher thing to do. But yes, I picked it up and stared at the photo of Brig standing in front of a bench in a garden. He had his arm draped around a beautiful woman with perfect features and a sweet smile.

I quit giggling, dropped the photo, then slammed the drawer shut again. For a moment I considered ignoring Brig's advice, heading back to my hotel, taking the airport shuttle, and flying standby to Manhattan if I had to, just to leave Bombay as soon as I could.

Then I reread Brig's sticky post and took note of the word "DANGER" underlined—in caps. Last night's nonstop perils had been enough. I didn't need to add to them today. I grabbed the duffel bag filled with the new clothes, tossed it over my shoulder, made sure the door to the hotel room was locked, and left.

I had about four hours to get to Film City. Since I hadn't had anything to eat other than those six samosas for the last twenty-four hours, I planned to spend at least ninety minutes of the time chowing down at the nearest restaurant.

The terraced Café de la Plaz was within walking distance of Brig's hotel. I could sit above the throngs walking below and keep a sharp eye out for anyone I knew in Bombay. Which, at this point, consisted of Raymond Decore, who might or might not be living, two sets of killers, who might or might not be living, one owner of a strip joint—pardon me, ladies club—and Briggan O'Brien. I assumed the latter two were still breathing.

I chose a table with a nice awning where I could hide, not only from the possible parade of miscreants, but also from the brutal Bombay sun. I settled in to enjoy the first moments of leisure I'd had since arriving two days ago and pondered how and where my so-called business trip had gone wrong.

Acting as interpreter for a businessman buying a piece of art should have been easy. I work as a translator for a large international law firm in Manhattan. The job pays well but it is not exciting. I read through contracts and help with correspondence. I often act as a hostess/interpreter for various clients and occasionally get sent out of the States on an errand. Such assignments have most often involved interpreting for clients engaged in lawsuits or business transactions. In a word—boring.

But my bills are paid on time. I don't have to share a studio walk-up with five other girls. It's my choice if I spend all the extra money left after paying rent and utilities to see the Broadway shows. My choice if I sit in theaters wishing I was on stage.

I know it's a dream thousands have daily. A dream my mother had instilled in me from my cradle when sounds of musicals filled the nursery instead of lullabies. A dream my father, divorced from Mom since I turned five, squelched at every opportunity. He did not want his daughter to end up a "penniless wreck in a loser's profession married to some sleazy actor." To appease him, I'd chosen linguistics. But my heart and soul felt a daily tug toward performing—somewhere.

Up until yesterday, the wildest trip I'd taken in my seven years at Tucker, Harrison and Deville, Esquires, had been to Paris. Jeremy Tucker, head of the firm, needed help springing his politically active, rebellious daughter from a French jail without causing an international incident. I'd eaten a lot of great food, toured a few famous museums, talked to some gracious gentlemen at the Paris Suréte, eaten more great food, and had seen two operas and one ballet. No one had tried to shoot me, knife me, or hit me over the head with a table. Nice.

Ray Decore's request had been out of the norm. Jeremy Tucker personally asked if I'd help his friend. I wasn't sure what Ray did for a living, if he even worked at all, and I didn't ask.

My temporary new boss had appeared to be somewhere in his fifties. Ray spent his time flying around the world acquiring objects of great beauty—including four ex-wives. Jeremy had warned me that Ray adored women and enjoyed collecting them along with Renoirs, Rembrandts, and Van Goghs. Ray claimed to be fluent in French, German, and Italian. He knew zilch about any of the languages of India and needed someone to translate during his negotiations to buy the statue of the goddess Saraswati. I wasn't exactly up on my Marathi or Maharashtra or Hindi, but I learn languages the way most folks learn a new software program. Pop it in the brain and it's mine.

The seller, Himali Khan, had assured Ray he topped the list of other hopefuls and the statue would be waiting for him if he could get to Bombay. Ray and I were soon flying Air India on the red-eye. I tend to get airsick, so I drug up on generic over-the-counter motion sickness pills. Most zonk me out. The few times I'd been awake, Ray had been trying out his powers of seduction on his temporary employee. So I'd pretended to sleep.

Once in Bombay, we'd checked into our respective rooms at the prestigious Taj Mahal Hotel. I'd opened the curtains leading onto my balcony and sighed over the gorgeous view. I'd eaten a light snack and taken a long nap in my own big bed. Alone. Ray had made whatever phone calls were necessary to send us to Hot Harry's Saloon at the appropriate time last evening.

The rest was history. Shouts, screams, bullets, knives, a great gymnastic routine executed by one Tempe Walsh, added up to landing her in a storeroom with one sneaky, vanishing, handsome Irishman.

I glanced at the clock over the entrance of the restaurant. Time to leave. The food-satiation point had been reached. I was now rested and filled with curry, briani, yogurt, and some sort of yummy pastry that has no equivalent in American cuisine.

I sauntered out of Café de la Plaz and hailed one of the cute little black and gold taxis—color scheme a Bombay law—within seconds. If anyone followed me, I couldn't tell and didn't care. Just let them try and stop me from finding, then thanking, Brig for the clothes, discovering whether my hotel room remained safe, retrieving my passport, then finding the next flight to New York listed on a dot-com site. My stomach was full. Tempe Walsh was rested and ready for action.

Chapter 7

"Film City." I checked Brig's note again. "Uh, Vivek Studios, please."

My driver turned and stared at me with admiration.

"You are film star? Were you in Jake Roshan's last movie? Very good, that one. I have seen it over three hundred times. I like the part where Asha Kumar tumbles off the cliff into the tiger pit and sings to Spot the tiger, while the pirate lowers the rope and sings to her."

I hadn't a clue. But the man seemed to know who this Roshan might be. A producer? Director? I'd rented DVDs of several Indian films before Ray and I left New York in hopes of gleaning fast information about the place where I needed to translate in more than one dialect, but I didn't recognize Mr. Roshan's name from the credits.

The movies had been very entertaining, although the violence blended with musical numbers packed with bad dialogue and stock characters seemed questionable as to the nature of Indian culture. Then I'd thought, *They're movies, idiot.* No more indicative of the Indian people than *West Side Story* is of Americans. Which, in some ways, was not a reassuring comparison. *West Side Story* is a damn good depiction of race and class problems in whatever year and whatever locale a director chooses to set it. But I always loved the dancing in *West Side Story.*

After watching several of the Indian movies, I also fell in love with the music and the dancing they featured. These were routines worthy of Busby Berkley. I sat through a film called *Chhurii Nartaki*—Knife Dancer—twice just to see the musical numbers.

I shook my head at the driver. "I'm not in the movies. I'm supposed to meet this Roshan though. He's what? A producer?"

"Oh, miss. He produces. He directs. He has won many awards. And he is now having big love affair with my favorite film star Asha Kumar. She is most beautiful. Very exotic. She even does her own singing with her wonderful voice. Maybe you can introduce me?"

I didn't even want to imagine what it would take to get a glimpse of a major star in the Bollywood firmament, much less arrange a meeting, first with me, then with an anonymous taxi driver. And the more I heard about Jake Roshan, the more I figured there had to be a lesser being with the same name. Brig's note made it sound like he was a close enough friend to ask Roshan for favors. I couldn't fathom in what circumstances a famous Indian film director might have met Brig. Then again, Brig and I had first exchanged greetings facedown in a saloon storeroom. The big Irishman did get around.

The drive took a bit over two hours. I found I was avoiding much of the scenery after I started shivering from shock and horror upon viewing the filthy shantytowns that served as homes for thousands of migrant workers.

Once I firmly removed my focus from outside, my thoughts leapt immediately back to Brig. His hand pushing me through the window at Hot Harry's. His hand in mine as we ran down the alley. The kiss we'd shared. What might have happened if that kiss had gone as far as Brig seemed interested in going. My fantasies were reaching an embarrassing stage in my visions when the cab driver announced, "Bollywood."

We'd arrived at the entrance to Vivek Productions Studios. A group of Indians stood quietly in front of huge entrance gates guarded by bigger sentinels, hoping to catch a glimpse of an admired actor or actress.

I paid the taxi driver, then looked around for a security guard who might be able to direct me to Roshan. Any Roshan. Or an O'Brien.

Briggan must have read my thoughts and known I was looking for him. Two men exited a Jeep parked near the gates, then headed toward me. My breath quickened as I watched Brig approach. He was accompanied by a small man with a mop of brown hair, skin the color of pecans, and a smile that almost made O'Brien's most charming appear dim by comparison.

"Miss Walsh? I am so pleased you were able to come to the studio today!" Like I had a choice? "Brig has been regaling me with your adventures since arriving in Bombay. I'm so sorry your stay has not been pleasant. But we hope to change that. Please, come inside. I want to show you our wonderful set for my newest movie."

The gates swung open. The three of us entered a lot filled with tents. Carnival tents, food-service tents, tents teeming with men arguing behind computers, and tents holding an array of colored costumes hanging on multiple racks. I wanted to dive in and rummage through each sector like an antique addict at an estate sale.

Brig politely made the introductions while I craned my neck to see what animals were braying, snorting, and chattering under the carnival tents.

"Tempe Walsh, meet Jake Roshan. Finest director in India. And he'd be the finest in America if I could ever persuade him to film there. Even just one or two."

Jake smiled. "Brig likes to tease. I'm quite satisfied making my Masala films, although I use much of what I learned in the States as far as dramatic content and how to create a script. Anyway, the people of India seem to like my movies. They're great escapist fare. And people here, as people everywhere, need entertainment."

I nodded. "My cab driver adores them. He talked nonstop about how wonderful you and your movies are the whole way here. He also seemed quite enamored of an actress named Asha something. You worked with her on a film that had tigers in it? And pirates?"

Jake's expression turned from cheer to doom. Brig shook his head at me. I felt like the mother who'd just taken the last bit of

Halloween candy from her child and thrown it away. The piece the child had been saving for later.

"I'm sorry. Did I put my foot in it?"

Jake shook his head. "Asha Kumar is a fine actress. I'd go so far as to say a brilliant actress. And she is a beautiful woman. We were supposed to get married in the spring. She called it off two days ago."

I may have stuck a foot in, but Brig went full out and added a knee and a thigh. "What the hell? That's just damn silly. You two are the perfect couple. Do I need to have a talk with your intended and set her straight? Why is it I can't leave the pair of you alone for two days without you mucking it up somehow?"

Terrific. Briggan O'Brien, couples counselor.

Jake saw the look I sent Brig. He smiled before responding with, "It's okay, Miss Walsh. I'm not offended. I know Brig quite well. We attended Yale University together. I'm generally wary of taking his advice. In fact, I might go so far as to say the day I listen to him in matters of the heart is the day I take a slow barge down the Mula River with a cargo of rabid monkeys."

I liked this expression so much I almost missed the rest of this response. Then it hit.

"Yale? You were at Yale? Both of you?"

Jake chuckled. "I was given a full scholarship to the Yale drama department and ended up with a Bachelor of Fine Arts degree. But I'm still not sure what Brig did there, and we were roommates for three years."

Brig smiled innocently. "Unlike Jake here, I had no scholarship money dropped into my eager hands. Nevertheless, I did step out of the esteemed halls of ivy with a degree in Liberal Arts. Plus, I have a Masters in Humanities from New York University."

I grinned. "What does that mean? Liberal Arts and Humanities? In other words, you have no discernible means of earning a living. Right?"

Jake roared. "She's sharp, this one. I've often asked the same question for the last ten years. And Brig has yet to answer with anything remotely sane. Two useless degrees. That's rich. I like you, Miss Walsh."

Our kidding did not seem to bother Brig. He preened and twirled and bowed and finally stated in a bit of his brogue, "I am a Renaissance man. I'm havin' knowledge of all things on heaven and earth, unlike you peasants who have only dabbled in one or two subjects in your lives. I shall therefore be takin' no notice of your attempts to belittle all me grand accomplishments."

"And what would those be?" Jake quickly asked.

Brig opened his mouth. I could see his mind inventing more than one tall tale, but just then, Jake's cell phone rang. He glanced at the caller ID bar and motioned us to silence. "I'm so sorry. This is an important call. People who want to finance my film. I have to take this. I'll be back shortly."

Brig and I tactfully retreated and walked toward one of the enormous carnival tents. Brig assumed the kind of narrator voice suitable for playing tour guide.

"Did you know that Bollywood films started with silent flicks? And that over eight hundred movies are made each year? And villages all over India have pirated films imported so folks can see what's what in Bombay? And that most of the actors don't do their own singin'? They lip sync and songs get recorded later at a studio usually by one or two people."

He winked. "But Jake has his actors do their own voice-overs and he even uses a script. And the plots! Wait till you hear Jake's latest with Asha Kumar. You think the duet with the tiger was wild? Hang on to your undies!"

I didn't listen to the recital about Bollywood for long. As a movie buff and sometime dancer, the topic fascinated me, yes, but right now I just wanted to know what Brig had done since leaving the hotel this morning.

"Brig. Stop with the lecture. I love movies, but I can't focus, and I boned up on Bollywood before I got on that plane two days ago. So, some other time we'll exchange info on all the Masala movies made in the last eighty years, plus all the celebrities in India, including Spot the tiger. Now, will you please tell me what's with the cryptic statement about learning a lot? Where have you been and what have you been doing and what have you discovered?" I groaned. "Great. I've known you for less than twenty-four hours and I'm already rattling on as much as you are. I shall endeavor to be calm and collect my thoughts. So, Mr. O'Brien, where on Shiva's good earth have you been?"

He looked around the tent as if expecting to see thugs popping out of clown cars or animal cages at any time. Not that either of us would have been surprised.

"I have been to the Taj Mahal Hotel. Your previous residence, albeit a short-lived one. Quite nice, by the way. First class. I see why the snotty Brits stay there."

"Yes? Can you dispense with the Irish political sentiments for a moment and get on with it?"

His face darkened momentarily, then he nodded.

"Ah. Well, then. Miss Tempe Walsh is listed as checked out. Raymond Decore is not."

"What?"

"I couldn't determine who did the actual checking out of the checkout, mind you. But I did learn that Miss Tempe Walsh's things had been removed from her room by a gentleman."

I wavered between stunned, ticked, and scared. Ticked won by a hair. "They got my stuff! Damn! I had a really cute little outfit I planned on wearing just for the Ganesh festival closing ceremony thingy two days from now. I'll bet it was Mahindra's ugly obese goon, Avi the knife thrower. I'm sure Fat Thug Avi will enjoy traipsing through Bombay in a multi-tiered skirt with a conch belt and a green tank top. Why did he have to steal my clothes? Oh crap. My passport too. I hid it in my suitcase."

Brig watched me with amazement. "Tempe. Don't you get the point of this? They knew where you were staying. Conch belts can be replaced. By the way, if you'd hinted you wanted one, I'd've included a nice belt in the basket of clothes from this morning. I saw several at Kemps."

"Oh, Brig! That reminds me. Thank you. I owe you a ton. And you have great taste. You picked exactly what I would have and I'm overwhelmed. But I can't keep the earrings, gorgeous as they are. Way too pricey. I'm no dope. Those are not rhinestones swimming just below the sails."

He shook his head. "First of all, you don't owe me. Secondly, thank you for the compliment. Thirdly, you are going to keep the earbobs because I got them much cheaper than I care to tell you. Those are tiny little diamonds, and they look lovely on you, and I owe you for making you dance at the ladies club last night."

I put my hand up to stop him. Pointless.

He went on. "Tempe, let me finish. I knew you weren't thrilled with having to get up there and wiggle. Although I must admit I enjoyed every bit of that performance. I'm hoping for a repeat sometime in private. With extras."

I glanced at him, started to comment on the brash assumption that I'd be doing any wild shimmies for the man anytime soon, but he interrupted me. "Tempe, are you listening to and understanding what I'm trying to say? Someone checked you out. Someone has your things. The very nice maid who told me this said she had a bad feeling, but she didn't want to complain to anyone."

I stiffened. "The nice maid? Which one? That cute little girl from the outskirts of Pune or the blonde from Sweden working her way around the world?"

Brig's eyes opened wide. I looked for a hole to dive into. I was jealous. I did not need to be jealous. I did not want to be jealous. But darned if I wasn't jealous. For an instant, I flashed on the photo I'd found in Brig's drawer back at the hotel. Well, the man was gorgeous. He attracted women the way the vendors on Grant Road attract flies and beggars. I didn't need to be one of them.

I tilted my chin with a bit of defiance, just as Brig said, "Miss Walsh. My, my. Where's that little diatribe coming from? Will you listen to me? The maid in question hit ninety years old a decade ago and must be the great-great-great grandma of fifty kids. But she's an observant old bird."

"Oh."

"Do you understand that you can't go back there? That these various goons have ties all over this city and that they're after you? Which is why we're here."

"Brig, you lost me. We're about to go touring the lots at the capital of Indian cinema because murderous scumbags are hot on my trail?"

He grinned. "That's a decent take on the situation. But we're at Film City because you, my darling talented Tempe, are about to join the ranks of the legion of stars working on Jake's next picture. You've just been given a job in a new Masala extravaganza."

"Say what?"

Brig nodded. "I told Jake about your expertise as both a dancer and a gymnast. I also told him you were quite beautiful and you had legs up to your lovely neck that would look quite nice in high-cut bottoms. He whipped out a contract on the spot. So, you're dancing in *Mela Manokamana*. Loosely translated it means—"

"Carnival of Desire? Lust? Yes?"

He beamed at me. "That's very good. Jake won't even have to have a script translated for you since you know Hindi. He'll love that. Saves costs."

"Right."

He hastened to add, "I'm also in the movie and will be more than happy to keep an eye on you. Or more."

"Brig. Keep the eyes to yourself, okay?"

"Fine. No discussion of eyes or other body parts. For now. Anyway, you'll be hiding out in an apartment about an hour's drive from Vivek Studios. With Asha Kumar, celebrity actress and ex-fiancée of Mr. Jake Roshan."

Chapter 8

Jake finished his phone call. He trotted over to where Brig and I still stood staring at each other.

"Good news! I'll have money coming in on the next film from a very legitimate group in New Zealand. I can rest easier now. I must admit, I've been concerned."

I must have looked puzzled because Brig interjected. "Masala films are all too often financed by what we might refer to as some of the more unsavory lads in Bombay. Boys of the Mahindra persuasion. They think nothing of making poor honest businessmen pay protection or shooting them if they, well, disagree. Our Jake here sweats buckets every time he starts a film until he can be certain his backers are legit."

I glared at Brig. "Ah. Super. I am now so thrilled. I can't tell you how much that reassures me. You've got me hiding right back in the middle of the same slimy group of thugs who want to kill me. Thanks so much."

Jake took over for Brig, which I knew could be a difficult task. "Tempe. Okay if I call you that?"

I nodded yes. "Miss Walsh" now referred to that girl in the buttoned-down business suit from New York. The girl who hadn't existed since about seven o'clock last evening. The girl I wasn't sure would ever exist again. Unasked for, yet storming right into my brain, rushed the thought, *The girl I don't want to exist again.*

"Tempe. Brig, for once, has the situation well in hand. He's told me about the gentlemen who seem determined to locate you and Shiva's Diva. Let me reassure you. Mahindra and Patel are not part of the gangsters who desire to take over cinema. Mahindra is one of the wealthiest men in India. Patel is a thug, nothing more. He wants to dive into whatever scheme seems most profitable. He has no interest in anything artistic."

I glanced at Brig. "Which brings up another point. Why are those guys so determined to have Shiva's Diva? They're not art lovers. Well, at least not Patel. Don't they know about the curse? Aren't they trembling under their turbans?"

Brig smiled. "Mahindra fancies himself a great patron of the arts. And remember, Tempe, there's a blessing attached that brings luck and prosperity. I think our boy Patel is too stupid to believe in curses or blessings. I imagine Seymour Patel wants to steal it, sell it in an overseas market, then retire to Pago Pago."

I focused on what, to me, was the most interesting part of that discourse.

I squealed, "Wait. Seymour? *Seymour?* The scourge of Bombay, the man whose sidekick missed killing me by an earring, the biggest crook this side of Gotti is named Seymour? No wonder he's so clueless. The one other person in the world named Seymour sings in a musical called *Little Shop of Horrors* and plays with a giant alien plant named Audrey Two. Jeez. Seymour. That explains a lot."

I would have gone on. I could have gone on. Anything to chat about trivial matters and stop thinking about the very real danger Seymour and Mahindra posed. But just then I heard Jake take a sharp inhale of breath and tense up like a pony preparing to receive a five-hundred-pound rider.

I lifted my brows toward him in a wordless question. He pointed to a very sporty, very attractive, very classic sky blue convertible racing in through the entrance gates of Vivek Studios. The driver zoomed into a spot designated "No Parking"— and for good reason. There was barely enough space for vehicles the size of small motorcycles, much less for an American car (even one so diminutive as this two-seater convertible). Even its fins were slender and sporty—and it was still a tight fit.

I squinted. A girl who looked like she had barely reached

puberty, much less legal driving age, jumped out of the convertible and began striding toward our trio.

"Jake! What the crap is this urgent crisis you had to see me about? I thought I made it clear we weren't on speaking terms. I'll talk to you on the set for *Mela* or *Carnival*, or whatever the hell the name is, but that's it."

Jake held up his hand for silence. "It's not *my* crisis. Brig needs help, as does the lady with him."

A tiny nose tilted upward with the regal quality of a medieval queen. Eyes the same shade of blue as the convertible stared at me.

"And just who the hell are you and what are you doing here?"

I answered with as much grace as I could. "Tempe Walsh. Lady in crisis."

I saw her lips twitch in what had to be the suppression of a smile.

"Interesting. Are you friend or foe of Jake?"

I bit my lip. "Um, neither yet. I just met him about fifteen minutes ago."

She snorted. "Plenty of time to discover that Mr. Roshan is a rat. A first-class double-A-battery-run rat."

I had no idea what a "first-class-double-A-battery-run rat" meant, but I admired the vivid image. And I understood her as only one female can understand another. Two minutes after meeting Brig O'Brien, I'd been struggling between the desire to strangle him or throw him to the ground and pounce on every inch of his delicious body.

I had no idea how to answer her about Jake. I was also intrigued by her accent, which seemed familiar. Her looks were a mix of Indian and English. Yet she spoke slang and without that overly correct grammar affected by folks trying not to make a mistake in a foreign tongue.

I shrugged. Might as well side with my new, if temporary, employer. "I guess . . . friend? Since Jake has agreed to help Brig and me with some trouble."

"Trouble? Whatcha done?"

Brig took over. "Nothing. We did nothing. It's what we *have* that's the problem."

"Stolen artifacts? Crown jewels? Or simply a nice portrait? A Degas or a Matisse, perhaps?"

Just what *did* Brig do for a living? Make off with priceless objects on a weekly basis?

I glanced back at Brig's diminutive accuser, who winked at me. "He's a modern day Robin Hood, our Briggan. Rob from the rich, give to himself."

Brig chimed in, "Now, darlin'. Don't be havin' Tempe thinkin' I'm some sort of thievin' villainous pirate."

I'd noticed his Irish brogue grew stronger in moments of stress, moments of deceit, or moments when Brig desired to be ultracharming. This moment seemed to encompass all three. I ignored him and turned back to the girl.

"We seem to have taken possession of a statue Mr. O'Brien calls Shiva's Diva. A statue both cursed and blessed and a statue every criminal within a fifty-mile radius wants to own. We've taken shelter with Jake. Although why we can't just take the darned piece into the nearest police station and head on a plane back to the States is beyond my comprehension."

She looked horrified. "You can't do that! There are tons of cops here as corrupt as the crooks. Poking out of mobsters' coat pockets. Now, the good ones are great, but it's the decision as to who's who that's the killer. Besides, if this sucker has both a curse and a blessing, you'd better find out which one is going to land on *your* head before you give it to anyone."

Brig nodded. "Exactly. Which is why Tempe and I came to Jake who kindly agreed to let us perform in his latest cinematic masterpiece. Tempe's a fine dancer and I'm no slouch myself in the martial arts. Not to mention I do a nice Irish clog."

She closed her eyes in mock horror. "Right. I'm sure *Carnival of Lust* needs the Irish-American doing the Riverdale dance in the middle of the scene where the villain blows up half of the temple. We'll stick you in a loincloth and tap shoes. Works for me."

"Wait," I interjected, "Riverdale? Don't you mean *River-dance*?"

She snickered. "Mr. O'Brien spent his depraved youth in Riverdale. The Bronx, girl. Probably clogged his way out of boarded-up windows while burglarizing homes every weekend."

I glanced at Brig. His grin widened. I ignored him and turned back to the girl.

"So? What do you think about us hiding out here?"

She shrugged. "Makes sense. As much as anything I've ever seen you do make sense, O'Brien. I guess my question is, where do I come into the equation?"

She still hadn't looked at Jake. He muttered under his breath. Three sets of eyes opened wide.

Asha yelled, "What? Yo? I didn't understand that, Mr. Roshan. Say again, please."

Jake did. "Briggan will be staying with me. And Tempe will be staying with you. You have a spare bedroom. If that's all right with you. Otherwise, I'll make arrangements for her to have a trailer on the studio lot."

My brain suddenly clicked onto the situation. This had to be Jake's ex-girlfriend, who'd dumped him days earlier. Miss Asha Kumar, singer, actress, and exotic star of Indian screen extravaganzas.

I must have looked stunned.

She grinned at me. "Just got it, huh? Since the guys were too damn rude to introduce me."

"Well, Jake had said he planned to ask you if I could stay. I just didn't expect Asha Kumar to be, um—"

"From Jersey?"

"You're kidding."

She giggled. "You're looking at a homegrown gal from Woodbridge. My mom's maiden name was Schwartz. Really. Married Daddy in Newark, then moved to Woodbridge and had me. Barbara Ashley Kumar. I changed it to Asha when I started working in Bollywood six years ago."

I couldn't help staring. "Damn. I can't believe this. A Jersey girl. I grew up in Manhattan. Hey, how old are you? If you don't mind my asking?"

She giggled again. "Thirty. Yeah, I know, I know. I look like jailbait on a stick. It's the minuscule height plus these rotten elf features. I used to get carded in clubs from Atlantic City to Brooklyn. At least in Bombay everyone knows my face so I don't have that problem."

My age. Jersey. I beamed at her. She beamed back, then grabbed my arm.

"Okay, Tempe. Let's get you back to my place and get settled. We'll let Brig and Mr. Roshan do whatever they need to do without us. Perhaps forever."

Jake looked pained. "Asha. Can you take two minutes and come talk with me? In private?"

"Nope. Bye."

She whirled around. I had no choice but to follow if I wanted a ride to her place—and the use of my right arm. Not to mention I wanted to remain on good terms with this explosive Indian-American actress from a city twenty-five miles outside of New York.

We'd made it to the car, chatting about Jersey outlet malls, before I thought to turn around and see if the fellows were watching. Brig and Jake hadn't moved. I had the impression they had yet to even speak since Asha preemptively took over my security issues.

I called to Brig, "O'Brien? Where is our little ivory singer just now, anyway? The statuette to kill for?"

He looked around the empty lot with horror etched on his face.

"Tempe! Hush. The lady in question is in a fine hidey-hole. We'll discuss this later, okay? On the set tomorrow. I believe Jake is putting us together for a dance number. We can talk while riding the Ferris wheel."

I knew I wouldn't get an answer out of the man even if I

hadn't stupidly yelled the question in a very public place. I whirled around, then jumped into Asha's convertible without bothering to open the door.

She snorted. "I can do that *if* I take a running leap. My legs are too short. I look like a junior high school track star pre-puberty trying to tackle the college hurdles. In other words, dumb and graceless."

I smiled. "There are one or two advantages to being tall. Until I turned nineteen, I was five-four. I swear I grew four inches in one year just in time to be booted out of the Olympic trials for gymnastics. No one believed any girl who wasn't less than five feet could manage the vault or the parallel bars. The fact that my specialty had always been floor didn't penetrate their bigoted skulls."

"So you lost out on being an Olympic champion?"

"Pretty much. But I was still considering becoming a professional dancer, and I knew height had advantages when auditioning for musicals, as far as a lot of choreographers are concerned. So I rejoiced that I wasn't a tiny elf anymore."

"Thanks. So much."

I laughed at her. "You've done quite well as an elf, Miss Kumar. I hear you're the premiere star of Bollywood. Not bad for a girl from Woodbridge."

I cringed for a second as the star almost sideswiped two taxicabs. I hoped the man who'd taken me to Vivek Studios wasn't one of them. I glanced at Asha.

"But you definitely drive like a Jersey girl."

She giggled. "Why do you think Jersey drivers drive the way they do? They learned in India. When, or if, you do get back to Manhattan, take another look at the woman in the minivan with the cell phone in one hand and the mascara in the other who's just cut into your lane. Bombay born and raised. License from Newark. Swear."

I liked this girl. I had a feeling we'd be great roommates. Then I wished I hadn't remembered why I needed a roommate. She seemed to sense that my thoughts had shifted from New Jersey drivers to something more serious. She glanced at me while she slipped into a tight spot in front of a delivery truck and behind a beat-up ancient sedan.

"Tempe? What, by the grace of Brig's little goddess, is going on?"

"That's a very good question. I wish I knew the answer to it."

I narrated the events of the last twenty-four hours, beginning with the shoot-out at Hot Harry's Saloon. She listened with true concern when I told her how Mahindra's men had sent me somersaulting into a storeroom to escape their flying bullets and how Patel's men had made me their private dartboard. She loved hearing about my bump-and-grind routine at C.C. Curry's and wanted more information about where, and in what circumstances, Brig and I had spent the night.

I skimmed over the details of kissing Mr. O'Brien but did say I was now dressed in clothes purchased by Mr. O'Brien because I had nothing else. She tried to interrupt to ask about my sleeping attire while at the Sea Harbor Hotel, but I cut her off by telling her Brig's latest news about a man resembling one of the thugs removing my stuff from the hotel.

She hit the brakes. Hard. At least we were at a red light. One of the few she'd stopped for. She twisted in her seat to look at me.

"Do you have any idea what Brig intends to do? I mean, he's got this statue, the bad guys think you've got it, you're both about to hide out—if appearing in a film that will be seen by millions can be considered going undercover. And where will this Shiva's Diva end up? Has Brig even said?"

I lifted both brows and grimaced. "I haven't a clue. Do you realize I still don't know yet if the man who hired me as a translator is even alive?"

"Well, hell, girl, time for the ladies to do a bit of sleuthing. Leave the boys out of it since they haven't done a real terrific job of managing this situation so far."

She grinned. "Besides, I've always wanted to be Nancy Drew. I have all the books. I can get in and out of haunted houses, up and down spiral staircases, and sneak behind hidden bookcases. I could hot-wire a car by the time I hit twelve. Not that Nancy ever did, but I thought it was a useful skill to acquire. So, whatcha say, Walsh?"

An invitation to embark on a bit of private investigation with India's latest cinema celebrity. A spunky, mad-driving starlet who thought her fiancé was a double-A-battery-run rat and who had a secret desire to be a covert operative. With Asha by my side, the previous twenty-four hours with Brig were about to look like a tea party with my great-aunt Geneva—a ninety-year-old agoraphobic who hadn't stepped outside of her house for forty years.

Chapter 9

Asha decreed our first stop would be the Taj Mahal Hotel. I liked this idea. I hoped to find the sweet little old maid who'd been so kind as to give Brig O'Brien all that information about my belongings, including my passport.

The Taj Mahal Hotel is an architectural wonder in contrasts. Old meets new. India meets England. It's a five-star hotel that offers restaurants, nightclubs, spas, aerobic classes, and a pool. It can best be described as a grand, expensive palace. Ray had paid for my room as part of my salary. There was no way I could afford such a luxurious hotel otherwise. I'd felt like a trespasser all six hours I'd spent there.

Not so Miss Asha Kumar. This was her turf. Accompanying Asha gave me a new outlook on how one navigates the snob factor at classy hotels.

To begin with, Asha didn't bother dealing with parking once we reached the Taj Mahal Hotel. She stopped the car inches away from an eager, trembling valet, then waited for him to open her door. I stepped out on my own, although I did use the door instead of jumping out the top. Asha tossed her keys at the kid, then she grabbed my arm and we sauntered into the Taj Mahal Hotel like two starlets in search of paparazzi to tempt.

I did not look like the same girl who'd checked in yesterday morning. That Miss Walsh had been groggy from airsick meds, rumpled and wrinkled, but still appearing professional in a brown business suit. I'd wanted to make it clear that this interpreter was here to do a job. Period. Which was why before I left for Hot Harry's, I'd changed into my navy two-piece suit, slapped on a tinge of mascara and blush, and pulled my hair back into a bun.

This afternoon I had on one of the new outfits Brig had bought for me at Kemps Corner. Tight black jeans with a matching cap-sleeved black silk top. My hair was loose and waving over my shoulders. While I hadn't quite matched the outrageousness of the cosmetics for my impromptu performance at C.C. Curry's, I did sport decent amounts of blush, eyeliner, mascara, taupe eye shadow, and a nice shade of apricot lipstick; all items Brig had thoughtfully included in the gift bag. The man might be a rogue, but his taste matched my own. All the colors had been carefully chosen for a true redhead.

I had to banish thoughts of Brig from my mind before embarking on this little exercise in detection with Asha, the thirty-year-old celebrity vixen loved by millions. Ray might have had authority and that distinctly American businessman swagger, but Asha had presence and panache. I took a deep breath and prepared to follow her lead, wherever it took me.

There were perks to standing beside Asha Kumar at a hotel counter listening to a voice that easily changed from pure Jersey to the refined tones of an Indian actress with an impeccable command of both Hindi and English. Within moments, Asha and I were in the luxurious suite of the hotel manager, a Mr. Chopra. The offices looked out over the harbor, and for a few moments I simply enjoyed taking in the view.

Then we got down to business. I'd warned Asha that since we still didn't know who all the players were in this game, it would be best not to reveal too much about Shiva's Diva. She showed me she knew how to take direction without losing control of the action.

She smiled at Mr. Chopra. Heck, she practically simpered.

"Mr. Chopra. This is Miss Tempe Walsh, a dear friend of mine from the States. She came for a visit and checked in here two nights ago. When she sent someone back for her things earlier today so she could come to my apartment, she discovered that someone not authorized had checked out for her, and her things had been removed. Naturally, I am most upset at this lack of courtesy!"

Asha was good. She'd given the basics. She hadn't really lied either. Barbara Ashley Kumar had become my dear friend about two hours earlier. So she told the truth at least in that. I liked knowing I now had three friends in Bombay.

Asha turned and winked at me. Chopra grabbed his phone, dialed someone at the desk, and tried to find out why such a mess had occurred at his hotel.

Asha whispered, "No biggie. Basic Improvisation 101. I teach it twice weekly. I can lie like a rug. Anyplace. Anytime. Not, however, with anyone. Regardless of what the tabloids say."

I tried not to laugh. Chopra turned and smiled at us both.

"I am so sorry, Miss Walsh. The desk clerk informs me that the mix-up appears to be the result of your traveling companion misunderstanding your plans."

I threw him a sharp look. "Traveling companion?"

"Yes. A Mr. Raymond Decore from New York City. Apparently, he told the clerk you had a friend in the city and would not be returning to the Taj Mahal." Chopra looked concerned. "Mr. Decore did not seem to know the friend was Miss Kumar, our beautiful lady of the cinema."

I nodded. "And did Mr. Decore happen to say where he'd taken my things?"

"The clerk did not know. He did not ask, you see, not wishing to insult the man. I believe he assumed, that you and he, that is . . ."

Chopra turned red.

Asha rescued him. "He thought they were a couple, yes?"

He nodded in the affirmative. "Yes. I am most sorry that he reached this conclusion. Apparently, Mr. Decore specifically gave that impression. I do apologize."

I stared at a small boat with sails gliding across the water.

What a nice place to be on a sunny afternoon. No worries other than how much wind would rise to allow the sailor to whip past the yachts and cargo ships and head for open space and freedom.

I touched my ear. Last night a pair of cute, inexpensive sail-shaped earrings had dangled there, then been destroyed. Today, fancy earrings swung in their place. A good trade all in all. But now it appeared Ray Decore's very identity had been stolen by one of Mahindra's or Patel's minions. I wasn't sure if I felt angrier over my things being missing or my reputation being sullied.

I smiled at Chopra. "Perfectly reasonable assumption. Mr. Decore and I are business associates." I giggled. "And Mr. Decore presumes too much. I'm sure you've seen that kind of behavior before at the hotel?"

He nodded, relieved I hadn't pitched a fit.

Asha launched back into the meat of the matter. "Mr. Chopra, do you have any idea where Mr. Decore was going? Back to the States?"

He looked surprised. "Oh, he did not check out. Perhaps I did not make that clear. He merely said Miss Walsh now had other accommodations."

Bingo. Mahindra, or perhaps Patel, had usurped Ray's room as well as his name. I opted for Mahindra. Patel didn't have enough class or English to fool a hotel desk clerk.

We thanked Mr. Chopra for his kindness in answering our questions, then Asha autographed several pictures of herself for him and his family.

Chopra beamed. "My wife adores you, Miss Kumar. We have seen *Pirate Princess* at least three hundred and fifty times. We have the DVD. My favorite part is you with Spot the tiger."

Asha whispered to me as we left, "The DVD just came out three weeks ago."

I had to rent this flick when I had a chance.

We left the enthralled manager and headed for the new wing of the hotel. Ray Decore's room was on the fifth floor, as was my original room six doors down from his. Each room on this side of the hotel had a balcony and a view of the harbor, amenities I hadn't used since I'd spent my first three hours in Bombay sleeping. After that my night had been taken up with dodging bullets, shedding clothes, getting kissed, and listening to O'Brien talk. The latter being the most time-consuming. The kiss had been the most. Just two words. The most.

I couldn't think about Brig right now. I stopped the elevator at the fourth floor. Asha looked surprised.

"What? I thought you were one up?"

"I am. Well, was. But it occurs to me that I can't just knock on the door and tell some poor stranger, 'Hey! This is my room and I want my stuff!' Right?"

Asha nodded. "True. We also can't go pounding on Ray Decore's door with the same question. I have a feeling a brand-new, innocent visitor from Finland or Russia now occupies *your* room. But, I'll bet money that one of Mahindra's gonzos is snoozing on Decore's bed."

She punched the Open button on the elevator and we stepped out onto the fourth floor. Teatime. We didn't see a soul in the hall. Everyone must be out at the cafés enjoying a nice brew and a scone. Sounded like a good way to spend this hour. My large brunch from Café de la Plaz had become a wisp of memory.

A maid passed by with a load of fresh linens. She ignored us, intent on making her delivery and perhaps heading to the hotel kitchen for her own tea break.

Asha nudged me with her elbow.

"Ouch!"

"Shh! Wimp! I have a plan."

"No."

"What do you mean, no? You haven't heard it yet."

"Asha, I've known you, what, two hours? Long enough to see wheels turning. Wheels grinding out little ideas like dressing up as maids and sneaking into Ray's old room."

Asha looked at me with admiration. "You're good. Actually my plan was to ask that maid if she'd mind checking to see if the so-called Mr. Decore is currently flat out on his back snoring, or fornicating, or chanting mantras in his room, but I like your idea much better."

I groaned. "Asha! I'm sorry I suggested it. This is bound to turn into one of those British farces where everyone and his brother are in maid or butler costumes and hiding under beds or in beds—with each other. I'm not ready for that particular production, thank you."

"I did six of those plays in high school, and they're a lot like Jake's movies. Easy. It's all in the timing. Now just hang here a minute."

She took off down the hall after the maid. I could see an excited conversation taking place but couldn't hear the substance. Asha sauntered back within minutes.

"I am *sooo* good. I told her I'm researching for a part and you're a new actress who's doing a scene with me. The red hair kinda bothered her, but I explained that Jake wanted more foreigners in this particular film. More than me, that is. And I have dual citizenship."

This business of taking off on tangents during moments of stress seemed contagious.

"Asha, you're worse than Brig. Get to the point."

"Oh. I asked where we could find uniforms and keys. And she told me."

Definitely perks to hanging out with a movie star.

Like most hotels, Taj Mahal used those ghastly ATM-style cards that force one to insert it and then in a mad dash try to open the door while the green light is still blinking. I suppose they're better for inhibiting robbers accustomed to jiggling nail files, bobby pins, or other sharp instruments into keyholes. Then again, I'm sure any clever thief can manage a way to insert his driver's license or credit card into the darn thing and gain easy entry.

We had to trek down to the basement to the maid's closet to get the uniforms and key cards, but we were back in the elevator and on the fifth floor within twelve minutes—with a passcard that should open Ray's door.

We looked ridiculous. A redheaded fair-complexioned woman towering over a tiny dark-haired girl who looked barely out of puberty. But the few people either entering or exiting the rooms on floor five didn't seem to notice. Amazing how invisible one can become in a black and white uniform. Especially to those folks who look on anyone in service as unworthy of attention.

Asha nudged me again. I nearly dropped the load of towels draped over my arm. If she continued poking me, I'd have bruises larger than my entire torso by nightfall.

"What?"

"I think it's best if I go into Ray's room first. The bad guys know you. They don't know me."

I stared at her. "Bombay's sweetheart of cinema? You don't think they'll recognize your face? Like it's not plastered over half the billboards in town? Like there's anyone outside of Mahindra, Patel, and me who hasn't seen *Pirate Princess* at least four hundred times? Why don't we just bring in Spot the tiger and stick him in a uniform while we're at it?"

She drew herself up to her full height of four foot nine and sneered at me. "Well, excuse me, but I can do this. I'm an actress. I'm in a maid's costume. Aside from no one bothering to see the face atop the collar, I'm about to do the veil thing."

I sighed. Asha had managed to find two veils amongst the starched uniforms and had sashayed out with them under her arm. She handed me one, then eyed me critically.

"Put it on. Plenty of Muslim women work in hotels. No one will think a thing about it. Really, Tempe, that stupid little cap will *not* hide Miss Flaming Carrot Top."

I did as asked. Even if Mahindra's and Patel's goons didn't quite remember my face, the red curls were enough to blow my cover. I felt certain my hair had been the tip-off to Patel at C.C. Curry's that all was not kosher last night.

I wandered around the hall pretending to look busy while Asha calmly inserted the passcard and entered Ray's room. I expected to hear shouts or guns or screams. Instead, Asha stuck her head out and motioned to me. The hall remained empty. I hurried over to the doorway.

"No one's home, Tempe. Come on in and we'll see if we can find any clues as to the whereabouts of Ray Decore. Not to mention discover who the hell took over his room."

This did not make me happy, but I quickly slipped inside. If a nonfriendly returned and found one maid in his room, either of us might be able to talk our way out. Asha knew Hindi, and I could say I was a European girl working my way across India. But two maids? Yeah, Taj Mahal was a five-star hotel, but hiring two maids to deliver one stack of towels? Not plausible.

We began to tour the room. Two suitcases had been placed on luggage racks but were closed. Asha headed right to them.

"Crap. They're locked." She looked up at me, now headfirst into the trash can by a large desk. "Tempe. Any good at picking locks?"

"Excuse me? Jersey girl? You think I spent my childhood in Manhattan hanging with juvies breaking into cars on Fifth Avenue?"

She grinned. "Well, yeah. You strike me as pretty resourceful."

"Resourceful, maybe. But my off hours as a kid were spent in dance or gym classes. My talents do not include breaking and entering. Although I think I now have to change my résumé to include that activity."

She ignored me. She headed for the bathroom. "I want to see if the key for the luggage might be tucked into a travel kit. And use the facilities while I'm here."

I whispered, "Asha? Try the shaving kit. Bad guys always stash their stuff there in movies. Maybe that's why they have permanent five o'clock shadow."

She rolled her eyes but nodded. I began digging through papers in the wastebasket, for what I had no idea. I did find yesterday's *New York Times* crossword half finished. In pencil, not in ink.

I snorted. "Wimp." Then I picked up the pencil and twirled it for a moment. I considered filling in twenty-six down—"a five-letter word for demented"—with "Tempe" and couldn't resist writing the correct one, which was "crazy." Then I stopped.

I motioned to Asha, who'd just peeked out around the bathroom door. The dismay in her eyes told me that she'd heard it as well. The muffled sound of a card key being inserted into the door.

I panicked. I ran to the balcony doors, threw them open, stepped outside, and immediately closed the drapes behind me. I prayed Asha could fake out whoever had entered. I knew our chances were better with one actress improvising than with two.

No voices. Either the guy who'd entered had ignored the new maid or the bed had provided a hiding place for the new maid, or the guy had just blown off all niceties and knifed the new maid. I stayed crouched on the balcony, unsure whether to pop out screaming and kicking or wait for the next sound to determine the course of action most appropriate.

The snap of something metal breaking surprised me so much I had to try and find out if Asha was in trouble. I parted one small edge of the curtain.

A man stood with his back to me, rummaging through a suitcase. Then he stood straight up and turned toward the window. I closed my eyes and willed the balcony to collapse, taking me with it.

The doors flung open. I clutched the pencil, my only weapon. I opened my eyes wide in the classic manner of the deer in the headlights. Then I blinked.

"Brig?"

"Tempe? What in the name of Saint Swithen are you doing on the balcony?"

"Hiding. Is there really a Saint Swithen?"

He groaned. "I thought you were safe and sound at Asha's. Giggling over tea and crumpets about what a fool Jake is when it comes to his ladylove."

The woman in question crawled out from under the bed.

"Yo! Brig. I'm so glad it's you and not some killer popping in to slash my throat."

He sat down on the edge of the bed and groaned again. Louder. Asha plopped next to him. I sank into the chair by the desk. The three of us stared at each other.

Brig finally broke the silence. "Ladies? Would you mind explaining what you're doing here? And just whom were you planning to kill with the blunt pencil, Miss Walsh?"

Asha smiled. I smiled. She said nothing. Brig glared. Fine. Up to me.

"We're trying to find out what happened to Ray and who's using his room and where my stuff is. You?"

"The same."

I squinted at him. "How did you get in?"

He smiled. "With a room key. Passcard."

I threw the pencil at him. I missed.

"And how did you get the room key? Bribery? Pickpocketing? You're still in civies, not decked out as hotel help. We managed to get two keys. Everyone thought we were maids."

"And lovely ya are, the both of you in the black and white. The veil is a nice touch, Tempe, but your hair is peekin' around the cloth. Looks quite exquisite in the sunlight. But very red, you know."

I might have known he wouldn't answer about the passcard. I tried a different question.

"Did you find anything interesting in the suitcase you managed to pry open?" I glanced at Asha. "Obviously, Mr. O'Brien did spend some quality time with the boys in the 'hood. His lock-picking skills are excellent."

He inclined his head. "Sadly, those skills did not yield anything of interest. At least in suitcase number one. Other than the knowledge that the user has fine taste in shirts. Armani. Mediums. Too small and I dislike the color."

He turned to Asha. "I know Tempe didn't find anything on the balcony. She'd never have been able to contain her joy if her own traveling case had been stowed out there. You discover anything under the bed?"

Asha pursed her lips, shook her head no, and then grinned. "Yes. Taj Mahal Hotel runs the cleanest accommodations I've ever seen. Not a dust bunny in sight. I'm very impressed."

I stood. "This is pointless, gang. Looks like it's time to turn in our uniforms. Maybe hang out in the lobby for the rest of the day and see if we recognize any of the players connected to this show?"

Brig put his hand to his lips. We froze. Once again we could hear the sound of a passcard being inserted into that door. And unless Jake had driven off in search of either Brig or Asha, this time the three of us might well be facing a killer.

Chapter 10

We had no time to dive under the bed, scurry to the balcony, hide behind the shower doors, or crawl into the toilet. The door opened. A gun entered. Well, a man holding a gun entered. But all I saw was the gun.

Brig sprang to his feet, intent on shielding me from that gun. Bless the man. How he figured he'd save me from blazing bullets was a mystery, but I had to give him high marks for chivalry and sheer guts.

I sank back down onto the chair. If death proved imminent, at least being comfortable would be nice. As I casually swung one leg over the other in an attitude of inappropriate nonchalance while also hiding my shaking limbs, I looked up at the newcomer's face. I sprang up again.

"Ray?"

He moved to one side of Briggan, who had planted his frame in the middle of the room, ready to defend honor, country, and all of our hides.

"Tempe?"

"Ray! Hot damn! You're alive! I thought Mahindra had killed you back at Hot Harry's, then taken over your room! Or Patel. Either. Or both. This is incredible! How on earth did you escape? You were just lying on the table there. I really did think you were dead."

Brig sat back down on the bed. Asha hadn't moved. She did let out a whoosh of breath.

Brig stood and extended his hand in greeting. "Mr. Decore. You don't know what poor Tempe has been through since

Mahindra's hooligans came burstin' through Hot Harry's with murder on their minds. Lord, man, we thought you were at the bottom of the bay communin' with the eels!"

Ray stared at Brig. "Do you mind telling me who the hell you are and why you've taken over my bed?"

Good question. One a large bear had once asked a wench named Goldilocks. He hadn't gotten a straight answer either. Since Brig was on the receiving end of this current query, I figured Ray had as much luck as that furry fairy-tale bruin for a sane response.

Brig glanced at me. I smiled. Let the Irish charmer come up with a nice reason for breaking and entering and tossing Armani shirts.

"We'el, ya see, Tempe here thought you were either dead or mortally wounded, as 'twere. And we larned that someone had gotten rid of her t'ings, ya know, and checked her out of the hotel. And so we all came here to see if we could larn where her t'ings had been stashed and also to ascertain the right or wrong of your demise."

Not bad for a spur of the moment pack of half-truths and blame-the-other-guy-to-protect-your-butt excuses, done up in a pretty package topped by a ribbon of brogue. In this case "the other guy" was a girl. Me.

I stood.

"Ray Decore. Meet Briggan O'Brien. Brig rescued me from the back of the storeroom where I'd been hiding to escape the barrage of bullets pelting around the saloon."

Brig nodded.

I continued, "And then kindly put me up at his place when we discovered that two sets of rather nefarious sleazebags were chasing me."

Brig nodded again.

I continued, "And then agreed to help me find the things I brought from New York, like my passport, and helped me gain access when we thought Mahindra had usurped your identity and grabbed your room."

Brig smiled.

Ray leaned up against the door of the bathroom and motioned toward Asha. "Who's the shrimp?"

Asha stood.

In her best Hindi accent she whined, "I am just the maid. These two forced me to find a uniform for the tall lady and give them the key to the room. I am not involved in this. And I have work to do. May I leave, sir? And please do not report my conduct to the manager. I need this job very badly. I am begging of you."

I kept silent. As did Brig. I had no idea why Asha hadn't fessed up to her true identity, but she had a funny expression on her face. Ray nodded at Asha without even looking at her. He seemed to want her to leave.

"Well, I don't want to be responsible for getting you thrown out of work. It appears you got smooth-talked into sneaking into a guest's room by a man who is obviously experienced at charming women. Please leave. Now."

Asha stood, bowed, then in a flourish of chutzpah pointed to the towels she'd deposited onto the bed. "Clean, sir."

Ray grunted a thin "Thank you."

Asha wriggled out of the room with not a single backward glance.

Brig held his hand out to me. "Tempe? Perhaps now that we know Mr. Decore is safe, we should be about leavin' the man to be gettin' his own good rest. I'm sure he had an exhaustin' night as well."

I took his hand and smiled at Ray. "We'll talk in a bit. I'm just glad you're okay."

Ray did not return my smile. The gun shook in his hand, but he hadn't dropped it.

I started to feel nauseated. "Ray? What's the matter? You have this strange look on your face."

"I've never shot anyone before, Tempe. I'm debating the best way to go about it."

"Excuse me? Are you nuts? Are you going to try and take on Mahindra or Patel, the goons who've cornered the market on villainy? Don't. You'd never stand a chance."

Brig squeezed my hand. "He's not talking about our Indian friends, Tempe. Are you, Mr. Decore?"

Ray gave a slight bow. "Very astute, Mr. O'Brien. Tempe, for a woman who earns her living through communication skills, you're not quite up to your usual intellectual standards today. And O'Brien? Please, sit back down. You are far too tall to suit me."

I shut my eyes. "Oh crap."

"Ah. She's finally caught on."

I had. I muttered, "You've somehow turned into another bad guy, haven't you?"

I turned to Brig. "Remind me to tell Jake, if we get out of here with limbs intact, that this is an okay plot twist for one of his films. Not very original, but not completely clichéd either."

With Brig's hand holding mine, I attempted to edge closer to the door.

Ray coughed. "Tempe, do not move. Now then. You're a beautiful young lady and perhaps I have a way you can avoid floating around Bombay's harbors. I'm even confident we can come to a nice arrangement as to a future relationship. But your newest companion? I'm sorry, young man. I can't see where you fit into my plans to procure the Saraswati statue, then head to my villa in Nice for a few years."

I held my hand up. "Whoa! Ray. Can we go back a frame or two? I'm confused."

"You are? Why? I should think the situation would be quite clear to such a supposedly brilliant woman."

"Well, let me see if I've got the rhyme and reason of this particular scenario. First, you hire me in New York to help you in negotiations for a statue you're preparing to buy but which you are, in actuality, planning to steal. Sorry. Not original, Ray. Half of Bombay feels the same."

Brig nodded. Great. He agreed with my assessment. He should. He was part of the half.

"Be that as it may, Ray, we get here after an excruciatingly long flight with you trying to hit on me, which isn't really relevant but I thought I'd throw it in anyway."

I turned to Brig. "Where was I?"

"Hot Harry's. Almost."

"Ah. Okay, there we are in the middle of transactions with Khan and all hell breaks loose. Ray supposedly gets shot. I hide, meet Brig, haul butt, and get an unofficial tour of the seamier side of Bombay, which is also not relevant, although it was certainly interesting, at least to me. Then today I come back here with Brig to try and discover how you are and learn that you have lost your mind. Have I left anything out? Is that about it?"

"Correct. Up to a point. And that point is where a large amount of rupees would have been exchanged. An amount, my dear linguist, that translated to a million five, as I'm sure you recall. An amount I had no intention of paying."

"Aye," sighed Brig. "There's the rub."

I threw a glance at Brig. Quoting Shakespeare in stressful situations. A fascinating, if annoying, trait.

Ray nodded. "Exactly. The rub. In a way, Mahindra did me a favor when he and his thugs came barging in. Except that forced me to, as you so nicely phrased it, haul butt and hide from Mahindra in a disgusting cellar while I held an even more disgusting cloth to my bleeding ear. I bled a lot."

"Not enough," muttered Brig under his breath.

Ray shot him a look but didn't ask him to restate his comment. Instead, he turned back to me. "Now you tell me there's another set of goons? Patel? Was he the ugly one who came over during negotiations and offered me a cigar? Not that it matters. When I returned to Hot Harry's late last night and discovered the statue had disappeared, I was not pleased."

Brig squeezed my hand a bit harder. I did not flinch. I did not want to betray any movement that smacked of communication between Brig and me to the man holding a weapon aimed in our direction. I knew without words what Brig wanted to say with that touch. In what Ray might call succinct language, it translated as, "Shut up." As in "Don't tell him that Shiva's Diva made it out with us."

Ray did not know who had ended up with the statue. Which could be the primary reason those bullets were still in that gun instead of lodged in Brig's chest. Or mine.

Ray glared at me. "Would you happen to know where that statue is now?"

"No, Ray, I don't. Honestly. I would imagine it's residing either in the Mahindra mansion or the Patel pit. Maybe Khan himself retrieved it."

I hadn't lied. Brig had hidden Shiva's Diva sometime this morning and hadn't filled me in on her most current location.

Ray took a step closer to Brig, who'd found a nice perch for himself on the edge of the bed.

"What about you, Mr. O'Brien? Would your knowledge be a bit more up-to-date than Tempe's?"

He whacked Brig on the head with the muzzle of the gun. O'Brien must have possessed one heck of a strong Irish temple because, although he swayed, he remained upright.

Ray sighed. "Idiot playing the hero. Why don't I just shoot Tempe and see if that refreshes your memory?"

He turned toward me. I sent up prayers to Saraswati, Shiva, St. Cecilia (patron saint of music), and St. Swithen (patron saint of what? Irish Robin Hoods?) to get us out of this.

A high-pitched keening wail sounded from just outside Ray's door. The noise sounded like a cross between a moose in heat and a wild boar during a roundup. It produced a painful racket and provided a great distraction.

Ray whirled. Brig kicked the gun out of his hand. I threw the nearest large object, which happened to be the suitcase full of Armani shirts, at Ray's head. The door burst open. There stood Asha, still dressed in the maid's costume.

She held the door for us and in Hindi yelled, "Go! Now! It ain't getting any better!"

Brig and I did not waste time congratulating her on either her award-winning performance as the subservient hotel em-

ployee or the hideous noise she'd just made in order to get that
door unlocked without Ray noticing.

I'd really whapped Ray with the suitcase. He was rocking
and swaying on his knees. His hands were clasping his head
where two pink silk shirts from the tossed luggage had
landed. Brig and I leapt over the kneeling, crying, newly discovered miscreant, then charged out of the room.

The three of us galloped with the grace of stampeding oxen
toward the fire stairs located at the end of the hall. A pair of
English tourists inched back inside the elevator from which
they'd been trying to exit. As one, we turned and yelled,
"Sorry!"

With true English aplomb, one of the elderly ladies called,
"Not a problem, dears."

I could hear her as she turned to her companion and exclaimed, "Elizabeth? Did you see her? It's that darling little
film star. Asha Kumar. From *Pirate Princess*. I wonder if this
is part of a scene? On location, as they say. And if we might
be in it?"

Chapter 11

We made it into the lobby and out of the hotel without further incident. Once we neared the parking area, Asha walked up to the valet and requested that her convertible be retrieved within the next thirty seconds. She stated that if it arrived sooner, the valet would be on the receiving end of a nice *baksheesh* (i.e., tip).

Our intrepid starlet had shed her maid's costume somewhere along the fire-escape stairs. So, even if Ray saw a small woman roaring out of the Taj Mahal Hotel parking lot in an outrageous blue classic T-Bird, he wouldn't recognize the keening lunatic who'd aided Brig and me in his room. And he clearly wasn't up on Masala cinema, since, unlike the English tourists, he hadn't recognized her to begin with.

Brig and I found shelter behind an airport shuttle van and watched Asha speed away. We saw the valet smile as he counted the wad of rupees Asha had given him. I tried to convince Brig to jump into the van, head to the airport, and find the first flight headed toward the States or other points north. Brig pointed out that his passport was in Jake's home safe and that mine doubtless now fed fishies at the bottom of the bay. He didn't bother to mention he also had no intention of leaving Bombay without Shiva's Diva in his hot little hands.

Brig picked the lock of the van. We crawled inside the shuttle van so I could change back into my black jeans and shirt in relative privacy. I'd clung to my clothes the whole time I'd been in Ray's room, along with the three towels that had "Taj Mahal Hotel" embroidered on the hem. I now sat on one of the seats facing the center of the van and began to remove the maid's costume.

"Wow."

I turned.

Brig had politely held the towels over the back window of the van-now-dressing-room. But he was looking at me, not outside. "I knew black lace was the right choice."

"Brig. Wait. This isn't the time. Brig. Oh hell."

Brig edged closer. He touched my face with gentle fingers, then let his hands travel down to black lace garment number one, the bra with the front-closure clasp. My breath was coming in short spurts now. He leaned down and pressed his lips to mine. The clasp gave way.

Sunlight streamed into the back of the van.

"Elizabeth! Look! It's those other two darling actors who were with Miss Kumar. This is so thrilling! To actually see a movie in progress. But I was under the impression that kissing wasn't normally done in the Masala movies?"

I'd dived for both the floor and my T-shirt the instant the door to the van had opened and the sun, plus the two English tourists, brightened the interior.

Brig turned and barred them from seeing me. A lot of me. I quickly snapped the bra clasp back together while inwardly cursing the English. No wonder the Irish were always pissed at them. Their sense of timing was nothing short of criminal.

Brig's brogue filled the van. The Brits might not like the Irish politically, but few females can resist that sexy baritone sound.

"Ladies, so good of you to be so enthusiastic about the film-makin' progress! Yes, indeed, you can be seein' us on-screen in a few months. *Carnival of Lust* is the name of the flick, and while Miss Walsh and I be naught but poor players, Asha Kumar and Raj Ravi will star. This one will also be distributed in the Isles."

By this time, I had my underthings back in place and my shirt back on. We all sat in the van while Brig and I graciously signed autographs for these ladies who seemed to think meeting us was the highlight of their stay in Bombay.

Brig jumped down from the van, then helped lower me to the ground as well. "We'll be off, then, Miss Elizabeth, is it? And you, lovely lady?"

The other woman beamed and squeaked, "Margaret."

"Margaret. A foin, name, that. We'el, ladies, you be enjoyin' yer stay, then, and we'll be wishin' ya well."

After a spate of farewells, Brig and I left the van (and the maid's uniform). After a short wrestling match with my conscience, I also left the towels.

We barely made it outside before the driver of the shuttle arrived. He was carrying Elizabeth and Margaret's luggage and announcing that they were due to leave for the airport momentarily.

Brig and I nodded to him, then ran across the parking lot heading for the nearest train station, the Victoria Terminus. It took us thirty minutes to weave our way through the crowd waiting to buy tickets. I checked from time to time to see if my ribs were still intact from the pushing, shoving, and less-than-polite nudging from everyone trying to make it onto the train.

Traveling by rail in Bombay is not like taking the subway in New York or Boston or Chicago. At Victoria Terminus, the starting point for most of the trains, one stands on the platform along with several thousand other travelers watching for the next train with an empty car to pull up. While that train is still in motion, one jumps on board between large open doors, rather like a cattle car, in order to find a spot to stand when the train pulls out again to the next destination.

What the heck. I'd done somersaults and swings off a chandelier at a saloon. This was easy. We even found two seats and wedged ourselves between two men wearing white Nehru hip-length jackets and cotton pants. Ignoring the two foreigners, they yelled across us about the latest stock-market dive and whether the Euro currency would take over the system of rupees in India.

One of the men shrugged, nearly knocking my chin into my nose, then hollered, "I bought the DVD of *Pirate Princess* last night. My wife and I watched it five times."

The other man nodded, hitting Brig's shoulder more than once. "I got it three weeks ago. I've seen it more than three hundred times now. I love the part where Asha is lowered down into the cave where Spot the tiger sits waiting."

Brig winked at me and I wondered if the film I had yet to start, *Carnival of Lust*, would garner as much attention. Businessman number one answered my unspoken query.

"I can't wait to see Asha's new one, *Carnival of Lust,* with Raj Ravi. They are so marvelous together."

The two men were still chatting about film and film stars when Brig grabbed my hand and motioned to me to follow him. Getting off the train was similar to getting on. One waited for an opportune moment when the train was doing less than twenty miles per hour, then one jumped.

We took refuge at a restaurant called The Queen's Quarter that overlooked Juhu Beach. Very British, except for the Hindi waiters. Teatime had ended but quite a few patrons remained at their tables enjoying the afternoon break. Including one lady who sat watching the boats on the harbor. In quiet solitude.

Brig ordered tea and pastries for us, then suddenly excused himself and walked over to the lady's table. He leaned down and began to chat. I'd been on the receiving end of Brig's chats. It appeared another willing victim had succumbed to the famous O'Brien charm. She seemed so entranced that she hadn't even responded with either words or a slap. She just kept nodding and smiling.

I wavered between confused and ticked. Brig and I had come close to giving two tourists a close-up view of a rather erotic scene less than an hour ago. Now Brig was chatting up another female. It didn't make sense.

The lady turned. My breath caught. It was the woman I'd seen with Brig in the photo I'd found at his hotel.

Beautiful did not begin to describe the spectacular features.

Her complexion was olive and it was clear. Her small nose wouldn't have been utilitarian had it been one whit tinier. Her mouth was full. Her eyes were huge and the color of dark chocolate. Natural highlights leaning toward chestnut glinted from her perfectly coiffed dark hair.

Brig motioned to me to join them. At least this was someone he knew. He hadn't been hitting on some babe just to torment me or keep from being bored during tea.

I stood. Time to meet the goddess.

Brig stated, "Tempe Walsh. This is Claire Dharbar."

She smiled at me but said nothing. I smiled back and said "Hello." She inclined her head toward me and said nothing.

Brig took my hand, bent down and kissed my palm, then whispered, "I have to talk to Claire now about the Diva. It's very important, believe me. Do you mind waitin' at our table? They've brought the tea things out. With scones, darlin'. So have at it. All you want."

What could I say? "No, Brig. I do mind. I'm sitting here with messy hair and bruises on my body, really wanting to call it a day, and you're yakkin' it up with Miss-I'm-too-Superior-to-Talk-to-You-You-Peasant. The woman didn't even bother to say hello. But thanks, Mr. O'Brien, for at least ordering tea and pastries for the food hound here. I'll just go now and gobble down the specials The Queen has displayed on the tea carts today."

I kept silent.

I sat. I drank tea. I ate two scones, one muffin, and two divinely decadent Indian pastries made of carrots and raisins and pistachio nuts all swimming in cream. I watched Brig talk and Claire Dharbar listen. I tried to stop visions of them entwined in one another's arms making passionate love in a dark room while Shiva's Diva smiled over their heads.

Nutty. Neither had done anything to warrant my having this lurid vision. Jealousy is not a nice emotion. I resolved to work on that less-than-admirable aspect of my personality. One I never knew existed until this day.

"Tempe? You done eating?"

I looked at my clean plate. "I'd say so. Unless they serve samosas here."

He laughed. "Sorry. This place is Western food only, except for a few desserts. We'll get you some at Jake's. His cook does a marvelous potato-and-pea samosa."

I sighed. "Okay."

He politely helped me up as he said, "Grand. We'll be off then. Ready?"

"Yeah. Sure. Whatever."

I followed him out of the restaurant. Claire sat and watched the bay. Brig and I hailed a rickshaw and took off in silence.

Chapter 12

Brig and I stared at each other across the coffee table in Jake Roshan's lavishly decorated living room.

"So, do we have a plan? Wait. Let me rephrase that. Do *you*, Briggan O'Brien, have a plan? Now that other surprise elements—who should have been good guys but are now bad guys—have entered the playground of this already crowded court?"

"Aren't you mixing your metaphors?"

"Don't start with me. Just tell me there is some way to get out of Bombay, alive. Soon. Oh crap. I still don't have my passport."

Brig leaned against Jake's luxurious sofa.

"Wish I did have a plan, Tempe. I wasn't terribly surprised that Ray had joined the ranks of the felons but, unfortunately, that raises the growing number of miscreants on our tails."

I muttered, "Not to mention another interested party on your tail."

"What?"

"Nothing. Just admiring the, uh, woodwork in the room."

"Oh. That's nice."

I glared at him. He appeared far too smug. Well, why shouldn't he? He knew where he'd hidden the darn statue. And now it seemed he also had a strong idea of her ultimate destination.

I took a sip of tea. One has to love the British and their traditions. Academic endeavors stop for tea. Divorces are stalled for tea. Scandals rock the world, rioters riot, but the island of

Great Britain, and consequently the nations they'd held close to their collective vests for hundreds of years, stop everything for tea.

In my own private world that had gone mad in the last two days, this example of the teatime polite ritual and civilized behavior had become a godsend. Be that god Shiva, Saraswati, or Swithen.

Brig took a sip from his cup, then grabbed a large bite of scone and crammed the full piece into his mouth. I plopped three scones on my own plate and took another look around my latest temporary residence.

Jake lived in the Juhu Beach area, not far from where Brig and I had met Claire Dharbar this afternoon. Juhu Beach, a place once famous for the *filmi* crowd and their wild parties, as well as for luxury hotels and houses, had settled into a predominantly middle-class existence but it still held appeal.

Jake Roshan was considered part of the *filmi* elite and his house reflected that status. There were five bedrooms, four bathrooms, two living room/den areas, a maid's quarters, a library, an office, a rec room filled with videos, DVDs, games, and a dartboard. In Bombay, this was palatial for normal folks, but not ostentatious for an award-winning cinema director.

Brig and I had taken one short rickshaw ride to Jake's. That had been fun. A kid of perhaps twelve took the scenic route and the three of us sang operatic arias, pop, and country and western hits. He'd parked by a pair of small iron gates, then escorted us to Jake's door, bowing and blessing and grinning widely over the tip Brig had placed in his hand.

I smiled, thinking about our teenage singing driver.

"We should have introduced him to Jake. He could probably use him on a film."

"Who?"

"Rickshaw Ricky. Or whatever his name is."

Brig nodded. "He gave me a business card when I was doling out rupees. You were busy gawking at Jake's house. I told the kid to show up on the lot and give the guard my name. I'll get him an audition with Jake during filming tomorrow. Then you can watch over him Thursday."

Brig took another sip of tea.

I squinched my eyes at him. "Hold on. I thought you were going to be dancing merrily through the back lots of the studio both days?"

Brig nodded. "Wednesday only. The men aren't in any scenes Thursday. And I have people to see."

"About the statue? Brig, are you going to sell her to another party I haven't met yet?" *Or to Claire Dharbar, who I guess I have met? Briefly.*

"Tempe. Trust me. I can't tell you anything just yet, but I promise, Shiva's Diva will be in very good hands if I get things worked out. And you and I may just end up blessed after all."

"Yeah, right. I feel blessed, hunted through the streets and alleyways and hotel rooms of Bombay."

I chewed on the scone. It was excellent. I wanted to steal whomever Jake had hired as his cook more than anyone in Bombay wanted the Diva. After two bites, though, the food suddenly tasted like sawdust. Tears welled up in my eyes. Brig's own eyes widened.

"Tempe?"

"Sorry. I'm just thinking about Ray Decore. Damn. Jeremy, my boss, had warned me Ray fancied himself a lady-killer. Little did I know that would turn out to be literal, not figurative. But I can't believe Ray is as corrupt and evil as the other brutes. You think he really would have shot us?"

Brig nodded. "I hate to say it, but I do. Although maybe it's just temporary lunacy due to the curse. Ray fancies himself an artist because he likes to acquire fine things. Right? But he's a collector. Period. And Saraswati has a way of dealing with poseurs. It's as though the lady knows whom she wants holding and keeping her. And she gets angry when it's the wrong one."

Saraswati wasn't the only female with this attitude. I myself had strong feelings about who did, or did not, hold me. I brushed that thought aside and instead pondered Brig's assessment of a statue bearing responsibility for changing a man from good to bad.

Not that Ray had been a saint; he'd been somewhat of a cad about pursuing a relationship, but that's different than killing an ex-employee. Brig's theory sounded a bit wacky, but nonetheless I felt comforted with his ideas concerning the why of Ray's treachery. Plus Brig's sweet attitude toward my impromptu crying jag. I smiled at him and offered him the last two scones from my tray.

"I feel better believing Ray is just misguided right now. Maybe he'll come to his senses when he gets back to New York. Thanks, Brig, for understanding."

He took the scones and flashed a take-your-breath-away smile at me. "I was about to say the same to you. Thanks. For the scones, mind you. I love them. Mum makes lovely cranberry-orange scones for the Christmas holiday."

"Sounds divine."

"I'll tell her to whip up an extra batch this year."

"Where does she live?"

"Most of the O'Brien clan is still in Riverdale."

"There're more of you?"

He nodded. "Four brothers. All older. There's a ten-year gap between me and the youngest of that first lot. And Mum and Da are still thriving. I keep them young."

"I would have thought your poor mother's hair turned stark white when you hit talking age. And no girls? She must have climbed the walls a dozen times a day when you and your brothers were growing up."

Brig closed his eyes.

"Brig? What? Did I say something wrong?"

He opened his eyes but the look in them chilled me. He gazed at the window overlooking one of Jake's gardens. He glanced at me, then back out the window.

"I had a sister. She's dead."

I wanted to jump through that window and forget my insensitive comments about O'Brien men and no girls.

"I'm so sorry. Oh, Lord, why did I say that about your mom and girls."

He shook his head. "You didn't know. It's okay. Really. Annie died when I was nine years old. She was fifteen at the time."

"Dear God. What happened? Was she sick?"

Brig stood and walked toward the window as if movement might lessen a hurt still fresh after twenty years.

"She was a gymnast. Like you. Tiny though. She took after my mother, unlike all of us boys. My dad's six-six and I'm the runt at six-four. Anyway, we lived in Dublin then. Annie would drag me along with her to gymnastics practices and to her meets. That's where I learned the moves I still can do."

He paused, turned, lifted his cup as if studying the design, then placed it back on the saucer. His voice grew husky.

"Annie'd been invited to a party up at the rec room at the church. The good priests had just received a donation of two pool tables and all the kids were coming in to play a few games."

He closed his eyes for a moment, then opened them and stared at the tea cup as though willing it to speak to him.

"Mum said it was all right for Annie to go alone, since it was a church function and in the afternoon and all. We were to meet her after, then go over to my aunt's for supper, so we got in the car and drove to the church, and we couldn't find a place to park except for about three blocks away. I get out and Mum gets out and—we hear the blast and see the smoke and the fire."

My tears had started falling the instant he said "blast." I knew.

"IRA? A bomb?"

He sat back down across from me. "Don't really know who set it. One of the radical elements who specialized in that sort of behavior back then. Remember me saying how the *gardé*, how any cops, can be a force for good or evil?"

I nodded.

"Well, the police never could seem to find any leads as to

where this particular bomb came from. Not who brought it into the church, nor how it came into Dublin. Mum and Dad suspected a group that had done more than one church bombing in and around the area the last two years or so, but the police swept it under the rug."

He looked at me. "It's a better group now, so I'm told. The coppers."

He then put his head into his hands and cried. I reached for him and held him, and we rocked together, clinging to each other until one of us was able to speak again.

Brig sighed. "It's all so stupid, really. A silly game of pool on a bright afternoon in May. And who gets killed? A bunch of young kids and two priests."

He smiled. "Those two were the sharpest pool players in all of Dublin though. I'm sure they've got a game going somewhere up in heaven. Hustling all the poor rabbis and ministers who come in lookin' for a match. Probably taking on Saint Peter himself."

We sat quietly, drinking our tea while Brig dealt with memories and I tried to banish the visions of horror.

Brig took another bite of his scone and asked, "What about you? You mentioned your mother being a film nut. Where does she live?"

I welcomed the opportunity to turn to a happier subject. "She is indeed a film nut. She also loves live theater and opera and ballet. She swears she'll never leave New York as long as Broadway and the Met remain."

"Ah. Your mum and mine have probably bumped into one another during Wednesday matinees a time or two. My mum is also a fan of musical theater and fine music."

He smiled. "And *Riverdance*, don't ya know. We'll invite your folks up for tea soon."

Riverdance. And tea. This sounded very good. Intimate. I began envisioning cozy chats with Mom and Mum beaming at their darling children. I sighed.

"Better make it my mom only. She and my father have been divorced for years and years, and they do not get along.

I think I'm the cause. My father wanted a male entrepreneur and he got a taller duplicate of my mother. Why they married in the first place is beyond me. And her. I think it was his blue eyes, which was the only thing I inherited from him as far as either Mom or I can tell."

I changed topics to avoid discussing my father.

"By the way, Mr. O'Brien, I keep meaning to ask this. The night we met in the back of Hot Harry's you were spouting Gaelic like, well, a native. Since then, you've stuck to English like you were born and bred in the Bronx. So, were those phrases the limit to your repertoire? Or were you trying to impress me while we did our duck-and-cover routine?"

He grinned. "A bit of both. I know more Gaelic than I use. Usually comes out in stressful situations. Also, and don't get mad, it was fun to test your skills."

"Test? Why?"

"Ray introduced you to Mr. Khan as his interpreter when you first entered Hot Harry's. Khan asked you, in Hindi, what languages you knew. And you rattled off the basics first. French, Russian, German, Italian, Spanish. Well, now, most opera lovers can spout a few phrases in any of those."

He winked at me. "Then you got this funny, wonderful smile on your face. You said, 'also Japanese, some Chinese, Parsi—and Gaelic.' Perked me right up. I wanted to know the truth of your relationship with Ray. Find out if you really knew these languages, or if you were some gorgeous bimbo he'd met in New York who'd read a travel guide on India and learned a phrase or two to impress him."

"So you tried out a few phrases in Gaelic."

"Aye. Forgive me?"

"What, for doubting me? Nothing to forgive, Brig. You didn't know me at all. I didn't know you. And let's face it, I thought you were one of the hordes of hooligans there to pillage and rob the poor Americans."

He winked. "Me? A hooligan? Never. I tell you what. I'll be happy to toss in a Gaelic word or two from time to time throughout the years just to give you sweet memories of how we met."

That statement, as had several he'd made earlier, implied a future between the two of us. A possibility that eluded me right now with the way things stood with the craziness about Shiva's Diva. Romance seemed difficult to sustain while one tried to avoid all the bad guys and get the statue delivered into safe hands.

I rose, then took the empty tray through five rooms to deposit it in Jake's kitchen. And discovered Jake himself at the end of this trek.

"Jake? I thought you were at the lot dealing with carpenters and sound men for tomorrow's shoot."

A morose Jake sat on a stool behind a bar counter.

"I was. For once, everything went smoothly. Too smoothly. No yelling, fighting, bruised hands, bruised feelings, or broken bones. I came home."

"So why do you look like Vivek Studios just burned down?"

He lifted his cup and stared at it. "Asha."

"This is why you're sitting here drinking hot water?"

"Beg pardon?"

I pointed to the empty tea holder and the clear liquid in his cup. "No tea, Jake."

He grabbed a canister and filled the strainer. "I cannot believe that woman has me so distracted I don't know my own name."

"Loser."

We turned. Brig had entered the kitchen, announcing his presence with that one word.

Jake snorted. "Loser? Is that what I am, or my name?"

"Both."

"Well, thank you, my friend. Loser. Just what I needed to hear."

Brig winked at me, then slapped Jake on the shoulder. "Jake, me boy-o, listen to me. You're letting the lady grab you by the, uh, nose and lead you to the end of a plank. Where you appear to be prepared to jump. Be a man, man! Stand up to the lass."

Jake sighed. "I would if I had any idea as to why my sweet intended has suddenly decided to perform the first two acts of *Taming of the Shrew*. I'm not sure there'll be a third."

He aimed his appeal at me. "Tempe? You were with her all afternoon. Did she say anything about me?"

I hated to disappoint the lovesick director, but I had to be truthful. "Honestly? We talked about Jersey and New York and clothes and my adventures in Bombay. Sorry. Maybe when things are calmer, she'll feel like confiding."

I snickered. "What am I saying? Calmer? When will that be? Sometime between Mahindra chasing me into the harbor, Patel throwing me out of a speeding train, or Ray shooting me in the back while I'm trying to do high kicks and turns in the middle of *Carnival of Lust*?"

Jake looked at Brig with concern. "Is she all right? Tempe, when did you last eat something real? Or sleep?"

I shook my head. "I'm all right. I won't break down. At least not today. I make no promises for tomorrow." I smiled at Jake. "And that's only after the shoot. No hysterical ranting or sobs while filming. Which reminds me. When do I learn these dances I'm in?"

Jake looked surprised. "Tomorrow. I have already choreographed them. I teach them on the set. Then we film the numbers. Much more efficient than days of rehearsal."

"Uh. Okay."

"You'll do a good job, Tempe. These are easy steps, especially for someone as graceful as you. And you took dance in college. You'll think you're in beginners class."

Brig poured water over the now-full tea strainer in Jake's cup and handed it to him. Then he winked at me.

"Just be prepared to do a few flips and handsprings as well as those high kicks."

"And that would be . . . why?"

Brig lifted his eyes to the ceiling to avoid meeting my gaze. Jake stirred his tea and answered, "Because Mr. O'Brien spent an hour regaling me with the tale of Tempe Walsh vaulting over bars and springing off tables. This is the first time I've had a real female gymnast in one of my films. I plan to make as much use of your talents as I can."

"Ah. Got it. Fine. I'll agree to any and all tricks as long as Briggan O'Brien matches me—trick for trick."

Brig walked back into the hall adjoining the kitchen. He casually placed both hands on the floor, then assumed the position of a handstand. He then balanced, first using only the left hand as support, then the right. He rolled out into a somersault, finishing on his back. He next executed a perfect kip where the "kipper" jumps to his feet from a flat position without use of his hands to aid him. Gene Kelly did more than one in *The Three Musketeers*.

I hated to admit it, but Brig's was even better.

Chapter 13

I scanned the lot looking for an expected cast of thousands for the dance sequences in Jake's movie. Or at least hundreds. The Indian videos I'd seen on cable back in Manhattan always seem to have a swarm of dancers wriggling down steps in front of fountains or temples. First the men hop in circles. Then the women swirl and bump and flip wrists and ankles. Then the leads end up superimposed over each group in the final editing of the film while a voice-over track provides the singing.

Today, on a set made up to look like a giant cave, I counted only forty dancers. Twenty guys. Twenty girls. Thankfully, I didn't have to deal with a mob, yet there were enough people to hide behind.

Tempe Walsh, the redheaded native New Yorker, trying to blend into the chorus of a group of dark-haired female dancers, none of whom appeared to be taller than four foot six in a temple set somewhere in a carnival. The mind boggles.

"Yo! Tempe. How's tricks, girl?"

Asha Kumar came striding toward me with a most unstarlet-like gait and a large grin over her pixie features. She was dressed in costume today. A sparse one. Her halter top barely covered essentials and the harem pants consisted of swatches with silk on top of them. Perhaps costumes like this were the reason all the men in Bombay were enthralled with this diminutive actress who showed a feisty attitude and superior figure.

"Asha! You should have stayed with Brig and me after our little run-in with Ray. I got to do a spectacular jeté onto the filthiest train in the filthiest rail station I've seen since they started the renovations on the subway at 168th street. I also met the Ice Princess of Bombay, but that's another story."

She hugged me, then stepped back.

"I always hated that street station. I'd walk half a mile to avoid using that ghastly exit. That horrible elevator never had less than fifteen too many people on it, and the stupid fan in there never worked. And there was no other way to get to the street because the damn stairs were always locked. When did they do them? The renovations."

"Over a year ago. Jeez. When were you last in Manhattan?"

Her face fell. "Don't ask. Let's just say the ball has dropped in Times Square a few New Year's Eves. Hey. Change topic. You look great in the costume. Isn't Reena a wonder?"

Reena must be the designer and seamstress who'd thrown together an outfit overnight for the new American dancer. She deserved the Edith Head award for fast sewing and the Richard Blackstone for most tasteless.

She'd decked me out in a two-piece creation somewhat like a bathing suit. Made out of gold satin, it moved when the wearer moved while still clinging to the body. A small tassel swung from the center of the bra top. A longer tassel fell from the waistband. In actuality, the tassel swung from a hip, not a waist, band if one were to get literal about tassels. My waist was quite bare. But at least, unlike my costume at C.C. Curry's, my feet were not. Go-go boots that must have come from a vintage boutique hugged my size sevens and added another two inches to my height.

Asha removed a thread from the strap of the bra. "By the way, Miss Walsh. I thought you were supposed to bunk with me last night. Where did you stay? Before I forget, I have your duffel bag. You left it in the car. So, didja stay with Brig? You guys get it together?"

I sighed. "Brig and Jake decided I'd be safer if I didn't try and get to your place. So I stayed at Jake's. Alone. In the maid's quarters. Not bad, really, although a definite odor of musk clung to the sheets and I had to borrow her nightie, which about hit my stomach and also reeked of musk. I didn't care. Exhaustion hit about two seconds after I saw the bed."

Asha snickered. "I know that room and that maid. Let's just say she has a few issues about her looks, so she overcompensates with scent. I sneeze for hours when I'm at Jake's."

This could be the perfect time to ask about Jake and the soured romance. Before I could frame a polite inquiry, we were joined by my soon-to-be dancing partner, Briggan O'Brien.

"Asha. You look fresh and raring to go. Did you enjoy playing the mad maid yesterday? Damn, but you've got some pipes on you. You could earn a good living keening at the wakes across Ireland."

Asha and I surveyed Brig like construction workers ogling the secretaries walking across a site in their spike heels. My pulse reached a max aerobic rate. Asha still had use of her voice, which was good since my vocal chords seemed to be taking a break.

"Yo, Brig. You look, um, interesting. That outfit really brings out the true you."

Brig was dressed in black. All black. Tight black pants, black blouse, black duster down to his knees. Black boots up to his knees. He looked every bit the pirate he was doubtless descended from.

He preened. "Like it? I think my presence in the ranks of the dancers caused a bit of consternation with the costume lady. All these lads under five-seven and here comes the giant. She actually screamed when she saw me. Scared the living fool out of me. I'm only sorry Tempe wasn't there to translate. I have no idea what language the lady used, but I do know it was colorful."

He bowed. "Miss Walsh. I didn't see you this morning at breakfast at Jake's. Missed you, luv. Where'd you go?"

"I had a fitting with that same costumer who spouted the same language at me. I think it was the color of my hair she really objected to. She also wasn't crazy about my height.

And if it makes you feel better, I didn't understand a word either. Probably one of the other seventy-five languages of India I didn't study before being crazy enough to get on that plane with Ray."

I wriggled my shoulders and grinned. "If I had to guess? I think Reena cursed both Brig and me with far worse than Shiva's Diva herself ever imagined. I'm sure there was something in her tirade about enjoying seeing my hair fall out and feet fall off. Oh yeah. That I'd end up with a nervous twitch twenty-four-seven."

Brig had a light in his eye. "Too subtle for Reena. She was probably praying to Kali, who is not known as a nice god, that our blood would soon cover the tents of the tiger and the elephant. Or that Ravana, the demon god, will send us flying into Chowpatty Beach just as the elephants are tossed in during the Ganesh parade."

He grinned. "Not real elephants, you know. Just big replicas. Let's see. Maybe our ears would grow like the elephants and cover our toes. Maybe . . ."

Before he could hypothesize another outrageous curse, I heard my name called along with Brig's and Asha's.

Jake stood on a chair about forty feet away. He was yelling through a cone-shaped old-fashioned megaphone that hid his lips.

We were in trouble. This became clear when his next words were, "Miss Kumar. Miss Walsh. Mr. O'Brien. I'm so glad you've chosen this moment for a reunion, but some of us are ready to work. If you would deign to favor the rest of the cast with your presence, perhaps we can start filming only forty minutes late."

He'd morphed into Jake Roshan, director. Not Jake Roshan, drinker of hot water and lovesick swain. Asha, Brig, and I immediately galloped over to join the other dancers and the male lead, Raj Ravi. Cast members ignored Jake's plea for timeliness and continued milling about, gabbing and chugging down coffee or tea from plastic cups.

Brig and I spent the next thirty minutes fielding questions

from the excited group of dancers as to why two foreigners had been so gracious as to join their ranks in this film. They wanted to know where we were staying. They wanted to know where we were from. They wanted to know what other movies we'd been in back in the States.

But mostly, they wanted us to say yes when they asked, "Isn't Asha Kumar simply the most charming, beautiful actress ever to grace the Indian cinema? Have you seen *Pirate Princess*? Where Asha is with Spot the tiger?"

There are serious problems in Bombay. They range from pollution, to Mafia-style crime, to extreme poverty accompanied by a frighteningly large percentage of homeless who beg in the streets. Muggers can outnumber the tourists. But the Indian people? Hospitality, warmth, and friendliness flow in abundance. And the dancers in *Carnival of Lust* tripled those last three qualities.

The female dancers wanted to know if Brig and I were an item. How they came by that notion I have no idea. The fact that I seemed to find it difficult to keep my eyes off the Irish bandit this day just couldn't have anything to do with their suppositions.

Brig winked at me when one of the young male dancers loudly asked if we were shacking up together. He didn't quite state it that way, but the intent of "You share space, yes?" seemed clear.

I couldn't hear Brig's answer. Just as well. Doubtless it was outrageous and filled with charming tales of his seduction of the tall American who'd fallen into his arms two days ago. We'd now made it to day three. No telling how far this relationship would progress by nightfall, at least in the eyes of the chorus.

Jake grew impatient with the chatter coming from his cast. "Enough! We're already behind schedule. Tempe, Brig, Asha, Raj. Front and center, please."

Front and center? That worried me. My understanding had been that Brig and I were supposed to blend with the masses, preferably in the back row where the tall folks get stuck.

Jake smiled at me. "Tempe. You and Brig will be doing a dance directly behind Asha and Raj while they sing. Tempe? Midway through this number, you will do an aerial flip off that low wall and then a series of leaps across the area in front of the Ferris wheel."

In keeping with the title of this flick, the setting included carnival tents. There was also a sacred temple, stuck behind the Tilt-a-Whirl for no reason I could think of. Ferris wheels, roller coasters, and carousels dotted the landscape of the lot. Huts lined with enormous stuffed animals and actors in carny workmen garb and top hats filled a lot about two hundred yards wide and long. Another lot held empty animal cages that would be filled with real lions and tigers and bears and the like in the coming days.

I gathered that my activities would consist of leaping and hopping and turning and darting between the various rides and—oh dear—the snakes and elephants and tigers and llamas that suddenly began arriving on the set and heading toward those cages. Well, the snakes and the tigers were headed that direction.

Asha shrieked, "Spot! It's Spot!" and headed toward the tiger cage, eager to greet and bond again with the tiger who'd shared the duet with her in *Pirate Princess*.

I watched the elephant ramble into a large cage. When it turned, I noticed a little cap on its head that read "Binky." Cute. The llama had ended up in a little open-air pen. She glanced at the cast of dancers she'd joined, then started chewing what little grass she could find.

I turned back to Jake. "You want me to do what? Where?"

He smiled, and explained again. I sighed. If I had to end up knocking off cartwheels in front of the large cobra now entwined around a stereotypical basket, I'd rather just go back to C.C. Curry's and see if they needed me for the night. I'm not scared of snakes, but I'd prefer not doing a slow waltz with one.

Jake then showed Brig and me the steps we were to do before I began my series of spectacular jetés and flips.

Jake had obviously been watching a good amount of championship ballroom dancing competition on cable, along with too many VH1 and BET videos. Within minutes, Brig and I were attempting to perfect a combination of rumba and tango, mixed with some homegrown hip-hop and a sprinkling of *A Chorus Line*.

Jake also liked lifts. That is, he liked having others do them. Brig had me in the air more times than the Ferris wheel had hit the top mark.

What Jake either didn't notice, or did but enjoyed, was the way Brig let me down from these lifts. Rather like one of the cobras, I slid over Brig's chest, clutching his torso, then slid farther. A process Brig prolonged. I became warmer and more flushed with each lift and drop.

The other dancers applauded and cheered when Brig lowered me into a deep dip, then stared into my eyes while I lay on the ground, hands held tightly within his. The gleam in Brig's eye grew brighter. He leaned over. His lips headed for mine. Jake yelled, "Cut!"

I didn't know whether to be glad or sorry. The exact memory and feel of the kisses Brig and I had shared since the night we met kept flooding through my mind and body. I stood up and walked about five steps away from Brig and tried to compose myself.

A Bollywood film set that was less than two hours away from a city filled with killer thugs was neither the place nor the time to conduct a romance. Especially with a man who was too charming, too handsome, too bright, too enigmatic, and possibly too involved with a lady of mystery and unbelievable beauty.

"Nice work, Tempe. Brig." Jake beamed at us both. "I knew you could do it. You two dance together as though you'd been partners for life."

Partners for life. I spied Asha giggling at me from a perch on a large carousel giraffe. I crossed my eyes at her, then gave my full attention to Jake.

"Actors. Please, take five. No. Scratch that. Perhaps we

will make it thirty. Or forty. Then we will start on the flips. Brig? You can do handsprings like Tempe's, right?"

Brig nodded and I thought about his sister, Annie, who'd dragged her little brother to gymnastic practices. I wondered if performing those handsprings brought up hurtful memories.

Brig winked at me. "Once I learned how to do spectacular handsprings, I used them to run from the coppers in Riverdale and all. Easier to jump from car to car. Off the hardtops, you know."

I was relieved he seemed to be taking a light look at these tricks. But I couldn't respond. I'd hit depletion for the day. Tired, dirty, and hungry were the best descriptions of my mood and feelings. If Mahindra himself had come flying onto the set doing handsprings and swinging from Ferris wheel to roller coaster using a king cobra as a rope, I wouldn't have cared. I wanted water and whatever junk food might be found at the service tables. Lots of it. Now.

I shuddered. I shouldn't have started thinking about Mahindra. I glanced around the set. So far, the day had been serene. If one could use that term for hours dancing in the arms of Briggan O'Brien and unsuccessfully avoiding hands that had a tendency to hit spots of the body not described in the Fred Astaire rule book. But at least no one had burst onto the lot with guns blazing and knives bared. Yet.

Chapter 14

By the end of Day One on the set of *Carnival of Lust*, I found I was grateful that my pragmatist father had steered me toward a linguistics job rather than dancing. I was ready to head back to the Taj Mahal Hotel and fill out an application to be a maid. Maybe hunt down Ricky the rickshaw driver and ask if he'd like to trade positions.

My body ached from the hours of endless aerial aerobics and splits and back and front walkovers and side crab crawls. In two-inch go-go boots and flying tassels.

I'd concluded that Jake Roshan was certifiable. Insane. Bonkers. No wonder Asha had called off the wedding. The man was a good two reels short of a full film.

One example of Jake's lunacy was his decree that I should spend the majority of the afternoon of Day One on the top of the Ferris wheel. This sounded rather nice until I discovered I wouldn't be reclining in one of the frantically rocking seats gazing down over my castmates on the ground. Oh, no. Jake wanted me standing on my head on top of those seats or springing from my hands to come bouncing off the seat just below. He loved the shots of me staring in terror at the huge foam mattress on the ground placed there to catch the crazy American should she not make the next seat.

I thanked Saint Swithen, for whom I'd developed an irrational fondness, that this Ferris wheel stood only half the size and half the height of most Ferris wheels one finds at fancy American amusement parks. So all my falls would be from only about twenty feet up instead of fifty or more. Besides, if

I crashed, no one would notice. They'd be too busy listening
to Asha and Raj mime singing love songs underneath me on
solid ground.

I considered asking Jake whether it wouldn't be more dramatic to have the film lovers crooning to each other half a
mile above and let the new lead dancer pirouette below, but
Jake seemed entranced by all the red hair flying in the breeze.

And what about Brig, one might ask? The reason I hadn't
yelled, "Strike! Call my union!" was that I could see Mr.
O'Brien doing the same ridiculous tricks on the other side of
the wheel. About once an hour we got to leap together. I felt
oddly reassured seeing the look of terror on his face. I knew
it mirrored the one on mine.

It was now 7:00 P.M. Brig had gone to Jake's for a much-
needed shower. Asha had whisked me into her convertible.
We were heading for her place for some extensive cleaning.
If the water at Asha's wasn't second-degree-burn-level hot, I
planned to head for the nearest bazaar, buy a long knife, and
personally kill Asha's plumber. First, though, I'd stop at Jake's
to carve up Brig for getting me into the movie business.

I closed my eyes when Asha nearly plowed into three bicy-
cle riders in suits who were trying to avoid her convertible by
staying on the side of the road. All three of whom began
screaming at her as they found themselves in the dirt after she
passed.

I began to muse about what little tricks Jake had in store
for tomorrow's shoot. I felt certain Brig could, and would,
supply suggestions. "I've got it, Jake! Have Tempe come
swingin' down off a rope to be landin' in front of the elephant.
Do a nice backflip off the llama, then somersault next to the
cobra under the tent. That would be so much fun on film!"

Asha, wisely, stayed silent. She'd had a fairly easy day. She
and Raj, her costar, had been on terra firma, gazing into each
other's eyes and warbling along with recorded music that had
sounded from my sixteen feet above like Sonny and Cher set
to a disco melody with a rap beat.

Amidst the curses of an elderly man, riding a ridiculously

large Harley motorcycle, who'd been inches away from being knocked into the bay across from Marine Road when Asha made a sharp turn, Jersey girl finally broke her silence. "Where do you suppose Brig is going tomorrow?"

I sighed. "Lord knows. Brig said he an errand, presumably one having something to do with Shiva's Diva. Which leaves me at the mercy of Jake Roshan, director from the Marquis de Sade School of Film."

Asha giggled. "He is a pain, isnt' he? But his movies win awards like crazy. Wait. What errands?"

"I don't know. Brig probably has unsavory associates in every continent from Bombay to Moscow. Although I guess those aren't continents, are they? Well, anyway, I'm sure he's about to wheel and deal and sell Shiva's Diva to the highest, sleaziest, closest crook who'll be crazy enough to pay his price."

"Ouch. You have such a high opinion of our Mr. O'Brien. I thought you two were hot for each other."

The memory of his kisses battled to overtake my senses. I sat up straight and tried to keep my voice even.

"Hot is Briggan's middle name. I imagine he has girls drooling over him in every one of those continents as well as the unsavory business associates. I do not wish to join the ranks of the 'loved-'em-left-'em' strewn around the world." I paused, then added, "One of whom I think I met yesterday."

I told her about Claire Dharbar and about finding that picture of her posing with Brig.

Asha avoided crashing into a stall at the side of the road by a foot. This was not due to her usual bad driving. Her laughter had become so raucous she couldn't see.

"Asha! Damn! Think we can make it home without carrying half a load of fruit or whatever with us?"

She straightened the wheel. "Sorry. No harm done. Didn't hit a soul. And see? He's already setting the stand back up. Not even an orange juiced."

"Right."

She grinned. "It's just thinking about you and Brig. Girl, if ever two people were nuts for each other? Well. Shall we say poster children for Lovers Inc.? And I don't know who this Claire chickie is, but if he met her at a restaurant with you sitting at a table nearby, it isn't likely they're going to go off and do, uh, anything kinky." She added, "By the way, that's both of you."

She turned her head and stared at me. Not a wise move given the way she drove. I yelled, "Watch the road!" as I hugged the sides of this passenger seat of doom, stared out into the streets of Bombay, and asked, "Both of whom? Me and Claire? Now that *would* be kinky. Can we shelve this discussion, Ms. Kumar?"

"For now, Ms. Walsh. But as you may have already surmised, I'm a nosy little girl. So expect the topic to come up again. And the both of you, as you very well know, is you and Brig. Think. Did he leave with the Claire babe? No. He left with you. Lordy, you are so lame. Two idiots nuts about each other and too stupid to admit it."

"And what about you and Jake, since we're on the subject of limping idiots. When do I find out what's the deal with the pair of you?"

She pursed her lips. "Later."

She punched the accelerator so hard I had to grab the dash to keep from flying over the back seat and onto the Bombay streets.

I turned up the car radio to a preset classic rock station. Strains of Cat Stevens's "Hard-Headed Woman" wafted around us. Perfect. Two stubborn females sitting in a car with no top sailing along Marine Road trying to pretend we weren't focused on the men in our lives.

We gratefully changed topics to the news from New York. Which Grammy winners were sleeping with other Grammy winners. Whether the new art exhibit at the Guggenheim would be removed or destroyed by the PETA activists who were angry it contained splotches of possum fur. Which Emmy winner had been jailed for sleeping with another underage same-sex Emmy winner. We contined discussing these important issues until we reached Asha's place.

Asha had done her own decorating for her flat in the Malabar Hills area of Bombay. Posters of her movies lined the walls of the den. The living room featured canvas artwork that looked like original masterpieces. They blended comfortably with the Queen Anne furniture that included large chairs and a huge sofa that invited visitors to sit and forget the cares of the day. I could have sprawled on that sofa within minutes and stayed forever, but as usual, hunger began to win out over rest.

My mother would have swooned with envy over the kitchen equipped with state-of-the-art gadgets and utensils. An expensive range topped the center island. A woman even smaller than Asha nodded at me when I popped my head in to inhale the scent of what smelled like lasagna. Asha's cook. I had already gathered that the words "Asha" and "cooking" were not to be used in the same sentence.

Hunger beckoned, but cleanliness now superceded all. Asha pointed me to the guest bedroom. Another treat. The bed was king-sized, dressed with a light antique quilt in shades of taupe and gold. I set my bag on a Victorian rocker in the corner beside an eight-foot-tall armoire.

To the right of the bedroom beckoned the joys of the huge guest bathroom. I had to wonder what opulence the master bath offered when I stepped into what I assumed was the lesser of the restrooms. A Jacuzzi sat right in the middle. And there would be no knife attacks on any plumber this night. Hot water spewed in abundance. The gods smiled. As did I.

An hour later, Asha and I were diving into what had indeed proved to be lasagna accompanied by garlic bread, salad, and a red wine that must have cost more than the Jacuzzi.

I glanced at her. "I have to ask you. How do you get a cook who looks like a Hindu goddess who's been dead for over two thousand years to make a dish worthy of Mama Leone's? Voodoo?"

She howled. "What? You a h*oo*t owl? *You. Who*. Hin-*doo. Who*'s. *Voo-Doo. Oooo!*"

"Quit that! I've had a long day. My linguistic skills deserted me somewhere at the top of that hideous Ferris wheel."

Asha grinned. "I won't be able to hear a word with an 'oo' sound for a week without laughing, but I'm letting *yooo* off the hook for now."

I crossed my eyes at her. "Tell me about this cook, okay?"

"Mala, my chef? Isn't she great? Actually, when I first hired her, she cooked curry, curry, and on alternate Sundays, more curry. With a bit of vinda*looo* and tandori chicken thrown in on holidays. Tasty, but limiting. When my parents came for a visit, my mother took Mala in hand and gave her every recipe Mom had kept from her wonderful dinner group in Woodbridge. Italian, Russian-Jewish, French, Norwegian even. Mala, bless her ancient little heart, was thrilled. I now dine internationally any night I *chooose* to hang out at home."

I nodded, then cocked my head. "As opposed *tooooo*?"

"Oh, heck, Tempe. I'm a film actress in India. I'm expected to do a bit of partying." She grinned. "Can't disappoint my fans, you know. So I try and hit the clubs at least once a week."

I did not trouble to stifle my laugh. "And I'm sure it's a great hardship on you, Miss Celebrity!"

She chortled. "Well, they used to call me the original party girl back in the States, so living up to the image isn't exactly a stretch. Speaking of which, want to go out in a bit?"

I stopped midbite and considered the offer.

"Yes and no. Yes, I need some kind of real relaxation after the last couple of days. No, because I'm scared witless that one of the various ruffians looking for me will hear about a red-haired American female carousing around the city, and suddenly I'll be forced to hide in a brothel taking tricks to keep from ending up floating around one of the beaches."

"Ouch. You do have a vivid imagination, don't you?"

I grinned. "At times. Also, if your idea of partying tonight has anything to do with dancing, count me way out. My aches have aches on top of aches."

Asha sipped her wine and studied me. "Hmmm. What say you to a few games of pool?"

"Pool? Like *The Hustler* or *Color of Money*? As in Gleason and Newman and Cruise, oh my?"

She beamed. "And solids and eight ball and cues, oh my!"

I giggled. "Racking and chalking and sticks, oh my?"

A wicked grin crossed her face. I held up my hand before the rhyme escalated into the obscene.

Asha winked. "Fine, I'll be nice. And you can just watch if you want. There's a great pool hall downtown. Mainly gets the office crowd and some college kids. I don't get hassled there, they play American music, and I really doubt it's the kind of place where the felons you've attracted since you've been here will be hanging out."

"I have to tell you, I don't play the game. Will that mess up your fun? I mean, it sounds terrific and I do want to come with you, but just to sit and watch. The operative word being sit. My feet have had it. I miss my bunny slippers I left back in Manhattan."

"Sitting is not a problem, Tempe. There's a group of guys from Dhava's College who regularly try to defeat the film actress here. I, however, am unbeatable thanks to an old Jersey boyfriend who preferred a night at the pool hall to a night in bed. I keep telling the kids this—well, not about the boyfriend—but that I'm invincible. They love getting whupped anyway."

"Uh, huh. Right. I'm sure."

"You can ask them if you come with me. And you're welcome to sip sodas or even sleep in the corner while I rack 'em up. Then I'll treat you to a frozen hot chocolate at this new American dessert place with the money I make from the boys."

This sounded even better. A chance to relax, listen to the sound of voices and music without needing to contribute, and watch Asha flirt with the college kids. And all while staying out of range of Shiva's Diva's pursuers.

Chapter 15

Unlike Asha, I had never dated a pool shark who showed me the finer techniques of "six ball in the side pocket." In or out of high school, college, or beyond. I was engaged, briefly, to an actor who confirmed my father's dire warnings about "creative sleazebags" when he took me to Atlantic City for a spot of gambling using my money. But most of the men who'd asked me out the last few years have been lawyers. Dates consisted of fancy restaurants, Broadway shows, the ballet, and the opera.

So going to the Pool Palace could be added to the growing list of Tempe's newest experiences. At least this one should be calm. I figured watching a few quiet games of pool would be a nice respite from crooks, filming, Ferris wheels, and killers. Not to mention Yale Liberal Arts graduates with intermittent Irish brogues and permanently seductive blue eyes.

I found a spot in a corner of the room where there should have been a sign reading "Tired Dancers Flop Here." The chair replicated the oversized, overpillowed monstrosities seen on such television shows as *Leave It to Beaver*. The I'm-watching-the-Jets/Giants/Yankees-so-don't-bother-me-now chair. This chenille-covered antique had been placed at an angle to allow the sitter to either watch the action in the hall or choose one of the numerous magazines littering the small table to its left.

I leaned back and plopped my legs over the armrest. I wasn't being rude; plenty of others sat in the same position. Asha was right. It was a comfortable pool hall.

I picked up a magazine with a cover featuring Asha Kumar

cuddled next to a tiger winking at the reader. (Asha, not the tiger.) I picked up another glossy. Again a magazine devoted to the film industry. Again, Asha smiling from the cover. Different picture; same tiger. I began searching through the piles. All fan magazines, all devoted to the stars of the screen. Asha was on the cover of at least ninety percent of them.

I glanced over at my new friend. Barbara Ashley Kumar, celebrity and one of the highest-paid actresses in India. She was clad in a pair of tight faded jeans and a plaid shirt I swear I'd seen prominently displayed at a Goodwill store in Manhattan two weeks ago.

India's darling pointed to the far right side of the pool table with her right hand, took a swig from the bottle of beer in her left, then reached up and set it on a mantle two feet over her head. She leaned over the table, adroitly sent the ball into that far right pocket, and howled in sheer glee. The four kids playing with her, none of whom looked over eighteen, groaned then grinned. They were not a bit concerned that they'd just been trounced by a thirty-year-old starlet with an accent out of *The Sopranos* and a bank account like a CEO headed for prison.

I snuggled back into the chair, closed my eyes, and let the music and the quiet chatter and the clanking sounds from the pool tables wash over me.

A pool cue jabbed into my ribs. Darn. I must have been snoring. I could find no other excuse for this mild assault on my person.

I looked up, prepared to do battle with Asha, who I figured had been the one doing the poking.

"Tempe. Up. Time to go." The voice was raspy and the face was pale.

Brig.

"Why are you here, Brig? Do you have built-in radar that tells you when I'm somewhere enjoying myself or resting or being involved in something that's safe and doesn't include you?"

"Tempe. No time. Take a look over by the bar and you'll see why an unobtrusive exit is highly recommended."

I inched to the left to see around Brig's impressive chest, then

I squeezed back into the chair trying to make myself as small as possible.

"Patel! Oh crap. Not good. How the hell did he know we were here?"

"Tempe, he hasn't seen us yet. Which is why this is a good time to find the door."

"And how do you suggest we sneak out of here without attracting the notice of sweet Seymour over there? And where's Asha?"

"I told her the bad news a few moments ago. But she's not in danger. As far as I know, none of the goons who are eager to get their mitts onto the statue, and/or us, are aware she's anything other than what she is. We're the ones in the soup."

"So? Do we have a Plan A to disappear? Is there some crazy costume tucked in your pocket I can wear that will allow us to leave without having to fight our way out of disaster?"

Brig's eyes glazed for a moment. I knew he was remembering another pool hall in Dublin. He smelled the smoke, heard the screams.

I grabbed his arm. "Brig. This isn't Ireland and it's not twenty years ago. We'll be fine, I promise. Plan A?"

He tried to smile. "Okay. There's a back way out from that room where Asha's now wiping the floor with those benighted college boys. She loves Plan A. She's going to be engaged in playing a very noisy game with the kids that will hopefully provide a very noisy diversion. Meantime, you and I will crawl under the tables and sneak through to make our way to that door."

As plans go, I thought it stunk, but I didn't want to say so. First we had to get to Asha's table without Patel's seeing us. Then we had to get down on the floor without the entire pool-playing population pointing at the two idiots and asking why those two idiots were bonding with the linoleum rather than standing and chalking sticks. Then we had to open that door and casually stroll into the street where, doubtless, Seymour had several confederates stationed and fully armed.

But I set down my magazine without protest, stood, then followed Brig toward the pool tables.

I was right. The plan stunk. No sooner had Brig and I hit the room where Asha anxiously awaited our arrival than Patel spotted us. Braying the Hindi word for yes—*"Haan!"*—he lunged across the room. The bodies of three jeans-clad kids lay in awkward positions on top of the table where they'd landed when Patel pushed his way through.

Brig grabbed my hand. "Plan B."

"Which is?"

"Run like hell."

We did. Plan B quickly ended as badly as Plan A. It appeared that Patel had backup. Four ugly guys who could have been sent over to Vivek Studios by Central Casting to play brutal villains. Scars down cheeks, scars on bald heads, scars on noses and chins, and expressions as nasty as the scars. And not a one (outside of Patel) was less than three hundred pounds of solid muscle.

They formed a semicircle around Brig and me, with Patel in the middle. Patel took a small knife out of his breast pocket. It looked too tiny to do a lot of damage, which was encouraging. But when the other four displayed similar cutlery, I lost any hope of getting out of this without an awful lot of bloodletting. Mine. And Brig's.

The same keening, screeching, harridan-from-hell sound that had forced Ray Decore to lose focus at the Taj Majal filled the Pool Palace. Asha.

I had to admire that set of lungs. I've heard fire engines in New York with less volume. All five thugs turned to see the origin of the racket. At the same time, a screaming elf in jeans entered the fray with a pool cue twirling like a lethal baton in the hands of a mad lead majorette.

The chalk end of the cue hit bruiser number one in the eye. Asha twirled the larger part of the stick around, then she hit bruiser number two in the chin.

This appeared to be the perfect time for Brig and me to go into our own improvised routine. Up came my knee into the groin of goon number three. Rude, but necessary. Brig went for higher ground. He popped an elbow into the nose of number four. This left Mr. Patel, at least until the four recovered, which would be in seconds. Patel snarled and lunged for me. I spun with a pirouette worthy of Pavlova and sent my foot into his chest.

It should have been a great move. But Patel expected it. He grabbed my foot and held on to my ankle.

The gleam in Patel's eye shouted "ankle twist imminent!" I knew this. I expected to hear a pop louder than Asha's wail when Patel suddenly dropped my foot, then dropped to the floor. One of Asha's pool-playing pals stood over Seymour. The remains of a heavy, ugly lamp lay around Mr. Patel in large pieces.

For a second no one moved. Thugs one through four seemed as stunned as their boss. A condition that was bound to change to rage very soon.

I looked at Brig and at Asha. "Okay, troops. Outta here."

They nodded. Asha bestowed a nice kiss on the heroic college student, then all four of us delivered simultaneous blows to the bruised gang awaiting word from their fallen master. Nose, groin, shin, chin. Didn't matter. We needed to injure them just long enough to allow us to get out of the Pool Palace without any of them recovering and then grabbing an appendage of ours or throwing another knife.

We ran to the front exit, then down to the street where three of Asha's fans stood guarding their beloved's car. With Brig aiming for the driver's seat, we jumped in, then threw kisses to the excited trio. With a squeal of tires guaranteed to make a mechanic cry, Brig steered the car out of its space and back onto the road.

I soon discovered his driving made Asha's expertise behind a wheel seem tame. I yelled, "Where did you learn to drive? Watching Bruce Willis in *Die Hard Three* going through Central Park?"

"I'll have you know I drove a cab in Paris for two years."

"Good God." With one voice, Asha and I bellowed, "Aagh!"

"Wimps," said Brig. "Both of you. You've got a problem with sidewalk driving?"

"Excuse me!" he yelled to the terrified street vendor who was trying to turn his cart before Brig clipped the front end. The vendor didn't quite make the full turn. He yelled and offered a gesture to us that was less than polite. It involved the middle finger of the vendor's right hand.

"Anyone following us yet?" Brig asked. I turned, which was difficult since Asha was sitting on my lap, a necessity in the two-seater. The streets were so jammed with vehicles I had no way to tell if any of them were interested in her convertible or not.

"Don't know."

He nodded. "I'm going to drop you ladies off at Asha's, then hide the car in Jake's neighborhood."

An indignant Asha rapped his shoulder. "Wait up there, boss. Why can't I keep my car at my own home?"

"Because it's very distinctive. How many blue two-seater 1957 T-Birds are currently driving through the streets of Bombay? If any of those boys back at the Pool Palace caught a glimpse of us jumping into this beauty, we've had it."

He didn't mention that even if the car went in for a paint job and a fin cut, and emerged fire engine red and finless, the T-Bird wasn't the only thing that had been recognized. Asha's picture flashed from the covers of half the magazines at the pool hall. If and when Patel and comrades recovered, they'd realize who she was—and further get the message that she'd been instrumental in aiding the two people determined to keep them from their precious statue. Asha had just joined the ranks of the hunted.

Chapter 16

"I'm hungry."

"What?"

"You heard me. I said I'm hungry. Yes, this is not a great thing at this point of our journey. And yes, while I hate to bring up the subject of food while we're speeding across the city wondering who's behind us with murder on the mind, I can't help it. My stomach is growling."

Brig and Asha both gave me looks that mixed amazement with disgust.

I sniffed. "Well, I'm sorry. Asha's cook laid out a wonderful spread about four hours ago, and it's been a really long day, and I tend to get an attack of the munchies when I'm stressed. Excuse me if I'm failing to live up to the high standards of heroines who are capable of going days without food, holding back tears after run-ins with bad guys, and leaping tall buildings in single bounds without mussing a hair on their bleached blond heads." I sighed. "Come to think of it, I did that already. Today. Well, not leaping a building precisely, but that Ferris wheel should qualify."

Brig rolled his eyes heavenward. "She's rambling. I think she may be right. She does indeed need food. It seems to be a constant and consistent problem."

Brig pulled over and stopped at the northern end of Juhu Beach at a place called Versova, which is near a fishing community. At this time of night all was quiet. We looked out over the water and stayed silent for a few moments. It was a gorgeous view. I couldn't enjoy one speck of it.

Brig nodded. "Okay. Five Flights to Go."

"What? More stairs? My legs are already killing me from dancing, flipping, and kneeing wiseguys in delicate areas. I can barely make it out of the car, much less up five flights. And what about food?"

Brig smiled at me. "It's the name of the place, Tempe. They did the touristy glamorous Three Flights Up two better. It's a nightspot for the beautiful people. Dancing to the latest tunes from the States. Though I don't think we'll want to hit the dance floor tonight. Best part for you? They have food. Plus the music is loud and it's always crowded and I doubt that we'd be seen, even if anyone we know happened to show up."

I nodded. "Sounds good."

Brig started the car up again and we were off. I tapped him on the shoulder. "Brig? Speaking of anyone knowing, how did Patel know we'd be at the Pool Palace?"

"I think it was a case of sheer blind bad luck."

Asha glared at him. "Unless he followed you from Jake's. Tempe and I were there a good two hours before Seymour showed up. Which, you may recall, was coincidentally right after *you* made an entrance."

Brig waved his hands in surrender. Not the best idea when one is driving. He placed them back on the wheel with a casual air. "Not my fault, ladies. Jake dropped me off at the rail station, and I took two cabs from there and checked behind me all the way."

I thought about this. "Hold up. No. Don't stop driving. Forget Patel knowing. Doubtless he had someone tailing you all day. I want to know how *you* knew Asha and I would be at the Pool Palace."

"I called Asha's house. Mala answered. She doesn't speak a lot of English, but she managed enough to tell me you ladies had gone to the Pool Palace."

Asha glanced back at me. I returned her look. We needed to have a chat with Mala, the helpful maid.

"So, Brig? Why did you want to join our girls' night out anyway?"

He bristled. "I didn't know you ladies had your hearts set on buddy bonding. It's Asha's fault."

She sat straight up. "Me? What did I do?"

Brig spat out, "You turned a normally intelligent male into a besotted dunce, that's what you did. Jake kept drooping around the house mumbling about how rotten you've been treating him. Not making a lick of sense."

"What else is new," Asha muttered.

Brig ignored her. "I had to get out. I planned to track you down myself and see if I could coerce you into throwing yourself at Mr. Roshan and doing whatever it takes to bring him back to the living. Damn, woman, the man's loony. What's this garbage about calling off the wedding? Will you at least talk to him?"

Cool. Maybe Asha would enlighten us as to her reasons for dumping Jake two days earlier. Or not. Asha settled back into her seat with a "Humph. Fat chance."

"Ouch!" Her seat happened to be me, and her elbows were digging into my rib cage.

"Sorry." She tilted her chin up. "Brig, drop it, okay?"

He did.

Brig stopped the car three blocks from Five Flights to Go. "I think it's best if you ladies proceed on foot. I'm ditching this baby at a garage. I don't want to park her on the street. I'll meet you at the club in ten minutes."

Asha and I started walking. Asha was a step ahead of me. She stopped. I ran into her back. She turned.

"You buy it?"

"What?"

"Brig's reason for tracking us down? All that cat poop about me and Jake. Mr. Matchmaker. Like he cares whether Jake and I exchange vows or not."

"Well, what else could have driven him out after a long day of gymnastic tricks and gliding through tangos with me? If he'd wanted a night out on the town, I damn well doubt he'd have ended up at a pool hall catering to college kids. First off, I don't think he plays pool. I mean, he might. Play pool, that is. But I think his list of teenage activities ran more to stealing hubcaps and hassling Bronx women than to shooting pool. Too tame."

I couldn't tell her about Brig's murdered sister and that I felt certain his blood had chilled when he learned another gymnast was at a pool hall looking for a bit of fun.

Asha threw her hands up into the air.

"Gad. I give up. Brig's right. You do ramble and run on when you're hungry. And you're also such a dope, Tempe. Brig was looking for *you*. Not me. He knows full well Jake and I will make up within the week. We break up at least twice a month and are back together before the florist even knows the wedding's been called off again."

"Oh." We were at the entrance of the nightclub by this time. "You really think he was looking for me? Not us, plural?"

She pulled me inside the doorway. "How old are you? Jeez! Did your mother let you date before you were twenty-nine? Damn, Tempe. For a bona fide born-and-raised-in-Manhattan businesswoman, you put the 'eve' into naive!"

"Oh."

Before I could think of anything polysyllabic to say, Brig joined us. His breathing was labored and his mouth was set in a scowl. Apparently, he'd run the whole way back to Five Flights to Go.

"What now?" I asked.

"I have good news and bad news."

"Which is which? You're gone less than six minutes and I already sense the hounds of hell after us. Am I right? What is it with you, Brig? Do you wear a scent every goon in Bombay sniffs and immediately knows where you are? And, by virtue of proximity and not choice, me too?"

Asha nudged me. "Will you let him speak?"

Brig glanced around us. We were in a dark doorway, sheltered from the streetlights, but I was not dumb enough to believe we were at all protected from prying eyes.

"Good news first. I discovered a nice stash of carb bars in the glove compartment of Asha's car. They seem a mite hard, rather than chewy, but they're all Tempe is going to get for a while because the bad news is I saw Ray Decore strolling down the street not one block from here."

"Oh terrific. Do these guys have us bugged somehow? This is insane!"

Brig urged us farther into the entranceway. "Didn't you tell me Ray has an eye for females of all shapes, sizes, and persuasions? This area is crawling with clubs and women. Hell, no more than half a mile the other direction are at least three places like C.C. Curry's where you made such a hit with your dancing. I'm sorry. It's just our bad luck that the man happened to pick the same street we're on."

I sighed. "You know, I've heard for years that India has a terrible people problem. As in, population explosion. And I've seen crowds here that make a Manhattan subway at rush hour look like a desert island. Can someone tell me why, in the, what, three days I've been here, I keep running into the same ten guys everywhere I've gone? And at least nine of them carry guns? Or knives?"

Brig ignored me. He whispered, "Asha. Go upstairs. Ray just turned the corner. Tempe and I will stay here until he passes. He hasn't seen you and wouldn't know you anyway unless you start keening. We'll meet up tomorrow."

I looked up at Brig in the dim light of the tunnel-like entrance. "How are we supposed to hide down here? Won't he see us in about ten seconds?"

Brig motioned toward the couples leaning up against every available space of the walls in this hallway. Every one of them was busily engaged in what I'd term serious making out.

Brig pulled me close. He found the darkest part of the entranceway. He leaned down and hid me from the opening with his whole body. A body that now pressed against mine with a firmness sending vibrations far different than fear throughout my whole being.

The man could kiss. I forgot that Ray Decore had wandered inside this entrance. That he stood barely two feet away. Woe to him, or anyone else, who interrupted the delicious taste of Brig's mouth on mine or stopped the hands roaming through my hair and down my back.

Brig then gently stroked my hair, then my forehead. He let his fingers travel over my eyelids and nose and chin, then rest for a moment in the hollow of my neck. I, in turn, was exploring the solid muscles of his shoulders, and his back, and heading down from there.

"Tempe?"

"Mmmm?"

"Tempe?"

Brig had stopped kissing and fondling. I started smoothing down more than one errant black hair off Brig's forehead.

"Hmm?"

"Ray's gone inside. We need to leave before he decides this isn't his scene and he needs wilder pastures."

"Oh."

"Tempe? Did you hear what I said?"

"Huh?"

"Ray. Here. We have to go. Now."

"Oh." I paused as the meaning hit me. "Oh!"

I quickly rearranged the shirt that had crept up under my bra as I managed somehow to snap out of the enraptured haze where Brig had kept me for the last few minutes.

"Brig, what about Asha?"

He shook his head. "I have to assume she'll be fine. She'll find a way to change into some wacky character upstairs. I don't think Ray would recognize her anyway. You and I, on the other hand, have to get out of here. No telling how long he'll stay, and the pair of us are a head taller than everyone else standing here. I'm rather amazed he didn't notice us when he walked in."

I smiled. "Our first piece of luck for the evening."

"Come on. We'd better hurry in case that luck turns again and Ray decides the women here are too young or accompanied by men bigger and better than he."

I followed Brig back outside, then put my hand on his elbow. He stopped.

"Brig. Any idea where we're going?"

"Not really. We can't use Asha's car because Patel's crowd knows it now. And walking in this area at this hour isn't wise even if we weren't already being chased by two sets of murdering thieves. I'm not in the mood to deal with ordinary muggers just now."

"So?"

Brig drew in a quick breath. "Holy Saint Pat! I don't believe this! Whatever we do, we'd best decide now! I think we must have offended a god today. Perhaps one who dislikes aerial flips beside a temple on a movie set."

"Why?"

"Because I just caught a glimpse of Kirk Mahindra under that lamp not two blocks down the street."

"Oh grand. It's now officially a three dog night."

"What? The old singing group? 'Joy to the World' and 'Celebrate' and all that? Are you loco? Is this what happens when you don't eat?"

I crossed my eyes at him. "Not the group! The *number*. Patel, Ray, now Mahindra. Hounds scenting blood. Ours. Three dogs."

"Uh, huh. Well, then, there's a train station half a mile from here. And blessedly, it's the opposite direction from where Mr. Mahindra has now been joined by two buddies. I'm not fond of taking the rails after midnight, but I doubt they'll be on to us as fast if we head there."

"They do seem to travel in clumps, don't they? The bad guys. Except for Ray. So far he's on his own. Stupid, really. Unless he was completely faking it, the man can't speak a word of Hindi. And Ray had no reason to fake it. He wouldn't have brought me if he hadn't been forced to hire an interpreter."

We turned and headed toward the train station. Brig stopped once to pull out a handkerchief from his shirt pocket. "It's not exactly the best disguise in the world, but if you can figure out a way to wrap up your hair, at least no one will see the color, Miss Redhead. These streets aren't near dark enough to suit me right now."

I did as he asked, fashioning a do-rag out of the square of cotton, then tucking my hair under it. "Yes?"

He burst into song. "Matchmaker, matchmaker, make me a match!"

I winked. "I'm glad you know the classics. Did you ever see a live production of *Fiddler on the Roof*? I saw the last revival in Manhattan. Super."

"I did too. We can sing 'Do You Love Me?' a bit later when we're not runnin' for our lives." He eyed me critically, then smiled. "Well, you don't really look like one of Tevye's daughters. Tell the truth, you could easily play the lead in *Playboy of the Western World*. Which reminds me, just how much Irish is in your background, Miss Walsh? You have the look, ya know."

"I have enough, Mr. O'Brien. Enough to recognize blarney when I hear it. And enough not to believe it."

He laughed, then took my hand in his as we tried to look like ordinary tourists out for a night on the town.

We made it to the train station without incident, paid our fare, and even found a seat in the crowded car. Trains in Bombay tend to give one claustrophobia during rush-hour conditions. They're not quite that jammed after midnight, but there were enough people to give me a sense of security from prying eyes. So much so that I relaxed and fell asleep on Brig's shoulder.

I had no idea how long I slept. I had no idea where we'd started, so I had no idea where we'd ended up. Brig squeezed my hand, then my shoulder.

"Tempe, lass. Time to get off the train. We have to take a cab or a rickshaw from here."

"Huh? Where we going?"

"The one place I could think of that's safe tonight. Vivek Studios. We're staying on the film set."

Chapter 17

Raj's trailer was a nice trailer, but it was still a trailer. Nowhere near the opulence of either Jake's or Asha's homes or even Brig's hotel by the harbor. But tonight it was going to be home.

Although picking the lock on Raj's trailer seemed a strange choice in accommodations for the night, Brig's suggestion that we camp there made sense, in a warped sort of way. Jake didn't have a trailer. Asha did, but we didn't know which one it was. There were smaller trailers, all occupied.

I gathered that Raj had told Brig during one of their chats on the set this morning (a very long time ago) that he'd be staying at his home for a few nights. His presence wasn't required early tomorrow. Which was now today, since it must be past three in the morning.

Raj had also told Brig that his trailer boasted a separate bathroom. That alone made Raj's home on the set an easy choice. The breaking-and-entering aspect bothered me, but since all we planned to steal was a night's rest and some toilet tissue, I felt sure once Raj learned about it, he wouldn't be terribly upset.

Once inside my latest residence, I kept dozing off. Brig appeared to be suffering from the same affliction. Exhaustion. We curled up spoon-fashion on Raj's narrow bed and fell asleep after one chaste good-night kiss.

We were awakened four hours later by the rude sounds of Asha Kumar yelling and pounding on the door. Sunlight streamed through the tiny window in Raj's galley kitchen.

"Tempe! Open up! I know you're in there."

I cautiously opened a second eye and gazed at the man lying beside me. "How do you do it?"

"How do I do what?"

"Not you, singularly. You, plural. Both. As in you and my new best friend out there attempting to beat down the door. How do either one of you seem to know where I am at any given moment of the day or night?"

Brig smiled. The thought struck me that waking up on a daily basis to that smile would be worth any grief that same smile might cause during the day. I pulled the sheet over my body. At some point last night I'd shed my jeans. I didn't remember doing so. Brig noted my movement.

The brogue returned. "You discarded the garment in Raj's bathroom somewhere around five this mornin'. Half asleep when you did so. And I, being the parfect gentleman I am, lass, did not take advantage of yer unclad state. Enticin' though 'twas, I can say without lyin'."

Brig stood. He'd discarded his jeans also, and I couldn't help but notice the large bump in the road between Wile E. Coyote and Road Runner on the boxers. Had I been aware of that before the knocking on the door started, I might not have stayed the "parfect lady."

I forced my attention back to the noise outside.

"Would you please open the door and let the girl in? She'll have everyone on the lot lined up outside wondering what's going on if she doesn't stop yelling. Watch. She'll start keening next just to keep herself in shape."

Brig's shirt lay on a chair across the room. I remembered the feel of bare skin on my back throughout the night. A sensual feeling. A wonderfully comfortable feeling. I could grow used to that feeling along with that smile.

The door opened and Asha breezed through. "Hey, guys. How ya doing this morning? Ready to dance?"

Obviously neither Ray nor Mahindra nor Patel had stumbled across Miss Kumar during the night. A pity. She looked far too bright, cheerful, clean, and rested. There was also a gleam in her eye that boded a fair amount of teasing in store for me all this day. I wondered if I could hide in Raj's trailer during lunch and tea.

Brig pulled his shirt back on.

"Ladies. 'Tis been a lovely night, but I have to be leavin' ya now."

"Where are you off to today?"

"Remember I told you I had a business errand for this day? One that will hopefully get us out of this pickle with the statue. I'll be back before close of filming."

He closed the door behind him. I lay back on the hard little pillow and groaned. "I hate that man."

Asha snickered. "Right. I see that. You look rumpled and far too happy for a girl who didn't enjoy a nice night of passionate sex with a hunk."

I sat back up. "Wrong. Wrong. And more wrong. Believe it or not, Brig did not touch me. Hell, we were both too stinking tired from beating up thugs and racing around train stations and picking locks to have been able to do anything illicit even if we'd had the inclination."

I threw Asha a sharp look. "Which I'm not saying we did."

"Did what?"

"Have the inclination."

I crawled out of the bed, headed for the small bathroom, and slammed the door shut. I had viewing privacy but not much else. Asha's voice could be heard echoing through the thin walls. "You are so full of it, Tempe."

"I beg your pardon?"

" 'Have the inclination.' What rot. The pair of you would be on each other like goats on grass if you ever had one night when you weren't being chased all over the city every waking minute."

I didn't answer. I turned on the water in Raj's small shower stall and stepped in. Maybe if I let it run for an hour, Asha the smart-ass would disappear. Go back to the set. Go back to the pool hall. Or New Jersey.

Asha was reclining on the bed when I stepped back out of

the bathroom. A current issue of *People* magazine lay on her lap. For once her picture did not grace the cover. She grinned at me.

"Did you know that Court TV is now the highest-rated cable show in America? That is so cool. They were barely able to get courts to allow them camera access when I left Jersey last time. Well, except in Florida. Either there are way more felons in Florida or the courts there were nicer to the TV people. They used to have a trial a week in Miami alone."

Tears suddenly filled her eyes. I forgot about being pissed at her for inserting her opinions about my love life into nearly every circumstance.

"Asha? What's the matter?"

"You keep asking why Jake and I broke up this last time? Well, it's simple. I want the wedding in Woodbridge. Mr. Director thinks it'd help both our careers if we had a big blowout here on the set of *Carnival of Lust*. With the dancers dancing behind us. Watch, he'll soon ask you to swing in on a rope and drop flowers overhead."

"Ah. Um. Would that be so awful? Not the flower rope trick. That would be beyond tacky, not to mention scary. But, I mean, you're both film people. The publicity would be great and everyone loves you here. Can't your folks fly out? Would they?"

She sniffed. "Yeah. They can. And Daddy would love to be back in Bombay."

One small tear trickled down her cheek. "But, Tempe? Hell. I want to hit Atlantic City for a crack at the slots. I want to go swimming down on the beach by Asbury Park. I want to eat really greasy burgers at the diner on Route 9 where I know every waitress by name. I want to head into New York and catch all the latest shows on Broadway."

I had to smile. "In other words, Queen of the Masala Movies, you're homesick."

She flicked her index finger toward me in a pure Jersey gesture of "you got that right." Then she rose.

"Thanks for understanding. Wish I could get Jake to do the

same. He's so wrapped up in movies all the time, he forgets that in real life, people need to visit the places where they grew up. Hey. Think you can get some of my feelings into his thick skull? Would you mind?"

I linked my arm through hers as we flung open the door of Raj's trailer and stepped into the bright sunshine.

"I'll be happy to make the effort for you, but I doubt I'd have much chance of success. Think about it. This is the man who blithely makes a girl he's known for less than a day perform feats of unrealistic daring and undeniable stupidity on large carnival set pieces."

Asha nodded. "True."

I continued my tirade. "And all these crazy stunts are simply to get the right look for his movie. You think he wants to be told he needs to forego publicity and thousands of worshipping fans adoring their beloved star as she becomes his missus?"

She sighed, then grinned. "Hey! If I do manage to persuade Jake to do the deed back home, will you be my maid of honor?"

"Hell, yes. Assuming I survive my stay in Bombay. Or even get home. I still don't have my passport."

Before Asha could respond, we were joined by the group of female dancers. Jake had scheduled women-only scenes for today's shoot. Jake also greeted us. As customary on the set, his manner remained professional.

"Ladies. Good morning. Tempe, today we're filming the sequence where Asha, as the princess, decides to fight her captives, including the ringmaster's mother. She discusses this decision with her women companions through the song. Asha. No dancing for you in this scene, remember? Tempe will lead the girls while you sing, sitting on the giraffe on the carousel. Tempe, the costumer is waiting for you."

This business of learn, rehearse, then shoot, all in costume and all in one day, seemed damned bizarre to me, but I knew Jake was short on money. At least we had a script. Most Masala movies don't. Cutting the budget meant slicing extraneous rehearsal, so I agreed with Jake's reasoning. Staying independent was preferable to ending up tied to the Indian Mafia business types who seemed to own most of the filmmakers in Bollywood. Or worse, ending up dead.

My outfit this day was a complete departure from the two-piece-bathing-suit-fifties-era gold jobby of the day before. Reena, the cursing costumer, must have joined Jake watching VH1 videos from the eighties.

I looked like a taller version of Pat Benatar in her wonderful video about girl runaways in the streets of Los Angeles. "Love Is a Battlefield." Funky short skirt with a handkerchief hem of many colors, hair tied up on my head, a ton of bracelets on my arm. Reena had also stuck me in a strapless tube top. I prayed it would stay on in case Jake had me doing backflips. I had no desire to start (and end) my career in Indian film as a topless gymnast.

Jake began taking us through the steps. The choreography seemed knocked off from the same Benatar video. Lots of low walks with snapping fingers, closed fist shaking, and hip pumps. Jake did add a few splits (for guess whom) followed by floor twists.

It reminded me a bit of break dancing, also from the eighties era, except Jake wanted a lot more wriggling and writhing. I'd been told to use the wooden floor stage for the latter. I worried about splinters ending up in tender places when I had time to be concerned about anything other than not snapping a bone or two in my back and neck.

Asha stayed seated on the giraffe on the carousel singing and wriggling. Envy overtook me. She definitely had the easier part of the number.

Then Jake motioned for me to climb onto the jaguar next to her and start thrashing and grinding on the beast. The well-oiled beast. I fell off the first three times I attempted to spin on the saddle. (Who puts a saddle on a giant carousel jaguar?)

Jake added one other touch. He hit a button. The animals, plus Asha and I, now began moving in circles. I clung to the neck of my jaguar and ended up with my body parallel to the ground. Next thing I knew, I went sailing off the carousel into the air. Twenty female dancers pulsed hips and shoulders and tried to avoid the red-haired missile rocketing through the center of their circle.

I landed on my butt, then glanced at the clock above the tent where Jake and the cameramen hid from the sun. Nine o'clock. As in A.M. A long day loomed ahead of me.

I wondered if Brig was spending his in an air-conditioned, stationary, Bombay restaurant seated across from a beautiful woman named Claire.

Chapter 18

I'd nailed it. It was a long, grueling day. I danced. I writhed. I twisted. I flipped. I flopped.

The plot of *Carnival of Lust* centered around a princess kidnapped by a pirate pretending to be a ringmaster at a carnival. The princess is tortured to reveal the whereabouts of a ruby she's hidden. After a great deal of running, hiding, slapping and kicking, the princess refuses to have sex with the pirate but gives up the location of the ruby.

The princess then keeps trying to get back to her true love, the owner of a cybercafé in Bombay. She prays to the goddess Parvati, consort of Shiva and destroyer of evil, to help her escape the privateering thug who has held her hostage. Parvati helps the princess evade the creep, then rains down fire, brimstone, and a few other choice plagues to smite the bad guy. The princess makes her way to Bombay (scene to be done at the Flora Fountain sometime next week) and is reunited with the love of her life, who, not surprisingly, has managed to get the ruby back. Everyone lives happily ever after.

Jake had written in a huge marriage scene near the end of the movie. That scene had given Jake the idea for what he wanted for a nuptial event with Asha. No wonder she was ticked. Life imitating art can be fun if one likes dancing around a carnival tent. For exchanging vows, it seemed somewhat less than romantic.

At ten till four, we took a break for tea. Asha waved me over to her table near the back side of the open-air tent. I sank into a chair. Since it was not made in the shape of an animal, nor did it stand over sixteen feet tall and go in circles, I sighed with pure pleasure.

"Killer, isn't it?" Asha smiled at me.

"What? The day, the dancing, or your once and occasional intended?" I shot back.

"Hmm. All three."

I took the cup she handed me, then drank it down with very unladylike speed. I handed it back to her and inclined my head toward the teapot for more. She smiled and poured another. I lifted the cup in a toast.

"I take my hat off to you, Miss Kumar. Or my bandana."

I reached up and pulled off the large kerchief and the scrunchie that bound my curls up into a high ponytail.

"This is tough work, Lady Starlet. Heck. I spend most of my time in an air-conditioned office looking over documents in the language of the day. I never realized how exhasuting a day in front of cameras could be. It never dawned on me that I'd find myself dancing on top of a giant jaguar moving in circles."

Asha winked at me. "Or sailing through the air when the giant jaguar moved a bit too fast?"

"Oh, yeah. Remind me to thank Jake for that little maneuver. Asha, this is worse than yesterday when visions of falling off that damn Ferris wheel haunted me the entire time I was flipping up there. Life less than sixteen feet in the air ceased to exist. I didn't even know I'd passed beyond pooped till Brig and I snuck into Raj's trailer."

She took a dainty sip of her tea, then ruined the effect by cramming half a scone into her mouth.

"Swy ah make da goo dough."

"Say again? You want a gooey doughnut?"

She swallowed. "That's why I make good dough. As in money, honey. Although the celebrity stuff is fun. It's great having fans asking for autographs. Getting seated before anyone else in restaurants. Seeing my picture on billboards all over town and beyond. But making a fantastic salary is important. And one reason why I can put up with the long hours of a shoot and the heat and the insanity and Jake being a jerk."

I reached for my second scone. "Ah. I wondered when his name would creep into the conversation. You guys still haven't made up?"

She shook her head. "Nope. And I'm not giving in. I want my wedding in Jersey. And if he can't see that, then he can just grab some little chorus wench and marry her right here on the lot."

"Right. Just after you scratch this mythical girl's eyes out."

"Pretty much." She smirked. "Tonight, however, I may get my chance to seduce Jake over to my way of thinking."

"Yes?"

"We're staying with a friend of Jake's on his yacht. Separate rooms, so far. But, on a nice yacht sailing around the harbor under the moonlight, I think I can convince that imbecile I adore how classy and romantic a more private ceremony would be."

"Sounds good."

She giggled. "Yep. Besides, Jake's really nuts right now. Normally when we break up, we make up within twenty-four hours. I've held out for five days. He's cuckoo. Clueless off the film set. Can't function. Can't form a coherent sentence. I've seen it. You've seen it. Brig has not only seen it, he spent an hour during the break yesterday afternoon telling me what a disaster his former roomie is without me."

The giggle turned into a belly laugh. "I like it! Jake is *so* ready to agree to any and all demands."

I chewed and nodded. Asha's talent for timing seemed right on. She understood it better than a watchmaker in Switzerland. A look of concern suddenly flashed across her tiny features.

"Tempe? Is this okay with you? I mean, us not being here? You're on your own tonight. One reason Jake accepted the invite on the yacht is because he figures he and I will be safer there. He thought you'd be fine staying at Raj's trailer again."

"Oh geez. That's right. Patel spotted you last night. And,

unlike Ray, who thinks movies and America are synonymous and exclusive and movie stars the same, I'd imagine Seymour knows who you are. You're not the most invisible babe around, Miss Queen of Bollywood."

She chuckled. "If that goon didn't know before, he does now. I nailed the sucker with a pool cue and some serious wailing. But now that he's been walloped by Asha Kumar? Well, it's not tough to get my address. I'm listed. And if they know *me,* they may know that Jake is, has been, and will be again, my best beloved. He's never made his address a secret either. Fans are cool. We have people over for tea all the time. I just don't think I'm including Patel or Mahindra in the next invitation."

"I'm so sorry I got you into this mess."

"Why? Hell, I'm enjoying the thrill of the chase, the adrenaline rush that comes with bopping bad guys and hauling A down dark streets. Seriously, Tempe, it's not your fault. I'm not even sure it's Brig's fault, although it seems to me he has a strange way of doing business. Whatever that business may be."

"Don't even go there. I keep waiting for the cops of several continents to join the chase here."

"I doubt it's that bad, but you might want to pin Mr. O'Brien down on his chosen profession before you guys post any banns. Anyway, don't worry about me or Jake. We're fine. Take care of yourself. Raj's trailer is clean; he's offered it to you for as long as you need it. I had one of the hired help at my place bring your stuff by today when they brought mine. You're set."

After a long afternoon spent repeating dance moves and doing handsprings off of carousels, an evening relaxing in Raj's trailer sounded divine. I opened the door, using a key this time, then sank down on the bed Brig and I had shared, all too innocently, last night. And I let the worry that had been with me since this morning invade my mind.

Brig hadn't shown up at the set. He hadn't called Jake. He hadn't sent a message by e-mail to Jake's laptop computer our director kept in his work trailer. No carrier pigeons had flown by and dropped a note, or anything else, on my head. I had no idea where Brig had gone this day, but I recalled his saying he'd be back before sundown. Or something equally dramatic.

"Before close of filming."

The shoot ended at seven. At seven fifteen, I had trotted over to eat at the service table still set up for cast spending the night in the trailers. After chatting with two of the dancers who'd wanted to know what America was really like ("Are there cowboys in the streets shooting at each other?") and devouring a dinner I didn't taste, I made a graceful exit.

It wasn't that I didn't want to be friendly or act as ambassador for the States. I needed to be in the shelter of the trailer. I needed to worry and curse and fume and wonder if Brig was lying with his throat cut in some dark alleyway near Hot Harry's or lying on Juhu Beach with the dark bewitching wench named Claire Dharbar.

A small TV sat on a table near Raj's kitchen. I turned it on, more for noise than anything else. U.S. president in France to discuss something vital like the price of croissants. American rock singer caught with his pants down in some sex-and-gun scandal. Stock prices dropping third day in a row. The usual. I turned it off and toured the trailer in search of reading material.

There was an assortment of magazines in a rack near the bed. I sifted through them. I found an article about Kirkee Mahindra, business tycoon and collector of *objets d'art*. Kirk had made his money in real estate holdings and ownership in big financial firms. The article described the original Matisse paintings and Rodin sculptures that decorated his penthouse apartment.

Great. The man was a celebrity. Ninth cousin or something to the Mahindra family who appeared to own half of India. Their wealth had been acquired in the tractor business, although Kirk did not seem to be involved in that branch of the family.

Ha! That was where Brig had hied off to. He was doubtless

riding down Marine Road on a tractor owned by one of the nicer and gentler Mahindras, waving to throngs of women who looked like Claire Dharbar. They were throwing kisses and tube tops with tassels at him while Matisse's *Blue Nude* did aerial flips off of Rodin's *The Thinker*.

Someone pounded on the door. I awoke, startled. Brig. Why he hadn't just picked the lock was a mystery, but maybe he thought knocking would be the wiser action in case Raj had decided to oust his visitor and stay at the trailer himself.

I opened the door—and hoped I was still dreaming. In front of me stood Mr. Kirkee Mahindra. Entrepreneur. Art collector. Killer.

Chapter 19

"Miss Walsh."

"Mister Mahindra."

We'd gotten the names right. Where we went from here I didn't know. I didn't really want to know. I wanted out, but there was no escape behind me. Raj's trailer had one window in the kitchen over the sink and one in the bathroom. Neither tiny piece of glass allowed easy exit. Assuming I could open one and try wriggling through before Kirk had time to squeeze off a few rounds at my derriere.

"Miss Walsh. I should like to speak with you."

This was new. Verbal communication as opposed to guns. I stayed silent. He smiled. Interesting. When the man smiled, he had a charm not unlike Briggan's. An incongruous thought flitted through my brain. Kirk Mahindra looked like he was in his midfifties. When this man had been in his thirties female hearts doubtless had shattered throughout India. He extended his hand to me.

"Perhaps you'd feel more comfortable outside this cramped space. Yes?"

Better and better. Talking in the open air where security guards might hear me scream when I needed to. Then again, Mahindra might have trussed up the night shift and replaced them with his cronies, who were now hiding in Ferris wheel seats with M16s aimed at Raj's trailer.

Mahindra motioned toward a bench about twelve feet away. I followed him, hoping he couldn't hear my knees rattling from fear, think there was a tommy gun behind him, and order the business associates to shoot first and ask questions later.

Mahindra waited while I sat, then placed himself at a proper distance from me. He smiled again.

"Miss Walsh. As well as being an attractive woman, you appear to be an intelligent one. A professional. I am going to appeal to you on those grounds."

What did that mean? He'd decided complimenting me could gain him more trust? He'd discarded the notion I was just some bimbo who wouldn't mind being shot or having her throat slit? I pulled my attention back to his words.

"I am a businessman, Miss Walsh. One who does not enjoy seeing a deal blow up in his face."

I held up my hand. "Wait. If I recall correctly, you were the one doing the blowing up right as Ray Decore was about to clinch his deal with Khan. Turns out he didn't care to go through with it as planned and actually hand over any rupees, but I didn't know that at the time and I doubt you did either."

"True, I did not know. But even if Mr. Decore had brought millions of rupees with him to the bar, it would not have made a difference. Khan originally promised the Saraswati statue to me. Me, you understand. Not Decore."

"Beg pardon?"

"Yes, Miss Walsh. Himali Khan lied to me. As your boss did you. Khan made a deal with me over a month ago. I came to Hot Harry's in order to give that cheater the money and collect the statue. *My* statue."

I looked into his eyes. Soft brown eyes that held only a hint of the anger behind them. Eyes that were likely to change and display savage fury if the man did not get what he wanted.

"Look, Mr. Mahindra. You were cheated. Sort of. I mean, no money had been exchanged as far as I saw. Ray got cheated, although he was prepared to do his own cheating. Sort of. I'm confused."

I sat up a bit straighter. "Not to change the subject, but I need to tell you, Ray wasn't really my boss. He hired me through the firm I work for. A very reputable firm. The firm who will wonder why Tempe Walsh is not in her office in a day or two."

He nodded. He was no dummy. He got it.

I continued. "Where was I? Oh. It sounds like Khan is pretty much a snake out to cheat everyone. But having you hunt me through every lowlife dive in Bombay is, well, not nice."

"When did I hunt you through a lowlife dive?"

I thought. "Oops. Sorry. I got you confused with Patel. Seymour Patel et al. The night I did the shimmy at C.C. Curry's. I can't keep everyone straight."

He seemed to be stifling a laugh. "I believe I would have paid good money to witness that 'shimmy' as you call it."

His face hardened. He sniffed. "Patel. Now he is indeed someone you would refer to as a lowlife. He has no business trying to retrieve the statue. He has no love for art. He wants to pawn the jewels. Imbecile. Barbarian."

Mahindra pulled out an elegant gold case from his breast pocket, lit a cigarette, then offered one to me. He politely blew the smoke past my ear once I'd made it plain I did not care to indulge.

I agreed with his assessment of his competition. "Patel must have bought Shiva's Diva over the same conference call that your slimy Mr. Khan seems to have made with you and Ray. But I have to ask. From what I understand, the legend states this statue comes with a curse. Doesn't that worry you guys even a little?"

Mahindra smiled. "I know about the curse and the blessing. Unlike Mr. Patel, I am a lover of the arts, Miss Walsh. Saraswati will bless me, of this I am certain. Patel is a swine. He will inherit the curse only, should he ever find himself in possession of the goddess."

I seemed to recall that Brig had claimed whoever owned the Diva needed to have a creative, gorgeous soul to be blessed, rather than end up without the use of one's vocal chords. Or wealth. Or ability to reproduce. I decided it would be imprudent to point out this particular component of the legend. "Generous and creative soul" didn't seem descriptive of Mahindra's character.

He dismissed both Patel's involvement and the curse. He inhaled the half-smoked cigarette. "The goddess. Shiva's Diva as you and Mr. O'Brien so cavalierly, and oddly, refer to the statue. That brings me back to the reason for visiting you this evening. Where is it?"

I almost laughed. The man had to be packing a gun in the other breast pocket. He'd already demonstrated no inhibitions as regards shooting at me in public places. Now the pair of us sat on a bench in the middle of the studio lots of Vivek Productions while we discussed this cursed statue as though we faced each other in a boardroom on Wall Street.

And I would have given it to him. The damn statue had come close to costing me my life. I'd seen it twice. First, when Khan had unfolded it from the bag plastered with Miss June displaying her wares. Then I'd seen the Diva peeking out of my old tote bag when Brig and I had collapsed at his hotel.

I had no desire to own the statue, sell it, or hear about it. My wisest course of action two days ago would have been to take it, and myself, to the American Embassy—instead of listening to Brig O'Brien, the vanishing Renaissance man, who hadn't returned by close of filming today.

"Mr. Mahindra? You're not going to believe me. I don't have clue number one where Shiva's Diva is. Really."

He stared at me. This time when he exhaled, the smoke came toward my face. Neither of us spoke. My back felt chilled. Ninety-plus degrees (even at ten-thirty P.M.) but I was freezing. Doubtless due to the many pairs of cold eyes staring at my back through rifle scopes.

"Then Briggan O'Brien has it. Of this I am now certain, Miss Walsh."

I looked him right in the eyes. "No. He doesn't. Brig sold it."

Mahindra stared at me. I gazed back and did not flinch. One of Asha's improv classes might have come in handy right then. Then again, I didn't need it. When one is trying to defend another's life, lying comes easier.

"To whom did he sell it?"

I shook my head. Seconds later, a demon overtook me. "I'm not sure, mind you. But I think Ray has it now. He really had the money all the time. He just didn't want to meet Khan's price. We were at the hotel and Brig stayed behind, so don't quote me on this."

Too much. I needed to shut up. Siccing Mahindra on Ray might not be considered charitable, but since Ray had tried to kill me not too long ago, I figured it was justice to let the bad guys fight it out amongst themselves.

Mahindra wouldn't resort to murder without first being sure he had the statue. Ray didn't have it, ergo, no slaying. Logical conclusion or not, it was one I had to sell in order to keep Mahindra from dislodging a weapon at any participants in this game of hot-potato-who's-got-the-diva.

Kirk Mahindra rose, dropped the butt of his cigarette to the ground, then mashed it with the same fervor he would likely extend to Ray, Brig, Patel, and, quite probably, me, should Saraswati not be in his hands by tomorrow.

"Thank you, Miss Walsh. I am sorry your stay in Bombay has not been a pleasant one. There are many places to visit, many I would love to show you. The David Sassoon Library, the Prince of Wales Museum. You are cultured. You would like these places very much."

I nodded, speechless. He turned to leave. I could see three figures about thirty feet away from our bench rise from the ground at the same time. He whirled around with the grace of any of the dancers in Jake's film.

"Miss Walsh?"

I looked up at him.

"If Mr. Decore does not have the statue, we will be closely pursuing Mr. O'Brien. You might tell him that, the next time you see him. And although it is obvious you did not heed my advice the other evening concerning Briggan, you should reconsider. He is not a fit companion for a lady. He is a scoundrel. You are a beautiful woman. You deserve a man worthy of you."

With that combined compliment and warning, he strode toward his waiting associates and headed off toward a white stretch limo parked near the carousel.

I have no idea how long I sat on the bench cursing my stupidity in fabricating a story to Kirk Mahindra.

"Dumb, Tempe. Unbelievably dumb. Kirk will now hightail it to Ray's hotel. He'll knock him around a bit, which might not be a bad thing since Ray deserves it, but he'll figure out in about twenty seconds that Ray doesn't have the Diva, because if he did, he'd have been on the first flight to the Cayman Islands or everyone's favorite resort spot in Pago Pago."

I moaned, then continued talking to myself.

"Okay. Mahindra will know I just lied through my teeth, and then he'll get right back to hunting down Brig. Which could prove difficult since Brig seems to have managed to make off with that stinkin' statue with no word to anyone who might possibly care about him. The rat. The stinkin' double-A-battery-run rat!"

Chapter 20

Mahindra had called me an intelligent woman, which might have been true once upon a time. I hadn't gotten into a spitting contest with Jake and Brig over scholarships and universities, but I currently boasted Bachelors and Masters degrees in subjects that guaranteed real jobs paying real salaries. I'd earned these degrees while also attending gymnastics competitions. Plus shaking my pom-poms for basketball games. Such activities left little time to study, yet I'd maintained an A average. Some people might call that smart.

In less than a week in India, that intelligence had turned to mush. Oatmeal brain. A nice description of Tempe Walsh. A bright woman would have walked away from Raj's trailer after conversing with a mobster, albeit a refined and polite one, and run to the nearest embassy.

Once there, that clever lady would have flung herself on the mercy of the cutest ambassador, then begged for asylum in a far northern land. Norway. Finland. Sweden. Somewhere with snow and ice cream and tall Viking holdovers. A place where the natives had never heard of Shiva's Diva and were too practical to believe in any curse or blessing not sanctioned by Thor.

She, Tempe Walsh—clever girl—might explain to this ambassador that, yes, she'd loved dressing up in outrageous outfits and performing gymnastic feats. Becoming friends with India's foremost actress had been a kick. Dropping clothes for the boys at C.C. Curry's ladies club and accompanying Robin Hood around town had been exciting.

She'd go on, though, to tell him that she, Tempe Walsh—oatmeal brain—would like to leave now. But she couldn't because one of several possible unfriendly parties had stolen all the goods she'd brought to Bombay. Including her passport.

I doubted it had dropped into Mahindra's possession. If he'd been the one to take it from my hotel room, he'd have returned it to me this evening. He had no reason to keep it. That left Patel or Ray.

Or heck, even Brig might have snatched it. I wouldn't put it past him to have managed to sweet-talk one of the maids into letting him in my room. He had no reason to steal my stuff since he already had Shiva's Diva, but that didn't mean I could rule him out as a suspect. He didn't have a reason for a lot of his actions.

So, did that clever Tempe Walsh opt for any of these intelligent strategies? Nope. I spent the night at the trailer.

Maybe I hoped Brig would come looking for me. Maybe he'd be so reassured to find me where he'd left me, he would throw himself at my feet. Beg me to forget all about goddesses and statues and run off to Pago Pago with him. Or maybe I didn't want to go anywhere near the heart of Bombay since Mahindra and associates were still sorting out who had what and what they planned to do to whoever did not.

The true answer to my staying put might have been that, once again, exhaustion ruled more than the wit to care whether any of the previous associates came bursting through the tiny window over the kitchen sink, guns and knives drawn and blazing, in the next six hours or so.

One of the major, or minor, goddesses did bestow a small blessing on me. I spent the rest of the night in peace, managed a good three hours' sleep, and was dressed and ready when Asha knocked on my door at seven in the morning.

"You don't have to be in costume today, didja know that? You get to watch. Me too."

"Hi, Asha. Good to see you. How's the yacht?"

"Oh yeah. Hi, Tempe. The yacht? Oh man. Super. Big, ostentatious, and romantic, and Jake and I are on again! So, I see you made it through the night alive?"

I grabbed the little black purse Brig had included in the shopping spree from Kemps Corner and followed Asha out the door. "Barely. I had a visitor."

"Brig? Is he back?"

I shook my head. "Nope. I have no idea where the elusive Mr. O'Brien is. Or whether he made it through the night either."

I stared ahead of me. Asha's blue car was parked by the carousel.

"The baby blue bomb is in the open. Aren't you worried it'll be recognized?"

She shrugged. "Hey. If anyone is stupid enough to chase me in the T-Bird, it's his bad luck if he catches me. I'm in no mood to hide from creeps. I have a life. Damned if Patel or Decore or that other clown is going to keep me from it. I'll call my parents and tell them to sic the guys from Tony's bar in Jersey City on 'em. They want to act like mobsters? Ha! I'll show 'em mobsters. So, who was your visitor, if not Brig?"

"Dog number three. Kirk Mahindra."

"Holy shit! Mahindra came out here?"

I told her about my conversation with the man.

"You told him Brig sold it to Ray? Wow! Talk about gutsy. What are you going to do when he realizes you just cooked up a major whopper? Which might be pretty soon."

"I did think about that. My reasoning is Mahindra knows Brig has, or had, Shiva's Diva. Even if he and Ray hash it out and figure that neither of them is in possession of the little charmer—the statue that is, not Brig—they'll try and find him. Not me. Mahindra seemed quite satisfied that Brig never came near my trailer last night."

Asha mumbled, "Which is why you're grumpy this A.M."

"Excuse me?"

"Nothing."

"I heard that, Asha. First, I am not grumpy. Sleepy, dopey,

even sneezy perhaps after all the cigarette smoke Mahindra blew in my face last night. But not grumpy. Second, even if I am grumpy, I don't want to hear your theories as to *why* I'm grumpy if they have anything to do with the fact that Brig is missing and did not spend last night lingering in my arms."

We smiled at each other. I switched topics back to her love life, not my lack of one. "Tell me. What's up with the wedding? You and Jake on again?"

She nodded, licking her lips like a contented cat sitting on a carton of Cool Whip. "I spent the first part of the evening gazing out over the waters with the foxiest man I could find on that yacht. And Jake spent that time glaring, muttering, and following us from stem to stern or whatever those parts of a boat are called."

"So?"

"So, about midnight, Mr. Jake Roshan decided he'd had enough. He politely told my semidate to take a long swim toward Chowpatty Beach, then he grabbed me and hauled me off to his room. Or suite. I'm not up on nautical terminology. Anyway, I think he's watched too many dailies of *Carnival of Lust*. Very forceful."

She grinned. "I loved it. There are times the alpha male has his place in the world. Last night was one of them. Anyway, he agreed that using the start of our marriage as a publicity stunt might not be the best idea he's ever had. He's just been really worried about budget for the film and he lost sight of the romance in the all-too-true reality that our wedding would rake in one heck of a lot of media attention, meaning great box office for opening."

"Yee haw! This is wonderful! So, Woodbridge is it?"

"Yep. I did agree to several massive, disgusting, gaudy, tasteless parties here, though. One to announce the engagement formally, one before we leave for America, and one when we get back, which will be just in time for the gala premiere of *Carnival of Lust*. I happen to adore gaudy tasteless parties. But I want to spend some time in the States before

I'm forced to take the seniors bus to Atlantic City for my gambling spree."

She glanced at me as we hopped into the car. "You have to come back for that, you know. Not the gambling spree. Unless you want to hit A.C. with me. We'd have a hell of a time. I'm as good at blackjack as I am at pool. Anyway. I meant the film opening. Not only since you'll be my maid of honor, and therefore part of this whole party scene, but so you can see the movie."

"Asha! Of course! Thank you. Believe it or not, I've never been a bridesmaid, much less a maid of honor. Just don't let Reena design the gowns, okay?"

We grinned at each other.

"Tempe? I also want you to get to tour the city when things are a bit less stressful. You haven't seen Bombay at its best, you know, and there are some terrific sites here. Like, the Sassoon Library is beyond cool, and the Prince of Wales Museum is gorgeous."

I sighed. "Funny. I had that same invite from Kirk last night."

"Yuck." She paused, then chuckled. "Although you realize the guy is loaded. Moneywise, that is. You could do worse."

I grinned at her. "I have. Remind me to tell you about the actor I dated who proved my father's point that men in creative fields are interested in money and sex and that's it. In that order. I'd rather not start another lousy relationship, especially with a man who lists 'shooting up saloons' on his résumé under 'hobbies'."

She giggled, I giggled, then I stopped when another thought struck me.

"Asha, you know, I might need to face some not-so-pleasant facts. Mahindra may, and I stress *may*, not be after my blood, but that leaves Patel and Ray. Neither of whom believes I'm not lugging the statue around in my purse. And since I don't have the beginnings of an idea where Brig hid the goddess, or himself, that still means I could be in danger."

Asha considered this. "Look. Shall we just whiz by the American Embassy today and see if they can straighten all this out? Which is what you should have done the night Hot Harry's bar got trashed." She fluttered her lashes. "They've got really cute marines guarding the gates. Always a treat."

I had to smile. "I thought about it. Really. And it's the sensible course of action. And we should do it right now. This morning. I know this. *But . . .*"

She swung the car around a sharp turn, missing a large SUV and an airport van by less than a foot each. I didn't even flinch.

"But. Damn, Tempe. I know that 'but.' I've used it more times in my life than I care to remember. It's the *but* associated with a male. And I'm not talking *but* as in rear end."

I nodded. "Brig."

She nodded. "Brig. You go to the embassy and you set the hounds on the man. And you get a new passport and visa or whatever and fly back to New York and maybe never see him again. And not know where he is or how he is."

"Or even *if* he is. Still living I mean. Crap! Asha. Where is he?"

"Girl, I wish I knew."

She swerved again to avoid a rickshaw loaded with tourists, and we both grew silent. Finally, she glanced over at me. "Tempe? I shouldn't say this, but I've never seen Brig act like he's been acting."

"What do you mean?"

"I met Brig when I first started working with Jake about five years ago. Brig periodically visits Jake, and I got thrown into the old roommate buddy stuff with them. Brig has brought girls out to the studio. I don't know the details of his relationship with any of them, if a relationship even existed. I didn't ask. But I'll tell you this. I never saw him with the same one twice. He'd show them the sights of the city, take them clubbing, whatever. That was it. The original no-commitment man."

"Well, duh. Why am I not surprised?" I blurted while I tried to choke back a few tears.

"Will you let me finish? You're different. Tempe, he stares at you all the time. And I saw how he looked when Patel grabbed you in the Pool Palace. Totally damn terrified. And it wasn't because you were just any old person he'd gone on the lam with. The man has it bad. With a capital *B*, *A*, and *D*! It's as if he's been looking for you for years and now that he's found you, well, he's not losing you."

I considered this. "Asha. All that doesn't mean anything. Not really. He and I sort of got thrust together with this nutty statue. A few kisses here and there were just the perks of keeping me alive. And his worry about Patel and his bruiser losers extended to you as well. Brig defended us both. And there are good reasons why he freaked over us being at a pool hall."

Asha nodded. "I know. Jake once told me about Brig's sister. But Brig's reaction at the Pool Palace was more than just fear of history repeating itself. If he doesn't care, why didn't he just take off with Shiva's Diva the first night you met him and leave you in the middle of Bombay? He had the statue. Why drag you around with him?"

"Unless he was afraid I'd report him to the nearest cop as one of the multitude of goons trying to get their hands on Saraswati. And I must point out, he seems to have done just that. Take the statue and leave me. I mean, now he doesn't have to concern himself as much with my safety since I know you and Jake. And crap, it would have taken a complete scum to have left me in that alley behind Hot Harry's."

"Well. I still think Brig has a thing for you. He looks at you with that look. That alpha male 'my woman' look. The one I saw most of last night from my man."

That did it. Asha had lost her sanity.

"Yo! Slow this thing down, Miss-Soon-to-Be-Married-to-Alpha-Male-Type. We need to find a garage. I think we've hit parade central for the Ganesh festival. Isn't this where Jake is shooting today?"

Chapter 21

Jake Roshan wanted to film one scene in the middle of a religious parade. Jake had decided the smart course of action would be to use an existing set at a real locale. He could climb up on a platform somewhere and shoot a few rolls of film and make everyone happy. Paradegoers would be thrilled to find themselves up on the screen. Jake's accountants would be thrilled Jake hadn't had to borrow money or go bankrupt building new scenery.

The Ganesh Chaturthi, a festival honoring the elephant-headed god of wisdom and prosperity, was a ten-day bash that had started nine days ago. Asha told me Jake had left the yacht before dawn to set up location cameras throughout the parade route. This last day promised to be the grandaddy of parades, outdoing Mr. Macy's annual Thanksgiving pageantry, the Rose Bowl march in California, and a New Orleans Mardi Gras all rolled into one.

I was still ticked that those first nine days of the festival were over, unattended in any capacity by Miss Tempe Walsh, whose mind had not been focused on a religious festival. The party atmosphere and general feeling of excitement that accompanies a festival of this magnitude lingered in the very air. But Asha, Brig, and I had been hiding out away from major or crowded thoroughfares each time we'd come into the city.

Asha parked in a garage across from Chowpatty Beach where the largest elephant replicas would be dumped later. As far as pollution was concerned, it was nothing short of dreadful. As far as the spectacle maintained from one year to the next, it was glorious.

I turned to Asha as we exited the blue convertible and grimly stated, "You know, I'd been looking forward to watching this parade from the sidelines as a good ol' American tourist just here to enjoy the sights. Now those dogs hounding us about the statue have just about ruined my even wanting to see the festival."

Asha slammed the door on her side. "Forget them, Tempe. Hey! If this hadn't happened, you wouldn't have met me, and let me tell you, I am the ultimate guide for this kind of stuff. Not to mention Jake can get shots of us leaping down the street and turning cartwheels in front of one of the Ganesh idols resting on the shoulders of paradegoers. Which Jake is apt to do. Be prepared for anything."

We walked over to a street already crowded with musicians and dancers and jugglers. Flashes from hundreds of cameras lit the area from every direction. Sounds of bells jangling and voices chanting added to the party atmosphere.

Asha and I bought some of the sweet carrot pastries called *gajar halwa* from one of the many vendors vying for attention. "Superb" didn't half cover it. And cheap. I went back for three more and would have gotten a dozen if Asha hadn't stopped me with the promise of a real lunch at a real restaurant within the next hour.

We spotted Jake standing on a platform high above the street. He waved at us to join him. We weaved through the crowd, then climbed the ladder leading to Jake's niche. Two cameramen flanked him, but Jake also held his own Panaflex to shoot footage.

Everyone nodded pleasantly to Asha and me. Jake motioned to the director's chairs placed around the platform; then we sat back and prepared to enjoy the festival. Thankfully I have no problem with heights. The ladder had been rickety at best, and the platform moved every time a small wind blew by. I ignored the swing and sway even though this perch made the Ferris wheel I'd been stuck on for the Day

One shoot seem firm and secure. At least today I had my butt in a real chair instead of balanced over my head while I balanced on my hands.

"Tempe!"

I turned to look at Asha. She and Jake were both staring down at a sight I couldn't see from my seat.

"Yeah?"

"It's Brig! Look! I can't believe this."

"What? Where?"

I rose, then joined Asha and peered over the edge of the platform.

Briggan O'Brien, the Irish American from Dublin, Ireland, and Riverdale, New York, was riding through the Ganesh festival parade atop an elephant. A real one. Not a Ganesh statue borne above the shoulders of honest worshippers. My first thought was Dumbo. Complete with tasseled saddle blanket and pink hat.

I blinked. And blinked again. The vision didn't change. "It's Brig."

Asha glanced back at me. "I said that. You okay?"

"Sure. I'm not even surprised that after leaving me to wonder where he'd gone, whether he'd been murdered or tortured or kidnapped or eloped, he should suddenly appear on an elephant in the middle of the biggest event of the year in downtown Bombay. Think there's any way I can jump off this platform onto Dumbo so I can kill him without breaking every bone in my body or hurting the elephant?"

Asha glanced at me, then at Jake. Sympathy showed in both faces.

Asha sighed. "She's hungry. All she had was that pastry. Well, four of them, but that isn't working. This is a girl who gets crazy notions when she's not regularly fed."

I scowled at her. "This has nothing to do with food."

She shook her head, and I muttered, "Well, maybe a little. But I really do just want to pounce on the back of that pachyderm down there and throttle the, uh, rider. What the hell does he think he's doing?"

Jake lowered the camera off of his shoulder. "Tempe. It's fine. This is my idea. I asked him to ride the beast. I need this for several shots. I talked to one of the organizers of the festival weeks ago and asked if I could get one of my actors in there. I wanted our stunt man Jervi to do it, but he has a bad fear of elephants."

"And Brig volunteered."

"Exactly."

I let out my breath. "Okay. I can buy that. But Jake, where's he been? Do you know? And damn the idiot, what happens if he's seen? It's not too easy to escape bullets from the top of a jungle beast."

Jake patted my hand. "I don't know where he's been. He was asleep at my place this morning when I left. But don't worry about him. No one is going to recognize him up there. I doubt that any of your thugs will be watching this parade. They're all too busy hunting through the city for where they think Brig might have hidden your statue."

"Not my statue," I quickly stated. "Brig's maybe. I don't want anything to do with the lady. Except to get her to whoever should own her, then wish them well."

Brig had seen us. He waved so vigorously from his perch it was merely by the grace of Ganesh he didn't topple to the ground. The elephant reached up and tapped him with her trunk. Brig caressed the snout with pure affection.

I sighed. "Must be female. He's obviously won her over with his charm. I wouldn't be surprised if she speaks Gaelic."

Asha and Jake both stifled their laughter, but glee remained in their eyes. I looked back down at O'Brien and his new friend. Brig pointed to the beast, then at me.

"He's either comparing me to Madam Dumbo there or asking me to join him. I think I prefer the first."

Asha nudged me. "Go. Get down there. I think it's very romantic. You and Brig riding through the streets of Bombay together. Jake'll get it all on film. You can show home movies back in Manhattan and impress your friends."

I fluttered my lashes. "If it's all that romantic, why don't you and the director give it a whirl?"

She grinned. "I'm right up there with Jervi the stunt man. Terrified of elephants. I love snakes and tigers and llamas, but these guys are just too big. Can't even feed the critters peanuts at the Bronx Zoo. Can't get that close to the cage. This is the perfect distance for me to admire them without interacting."

Jake held my hand for a moment and looked into my eyes. His held a twinkle, plus an entreaty. "Tempe? I had not planned this, but it's truly perfect for the movie. You and Brig have been dancing partners for several scenes. It would be fitting to continue that relationship in the parade. Will you do it for me? For *Carnival of Lust?*"

How could I resist a man who gave me those big sad brown eyes? He'd just delivered the film equivalent of "the show must go on." Besides, I would never tell anyone, but my pulse raced with delight that Jake had asked me to hop into the parade. Riding that animal with Brig had been a serious itch in my brain since the pair first came marching into view. This was much better than just having my photo snapped next to an elephant.

I scurried down the ladder, then tried to dodge through the crowd that merged around me. A group of dancers swirled and shimmied and shook and raised arms and tiny idols of Ganesh over their heads.

There were too many people in the street. I couldn't see over the heads of most of them, since they had statues of Ganesh held high. I bumped between dancers and clowns and men clad in robes who chanted in Hindi. I couldn't even see Brig. My breath started coming in spurts.

One of the clowns knocked me to the ground. Great. This was it. Death by Bozo in an elephant parade in Bombay. Couldn't wait to see my obit back in Manhattan. I tried to ooze through the legs and feet pressing in on me but made no progress.

A hand reached down and hoisted me over the crowd.

"Bit of a press, isn't it, luv?"

"Brig! Nice of you to grab me before the guy on stilts over there put permanent holes in my side. I appreciate it."

"Not a problem. Ready to meet Bambi?"

I nodded as I stared at my rescuer, who escorted me back toward Bambi. He was dressed in tight black silk trousers and a vest. Nothing else. Most of his chest was bare, as were his feet. A bracelet that had to be pure gold encircled his wrist. He was the definition of gorgeous.

The elephant knelt at his command. Brig leaned over and gave her a light kiss between the top of her trunk and her head. He then helped me up onto the back of the beast. He grabbed a fist of blanket and hoisted himself up beside me in a single, graceful move, then tapped Bambi with a stick. She slowly rose to a standing position.

She lifted me higher and higher above the crowds until the music, the voices, the laughter, and the prayers seemed far away. I held on to Brig's waist as tightly as I could, then peered around him.

"This is so cool! I can't believe I'm riding an elephant in a parade in India in the middle of the biggest festival of the year. And I'll be able to prove it since Jake is filming every bit. Although I hope he didn't get that view of my rear end as I climbed onto your new buddy here. Wow! Look! We're even higher than that tree with the idiot tourist leaning out."

We both waved at the idiot tourist who was now clinging in panic to a branch that seemed unable to hold his weight. Then Brig turned around, leaned in, and kissed me between my nose and forehead. Rather like he'd done with Bambi, who seemed to need steering. He leaned back over the elephant's head and whispered to her.

I forgot the crowds and the excitement. I nudged his shoulder and growled, "Where in the hell have you been?"

Chapter 22

The minute I asked where he'd been, he turned again. The gleam in his eyes made it obvious he was hatching a good Irish tale to distract me from my question.

I let out a woof of breath, then stated, "Wait. Don't answer. I don't want to know. Whatever you think up will have more holes than a tattoo artist's model. I do have a news flash for ya though, Mr. O'Brien."

"Yes? And what might that be? By the way, it's more than lovely to see ya today, Tempe. You're lookin' fair and fine, if ya don't mind my sayin' so. The crowds below are thinkin' the same. Blow them a kiss, okay?"

"No! I am not some cheerleader riding a float in the home-coming parade."

"Ach, you're prettier than any homecoming queen ever had a right to be. I must tell ya, I missed ya."

"'Lovely.' 'Pretty.' 'Missed me.'"

I forgot trying to be tough. I smiled and blew kisses to a crowd of teens waving flowers at this trio of boy, girl, and pachyderm.

"Ta, Briggan. I do appreciate the compliments. But there are important things to tell you. Ready to hear with whom I had a delightful little chat last night?"

"Kirk Mahindra."

I removed my other hand from his waist then put both back within milliseconds. Elephant riding requires a different balance I hadn't mastered yet. Until I did, I'd rather keep company with the all-knowing Brig O'Brien than tumble onto the street below to land in elephant goo.

"Brig. How did you know that?"

"Saw you. Very cozy you looked, too, sitting on the bench under the stars. Smoke floating around you both. Nasty habit, that. But I was jealous, I have to admit it."

"Why were you sneaking around anyway? Why didn't you just come to the trailer?"

Brig patted the elephant, who continued to wave her trunk, consequently knocking down small idols of Ganesh from the shoulders of three dancers below. "Hush, now."

I didn't know if he'd aimed that at the elephant or me. I poked him in the ribs. "So?"

"So let me quiet Bambi down and I'll tell you."

"Is she really named Bambi?"

Brig twisted in the saddle and smiled at me. "I think her real name is Bamnechokramurti or something like that. But she's Bambi to me. Just look at those sweet eyes."

No surprise. The elephant was female and she was preening under the gaze and touch of Briggan O'Brien. I patted the closest part of Bambi that felt like Bambi and not the blanket, then nudged Brig again. "You *do* realize that the original Bambi was a boy? Come to think of it, so was Lassie. Never mind. How do you know how to ride one of these beasts, anyway?"

I had visions of Brig at age fourteen or so running off to join a traveling circus. Or perhaps bribing the keepers at the Bronx Zoo to let him come inside and sing lullabies to the animals, elephants included.

Brig didn't answer, which was no great surprise. I patted Bambi again.

"Well, Mr. O'Brien, now that your darlin' lass is calm, can we get back to last night?"

"Sorry. Where did I leave off?"

"Spying on me."

"Well, if you must put it that way." He winked, then turned back in time to steer Bambi away from a frightened vendor below us. "I was not sneaking around, simply making sure that neither Mr. Mahindra nor his acolytes would detect my presence."

"I suppose that means you were lurking in the bushes?"

His shoulders shook slightly. I assumed he'd been stricken with a fit of laughter. He sobered a bit.

"It might if there'd been bushes to lurk in. Unfortunately, as you may or may not have noticed during your little chat with Kirk, it's pretty open between that bench and the trailer. Vivek Studios is one big desert."

"So?"

"So I perched at the top of the roller coaster, which ended up as a nice place *not* to be detected. And Tempe, neither you nor Mr. Mahindra were blessed at birth with quiet tongues. I could hear every word."

"Did you like the way I sicced him on Ray?"

"I did. Nicely done. Mahindra is not stupid. He knew I had Shiva's Diva in my possession. Trying to pretend you didn't know it as well would have been sheer folly. Dangerous folly. If I had a hat, I'd tip it to you for such a savvy prevaricatin' tale, lass. 'Twas worthy of the wee folk themselves."

I disliked having to address my questions to his back, but Bambi seemed intent on nosing through the crowd in search of a snack, meaning Brig had to concentrate on steering his latest conquest. It forced me to converse without benefit of seeing his face.

"Why didn't you come to Raj's trailer after he left?"

"Because I followed Kirk and the lads all the way to the Taj Mahal Hotel to have a listen in on his visit to Ray Decore. I imagine having Kirk pop up at his door might have been bit of a shocker for Raymond."

I saw no point in asking how Brig had managed this without transportation at hand. It didn't matter. Brig hadn't needed to follow Mahindra. He knew right where he'd be going, which was right where I'd sent him.

"What happened? Could you get into the hotel? Well, not

the hotel, of course you could, but up to Ray's room? Could you hear anything? Did they fight?"

He did laugh then. A rich laughter echoed by the roar of Bambi. It appeared she thought Brig was talking to her.

Another round of patting and caressing behind the elephant's ear ensued. I waited patiently for the bonding to halt. Once all was calm, Brig told me what he'd heard. Or not heard.

"I have to grant the Taj high marks for soundproof walls. I hid in the hall behind a large luggage rack and couldn't hear a blessed thing. I did see Mahindra rapping on Ray's door. Ray answered and Mahindra walked in and came out no more than six minutes later. I waited till the man had gone down in the lift, then I knocked on Ray's door and announced room service. To my relief, he answered he hadn't ordered any."

"Why relief?"

"I knew the man was still alive and well. Mahindra hadn't murdered him."

This was good and bad news. My conscience felt easier knowing that my fib hadn't caused injury to anyone, even someone as despicable as Ray Decore. But I was worried. Mahindra now knew Miss Tempe Walsh possessed a prevaricating tongue. He also must have surmised Brig still had Shiva's Diva. In which case, Mr. Mild Mellow could turn into Mr. Testy Terror should Kirk care to visit me again.

I sighed. "Okay. Great. We're back where we started. With the whole lot of them on our trail."

"Now, now. We've made some headway. We know that Ray is alive and one of the villains. We know Patel doesn't know about Ray. We know that Mahindra knows where you're staying and that he fancies you. So does Ray. You've got quite a way with the older men, Tempe. Too bad Seymour is a mite closer to our age. Otherwise you might be able to charm him as well."

"Huh? Go over that last again. Have you lost all your wits? Breathing in too many high altitudes lately? First the Ferris wheel, then the roller coaster, now Miss Bambi here. It's blunted your brain."

"It's not the heights, lass. 'Tis your own sweet self that's got me fair not knowin' which way is up or down. If 'twere only Ferris wheels and such, well, you've also been climbin' them. So your brain would be just as befogged."

Brig halted the elephant. He turned and wrapped his arms around me. "My brain *is* completely befogged, Tempe. And you're the cause."

Scents of curry and almonds and fried vegetables wafted up from the various vendors who'd entered the parade at this point. Shouts, prayers, and voices raised in song should have been deafening. The blanket on which I sat was rough. At any other time, I'd be complaining about the chafing and itching. But at this moment, every one of my senses was in tune to this man as he ignored the crowds below, leaned down and pressed his lips to mine.

I returned the soft pressure. I let my hands roam under the vest across his bare back and let my tongue explore his mouth and let my body shiver in anticipation of where this moment had to lead.

I could dimly hear shouts coming from somewhere to our left.

"Brig! Tempe! That's really nice! Can you keep it up for another minute or two?"

Jake and his Panaflex were following us. Brig and I drew apart. Brig's eyes took on a wicked gleam as he waved his hand to the omnipresent director and again pressed me close to him and kissed me with an intensity no camera would ever catch.

We might have continued the activity to an X-rated level had Bambi not been jostled by another elephant who let out a large roar of dissatisfaction. Or greeting. Perhaps mating. I'm not up on elephantspeak.

I adjusted my seating so as not to end up in the street if Bambi decided to play bumper cars with the other pachyderm. I tapped Brig on the shoulder after he turned to calm the girl.

"Brig? Any idea where Jake wants us to end up? Uh, geographically, that is."

"Chowpatty Beach. Jake wants to film the ecological disaster when the seventy-foot statue of Ganesh gets dipped into the water. I've heard that the good people of India have started using recyclable materials to build the statues that get baptized at the end of the festival. Then again, I wouldn't want to go snorkeling down there for a few years yet."

For some ridiculous reason I assumed the dunking place would be in, say, another hour or so. Tops.

Six hours later, we rode up to Chowpatty Beach. The actual dunking of the statue wasn't due until late evening, but by that time, it wouldn't matter to me if the EPA itself came storming in to protest. Excuse the crudity, but my butt hurt. I wanted off the elephant. Now.

Bambi's trainer, or keeper, or significant other was waiting for his darling at the beach. Brig climbed down, then helped me off the elephant's back. We gave Bambi a few fond hugs, pats, and peanuts, then looked around for Jake and Asha.

Jake waved to us from a terraced café. Great. Perhaps the restaurant would have more than tea snacks. I needed a hot meal and a glass of wine. Or more. Asha had promised me a decent lunch hours ago.

"Hi, Jake. Where's Asha?"

"She'll join us soon. She saw some snake charmer doing a hootchy-kootchy dance behind that clown with the cymbals." (And he meant clown literally.) "She ran off to see if she could entice him to do a scene in *Carnival of Lust* or lend her the serpents so she might perform herself. She wants to outdo the tiger scene from *Pirate Princess*."

Brig made a wry face. "Just make sure I'm back on the Ferris wheel or roller coaster or something way above the ground for that shoot. Snakes and I do not get along."

I saluted Brig with my glass of pineapple soda. I decided to let thirst win out over the need to relax. Perching on an elephant's back all day makes one hungry, thirsty, and smelly. I avoided thinking about the latter.

I smiled. "What's this? The intrepid Briggan O'Brien, jujitsu expert, rival of Michael Flatley for the lead in the next installment of *Riverdance*, victorious in battle over villains, and charmer of beasts and beauties throughout the world, is scared of a little old cobra?"

"Yep."

"Ah."

I turned to Jake. "Whatcha think? Can we hire a few anacondas or copperheads as extras in the film? Then just sit back and watch Mr. O'Brien dance a few steps not originally choreographed?"

Jake didn't answer.

"Jake?"

"What? Oh, sorry, guys. I haven't been listening. What did you say?"

I glanced at Brig. Other than the time Jake had been pouring hot water into his cup sans tea bag, he'd never appeared distracted. He was always on. Always sharp.

"Jake? What's wrong?"

He glanced at his watch. "Asha should have been here by now. She knows this place. The crowds are thinning, at least where the bulk of the festival has been held. There are so many different statues of Ganesh thrown into so many different venues of water. Chowpatty Beach is just one. The biggest, but still just one. And Asha is good at maneuvering through crowds."

He tapped his watch again. "She should be here."

Brig offered, "Maybe she decided to take the car?"

I shook my head. "Not in this mess. We parked here this morning specifically so she wouldn't have to deal with it later."

I glanced at Jake. He'd bit clean through his lower lip. Blood dripped onto his shirt. He ignored it.

"Jake. I bet she's engaged in a very prolonged discussion with the snake guy. Or she's autographing headshots of herself from *Pirate Princess*. I swear everyone I've met in Bombay has seen it four hundred times."

He nodded, then chugged down an entire bottle of beer.

"There's just one problem. Asha is indeed a talker. She's a pain in the you-know-what when she wants to be, and she loves practical jokes. She also loves her fans and will talk to them for hours outside the studios or invite them to her flat for tea."

Brig and I grinned. That was our Asha. But the grins turned to frowns when Jake continued his assessment of his fiancée.

"There are two rules Asha swears by. One is being ultimately professional when she is working. The other is an almost fanatical adherence to promptness. In the five films we have done together and even in our personal life together, I have never, not once, known her to be late. She said she'd meet me here at six. It is now six forty-five and no sign of her."

Brig stood, threw down a few rupees on the table, helped pull my chair back, then stared at Jake.

"Time to go. Normally I might agree that Asha just lost track of time with the snake man. But with everything that's happened in the last few days with the statue, I think we need to find her. Tempe? Any ideas?"

"Um. How about checking her car? It's close by, and I think she left her cell phone in the glove compartment. If she's okay, just off communing with the snakes or something, she might have called that phone and left a message knowing you'd be worried."

Jake brightened. "Good thought. She knows I had to leave mine at home today to recharge batteries. So she couldn't call me if she needed to. Tempe? Lead the way. Do you remember which garage?"

I did. When Asha had parked earlier this morning, she had suggested I make note of various landmarks in case she and I got separated and I needed to make my way back to the car alone.

The first thing I'd noticed had been the street vendor who'd printed the words "Best bhelpuri in Bombay" in English on the awning of his immobile cart. Down the block stood a stall that sold balloons. Next to that stall I'd seen a small boutique advertising pendants and other jewelry from the States. I remembered it because the whole place had been painted colors of red, white, and blue.

Brig muttered to himself as we walked to the garage. "My fault. It's the Diva. I know it."

Asha's car still sat in the same parking spot. But there was no Asha inside. She never closed the top, so we reached in and opened the glove compartment. Success. Her cell phone lay nestled inside a wad of tissues. The light blinked, signaling that she had messages.

Jake punched in the code necessary to retrieve the calls. We heard Asha's voice quivering, "Uh. Mr. Roshan? If you're getting this, I've run into a bit of trouble. I can't make our business meeting."

The message continued. "I ran into, uh, an acquaintance who has, uh, persuaded me to accompany him for the evening. Perhaps longer. I'll be in touch."

Brig began shouting, "Damn them! It's one of our stinkin' thugs. Bastard! He's got her!"

Brig continued to yell while he kicked the side of the car again and again and again until a large dent appeared. His face had turned bright red. I worried that between his intense anger and the heat of the city he'd have a stroke.

"Stop! Brig. Brig! Calm down. It's not going to do her any good if you wreck her car."

He stared at me for a long moment, half-heartedly kicked the tire, then sank to the ground.

"My fault. All my fault. She's gone."

He was right about the last two words. Asha, just like the princess she portrayed in *Carnival of Lust*, had been kidnapped. But this was no movie.

Chapter 23

"Where does Jake keep the sugar? Do you know?"

Brig absently waved toward the top of one of the cabinets in Jake's kitchen. "Up there. Canisters. Flour. Sugar. Coffee beans. Chocolate chips. The basics."

"Thanks."

I opened the pantry and hit the jackpot. All the basics indeed, plus flavored coffees and teas. I grabbed a handful of chocolate chips and stuffed them into my mouth as I began grinding coffee beans. Within minutes I had a nice pot of hazelnut Kahlúa coffee brewing for any and all who needed it. Which meant Jake, Brig, and me.

After we'd heard Asha's guarded message, we'd jumped into the convertible. Brig hot-wired her car while Jake replayed the call, and I prayed no harm would come to my friend. I wanted to throw myself into the water with the elephant statues for not going to the American Embassy and turning the problem of the Diva over to them. My fault.

Brig had wasted no time driving to Jake's. He'd stayed silent except for occasional obscenities directed toward whichever scumbag had snatched Asha.

We'd been back at Jake's about an hour. Brig and I had gone off to shower for significant lengths of time to get the pungent odor of Bambi removed from our bodies. Since I returned to the musky maid's room and had to use her fragrances, I ended up smelling like a hooker in heat. Which I suppose was better than the previous odor of a pachyderm in a panic.

Jake had spent that time pacing and cursing. Sounds of a fist smashing against the wall in the living room could be heard periodically during the fifteen minutes I spent digging through Jake's closet searching for something to fit me. I refused to don the now-ripe elephant-scented jeans and shirt I'd worn for the festival. I found a pair of sweats and a T-shirt, dressed, then followed the sounds of swearing coming from the kitchen.

Both guys were popping tops off beer bottles and checking the wall phone every five minutes to make sure it worked.

"No word, I guess?" I asked.

"No," had been the terse answer from both men.

I poured the coffee. The three of us sat on the stools behind the counter where just days ago Jake had sipped hot water and mooned about his latest breakup with Asha. It seemed so silly now.

The phone rang. Three mugs slammed down on the counter as one. Hot coffee spattered.

Jake hit the speaker button. Before he could say hello, we heard, "Roshan?"

I closed my eyes. I knew that voice. Last time I'd heard it, those dulcet tones had been screaming vile language at me at the Pool Palace. Seymour Patel. Damn. Of the three primary players in this game of hide-the-statue, Patel, in my opinion, took top honors as the nastiest.

Jake made no pretense of misunderstanding the reason for this call. "You want Shiva's Diva."

"Yes." Hindi curse word, curse word—I blushed. "We know O'Brien stole it at Harry's. We want it. Simple. I trade. The statue for that"—curse word, curse word—"Miss Kumar. We know she is lover even though she pretends all business."

Brig tilted his chin, then motioned to Jake. The motion declared "Yes."

Jake closed his eyes, took a deep breath, then spoke into the receiver. "Where and when?"

"I call three hours with orders."

Jake began to scream in the Marathi dialect. Since Hindi

had been my main language focus before I came to India, I could grasp only half of it.

Jake put Patel's curses to shame. He called the man a "filthy son of a camera." Wait. That might mean camel. Wrong translation. I shook my head and opened my eyes wide when Jake told Patel that his ancestors had never married. Or if they had, they'd married their sisters. Or brothers. I interpreted something about a hanging and a stretching and burning in there as well. I believe the words "draw and quarter" and "hot tar and sticky feathers" were used.

Finally, Jake returned to English and told Patel that if he hurt one hair on Asha's head, he, Jake Roshan, Yale graduate and award-winning film director, would chop off several essentials of Seymour's anatomy. Essentials that would make it impossible for Patel to create progeny of his own, whether with his mythical sister or any other female.

Patel took it well. Doubtless Jake's epithets were mild compared to what most of Seymour's confederates, or his enemies, called him on a daily basis.

He even laughed. "Three hours, Roshan. You listen to orders. I say once."

Jake yelled, "Wait!" but I could hear the click as Patel hung up on him.

Jake turned to Brig and me with tears in his eyes. "I just wanted to see if I could talk to Asha to make sure she is alive. I guess I ticked him off too much?"

Brig reached over and laid his hand on his friend's shoulder. "Jake. Patel won't kill her. He wants that statue too badly. And he knows he won't get it until you've been assured that Asha truly is unharmed. When he calls next, don't give him time to start what that idiot called 'orders.' I swear, the man needs a translator. His English stinks."

"I'm not volunteering for the job," I interjected.

Brig threw me a not-now-with-the-humor look and continued to tell Jake what to do.

"Ask him to put Asha on the phone and tell him you'll throw Shiva's Diva into the water of Chowpatty Beach to bond with the latest Ganesh idol if you don't hear her voice pronto."

Jake nodded, then laid his head down on the table. He looked like he planned to stay there every minute of those next three hours. Waiting. Brig motioned me to follow him and let Jake worry in peace.

In silence, we took our mugs into the den. I looked up at Brig as he leaned against a mantel, then began cleaning the pieces on it with a feather duster he'd found on a small table nearby.

"Brig? Thanks for agreeing to give up Shiva's Diva. For Asha."

He stared at me. "Did you really think I wouldn't give up the goddess, with Asha's life almost in my hands?"

I shook my head. "No. I didn't. I don't know what your usual modus operandi is for snatching stolen goods, but I do believe you'd never jeopardize another life just to keep a piece, no matter how precious."

He bowed. "Thank you for that somewhat mixed opinion of me. For the record, I don't steal. I know it appears that way to you, but I promise you I don't."

I looked into his eyes. "So, that being made clear, where is our little dear? I still can't figure out how you've managed to keep it hidden all this time. I mean, you gave me back the tote bag on the set the other morning, but I didn't notice any figurines coming along with it."

He smiled. "*Purloined Letter*, luv."

"What?"

"Poe's classic. Didn't you read it in high school?"

"Yeah, yeah. I've read it. More than once. The gist, if I recall, is that to hide something of value you must put in plain sight along with similar items. In Poe's story, a letter."

Brig nodded and continued to dust. I narrowed my eyes at him. The man didn't strike me as being a model of domesticity, and Jake's servants were more than adept at keeping a clean home. I focused on the shelf as the duster swept the objects clean. And saw it.

Jake's mantel had been decorated with a hodgepodge of film-award statuettes, idols in the form of Shiva, Ganesh, Lakshmi, and at least three other Hindu gods or goddesses. Five carousel music boxes shaped like horses formed a circle around another idol. Not any idol. Shiva's Diva.

"Sweet Saraswati! It's her."

"Exactly."

He took the piece off the mantel and gently ran the duster over it. "She's a beauty, isn't she?"

I hadn't had much of a chance to see Shiva's Diva close up. While Ray had been wheeling and dealing, I'd been translating and not terribly concerned with the object of the negotiations. The only part of her I'd really seen had been the upside-down lute, which had caused me to question her authenticity.

Brig handed her to me. She stood no more than twelve inches high, with fine, sculpted lines and features that spoke of nothing but serenity. Rubies glittered over the upside-down lute, and diamonds and rubies decorated the weapon this goddess would never have carried. Shiva's Diva. The lady who'd caused such a fuss. A lady who blessed the creative in life and cursed the greedy.

"She's beautiful. I see why everyone wants her, aside from the price angle and the blessings. Should one be so lucky as to earn them rather than their opposite."

Brig's eyes narrowed. "Much as I hate to deliver Saraswati into the hands of a swine like Patel, I cling to the lovely thought that he'll be a penniless, speechless wreck within weeks. And if he keeps our goddess, that's what will happen. Though he'll more likely just sell her fast for big money."

He sighed. I handed him the statue. Jake entered in time to see Brig take the goddess back.

"That's her? The statue the three hounds are hunting?"

We nodded. Jake walked directly over to Brig. For a second I thought he would strike him. Jake's life had been turned around because of Brig. His house had been put in danger. And not just his physical abode. Asha, his love, might not make it to the wedding she'd been so determined to have in America.

Jake reached out and hugged Brig so tightly I expected to hear bones snap.

"Thank you for agreeing to give it to Patel. That *biimaar jhiigaa*."

Jake had just called Patel a "sick shrimp" in Hindi. I nodded in agreement with the sentiment, but I couldn't help wonder why he and Brig seemed to want to defile innocent cephalopod mollusks (squids) and hapless crustacea.

Brig turned red. "Jake. I'm so sorry I hid it here. Sorry you and Asha ever got involved. You're my best friend, but I've brought nothing but disaster to you."

I didn't get included in this little apology. Perhaps Brig thought his game of hide-and-seek had enthralled me. And, thinking about it, maybe it had. I could have forced him (how, I'm not sure) to hand it over to the authorities. If not the police, then the embassy. I almost smiled thinking about Asha lusting over the marines who guard the gates. We could use a troop of them in full battle mode just now. Or the good old British cavalry riding to the rescue.

Jake shook his head. "Brig. This is not your fault. The villain is Patel."

"Not to mention Mahindra and Ray Decore," I muttered. The men glanced at me. Both of them had the same expression of sheer panic on their faces.

Brig spoke first. "Damn! I'd forgotten about them. We've got to stick Shiva's Diva into Patel's hands and get Asha back home safely without either of that lot barging in and taking the statue from us before we can deliver her."

As one, we sank onto Jake's spacious sofa. After a moment or two I stood again.

"Guys. Let's not borrow trouble, okay? Look, we don't even know where Patel plans to meet. And Mahindra and Ray would have to be on our tails from the moment we leave here and follow us to figure it out. Plus, they'd have to have dis-

covered this is where the statue's been kept. They don't even
know Asha's been kidnapped. At least I guess they don't."

I paused. Mahindra had an uncanny ability to figure out
who'd gone where and what had happened. For all I knew,
he could be camped under the window pretending to be a
shrub in order to eavesdrop. I glanced toward the large glass
sliding doors leading to Jake's patio. No movement from the
banyan trees. I needed to do something before my imagination had the man popping out of Jake's coffeepot.

"I'm going to make some more coffee. And some dinner.
We've got two hours and thirty minutes to wait."

I tried to smile. "We need to keep up our strength for dealing with Patel. No one needs to pass out and faint while we're
in the middle of our big rescue of Asha."

Brig rolled his eyes, smiled, then said, "In other words,
Tempe's hungry."

Chapter 24

Midnight. Brig, Jake, and I were still in the kitchen, still sipping coffee, and still trying to finish the food we'd been pushing around our plates for three hours.

Jake had used the time to give us a nice lecture on the history of Bombay. He started with the century it was home to Koli fishermen, then took his audience of two through various Hindu dynasties. He explained that Muslim sultans, then Portuguese conquerors had been next up in the we-want-this-city parade. He talked about the British naming the city Bombay, and then Gandhi and the move for independence, and finally the renaming or reclaiming of the name Mumbai in 1995.

It was all interesting and informative and I was damn glad there wouldn't be a test because I hadn't retained one word of it.

The phone rang. Jake picked it up and punched the speaker button. "Yes?"

"Roshan?"

Déjà vu.

"Yes, Mr. Patel."

Silence.

"I did not tell you my name. Where you hear name? I do not like you know my name."

Jake, though a drama major, had never quite mastered the art of deception. Perhaps he'd always just directed others and so he'd skipped Improv 101 himself.

He now glanced in terror at Brig and me. "Uh. Brig

O'Brien thought you might be the one who had Asha? So I figured it was you?"

Brig rolled his eyes. Jake panicked and stared at the phone like a man seeing such a device for the first time.

I grabbed it from him. "Mr. Patel! Seymour. Do you mind if I call you *Seymour*? We're such old pals now. Listen, Seymour, Jake is coughing in the corner right now and can't speak. Too much curry in the, uh, curry."

Brig tried to take the phone from me, but I wouldn't let him.

"Seymour? I'm authorized to take instructions. 'Orders' as you so badly termed it. But before I do, I really think you need to put Asha on the line. And don't even start any business of telling me she's fine and assuming I'm going to take your stinking lying word for it. Understand this, you filthy squid. The Saraswati statue is currently sitting no more than two feet from me at this very moment, and if Asha Kumar's lilting tones aren't sailing over the wire in ten seconds, I will personally toss the statue into the nearest, deepest, most polluted lake and let her swim with Ganesh elephants. Got that, *Seymour*?"

I didn't wait for a response. "Now put her on the phone, you scumbag. Five seconds have passed."

I took a deep breath. Jake and Brig were both staring at me with a mixture of horror and admiration. I hoped my bravado would warrant the latter. Where it came from in the first place I had no idea.

"Yo! Tempe!"

"Asha! Hey, girl. Where are you?"

"Good question. One I don't have an answer for. But do let Jake and Brig know that I'll be fine as long as that statue gets delivered per ol' Seymour's instructions."

A cry sounded as the phone must have been twisted from her hand. We heard one more word from Asha. "Shit!"

Patel came back on the line. "You being satisfied?"

"Well, that's not quite the best description of my feelings

at the moment but at least I'm a bit more reassured that Asha
is okay. A condition that had better remain just that."

"Put man I know is still in room back to phone."

Jake hadn't recovered enough to be coherent, so I handed
the phone to Brig. He grunted, "Patel."

"O'Brien. So nice hear voice. Now you stay silent while I
be telling you where you bring Saraswati."

Jake and I listened as Patel ran through a complicated set
of directions that ended up at some place called The Fort.

"One hour meet," was Patel's good-bye phrase.

I pursed my lips. "Male chauvinist."

"What? Who? Me?" Brig asked.

"No. Seymour Patel. Grabbing a girl and keeping her
hostage like she's some weak floozy in a melodrama. And
then not giving *me* the directions to The Fort. Like I'm too
stupid to understand them."

Brig hugged me. "Darlin' Tempe, we admire your talent
with words in all languages, and you're a damn terrific dancer
and you make a wonderful cup of coffee. You also kiss divinely. Something to explore further when we get home
tonight. Or, just a bit now."

He kissed me, then casually continued his monologue.

"Where was I? Ah. Mr. Patel is indeed a rotten chauvinist
of the worse sort. But no matter how brilliant and independent you are, you've been in Bombay less than a week. I'm
sure Patel believes, as do Jake and I, that you can rescue Asha
single-handedly while singing disco tunes and dancing a fine
gig at the same time. But your navigational skills are not quite
the ticket just now."

He had me there. He could have me in a few other places
if he set his mind and body to it, but dwelling on that thought
seemed inappropriate just now.

"Okay. Fine, I think. So, The Fort. Is this some military en-
campment? How do we break in?"

Brig and Jake exchanged a look. I intercepted, immediately
set my mug on the table, then headed for the den to hunt for
my shoes.

I paused in the doorway for a moment to state, "I know that look. It's the women-and-children-into-the-lifeboats-and-let-the-brave-men-fight look. Forget it, guys. I'm going."

Brig scooped up his own boots and began pulling them on. "Never said you weren't. And looks to the contrary, never intended for you to stay here. The Fort is what the general area is called. We're actually making the exchange at the Flora Fountain."

Eerie. I remembered talking to Ray Decore back at Hot Harry's Saloon, telling him that I wanted to visit Flora Fountain. I had intended for that trip to be part of a nice afternoon tour of an older area of Bombay. Rescuing a friend at Flora Fountain had not been part of the original itinerary.

I nodded at Brig. "Good. Grand. Okay. I'm dressed and ready. You're dressed and ready. Jake's been ready for the last three hours. So. How do we get there?"

Jake had finally snapped out of the fog he'd been sucked into upon hearing his beloved's voice over the speakerphone. He grabbed Asha's extra car keys and growled, "We drive. We might as well take Asha's car. Once we hand over the statue, Asha will be spitting mad if she doesn't get to work off some steam by tearing around town running over curbs and dodging carts."

I tactfully refrained from mentioning that, if we got Asha back and Shiva's Diva delivered, there would be no room for anyone but Asha and Jake to do that tearing.

I glanced at Brig. He whispered, "We'll get back by means of public transportation. I doubt the engaged couple will want the pair of us trailing them about all night anyway."

Shiva's Diva again rested inside a tote bag. This was one of Jake's he used to lug tons of notes and sketches to and from the studio lot. Pictures from *Pirate Princess* had been plastered all over it.

The goddess herself had been wrapped in a T-shirt with a picture of one of Jake's older movies silk-screened on the front. I shuddered every time I looked at it. The film had a Hindi title that, when translated, meant *Fountain of Death*. I doubted whether either Brig or Jake had noticed in their haste to dress Shiva's Diva.

Taking Asha's two seater meant I got to sit on Brig's lap. A location that would have proved enjoyable had not both of us been so worried about Asha. Even so, I found it difficult to keep my mind focused on anything beyond the feeling of Brig's thighs under mine or his strong arms encircling my waist. I smiled, knowing Asha would understand and approve.

I turned as best I could and asked Brig, "Think we'll get to see Asha, before we hand over the statue?"

"You mean will Patel let us, or is there a spot for viewing the prisoner? Since he said to go to the top of the fountain, no doubt he'll have her up there with him, though how is a mystery. There are no stairs leading to goddess Flora. Anyway, I'm sure Seymour has Asha bound, gagged, and trussed up tight."

Brig winked at me before continuing. "But if you're worried Jake and I will just deposit Shiva's Diva on the ground without bringing Asha safely back with us, forget it. First her, then the statue. Those are the rules and I made them quite clear to Patel."

The Bombaby Fort area had begun its existence as a British military stronghold built in the 1700s. Fires and natural decay had ruined most of the actual fort, but according to Jake, who acted as tour guide and chauffeur, a few of the walls still stood. The Flora Fountain had been built on the site of one of the former entrances of the fort itself and was the center of a Y-intersection.

On various sides opposite the fountain were the offices of American Express, the Bombay High Court, and St. Thomas's Cathedral. Doubtless Patel's goons now occupied the bell tower at St. Thomas (if there was one) and had pots of oil boiling and ready to dump over the heads of Asha's brave rescuers.

Patel had set the time for the exchange at three A.M. No tourists would be lingering to listen to political radicals expounding their views from the base of Flora Fountain. No taxis would be circling the area waiting to take those tourists off to the National Park or the beach or a quiet museum.

I wondered if the ghosts of soldiers from centuries ago still haunted the place. If so, would they look more kindly on Patel or on the three desperate people about to invade their privacy at such a late hour?

I still didn't like the Tempe-stay-in-the-car-and-wait scenario, but Brig claimed we'd look like an amateur religious revivalist singing trio if all of us went barging around the fountain with our hands waving in the air screaming Asha's name. The man had a unique way with words. I knew he simply wanted to keep me safe. I would listen to him this one time and not grouse.

We parked in the street by a vegetable market, opened the doors to the convertible, then stood outside for a few moments, waiting until the precise hour.

I took the opportunity to stretch. Half my day had been spent riding on the back of an elephant and a quarter of it riding in Asha's car. Neither mode of transportation had done my rear end any good.

Three o'clock in the morning. Time to let go of Shiva's Diva and bring Asha back to the safety of friends and fiancé. Brig and Jake grabbed the tote bag, then began the three-block walk toward Flora Fountain. I stayed.

In our haste to get there on time with Shiva's Diva securely wrapped and ready to become part of Patel's personal art collection (or immediately sold by the creep for a large sum of rupees), we'd forgotten something. Two things, actually. Well, not things if one wanted to be literal.

I'm getting to the point. Really. What had slipped our minds were the other two players. One of whom now approached from a limousine a block south from where I stood. The second headed in from the north. Kirk Mahindra and Ray Decore. It was another three dog night.

Chapter 25

I dropped to the ground next to Asha's car.

Brig and Jake were close to the fountain now. I wanted to try to whistle to get their attention, but that particular sound technique has never been listed in my arsenal of talents.

To hell with it. I stood and started walking toward a cluster of vendor stands at the edge of Flora Fountain's park. Kirk, Ray, and I all reached the fruit-seller's cart at the same time from different directions. Kirk and Ray stared at me. Then at each other.

After a good thirty seconds of silence, I couldn't stand the tense quiet.

I coughed politely, then said, "So. What's the plan, guys? You both came out for an early morning stroll to check historic sights? Just like me? Nice here, don't you think? Quiet, peaceful. The way fountains and parks should be."

Mahindra smiled. "I am sorry, Miss Walsh. I had not imagined I would run into either you or this man tonight. I do not know what your plans are. And frankly I do not care what Decore has in mind. I intend to cross to the base of the fountain where Mr. O'Brien is now standing with a bag I presume holds my statue. I shall retrieve it, then leave."

"Right. Ray?"

"About the same, except that bag is going to end up in my hands, not his."

"Can we talk about this for just a second?"

Ray sighed. "What's there to talk about? I want the Saraswati statue. Brig O'Brien has it. I don't really give a damn if a few bodies get tossed through that archway over there next to the plaster clown with the torch. Especially Brig's body. I owe him for the black eye."

Mahindra grabbed my arm and faced me back toward the street. "Miss Walsh, in less than two minutes, there will be guns firing and knives being thrown and fists flying. I say this to give you the chance to turn and run before any blood is shed this night. Most particularly yours. You are a pretty girl. I would not like for you to be a dead girl. I cannot say the same about your male companions. Either of them. I despise Briggan O'Brien. And quite honestly, I do not care for Jake Roshan's films. Too violent."

"Oh."

Ray pulled a large gun out of a brown bag. "I'm not as accommodating as Mr. Mahindra. Enough chatter. Now, shut up, both of you."

He grabbed me, then held me in front of him. He pushed me closer to the fountain. I could see Brig and Jake standing in an empty archway. But as yet, there was no sign of Asha or Patel.

I had to let Brig know we were here before one or the other of my escorts shot him.

"Three dog night!

He got it. Not that he could do a heck of a lot about it. Brig nudged Jake and both men turned. All five of us stared at each other.

From up above, standing by the statue of Miss Flora herself, stood Asha. She was yelling, "Martyrs!" I thought she might be telling me it was time to die for the cause, but then I remembered the statues of the patriots on either side of Flora Fountain. They gaze upon tourists in an area known as the Martyrs Memorial.

Patel stood beside one of those martyrs shouting at Brig, "Drop it! You must drop statue now and be leaving or girl dies! You hear? She dies, I swear. She dies!"

The next thing I knew, a volley of knives came flying into

the park from every direction. They were followed by the sound of gunfire, also from all sides.

Patel's raspy commands had created a diversion, albeit unintentionally. Mahindra dodged several knife attacks from the area of the High Court as he struggled to get his gun out of his breast pocket. Since Ray already had his pistol in front of him, he simply started shooting in all directions. Then he screamed. One of the knives had made its way into his thigh. Or maybe it had been a bullet.

I didn't stop to ask which one or to offer assistance. I dropped to the ground and did a low somersault that landed me by Brig's feet.

I looked up. Brig looked down. Jake looked at us both, then pointed to Asha who was hanging on to Miss Flora herself looking out over Bombay.

Asha leaned over the edge of a railing and waved her bound hands. She kept yelling, "Cherry picker!"

It had never occurred to me back when I played *Sweet Charity* that the experience could ultimately save my, or someone else's, life. Besides having a great time performing that summer, I'd learned the names given to the hydraulic lift the tech crew used to hang lights or place railings at the top of our set. "Cherry picker" is another term for that particular piece of construction machinery.

I turned and saw the vehicle behind the fountain. Patel must have stolen this particular lift from a hapless worshipper at the Ganesh festival, since cherry pickers with cranes and grappling hooks hoist the elephant statues in preparation for dunking. I headed directly for it.

Either the goddess was on our side or the various felons shooting and tossing knives were afraid to get too close to Saraswati in the tote bag, because all the weaponry was currently aimed at villains and not at me.

Patel was throwing knives at Mahindra. Mahindra was shooting at Patel. Ray was shooting at a collection of thugs surrounding the perimeter.

I glanced over at Brig and Jake who had taken shelter from

the battle behind a vending cart. Brig shouted "Churchgate" and I nodded. I assumed this meant it was everyone for his or herself, and we'd meet up at the Churchgate train station if we lived.

No one was manning the cherry picker. I hopped aboard and nearly jumped right back off when I looked around the cab and saw the array of gearshifts and pedals. This wasn't like the smaller vehicles I'd watched the techies drive around the theater with the ease of small golf carts.

I turned the key Patel had stupidly left in the ignition, then started pulling levers and sticks and mashing pedals. Within seconds I'd destroyed two fruit stands and an herb cart. I finally figured out which lever aimed the lift in the direction I needed it to go, which one took me in reverse, and which pedal sent me careening into another cart. This vendor advertised cell phones and computer gadgets. I hoped the dealer had taken his unsold wares home for the night.

Asha spotted me (how could she not?) and began waving her arms trying to guide me toward her position next to the top statue.

I glanced down at the activity continuing around the fountain. Goons of all sizes were sliding and slithering in the stagnant water that surrounded the bottom tier, intent on keeping their footing while trying to kill each other. They hadn't noticed the cherry picker lurching its way toward the actress emoting above them. They didn't even see Asha grab the grappling hook at the end of the crane lift, then sway twenty feet in the air while her buddy, the unlicensed driver, struggled to hold the machinery in place for this rescue.

I sideswiped three more stands but finally managed to drive that piece of machinery away from the fountain. In reverse. Asha continued to cling to the hook. The thought struck me that it was a shame Jake was trying to escape the battleground with Brig. If he'd had his camera, this would make a great scene for *Carnival of Lust*.

I couldn't figure out how to bring the cherry picker to a halt, so I crashed into a garage near the offices of American

Express. There was no damage done except for a few paint chips flying. The American Express folks would assume some drunken festivalgoer had been out joyriding in a construction vehicle. I stayed in the cab and fiddled with a few more pedals and levers until I was able to lower the crane to the ground without flinging Asha into the street.

Once down, we stood and grinned at each other.

"Nice drivin' there, Manhattan girl."

"Thanks. My first attempt. I may even have to get a license if we're ever back in the States. So, how you doin'?"

"Not bad. You?"

Enough. We hugged each other, then ran toward Asha's car before either of us actually burst into tears. Jake and Brig met us about a block from the convertible.

"Is the war still raging?" I asked Brig.

"Oh yeah. It's almost scary. I haven't seen any casualties. Either they're all incredibly inept or they just want to wound each other to keep the cops from snooping because they found dead bodies in the fountain."

Asha and Jake ignored this exchange. They were too busy reuniting. After three minutes watching the lovers display very public affection, Brig leaned over and tapped Jake on the shoulder.

"Time to go, crew. Kisses later. You and Asha take the car. Tempe and I will hop the train."

Jake didn't even hear him. He hadn't stopped staring at his beloved. Asha nodded, then waved at Brig and me with an air of casual disinterest.

I tugged at Brig. "Come on. If we're going, we'd better go fast."

With another wave of hands and Brig's cry of "Back at Jake's!" we took off, headed for Churchgate Rail Station.

Since it was now almost four in the morning, we found a seat without difficulty.

For the next twenty minutes we stayed silent. For good reason.

I couldn't stand it any longer. I squeezed Brig's hand and

looked into those blue eyes. Eyes that mirrored my own expression of stupefaction and anger.

"Brig? She's still there, isn't she? Shiva's Diva. Somewhere at the Flora Fountain?"

He nodded. "She got dropped when the shooting started. Probably somewhere behind a cart or in the fountain. Damn, damn, and damn. And the worst part is that we have no idea who ended up with her."

Chapter 26

We were back where we'd started the night, sitting in Jake's kitchen, drinking coffee and snacking on leftovers. Well, I was snacking. No one else seemed hungry. This time though, Asha sat with us.

"One diva for another," I'd kidded her as I pulled pastries from the fridge.

We should have been happy. But all four faces reflected nothing but doom and gloom.

"Crap. They've got it. Shiva's Diva. Damn."

This refrain had been repeated for the last hour with different forms of cussing issuing forth from each one of us. Asha got credit for the most colorful verse. I imagined Asha had learned most of her highly obscene vocabulary from friendly wiseguys back in the infamous Tony's bar somewhere in the bowels of Jersey City.

I glanced over at Brig. He picked up the feather duster he'd used earlier this night to clean the statue with such loving care. He began waving it through the air like a wand. Maybe he thought the vibes from the duster would send out a signal to Shiva's Diva and send her back to us.

"We don't even know which of those cretins has it," he moaned for the tenth time.

I stood. I had pigged out on coffee and pastries and fruit and potatoes. But the adrenaline rush that had seen me through a night of facing the "three dogs" all at the same time had vanished. I felt tired, sleepy, and cranky.

"You know what, gang? I hate to be the one to break up the

pity party, but may I remind you that Asha is here? Alive and kicking and talking? The whole point of tonight's little gathering was to give Patel Shiva's Diva. Right? Exactly so that the end result would be Asha back here alive, kicking and talking. It's done. Let the three miscreants fight over it now. Become mutes or mutants or mutilated. We can't worry about it anymore."

Two sets of eyes gaped at me as if they were staring at a Tempe with as many heads as Ganesh. The third set, Jake's, reflected some empathy for my feelings. But he knew the other two too well. Especially his darling bride-to-be, who now glowered at me. One of her daring rescuers.

"Tempe, I want it. Got that? I do not want the prize going to that slime bucket who grabbed me today."

Brig nodded in full agreement with Asha. "Tempe, don't you see? If we'd given the statue to Patel as planned and he'd shoved Asha into our laps, so to speak, well, that would be one thing. We expected it. But this just seems like we were cheated. And the Diva needs a better home than with Mister Seymour Patel, creep personified."

"But—"

I got no further. The kidnappee herself sprang to her feet, then began waving a fork with the remains of potato curry on the tip.

She growled, "Ms. Walsh! Do the words 'matter of honor' mean anything to you? Or, hell, screw honor. How about just sheer revenge? Those guys chased us all over the city. I got trussed up like a Thanksgiving turkey and dumped into the back of a very smelly van. I was blindfolded and tied up all day, then stuck at the top of a dirty fountain next to a dirtier statue, and let me tell you, I didn't like it one flippin' bit!"

Jake and Brig applauded.

She growled, "I'm not finished. I don't know who's got the statue, but I'd rather be tossed into the East River to float toward one of the nastier landfills near Staten Island than let them get away with doing this to me. And you know what else? I think any one of us has as much right to that statue as anybody. We're all creative. Saraswati is not going to be happy on the mantle of any of the three who might have snatched her."

Brig quickly chimed in, "I agree!"

Not surprising. He'd been a gentleman and a brave hero when he needed to give up Shiva's Diva to save Asha's life. Now that Miss Kumar was bouncing and full of fury, he wanted that statue back under his watchful eye.

Jake walked over to me and hugged me. "It's quite useless, Tempe. Both of them are mad. And I use the term with both meanings—anger *and* insanity. There's nothing we can say." He chuckled. "I also must admit, they're right. I do not want Patel, Mahindra, or Decore claiming Shiva's Diva. Or victory. And I'm damn incensed that Patel had the nerve to treat Asha that way."

He had joined the crazies. Three sets of eyes now stared at me. Jake had pegged it. Useless. Mad. Insane.

I sighed. "Fine. Fine. We shall hunt down all of the felons like the dogs they are and bring the goddess back to somewhere she'd prefer living. How's that? But can we get some sleep first?"

A sane person might be wondering right now why none of our recent attackers or kidnappers had come storming up the gates, or driveway, to continue the battle started at Flora Fountain. We were at Jake Roshan's residence; a house listed in various directories. Asha's flamboyant vehicle sat parked right outside, unguarded. Naked. We were doubtless crazy.

But, without delving too deeply into the sanity issues of this crowd, none of us were worried for one simple reason. We didn't have the statue. Ergo, logically, the pursuers would now be chasing down the one who did.

Jake gave Brig the large guestroom. I got a study with a nice couch instead of the maid's room. I couldn't stand inhaling the scent of musk again. I didn't ask where Asha would sleep. Not my business. But I felt sure she'd be a lot more comfortable and more satisfied than I.

At some point during the wee hours of the morning, Asha had managed to call her cook, Mala, and get the woman over to Jake's. When I awoke around nine, wonderful scents were coming from the kitchen. I threw on my battle-stained old sweats, then followed my nose.

I spent the next hour blessing Asha's mother and her recipe book. Mala had whipped up a down-home American diner breakfast. Eggs, bacon, English muffins made from scratch, home fries, jam and Danish. There was even fresh-squeezed orange juice on the side. Plus more flavored coffee.

I ate. The more I ate, the more I agreed with my compatriots. The Saraswati statue did not belong in the hands of thugs. It might not belong with the three of us, but we were far more worthy of giving the Diva a temporary home than Seymour Patel and his lackeys. Or even Mahindra, who might act like a gentleman but had the instincts of a career criminal. Or Ray, the cheating businessman who'd aimed a gun at me on two separate occasions. The creep.

Brig had wandered into the kitchen sometime during my third cup of coffee. He had then proceeded to gulp down his breakfast with frightening speed. I waited till he'd finished before I asked, "Where do we go from here?"

Jake and Asha walked in at that moment. Jake answered, "Tempe. You, Asha, and I go to the studio. We have filming to do today."

Asha and I yelled, "What?" at the same time. Jake shook his head. Firmly. No discussion there.

"Ladies. You enjoyed a break yesterday for the Ganesh festival. But we have a dance sequence in the carnival to complete by close of shooting today."

"But what about the statue? I thought we were going to find her. And *pardonez moi*, but that was no break. Asha got kidnapped and I got saddle sores riding Bambi."

Jake looked at me. "Weren't you the one who wanted to let it be? Let Shiva's Diva work her curse on whichever one of those jerks grabbed her last night?"

"Well, you guys convinced me otherwise. And tempus is fugiting, folks. Unlike me, Ray has his passport. There's nothing stopping him from getting on a plane and flying off back to

New York even. Who would know he stole Saraswati? Or Mahindra and Patel could smuggle it out of the country and we'd never find it again."

Brig put his hand on my arm. "If Seymour has it, he's looking for the highest bidder. If Kirkee has it, he's going to put it in his flat, admire it, and pray for its blessings before he sells it. If Ray has it? He's dead. He's way over his head in this deal. The point being there's no great rush to get the goddess this morning."

"Oh. Okay. But I hate to go off and dance when I feel like I should be taking some kind of action."

Brig stood. "That's where I come in. While you three are doing your thing on camera, I'll be trying to learn what I can. I know people."

I started to ask who, what, and why, but Brig held up his hand. "People who know things and owe me. Okay?"

I took off with Jake and Asha. Jake had wisely scheduled the shoot for a later hour than his normal working day, knowing most of his actors and dancers would be attending the closing day of the Ganesh festival, then hitting the party circuit after. I settled into the back seat of Jake's second car, a huge sedan, grateful we were not trying to squeeze into Asha's two-seater again.

Heaven smiled on me. This particular sequence in the film called for less aerobic activity than any of my other scenes this week. I had one small dance number listed, set in the carnival tent where the animal trainers would be showing off the tigers and lions and elephants and their tricks. I expected to see Bambi the elephant come strolling in any moment and start a tap routine behind me.

Most of the day I spent watching Asha and Raj go through a series of love scenes that made me blush and made me wonder how Jake dealt with watching another man's hands roving around his intended's softer parts. I started imagining Brig and me in similar circumstances.

I missed him. I missed his laughter and the thick Irish brogue he assumed when he thought the occasion suited it. I missed his quick mind and his lack of fear and his concern for his friends. I missed the taste and feel of his lips. I missed the warmth of his body beside me. I needed much more than one brief, chaste night in his arms.

I sat up. What was I thinking? I'd already concluded that the man put the *K* in crook. I mean, really, only today he'd gone off to see "some people." Black marketeers? His Merry Men? Burglars-R-Us? Even if he felt the way I did, there was no future in this relationship. I could see it now.

"Hi, Mom. This is Briggan O'Brien. I'm not sure what he does for a living, but he has friends on all continents. And his picture is up in a lot of post offices and train stations throughout the Western world. Oops. Make that the East as well. Not to mention all points north and south. Rather like the witches in Oz. But, hey! He spent his teen years in Riverdale even if on occasion he sounds like a charter member of the Society for the Preservation of Leprechauns."

Actually, Mom would love him immediately. It would be the discussion with my father that would send me into an arranged marriage with the first Wall Street mogul my male parent hauled in while dining at Twenty-One.

Mom would be singing "Over the Rainbow." My father would be hiring detectives. I would then cajole with "Father, you always wanted me to bring home a nice man who grew up in Manhattan. One who has eclectic tastes and can speak more than one language. Well, here he is. Yes, he lists robbing the rich and giving to the poor on his tax returns under 'Occupation,' but he's truly a sweet guy. Practical. Stable."

In the midst of this absurd daydream about this unlikely, silly, and just plain stupid scene, the man himself appeared. He couldn't just walk up and greet me though. Oh no. That would be too simple, too plebeian for Mr. O'Brien. He had to make an entrance, even if he was seated as he did so. He waved at me from the top of a glassed-in animal cage stored at one end of the carnival tent. He looked very pleased with himself.

I wondered if he'd look that pleased if he realized the cage was swarming with snakes.

Chapter 27

I lied. Yes, I'm a linguist. And yes, I do have a decent vo-cabulary. I take a special interest in the meaning of words. Which is why I was pretty darn certain snakes do not swarm. Bees swarm.

To be honest, I'm not sure what snakes do when two or more get together to chat, but even if that activity could be called swarming, I exaggerated somewhat. There were two snakes, total, in the cage. I don't believe even two *bees* con-stitute a swarm. Nonetheless, if Brig realized he'd chosen a spot above two cobras, swarming or not, he'd be less than pleased. He'd be paralyzed. Or passed out entirely.

"You look a bit too content with your lot in life, Mr. O'Brien. Did your buddies direct you to whoever is currently holding Shiva's Diva, give you tea, then send you out to re-trieve the goddess without incident?"

Brig shook his head. "Cynical. Bless your heart. I'm gone four hours and you've turned cynical. It's because you need me around to keep you sweet and trusting and lovely and sexy and—"

"Brig? What did you find out? And you can stop the list of compliments you're *apt* to be tryin' on me, lad."

"I'm just getting warmed up, you know. On the list of your better attributes."

"Well, hang on to them to warm you on a cold winter's night. I swear, trying to extract info from you is like trying to milk Bambi the elephant. What did you find out?"

He sighed. "Not a blessed thing."

"Beg pardon? You're looking like the proverbial cat with a whiskerful of cream on its mug, but you don't know diddly?"

"You're doing it again."

"I'm doing what?"

"Mixing your metaphors. Slaying your similes. Pounding your paradoxes. Ousting your oxymorons."

"Brig!"

"Sorry. What were you asking? Ah. If any discoveries were made. Actually, it's been a most frustrating day. I hit Ray's hotel. No statue."

"He still there? I mean, checked in and all?"

"Oh yeah. Very much there. I could hear him snoring all the way out in the corridor."

I threw him a quick glance. "I thought you told me the rooms were so soundproof you hadn't been able to hear anything when you were eavesdropping on Mahindra and Ray the other morning. Yesterday?"

He looked not the least ashamed to be caught in a fib. "We'el, I might be stretching the truth just a wee bit there about hearing actual snoring from the corridor. But, Ray Decore was inside and definitely asleep. I peeked in on him from the balcony doors and saw him lyin' on the bed and whispering sweet nothings to his pillow."

"You were on the balcony? Are you nuts? How in hell did you get up there anyway? I don't remember a fire escape nearby."

"You've got good eyes. As well as beautiful. And you're right, there are no stairs by the balconies. But I've done a spot of mountain climbing in my time. I simply shimmied up to floor five."

The lunatic truly was a second-story man. And today he'd added another three stories.

"You did this in broad, blazing daylight?"

He seemed surprised. "Well, naturally. If I went sneaking up the side of a luxury hotel in the middle of the night, it'd look quite suspicious. Daytime? Who cares? Anyone not busy with their own business would assume a man climbing outside a building had a damn good reason to be doing so. Checking security. Washing windows. Having an assignation. Avoiding a spouse. Any number of innocent explanations. Who's to notice a man rappeling in reverse?"

He had me. It was so ludicrous it made sense.

"Okay. So you do your Spider-Man routine up the side of the Taj Hotel and peek in through the doors outside Ray's balcony and see him snoozing. How do you know the statue wasn't there with him? Or packed with the Armanis?"

Brig studied the top of the carnival tent with intense interest. He didn't answer.

"Brig?"

"Well, if you must know, I searched his room."

I groaned. "You went in and tossed his things and he just lay there?"

"The man's a world-class champion sleeper. But I think this particular nap might have been kicked up a bit thanks to the stash of morphine on his bedside table."

"Morphine?"

"He got shot last night, Tempe. Or knifed. Leg? Thigh? Remember? Which is how you were able to squirm out of the way of Ray's nasty gun while he howled. I hate to ruin any previous impressions you might have from TV. Regardless of how heroes in crime shows pop up and run away after being riddled with bullets that would take down a charging moose, getting shot hurts. One hell of a lot. Wee bottles of children's aspirin won't end that kind of pain anytime soon."

"Ah." I paused and remembered the cry from Ray last night when whatever got him tore through his thigh. I winced.

Brig motioned for me to join him on top of the glass cage. It was apparent he still hadn't noticed the inhabitants. I politely declined his invitation. I'm not terribly afraid of snakes, especially when they're behind a sturdy partition, but the idea of conducting a nice tête-à-tête on top of a nest of crawlers made my skin crawl more than the serpents, who at this point still seemed to be asleep.

"Uh, Brig?"

"Mmmm?"

"Do you know what you're sitting on? Do you have any idea at all?"

Both eyebrows raised in an attitude of bewilderment.

"Well, this *is* a carnival tent. And I'm on top of a cage of some sort of animal creatures. I don't know. Whoever they are, they seem pretty quiet. A lot like Ray. Sleeping tigers? Sleeping monkeys? Sleeping gorillas?"

"Want to try sleeping cobras?"

Expressions of intense panic followed by intense fear flooded his face. He froze. For a moment I thought he would faint right there onto the cage itself.

"Brig? You don't look too happy. In fact, you look rather sick. No offense. Brig! Brig! Snap out of it! Hey! Do you need some help climbing down?"

He continued to stare at me.

"Brig? You okay? Brig! Listen. It's okay. They're behind glass. The snakes. They can't get out. Honest. And I'm sure they're defanged anyway. Um. Brig. Listen to me. There's a ladder on the side. Just take it, stay quiet, and come down."

He hadn't said a word. But he followed my instructions and inched down the ladder.

We stood in front of the glass prison and stared at each other for at least two minutes.

"Why didn't you tell me?" Brig finally choked out.

"I thought you knew. How did you get on top of the damn thing in the first place if you didn't crawl up the ladder? Where, quite plausibly, you would have seen the serpent critters inside?"

He pointed to the top of the tent. A rope swung leisurely from a tightrope that was stretched between two small platforms.

"You didn't."

"I did. I wanted a bit of practice."

"So you did a swashbuckler with the rope? You are so nuts."

He looked hurt. "I did not use the rope. Not till I decided

to land on this evil cage. I used the tightrope and walked. Then I jumped down."

"You can balance on a tightrope?"

"Well, certainly. You're a gymnast. A tightrope is a lot like those tiny little balance beams. You yourself have done hundreds of spins and splits and leaps and flips off them without a care."

I didn't bother to point out that a balance beam is only four feet six inches off the floor, whereas a circus tightrope is yards above the ground, and there wasn't a safety net anywhere in sight.

I debated whether it would be better to ignore his more outrageous exploits or lecture him on the value of safety. If I dismissed his tightrope routine as no big deal, he'd be convinced I wasn't impressed. So he'd try and top himself with something crazier and more dangerous.

Then again, if I told him he was deranged, he'd do something worse to prove I was being foolish by worrying. He'd trot back to the snake cage, be brave enough to grab one of them and use the serpent to swing himself over to the cannon in the back of the tent. There, he'd light a match and shoot himself out of the cannon, grinning all the while.

I shuddered. "Okay, ropes and balance beams aside, you searched Ray's room and didn't find the Diva. Right?"

He nodded. "Do you mind if we move away just a tad from the serpents? They freeze the bloody blood in every one of my veins. I'd love to tell you about the rest of my day, just not next door to the lads here. Or lasses. I have no desire to get close enough to check name tags."

One of the snakes must have heard him. It uncoiled itself, raised a flat head, then butted the cage. Brig grabbed me. "We'll be off then, before this one learns how to get through the feeder."

I gazed at him as we hurried away from the snake cage.

"What is it with you and snakes? A holdover from *Indiana Jones* movies? Or is it an Irish thing? Saint Paddy ridding the island of the slithering evil serpents?"

We were outside of the tent. Brig took a deep breath.

"Nothing so glamorous. I got bit by two rattlers in the wilds of Texas about two years back. Not a pleasant feeling, I can tell you. And it stayed with me. As did the treatment to get rid of a few poisons. Ouch and ouch."

"What were you doing in Texas? Aside from bonding with rattlesnakes, that is."

"Work."

Terrific. Doubtless a tale of infamy and deceit. I pitied the rattlers. One bite out of Brig O'Brien's treacherous, albeit muscular and tempting, ass had undoubtedly sent them into shock for the rest of their natural lives.

With much effort, I pulled my thoughts away from the bottom portion of Brig's anatomy. He kept smiling at me. I was certain he was reading my thoughts and storing them up to use against me some wild night. Which could be fun.

"Did I tell you the other part of the Saraswati legend? The one concerning the snakes?"

I groaned, "There's more?"

"Oh yeah. When the statue hears a snake hiss in her presence, she makes the choice as to her true owner. Immediately. So if a snake hisses and there are two people present who want Saraswati, one might get hit with the curse and the other blessed on the spot. She's a very smart goddess, our Diva."

"Right. Like I really buy this particular tall tale."

Brig smiled. "Ah, Tempe, you'll be a believer by the time we get Saraswati into the right hands. And hopefully I'll be well out of range of any serpents helping the Diva choose. Which she will."

"And that's coming when? Oh, never mind. I know you won't tell me. Okay. No more talk of curses or blessings. And definitely no more snakes. So, what happened after you left Ray's? No, wait. Back up. How did you choose to exit?"

"The balcony again. In case any of those suspicious types you were so worried about might be gazing up at the building. Better to leave the same way one comes in."

Frightening, but logical. I nodded. "Go on."

"Ah. Yes. I next paid a visit to Mahindra's flat."

I groaned. "You know where he lives?"

"Well, certainly. I know you think everyone involved with Shiva's Diva has psychic powers. That they gaze into some crystal ball and the whereabouts of all concerned pop up on demand. I considered trying to impress you; make you think I came by Mahindra's address through brilliant means of detection, but the truth of it is quite simple. The man's listed in the directory. I looked him up."

We smiled at each other. He continued, "I will admit, Mahindra's place of residence made it a bit trickier to do any spying. First off, Kirk's flat is in a high-rise. Close to Flora Fountain. A bloomin' twenty-nine story tower. You might know the man would choose to live in an ostentatious skyscraper. Painted gold outside, mind you. So much for taste. At heart he's nothing but a showy gangster."

"So?"

"So, what?"

"Honestly, O'Brien, you are an annoying man. Did you get into Kirk's flat, and if so, how? And if you did, did you find Shiva's Diva?"

"No."

"No, what?"

"No to all of the above. I did not get in. Consequently, I did not find Shiva's Diva."

"Oh poo. So Mahindra may have it. Well, I guess that's better than Patel, who doesn't even have the wit to try and be genteel about his crimes."

Brig shook his head. "You're jumping to conclusions. I said I didn't get inside. What you didn't let me get to is that I *did* meet Mr. Mahindra outside. He very kindly informed me that the statue did not reside in his possession and that he had no idea who'd claimed the prize at the end of the battle."

"I guess that means Patel got her after all. Damn."

"I'm not so sure. I saw our Seymour today as well."

"Is he listed too?"

He laughed. "I don't know. I saw him outside Mahindra's

high-rise. Patel walked right up to both of us as we stood chatting near the flower garden. Demanded that whichever of us had the statue give it over."

"Wait. This doesn't make sense. Was Mahindra lying? Was Patel faking you guys out? Or did Ray manage to hide her so well you couldn't find her?"

"I don't know. Could be any of the above. I left Mahindra and Patel arguing about that very subject when I went tippy-toein' down the lane with none the wiser as to my absence."

"Arguing?"

"Well, the debate seemed likely to turn into fisticuffs when Patel's bruisers showed up and were met by Mahindra's backup. I decided it would be a sane thing to exit fast and on my little fleet feet."

"And you came back here."

"Precisely."

He inched closer to me. We'd found a table a few yards from the carnival tent and were sitting across from each other during Brig's recounting of his activities. Brig ooched his chair next to mine, then casually wrapped his arm around my shoulders.

I couldn't move. His very touch was hypnotic.

He moved closer and his lips met mine. His hand traced down my cheek to my chin and the nape of my neck. I wanted to wind my body around his like one of the snakes. I pulled closer within the circle of his arms. And then heard, "Brig! Tempe! There you are. I thought you were watching the shoot."

We pulled away from each other.

"Hi, Asha. I was. That is, we were. But it got too crowded inside the tent to discuss whether Brig had learned anything about the whereabouts of the statue. This seemed a better place."

Asha smiled sweetly. "Of course."

She plopped down on one of the vacant chairs. I ooched mine away from Brig's. For an actress, Asha had crummy timing. Which might be fortuitous. Another two seconds looking into Brig's eyes, and our next moves would be on the ground engaging in serious unsafe sex in the middle of a carnival set on a studio lot. Jake would pop up with the Panaflex to film us in the act. Maybe I could ask for a copy to take back to the States. A nice souvenir video of my trip to Bombay.

Chapter 28

A wizened gnome of a man appeared from the direction of the service tables bearing a tray stacked with tea, cups, and an assortment of goodies. Asha, Brig, and I helped ourselves, then spent a few minutes enjoying a respite from thoughts of filming, kidnapping, cursed statues, and shoot-outs. Jake joined our group about ten minutes later. He sank down next to Asha.

"I am tired. I freely admit this. I must say I dislike a schedule of filming during the day and tracking down felons at night. It is very disruptive."

Asha, Brig, and I held on for a moment, then we lost it. We laughed until the tears came.

Jake scowled at us. "Did I say something humorous?"

I wiped my eyes. "Nothing. Really. We all feel the same. Disruptive. I like that. Pretty much describes my life since landing in Bombay."

I glanced at this little group of friends and treasure seekers. My new friends.

I took a deep breath. "Know how my days are spent in Manhattan? Well, let me tell you. I generally slap on my sneakers in the morning and walk twenty blocks to work. Since I sit most of the day, I keep my shoes off, although I have heels in a drawer. About ten blocks into this trek, I pick up a copy of the *Times*, along with a cup of coffee and a bagel. I then look at mounds of papers all day containing legalese in about ten different languages. I translate them into English.

"I normally eat lunch at a deli two blocks from the office. Come back and sift through more papers. Sometimes my boss has me sit in meetings with clients if a translator is required. I leave work. I go to a dance class two blocks away from our offices or take a martial arts class at a studio in the Village. Or yoga."

I winked at Brig. "Power yoga. Now, some days are truly thrilling. That's when I go out for dinner with a buddy or two from class. Most days I go home, cook something nonfattening, then either watch TV or read."

No one spoke. The more I'd talked, the more I'd realized how boring my life had become. In the week I'd been in Bombay, I'd been shot at. I'd had knives thrown at me. I'd wriggled my butt and torso at a place that in any other country would be called a strip club. I'd done handsprings off Ferris wheels and gyrated for the cameras in dance sequences rivaling *Ziegfeld Follies* routines. I'd used techniques from martial arts classes to inflict injury on thugs. I'd fallen for the Robin Hood of Riverdale.

And felt more alive than I had in ten years.

Asha patted my hand. Jake patted my other hand. Brig smiled his seductive smile. I had nothing left to say.

Asha turned to Brig. "So, O'Brien. Did you accomplish anything today?"

He sipped his tea, then replaced the cup on the saucer. "Yes and no. I did discover that if any of our friends is currently in possession of Shiva's Diva, not only do the others not know, but it's also still in that particular person's possession."

Asha squinched up her nose at him. "Would you like to explain that in English? Or Marathi? Or Hindi? Or in some language we can all understand? Break it down, man!"

"What I meant to say is the good lady hasn't left the country. Nor have any of the boys in attendance from the Flora Fountain fiasco. All of whom at last count were alive and pissed. Well, I'm not sure about Ray, since he was sleeping and pretty out of it, but I imagine he's not too happy over last night's disaster either."

Asha bit her lip. "Thanks a lot."

Brig flashed a smile her way. "I don't mean the rescue. That was great. Think about it. None of us got injured or killed and you're back safe and sound. That's a good night's work all the way around. I just meant we lost the Diva. And I blame myself since I had the tote bag and dropped it. A muddled job, that."

Jake shook his head. "You did the smart thing. Diving under the cart was what saved our lives. And the point of the whole night was to release Asha from that despicable Mr. Patel with none of us getting hurt. We did it. That in itself is miraculous."

Asha and I nodded. All of us sipped our tea for a few moments. We didn't speak. Then I nudged Brig's hand with mine, intending to ask him what we needed to do. Even that light touch sent a tingle through me. I focused on a half-eaten *chikki* confection made with sugar and nuts and addressed my next question to Asha only. I could not look at Brig while pure desire showed in my eyes.

"So? What's the next step? Do we let the statue go? I mean, let her stay with whomever grabbed her last night? Call it a done deal and get on with our lives?"

Asha snorted. "Hell, no! I want Shiva's Diva back."

I sighed. "Did I just hear the Round Two bell? Are we about to get back into the ring?"

Jake took her hand. "Asha. It's not ours. You know this. We can't keep her."

"I know that. I do. I just want to have her for a while before we figure out the permanent home. Really."

The woman had fallen under the spell of the ivory goddess. And she hadn't even seen the statue.

I interjected, "That brings up another point. Who, legally, owns Shiva's Diva?"

Brig tensed, then relaxed. "Definitely not Patel, Mahindra, or Ray Decore. Nor that misbegotten son of a seller, Mr. Khan, who figured he'd get a nice price by auctioning her to several different buyers at the same time."

I frowned. "That's why the fink didn't want me talking to the other guys there. He knew I'd discover they also thought they'd bought her."

Brig nodded. "Ray wasn't aware of this, but he didn't really need you in Bombay. Khan speaks English better than a London native. He prefers to let people believe his one language is Hindi. Thinks it'll fetch better prices for him. Man's an idiot as well as a thief."

His voice held sheer seductiveness, although Asha and Jake could still hear him quite clearly. "But I'm very glad Ray didn't know about Khan's English skills. Otherwise he'd've never hired you and you'd've never ended up in that storeroom in my arms. I should thank him."

I turned red and ducked my head as far into my cup of tea as I could manage. Jake and Asha merely smiled fondly at the two of us like a pair of proud parents.

I loudly declared, "Well then. Himali Khan had the statue at Hot Harry's. And we got it. And the others want it. Leaving Shiva's Diva as, what, fair game?"

Asha brightened. "If we find her, we can keep her?"

Jake's eyes widened. "Not a wise thing to do, my love. Even if I felt we had any claim to the statue, I'd be afraid to hang on to her."

I smiled at him. "You'd be okay, Jake. You and Asha are artists. You'd be blessed, not cursed. Assuming you buy into the legend."

He shook his head. "It's not that. I'd be in constant fear that a thug like Patel would be forever waiting to pounce and grab Asha again. Anything to get the statue for himself."

Asha fluttered her lashes at Jake. "We could hide it really, really well. Maybe let my mom keep it in Jersey? Plop it out during bridge games in hopes she'll win."

Brig stated, "If and when we get the statue back and deal with this particular set of avid acquirers, Shiva's Diva will have a good home. I promise."

Asha glared at him. "With you?"

"No."

He clammed up. I somehow felt this home would be with Claire Dharbar. Perhaps that's why he'd been meeting her at the restaurant. All business. I held up my hand.

"Peace, children. This is all kind of academic anyway since we haven't the slightest clue where the statue spent last night. And is resting today."

Jake nodded. "I think Patel must have gotten it."

Brig stared at him. "I've been trying to recall. Did I drop it at the base of the fountain, or did I still have it when we left you two at Asha's car?"

Jake shook his head. "I honestly don't remember. Once I saw the first knife fly through the air and heard that first sound of gunfire, I wouldn't have known or cared whether Shiva's Diva was seated in a lotus position on the floor, in the bag, or on my head. Tempe?"

"I was illegally driving a stolen cherry picker. I barely even saw you and Brig. Or the tote bag. Asha?"

She pouted. "Trying to balance with my hands tied and screaming at getting you guys to come and get me, then riding on that same picker. Brig?"

"Looking for the exits, luv."

That figured. Brig knew more ways out of storerooms, saloons, hotels, pool halls, fountains, and rail stations than I knew languages.

I grumbled, "So we're back where we started. Any one of the three goons or their ardent disciples might have ended up with it."

Nods all around. Again, we lapsed into silence.

Jake glanced at his watch. "It's late. And we have an early call for the shoot tomorrow, and it's very athletic, so I suggest we get some rest. No more wild trips into Bombay this night."

He turned to me. "I've got a trailer for you for the next few days since Raj is back in his." His eyes twinkled. "And I doubt Mrs. Ravi would be pleased if Raj shared his trailer with you."

Brig glanced at Jake. "Am I bunking back with you?"

"I've got trailers for us all. That includes you."

I suppressed a grin. All could be four, or three. I politely refrained from asking whether Miss Kumar would be sharing space with Mr. Roshan. I was happy that at least for this one night, I wouldn't be roaming the streets of Bombay looking for accommodations, hiding under a vendor's cart, or worse.

Jake gave me quick directions to my latest abode, then did the same for Brig. We'd be separated by a Ferris wheel, a roller coaster, the snake cage, and two vacant soundstages. Not that distance or locks would deter Brig from visiting me should he so choose. Although the snakes might.

The four of us stood and began our good nights.

"Mr. Roshan! Mr. Roshan!"

We turned. A man wearing a long white smock over beige cotton pants jogged toward us. A beat-up van fifty feet back could be seen behind the tiger tent.

"Mr. Roshan?"

"Yes? I am Jake Roshan. May I help you?"

The man looked as if he'd just reached the pearly gates and St. Peter himself had offered him a golden key.

"I am so happy to have found you."

Jake's brows lifted. He remained polite, but his voice was strained. "If you're looking for work on the movie, I don't do the casting for extras. You are welcome to return in the morning and talk to the gentleman who handles that end of the business."

The man shook his head. "No, no, sir. I am not an actor. I am a vendor. I have a cart at Flora Fountain."

At the words "Flora Fountain," four people stiffened. The dusty-looking man continued. "This morning I was setting up for the day and I found this under my cart. It has the picture of your wonderful film *Pirate Princess* on it. I have seen that over four hundred times. Miss Kumar's duet with Spot the tiger is magnificent." He bowed to Asha. "You are my favorite film actress."

Asha smiled. A little flattery is nice to hear after a day filming and a night spent bound and gagged.

The man continued. "But there were papers inside this bag

with your name on them, Mr. Roshan. And your wallet. I had to think this is the property of Mr. Jake Roshan, the famous movie director. And so I have brought it to you."

None of us dared to breathe. Jake reached inside. He pulled out a heavy object wrapped in the T-shirt with the *Fountain of Death* silk screen.

Jake tried to hand the man a wad of rupee notes, but the vendor would not accept them.

"No. No. It is such an honor for me to do this small favor for such a wonderful man. I have seen all of your movies. Over and over again." He turned to Asha. "And to be in the presence of the most beautiful actress in films. I am so honored."

Honored. He'd just made a good two-hour drive from the fountain to Vivek Studios. And now had to head back.

Asha grabbed her own tote bag, reached inside, then pulled out one of her publicity photos and a battered script of *Carnival of Lust*. She autographed it, then passed it to Jake, who did the same. They gave the photo and script to this kind man who then blessed them and their children and their children's children and on through the centuries.

After the man returned to his ancient vehicle, Jake quietly sat back in his chair. He unwrapped the T-shirt.

Shiva's Diva. Home.

No one spoke. For at least three minutes, all four of us just stared at the statue. Then I began to laugh. I laughed until the tears flowed. I laughed until I coughed. I laughed until my knees wouldn't hold me up and I nearly fell back down onto my chair. Brig stared at me.

"Are you all right? Do you need water? A swift tap to the back? Anything?"

I held my hand up and motioned that I would live. I wiped my eyes, then croaked, "I'm okay. Just a bad fit of giggles. It's the utter silliness of the situation. Our little goddess dropped into our laps after Brig spent the day sneaking into hotel rooms, chatting with Mahindra, and evading Patel's goon squad. And suddenly, in comes the Diva after a day's filming where three of us were dancing and singing and acting and directing and never once focusing on what we were doing. Sorry. It's just—?"

Brig grinned. "Silly. Daft."

"Precisely." I grabbed my cup. There were two sips left. I slugged them down before I started coughing again.

Asha hadn't said a word. Not that she'd had a chance what with me having hysterics, but she kept staring at the statue with a look bordering on lust.

Jake's tone was firm. "Asha. We're not keeping it. I don't even want to know where Brig takes it. Understand?"

Asha glared at him, then at Brig. "So O'Brien gets to waltz off into the sunset with the Diva? When did he get appointed guardian of Saraswati?"

Brig smiled. "Since I've managed to keep her safe since Tempe and I found her in the bar. Did anyone even have the first idea she'd been at Jake's till last night?"

Asha gave a "humph" but had to acknowledge Brig's skill at concealment.

Brig rewrapped the statue in the T-shirt and placed her back in the bag almost tenderly. His eyebrows lifted.

"What's wrong?"

"There's something else in here. Hang on. There's *several* things in here. I'm afraid to bring them out. What sort of vendor did that chap say he was?"

Asha, Jake, and I looked at each other, then shrugged.

"He didn't," I said. "Why? Is anything moving?"

Brig lifted out three objects and placed them on the table. All four of us stared silently. All four of us laughed until we were hysterical and exhausted.

I lifted up a pair of red thong panties. "Dessert anyone? These appear to be cinnamon flavored!"

Asha ignored me. She was too busy swinging something off a string that appeared to have a clasp that attached to one's rearview mirror in the car. Like dice. But these weren't squares with numbers.

"Boobs!" she shrieked. "Bouncing, bobbing boobs!"

Brig shoved the last two articles back into the bag before either Asha or I could get a look. He whistled through his teeth, then said, "Sex toys. Shiva's Diva has spent the day in a bag filled with sex toys!"

Asha was trying to wrestle the bag away from him. "Come on, O'Brien. Let us see the rest!"

He shook his head. "Nope. You're too young. Both you and Tempe. Now then, I'm going to finish wrapping the Diva up and I'll be off."

It was no use. Brig was too tall and too solidly built. Asha and I would remain ignorant of whatever little erotic goodies remained in the bag.

I gave up. "So, Mister Protect-the-Virgins-from-the-Fun-Stuff, dare I ask where our goddess is off to now?"

Brig grinned. "No. You dare not. I promise though that she'll be safe and sound. Jake, can I borrow a car?"

Asha assumed a tone of sheer seduction. "You can take mine but only if you give Tempe and me a glimpse of what else is in the bag."

Brig howled. "Thanks, but no. I appreciate the offer, but your bad, bold, blue convertible is too well known by every other party concerned. I'm surprised Mahindra hasn't put out an all points bulletin on it, seeing as he's so friendly with the cops. As to the bag? Jake and I shall talk and decide what else we might be willin' ta show you ladies."

He nudged me. "In private."

Jake handed him a set of keys. "Take the Jeep. The one I use to get around the studio lots. It's pretty inconspicuous."

Brig rolled his eyes. "It's a fine wreck is what it is."

Jake grumbled, "But it runs and doesn't guzzle gas. Amazing for an old heap."

I stood again. Brig picked up the tote bag and I laid my hand over that arm.

"You're not going to tell us, are you, or let me go with you?"

"That I'm not."

He plopped the bag back on the table. Impervious to any

and all watchers, he took me in his arms and gave me a kiss that curled my toes. He released me, grabbed Shiva's Diva, and took off at a nice trot toward the direction of the garage that housed Jake's Jeep.

He waved and yelled, "Later, lass! Wait up for me!" then disappeared, ironically, into the setting sun.

Asha and Jake were gathering the cups, saucers, and spoons with more concentration than such an activity warranted.

I leaned over and placed my empty cup on the tray with a crash. "That man is . . . well, he's . . . he's . . . !"

Asha nodded. Jake nodded. In a brogue matching Mr. O'Brien's, Asha said, "Aye, lass, that he is."

She and Jake walked me to my new abode, a trailer half the size of Raj's. Well, after all, Raj Ravi was a star. I was merely a dancer/gymnast/stuntwoman/translator who needed a safe haven. I didn't mind. The size of the trailer didn't matter.

I found a clean bathroom, a kitchenette with a one-burner range, a sink and a fridge as big as a small nightstand. I pulled the single Murphy bed down from the wall without much effort and threw myself on it as soon as the happy couple left.

I didn't even care where Brig planned to hide the statue. He needed a car, which meant he required a better way than the trains to get to his destination.

Thoughts of Brig and Claire flooded my brain. That's where he'd gone. I knew it. Maybe he'd give the Diva to her; maybe he'd just camp for the night in her perfect arms. Inhale the fragrance of her fine, dark, fresh, clean hair.

Claire. Who probably had never heard of a "pirouette" outside of the cookies. Who still possessed more grace in her lithe, long fingers than I had in my whole body. Who would never be coaxed into climbing onto the top of a stinky, oily elephant and spending the day peering at the heads of festivalgoers.

I had to stop this. I had no claim to Brig. He was free to conjugate with any female over the age of twenty-one in any one of the many countries where he seemed to have done business for the last ten years. And doubtless he had done just that. Charmed and smiled and kissed and conjugated. And I'm not talking verbs.

Then again, it seemed absurd to assume that Claire was anything other than a friend. She might be no more than a business partner in this venture of acquiring the Diva. The pair had looked quite serious when they'd had their heads close together. While Brig had been explaining whatever he'd been explaining. It had not looked like a lovers' conversation. Business, yes.

I slid off the bed, then paced around what little space I had in the trailer. I made a pot of tea on the miniature stovetop, then opened the fridge and discovered sweet pastries filled with honey and coconut, plus bags of veggies and fruits. I ate six pastries and two oranges.

Midnight. I tried to sleep. Images of Claire entwined in Brig's arms warred with images of Brig entwined in rope as small knives were thrown at him by Patel.

One o'clock. I headed for the fridge and ate the rest of the pastries and an apple. Might as well stay healthy.

Two o'clock. I cried. Brig was dead. I knew it. Mahindra had found him sneaking around Bombay. He'd shot him. Or poisoned him with a blow dart. Or thrown a snake at him. Either that or he'd eloped with Claire. Brig. Not Mahindra. It was one of those scenarios. Either way, Brig wasn't coming back. Not ever.

A soft rap came from the door of the trailer. I wiped my face on the pillow, then crossed to the door, wishing the designer had provided a peephole. A couple of nights ago, this same scene had occurred. Kirk Mahindra had been the visitor outside. Tonight's guest would be Ray. Or Patel. Carrying Brig's lifeless body in a gunnysack. Then again, Patel wouldn't knock. He'd just let one of his giant goons rip the door off and come on in.

"Who's there?"

"It's Brig, darlin'. I told you I'd be back tonight. You didn't think I'd gone back on my word, now, did you?"

I flung open the door and threw myself at him. I buried my face into his chest and hugged him. He lifted my chin, bent down, and kissed me. What started as gentle pressure from lips to lips grew more intense. Hands were roaming and stroking and caressing. We had yet to release the kiss. I couldn't stop touching him.

Brig slammed the door shut using one foot. A half second later, we were on the bed. He looked down at me.

"What do you say, luv?"

The only thing I could. "Aye."

Chapter 29

Brig and I made it to the carnival set bright and early the next morning. We reported to our costumer for whatever cute, tasteless, little outfits she'd planned today. After listening for a good fifteen minutes to Reena swear in a language I still couldn't place (and realized I didn't care to anyway) we strolled arm in arm toward the roller coaster where we were filming today.

Jake and Asha were having a discussion about the song Asha and Raj would be singing. They looked up, saw us, then hastily turned their backs and buried their heads in a script held in Jake's hand. Both backs shook.

Brig squeezed my hand, then leaned down and whispered, "They're jealous. Ignore them. Complacent engaged blighters, you know. Have no idea what true passion is."

I nodded, giggled, then immediately felt a pang. "Passion." That's what he'd said. Not "true love." Passion. Well. It sufficiently described what had transpired over the night and into the morning, but it still jarred me more than I cared to admit.

I was in love with Briggan O'Brien. I had been since our first meeting in the storeroom at Hot Harry's Saloon. I'd known him less than a week, but the feelings were there and they were solid.

His were another matter.

"Jake. Asha. Mornin'. What's on the agenda for today? Am I swinging through the carnival tent on a rope? Doing a fine trapeze act? I'm up for anything."

Asha muttered, "I'll bet." Then she smiled. We ignored her. It took some effort.

Jake politely explained precisely what he had planned for the dances today. Asha politely explained precisely how these dances fit into the overall story of *Carnival of Lust*. Brig politely explained precisely why he needed to be on the top platform of the roller coaster doing the steps Jake had designed. I politely explained precisely why I needed to be on solid ground to complete the series of turns Jake had in mind.

All in all, the four of us maintained a polite, precise discussion. We made no mention of Shiva's Diva. Nor of where she might have spent the night. Nor of where Brig and I had spent the night.

My outrageous Tempe-costume-of-shame-for-the-day replicated the two-piece tasseled job Reena had stuck me in on my first day filming. This one was in silver. And the top seemed much smaller. Jake and the hideous Reena were either being frugal or were going for sex. On camera, that is.

Today's dances were *West Side Story* Jets-versus-Sharks routines. The women were Jets and the men Sharks. Or maybe it was the reverse. Asha and the girls came dancing across a huge fountain set while Raj and the boys turned and leapt by the tiger cages.

Neither group seemed to be doing anything in the least related to the story line. No one, including Jake, noticed or cared. It would make for great entertainment and pure escapism for the crowds of Bombay film enthusiasts who would line up this spring to see the finished product.

Jake taught the routines in the morning. The plan was to film first thing after a long lunch break. I spent that lunch with four girls from Bombay who wanted to know everything I could tell them about America. By the time I finished my rice and curry and the korma veggie dish, I felt like a travel agent for Air America.

All these girls assumed I'd been starring in every musical film that had come out of Los Angeles in the last five years. Or at the very least that I graced the stages of Broadway and had taken this detour to Film City so I could soak up the culture and the tandoori chicken.

I'd seen Brig exactly once since we first met with Jake for the morning to-do meeting. Mr. O'Brien had been on his hands balancing on top of a tiger cage, then leaping off and doing some sort of tap dance in front of an elephant. Not Bambi. This was the one I'd seen a few days ago wearing the little cap labeled "Binky."

Brig and I had never gotten around to discussing the whereabouts of Shiva's Diva last night. We'd had better things to talk about—and do. Frankly, if a chorus line of dancing statues had done a Rockettes-style kick line in the trailer, we wouldn't have stopped our own vigorous routine.

I did manage to push thoughts about the statue out of my mind until I'd taken the last bites of several delightful dessert pastries. The same as those that had been stored in my fridge the night before and devoured by morning. I had no idea what they were called, but I was already addicted to them. I waved at Asha who sat two tables over from me. Maybe she'd know the name of the goodies and where I could get them on a daily basis while I was here. She motioned for me to join her and Raj Ravi, her costar.

Introductions were made. Then Raj excused himself to go call his wife, who seemed to be in the middle of preparations for a trip to her mother's in, of all the strange coincidences, New Jersey.

"So?" Asha asked.

"So? What?" I answered.

"You and Brig? Was I dreaming or did the two of you exit your trailer together this morning? And did I not see that trailer rocking late last night?"

"No comment except to say the rocking you thought you witnessed was doubtless due to Binky the elephant trying to break down the trailer to see Brig. They all adore him. Bambi, Binky, Buffy, if there is one. Is Spot female? No, wait, she's a tiger. That's a different story."

"Fine. I don't want to know anyway. Did the man at least

tell you the latest news on where he hid the Diva? In between that no-comment activity that shook the earth."

"I didn't ask."

Asha shook her head in sheer disgust. "Tempe Walsh. Shame. For a career woman, you are so, what's the word?"

"Stupid? Naive? Gullible? Dumb? Um. Easily seduced? Easily misled? All of the above?"

"Well said."

We smiled at each other. "Asha. He's not going to tell us. I think he has this notion that what we don't know keeps us safe. Women, elephants, and llamas into the lifeboats first."

"Right. Like that really worked when Patel grabbed me in the middle of a crowd of people during a religious festival."

"Good point." I nodded. "Shall we remind Brig? See if we can convince him to part with the info?"

"Nope. I've got a better idea. We're gonna follow him at close of day. He'll lead us right to the Diva."

"And why would he do that, Miss Kumar?"

"Because he has some ultimate purpose in mind and I don't think he achieved that purpose last night."

She snickered. "Well, not the one involving the sale of the statue."

I ignored the not-so-subtle innuendo. "Sale? So, you *do* agree with me he does have a buyer? May have had one all the time?"

"Yep. Let's see; you and Brig met at Hot Harry's where Mr. Khan performed his juggling act selling one statue to four customers. Neat trick. Okay. Brig's in the bar to get his own hands on Saraswati. I doubt if it's for a private collection. He doesn't have the kind of money Khan wanted. And, much as I tease about Brig's actual profession, I don't truly think he's a thief. So. Mr. O'Brien is acting as agent for an unknown buyer. That's what I think. And don't try and tell me it's not exactly what's been in your head too."

There were a few holes in this hypothesis, but I didn't try and plug them. Mainly because I agreed with the ultimate conclusion. Brig must be acting for someone else who wanted the statue.

Claire's face flashed in my mind. She was the buyer. I knew it like I knew my own name. "Whoever it is, Asha, I think Brig believes they deserve the statue. He's had a lot of chances to take off and sell her. But he hasn't. He's been waiting for the right moment and the right person."

Asha agreed. We began to speculate on whether Claire Dharbar might be that person and if so, why.

Jake's assistant bellowed from the roller coaster. "Asha! Tempe! Stop the chitchatter now. Time to work."

I didn't have time to delve into the relationship between Brig and Claire. The co-choreographer made Jake look like a preschool teacher as far as the girl dancers were concerned. She had a real fondness for backflips and front walkovers.

I didn't mind performing them until the last flip landed me in front of the snake cage and two girls grabbed me by my hands and feet and started swinging me parallel to that snake cage with the ultimate purpose of flinging me on *top* of that snake cage.

The easiest move the woman gave me all afternoon was when I was perched on the seat of the roller coaster. I waved my arms in moves meant for King Tut and a chorus line of pharaoh groupies while simultaneously kicking my legs. Need I mention the ride was moving at the time?

Filming closed at seven in the evening. The men, again, had been shooting their scenes in a different area than the women. I looked for Brig at his trailer, then at mine. I couldn't find him at either location.

Since the majority of the cast were staying on the lot for the night, tables had been set up for dinner. Jake had a few scenes planned for later. The nearly two-hour trek to Bombay meant anyone involved in the shoot would make it into the city about five minutes before having to immediately return.

I saw Jake and Asha sitting together but no Brig.

"He's off again?"

Jake smiled at me. "It's an innocent errand, Tempe. I

needed a few things from my house and sent Brig to get them. You were still working or I would have let you go with him. He also had to retrieve his clothes."

"Oh." My feelings for the man now must be clearly stamped on my forehead in bright gilded lettering.

Asha winked at me. "We'll take care of that errand I told you about when he gets back. Since neither of us are in the scenes later tonight."

Jake frowned. "What errands?"

Asha shrugged. "Nothing. Girl stuff. Don't worry about it."

Jake began to interrogate her as to what constituted "girl stuff." Fortunately, one of the cameramen ran over to discuss a problem with the lighting for tonight's filming. Jake kissed Asha on the top of her head, then left.

She whispered, "Ready to play Nancy Drew again?"

"Asha, I don't know if this is such a great idea. What if Brig isn't even planning on going to where he stashed the statue? If he doesn't stay here tonight, he might be off, um, seeing a friend. Or someone else."

Asha sighed. "Tempe. He spent last night with you. Don't deny it. And Brig might even be involved in something we'd call a shady undertaking, but Brig is not going to go off with another woman. I've seen how he looks at you. Infidelity is not an issue. I swear. But sneaking around and delivering Shiva's Diva to one of the many nefarious types he seems to know is another matter."

"I still don't see why he'll need to come back to the lot. Why not just take off from Jake's to wherever he's going? I'll bet it's somewhere in Bombay."

Asha shook her head. "Look, he's gotta come back here first. He took my car for his trip to Jake's, so unless he wants all the villains of Bombay on his trail, he'll be back for the Jeep. We wait, then we follow. I asked that girl who kept hanging on to your feet during the roller coaster sequence if we can borrow her sedan. It's brown and ugly. The perfect nondescript vehicle for tailing someone. And she owes you for stretching your height another two inches with her pulling."

"Okay. I'm with you. After all, we had such fun the last time we played Kumar and Walsh, girl detectives."

We smiled. Less than a week had passed since we'd gone to Ray Decore's room dressed as maids and had to engage in a few choice kung fu moves to escape unscathed. Our first adventure as sleuths. Of course, that little routine had ended with both Brig and me almost being shot.

Asha and I agreed to meet in thirty minutes at the garage where Brig was parked. I jogged to my trailer and changed into black jeans and a black shirt—the correct outfit for spying or getting into trouble. I threw my black purse over my shoulder, added some makeup (I wanted to look good in case we got caught), then headed back to the garage.

The appointed hour for our meeting arrived. No Asha. No Brig either. Ten minutes passed. Then another ten. This was ridiculous. A sensible person would just give up, go back to her trailer, and watch the minitelevision on the teensy table in what passed for a den.

A baby blue convertible suddenly came whizzing into the garage. I ducked behind an enormous limousine. Brig got out of Asha's car and quietly left the garage.

Brig wasn't going anywhere. The man had experienced a full day. He'd been dancing and balancing on amusement park rides, running errands, and he had to be tired. He'd experienced a full night last night as well. I smiled.

The garage doors opened again. Brig. Damn. Asha was right. He was heading out to wherever he'd stashed Shiva's Diva. He'd retrieve her, then turn her over to the buyer. I didn't stop to wonder why he hadn't done just that all those days the statue had been peacefully reigning over the other figurines on Jake's mantle.

If Asha showed up, tailing Brig around Bombay might be fun. But Nancy Drew had deserted me. The whole thing now seemed silly.

Which is why the actions I took were even sillier. The dark-colored sedan sat in the spot next to the old Jeep. We'd planned to hide in the sedan until Brig brought back the convertible, then tail him once he set out in the Jeep. I had no key. Asha did. And since, unlike certain Irishmen or Jersey girls I could name, I had no skills in picking locks or hot-wiring cars, I had no way to get into the sedan and start her up.

Instead of waiting in the dark for Brig to leave, instead of waiting in the limo for Asha to show and tell her that Brig left already, I waited until Brig stooped to pick up the keys he'd dropped on the floor of the garage. Then I executed a high hurdle right into the back seat of the Jeep and hid as far under the seat as my body allowed.

Within seconds, Brig was in the driver's seat. I heard the key turn and the radio turn on. We backed out of the garage, then wheeled onto the dirt lot that ran beside it. The bumpy, rocky, pitted dirt lot. My rear end screamed, "Ooch, ouch, owie, ow!" but I kept my mouth shut.

We reached the paved road after what seemed like hours. By that time, my bruises had bruises. I made a silent memo to myself to bribe Reena for a costume that would have enough material to cover purple elbows and knees. Thankfully, my rear end wouldn't be seen.

We were now gliding down the open road. The two of us. Briggan O'Brien, the man preparing to sell a cursed statue, and Tempe Walsh, half of the new girl detective team known only as Kumar and Walsh. Tempe Walsh, stowaway.

Chapter 30

The radio blasted out disco tunes from the seventies sung by Hindu vocalists. The night air felt cool for India in August. It would have been a nice night for a drive, if one were indeed driving and not cowering under a seat.

"Are you planning on staying there all night getting cramped or would you prefer the passenger seat next to me?"

"Oh crap."

"Hello to you too, darlin'. Come on up, Tempe. It can't be a comfortable position you're in. And for the life of me, I don't know why you're in it."

I crawled over the passenger seat's back and sank down into the seat itself. If Brig had stopped the Jeep, I would have thrown myself out the door. Humiliation. Embarrassment. Mortification. Stupidity. Waves of them all flowed over me.

"Hi, Brig. Um. I guess I need to explain, don't I?"

"Pretty much. It's rude not to, you know."

"Yes. Well."

I related the convoluted and twisted steps Asha and I had taken to reach our conclusion that Brig planned to sell Shiva's Diva this night. Steps that now made about as much sense as my hiding in the Jeep. Brig stayed silent even after I finished.

I opened my mouth again and said, "You can just drop me at the nearest rail station. If there is one. I'll catch a train and a cab back to the Vivek lot."

He shook his head. "You are so quick to jump to conclusions. I've no intention of dumping you at some filthy train depot at this time of night. What kind of rotten fiendish lout do you take me for? And what makes you think I don't want your beautiful face sitting beside me on this fine evening?"

"Because Asha and I were nuts to think you'd be joyriding around Bombay and parts north to retrieve Shiva's Diva and sell her tonight."

"Well, you're both right and wrong on that little assumption, luv. And not terribly brilliant about your execution of that assumption."

"What do you mean?"

"I *am* on my way to rescue the Diva. You and Asha got that right. I don't want the statue sitting in one place longer than a day, what with the various bloodhounds sniffing about for her." He glanced at me and smiled. "Including two snoopy females who should know better."

"Oops."

"It's all right. I know Asha. She gets a thought stuck in her head and the devil's own brigade can't budge her. And you're still thinking this is some grand adventure instead of the deadly game it is. So you're letting Asha talk you into playing Charlie's Angels. Badly, I might add. I knew you were in the Jeep long before I ever got in."

"Oh."

I seemed incapable of uttering anything but one-syllable exclamations. Or prepositions. Or whatever "oops" and "oh" constituted since I didn't remember those words covered in Linguistics 101.

Red faced, I looked up at Brig's profile. He focused his concentration toward getting past two huge trucks that were hogging two full lanes and driving at speeds under twenty miles per hour. He seemed to be waiting for me to say something. So I did.

"Um. How did you know I was in here?"

"Your scent. I know that scent. It's a heady scent, Tempe Walsh, far stronger than any Paris perfume. It's filled my senses for the last week. And I'm not referring to any musk left over from Jake's maid's quarters."

"Oh."

I was back to a one-syllable word but with a different meaning this time. I settled back in the passenger seat and took a deep breath. He didn't sound angry. Amused, yes, but not angry.

"Brig? Where were you—now we—going? Where did you stash the statue?"

"Mahalaxmi Racetrack."

I stared at him. "Wait. I know that name. I read about it in my guidebook. It sounded like a fun place to see. But I thought it closed summers and was only open for the winter season. You hid the statue there? Where? I mean, the in-plain-sight thing worked at Jake's with all his little statuettes and idols and dust collectors, but at a racetrack? Even if they have trophies, I don't imagine they have Hindu gods and goddesses resting in the case."

"As to the first question, yes. And no. The track is closed until November. Which is perfect. No tourists, no business tycoons or die-hard gamblers swarming around. No one except groundskeepers and a few hosts to show the tourists around. And I didn't hide it in an awards case."

"No?"

He patted my hand. "You'll see."

"As long as it's not resting under a bundle of hay filled with horse, uh, hosties." I thought about that. "No. I can't see you stashing our beloved goddess in a nasty place."

"No horse stalls." He inclined his head as he continued to weave in and out of what had now turned into traffic on the order of commuter hell in any big city.

I glanced at Brig. "Do you mind if I ask why, if you planned on moving the Diva tonight, you didn't just hide her better the first time after the sex-toy guy brought her back? Oh hell. I'm sorry. I didn't mean that to sound as snotty as it came out. I just meant, uh . . ."

"I know what you meant. Why not just find a place to conceal the goddess that's a mite more permanent? So I don't have to keep running all over the city hiding, then out of the city, rehiding. If that's a word."

"I'll look it up sometime. So?"

"Simple really. I didn't want to alarm any of our gallant band of Shiva retrievers—that's you, Asha, and Jake—but last night someone followed me from about midway across Bombay all the way out to the trailers on the lot."

"Oh, terrific. Could you tell which one of our dogs sniffed out your trail? I assume it was one of the three. Please don't tell me we've managed to attract a fourth. Or maybe Khan has reentered the hunt?"

He nodded. "No, no. It's still one of the Terrible Trio. I can't be absolutely certain, but I'd say it was Mahindra. Whoever it was had hired a cab. Mahindra's smart enough to do that, knowing I wouldn't be able to see who was in it."

"Do you think he tailed you to the racetrack?"

"Honestly? No. I did a stupid thing, though. After I stashed the Diva at Mahalaxmi, I headed into Bombay for a stop at Claire's. The lady you met earlier this week at the restaurant, remember?"

My heart took a dive deeper than the statues resting in the lakes and bays of Bombay. Claire. Well. How honest of him to tell me he'd seen her. But the fact that he'd visited her first, then headed over to my trailer to do what we'd done all night?

Every thought and feeling I had was leading me back to another one-syllable four-letter word. An extremely unprintable one ladies aren't supposed to use. I substituted "ouch" in my own mind instead.

I tried to focus on Brig's actual words and eagerly honed in on the mention of "pot of tea." That sounded pretty innocent.

"So, you think he followed you from Claire's? Right? Um. Where does she live?"

"This isn't a permanent residence for her. She doesn't live in Bombay. I drove to her hotel."

Double ouch. A hotel. Around midnight? The hour for romance. I had to stop thinking this way.

"Um. Where is she from? The permanent home, I mean."

He didn't answer. Instead he pointed just ahead of us around a curve. "Mahalaxmi Racetrack."

I squinted into the darkness until I caught a decent glimpse of well-kept grounds and a luxurious clubhouse. Row after row of trees I couldn't even name (other than palm or banyan) bordered the entrance to the parking area.

"Oh, Brig! This is nice. I'm not a betting person, but I love watching the Derby races on TV, and I visited Hot Springs, Arkansas, one time during a college break. Just seeing the horses that close while they're running is a thrill. Gorgeous creatures. I wish the track was open."

Brig smiled. "Did you bet at all? Down at Hot Springs?"

"Three dollars on the daily double. I lost. So much for the career of a budding gambler."

I peered out into the night at the track. Quiet. Dark. Peaceful. A total switch from our usual nightspots.

"Hey! We passed the parking area. Where you going?"

He pointed to another building about a quarter mile away from the road. "There."

"Is that part of the track? Stables or something? Doesn't look big enough. Wait. Is it a clubhouse?"

"Tempe, um, don't get mad now. First, let me explain that when I got back this evening, I *did* go to your trailer to tell you I'd be off to retrieve our Diva. I wanted to ask you to be patient and not to come with me. For damn good reasons, darlin'."

"Uh oh. I don't like the sound of this."

"You won't like the rest either. It gets worse. Last night I hid Shiva's Diva in a new club for gentlemen. Brand-new. I heard about it from one of the dancers on *Carnival of Lust* while we were balancing on our heads."

"Is this another ladies club? Faux strip joint?"

He nodded. "Not so faux. It's sort of theme based on the Masala movies. Posters of various films all over the place, music from the soundtracks as well."

I brightened. "That doesn't sound too bad. You know me and movies. What's the name of the club?"

"Acchaa Nasal Garam Cheez. And I'm no expert in Hindi, but loosely translated I believe it means 'Hot Things Thoroughbreds.' Or more simply, 'Hot Mares.' "

"Well, that makes sense around the racetrack."

"Tempe. Now listen to me. You do not want to go in there. I promise you. Which creates a bit of a problem."

"Why? It sounds kind of fun. For a strip joint I mean. Like a fan club for film buffs and horse lovers."

"You're thinking of C.C. Curry's. Women in saris wriggling and not really doing much else. This place is about four steps removed. Just like their clothing. Think New York. Eighth Avenue. The old Forty-Second Street hangouts. Before it got Disneyfied a few years back."

"Oh. We're talkin' down to the skivvies then?"

Brig laughed. "You might say so. Skivvied and then some."

"Well, maybe I'd just better hang out by the Jeep. Do my nails. Keep the radio on and sing 'MacArthur Park' along with Donna Summer's Hindu duplicate in Bombay."

Brig assumed his brogue. That meant trouble coming.

"We'el, that's where that problem comes in. From my understandin' of it, you see, some of the, er, clientele here like to take the girls out and do a bit more than just look. I might have to be sluggin' a few faces who thought you had a 'For Sale' sign on you just because you're outside hangin' by a car."

"Ah. In that case, I'll go in with you. Hang tight to your manly coattails and we can make it quite clear that I'm already sold. So to speak. Will that work?"

He smiled. "Perhaps. And I would feel better with you by my side. I always do. I might also be sayin' you're by far the grittiest lass I believe I've ever had the pleasure of knowin' all my thirty years on this earth."

I beamed. It might not be the most romantic declaration of love, but I felt warm all over and not just from the summer night.

I leapt out of the Jeep. "Lead on, O'Brien."

Chapter 31

The doorman at Hot Mares put the snoot in snooty. Or snotty. Either way he had a bad attitude. Impeccably attired in a uniform with more gold-trimmed tassels than my first costume for *Carnival of Lust*, he looked down his nose at the two visitors daring to ask to see the owner. The nose comment is figurative. Both Brig and I were considerably taller.

But Mr. Doorman made up for his lack of inches with an attitude straight out of *The Wizard of Oz*. "What? You dare ask to see the great Oz? Or in this case, the Ozzettes? Are you flippin' nuts?"

Brig assumed his best Irish brogue. He told the man that we were "inquirin' about a job for the lass here who's a well-known exotic dancer from the States and Great Britain." Brig claimed to be my agent.

The doorman's demeanor changed. "From the States? I am so sorry to have been delaying you out in this heat. Please. You must come in at once. I shall personally find Mr. Bombay and bring you to him for introductions."

I almost missed this shift in demeanor. By the time he'd gotten to the name Mr. Bombay (they had to be kidding) I'd been escorted inside, had taken a look around, and started hunting for the nearest closet. I wanted to hide there until Brig brought Shiva's Diva out from wherever he'd consigned her last night. The goddess herself must now be casting curses over this damnable den of decadence, depravity, degradation, and degeneracy.

This was indeed not C.C. Curry's. No delectable odors of

samosas or curried rice wafted through the air. Air? Did I say air? No air existed. Just lots of cigarette smoke. I clung to the safety of Brig's hand. We passed between tables filled with men stuffing rupee notes into what scraps of fabric remained on the women writhing above them. No one smiled. Not the men. Not the women.

"Brig," I murmured. "We're about to meet a manager who thinks I want to end up on a tabletop in less than skivvies. This is not what I had in mind for my next job interview. Any ideas? Plan A or B?"

Brig didn't answer me. He was continuing a running commentary for the doorman, who'd cleared a path for us toward Mr. Bombay's door.

Finally Brig squeezed my hand and muttered, "Not a one. Yet. But Plan A will hit before you find yourself auditioning in the buff. I promise. If I have to fight every despicable beggar in the place while you run like Spot the tiger with the Diva."

Oh good. He did have a Plan A. Which would undoubtedly turn into one of those Plan B scenarios that usually sent us flying into worse pickles with more bruises than Plan A.

The doorman couldn't have been more than five-two, but next to Mr. Bombay, he loomed. Bombay came up to my chest. The little creep ignored me completely. Except for that aforementioned chest, which he stared at so long I considered smacking him in his overly large nose and forgetting why we were there. Bombay pumped Brig's hand, then rudely asked just what we thought we were doing walking into his club with assumptions he'd be interested in some unknown girl.

Brig oozed out every bit of Irish charm he possessed. The brogue had grown thicker than a fog on a Celtic moor. I waited for the Gaelic phrases to pop out next. Not that he'd need them. I doubt Mr. Bombay caught more than two words of Brig's monologue, but the two he did catch were vital: "Top dollar."

I gathered that meant my services. Top dollar for Miss Tassels la Tour. I almost ruined Brig's pitch by breaking into loud guffaws over that one.

It was silly and clichéd, but it impressed Mr. Bombay. He looked me up and down with a thoroughness that made me feel like one of the horses at the racetrack. Even digging through whatever remained in the horse stalls would be preferable to enduring this kind of stare. I felt naked. Nauseated. When Bombay licked his lips, I considered diving through the one small window in his office to head for the stables.

"When can Miss la Tour start? I believe we have an opening tonight?"

If Brig had said yes I would have killed him with my bare hands. But the King of Prevarication took over.

"No, no! Miss la Tour is not some cheap understudy, mind ya. We'll be wantin' the contracts signed. And she has to have her own costumes. No sharin' with the other lasses. And dressin' rooms as well, don't ya know."

"Yes, yes. This I understand. My best girls have both. And no, she will not table dance. Stage only."

Brig had done it. After a few more minutes of business negotiations, we had a deal worthy of one of India's film stars. No Shiva's Diva in hand as yet, but I felt confident Brig would get us out of Hot Mares with the goddess wrapped in a box with a bow. Which was more than the strippers were wearing.

We paused at the door of Bombay's office. Brig turned and smiled at the little toad. "One other bit of a t'ing."

"Yes?"

"I'll be wantin' ta inspect the sound system yer lads have here. 'Tis most important for Miss la Tour's music ta be hard over bettar speakers than we've been subject ta dealin' with at lessar cloobs about the city."

The brogue had passed beyond dense. But Bombay got the gist. As did I. Brig had hidden the statue somewhere in the sound booth. How he'd managed it the night before with the doorman from hell standing guard I didn't care to imagine. Probably disguised himself as an electrician come to check the wiring. Then actually *did* check it.

Everything was going great until Mr. Bombay stopped me at the bottom of the stairway leading to the booth.

"Miss la Tour will stay here with me while you are shown around upstairs. There is little space in the booth. She can see what some of our other ladies are doing onstage here. Learn from my dancers what my clients want and expect."

I had a damn good idea what his clients wanted and expected. Cable blue channels show the activities nightly unless one's TV set contains child locks. I tried not to smack Bombay across the room.

Neither Brig nor I could come up with a good response to a suggestion that made me want to toss my tea pastries. Brig gave my hand a quick, inconspicuous squeeze, then turned and galloped up the stairs.

Mr. Bombay and at least a hundred other leering males aimed their eyes, thoughts, and lust in my direction. That meant they were now ignoring the girls on the tables. Suddenly female eyes became hostile.

I was a deviation from the typical girl these men saw every night writhing and grinding. All the brown-skinned, brunette, tiny Indian girls. In walks the tall, pale-skinned, red-haired foreigner. A new toy to ogle. To take home. To use.

I blessed whatever instinct had made me dress in basic black. Especially jeans and a long shirt top. Sweat trickled down my forehead and all over my torso. My already pale skin turned ashen. Bombay stared at me.

"You appear uncomfortable, Miss la Tour. Is this different from the clubs in America where you have danced?"

An excellent question. There are topless and "all nude" joints up and down certain avenues in Manhattan. I'd seen the posters and the neon signs outside as I scurried past. I'd never gone in and had never wanted to, so if this differed from "clubs in America" I hadn't a clue.

And I needed to respond to the creep's question.

I faced an improv, and improv fast, situation. Where the

hell had Brig disappeared? Was he having to talk his way around some arrogant sound tech to get under a board filled with wires so he could pop out with a tote bag he hadn't brought up there with him only two minutes ago?

I tried to smile at the manager. Owner. Sleazebag. Whatever his claim to fame. Filthy pimp came to mind.

I had to say something. I had to move somehow. But I had suddenly morphed into some kind of woodland creature being hypnotized by one of Brig's dreaded snakes. Any moment now the silent intensity would stop. The venom of the lust in this den would bite into me. Destroy me.

That thought made me remember Brig on top of the snake cage at the set and his bravery in getting down without hysterics or staying frozen and making someone come and rescue him. I took a deep breath and prepared to dazzle Mr. Bombay with one long, nonsensical bit of monologue.

I winked at him, then said with my most obnoxious and outdated American slang, "Yo, dude! You have, like, a rad club. Awesome, doncha know. I just *love* the posters of all the films everywhere. Excellent of you to do this up like a Masala movie set. Do you get out to see many of them? They're truly cool, like rad, man? Extreme phat. And so many made every year. Quite a money-maker for the country, like wack? What's your favorite flick? Or do you have one? I, like, haven't had a chance to go, dude, but you know, me and my homeys do get them on DVD back home at the video stores, so, like, I'll just have to check them out when I'm back in the 'hood, doncha know?"

Bombay had gone as speechless as one of the Diva's cursed. Admittedly, I hadn't given him a chance to say much. If Brig could blather to squirm out of a tight situation, well, then so could I.

Brig stood at the bottom of the stairway. His eyes were wide. He chewed his lip to hide his laughter, but his shoulders shook. Mr. Bombay appeared stupefied.

Briggan O'Brien was amused. Briggan O'Brien was also laden with a little extra baggage. The infamous tote bag, which had been nonexistent when we walked in, now rested over his shoulder.

Bombay remained in the trance I'd put him with my spate of words. He wouldn't have noticed whether Brig had brought a new bag with him or was starting a conga line with the customers.

The manager quickly ushered the pair of us to the door with assurances that the contracts would be drawn up within the next two days and that he would be most pleased to have Miss la Tour dance at his club for the three weeks of her stay in Bombay. He didn't add "as long as she shuts up," but the meaning was implicit.

I smiled and called, "Peace out, bro!" as we left. Mr. Bombay closed his eyes. I assumed he'd begun entreating Saraswati herself to remove my vocal chords before I hit his stage.

We were out. I breathed in the night like a marathon runner breathes oxygen. Brig opened the door to the Jeep, although I could easily hop in. I appreciated the courtesy. I didn't feel too kindly toward the majority of the male sex just then.

Neither of us said anything for the first mile. But once I felt safely away from Hot Mares, I turned to Brig.

"Thanks for trying to keep me out of there tonight. And thanks for getting both of us out with all parts intact."

"I am so sorry. I should have dropped you at the racetrack. You'd've been safer and happier in the stables. I knew this place had sleazy written all over it. Although I honestly didn't know it was this bad. Last night they were closed. I did see the posters for the films and the ads and thought it might be a bit, um, tacky. But not quite so hostile. I'm truly sorry."

I waved my hand at him. "It's okay. I'm just glad I didn't have to audition for our Mr. Bombay. A man whose mama is doubtless so proud of the profession chosen by her baby boy. And you got the bag. Cool."

He nodded. "I stashed her under the sound board. No one

ever looks under something like that. Unless there's a problem with the music."

We pulled off the road. I lifted the tote bag off my lap. It felt heavy but not painfully so.

I handed it to Brig. He reached inside, then brought out the statue, still wrapped in the T-shirt with the film logo for *Fountain*.

He removed the cloth. We both stared at the winning trophy for a horse named Miscommunication.

Chapter 32

"That's not her!" I exclaimed inanely and unnecessarily.

"Great Saint Anthony! She's been switched."

We looked at each other, then back at the trophy. Same size and relative shape as the Diva. Brig hadn't had a chance to check out the bag. He'd been bandying words with the sound techie so the man wouldn't notice Brig sneaking the carryall from under the booth.

"Who do you suppose got her?"

Brig sat back in the driver's seat. "Patel."

"Why him? Why not Ray or Mahindra or even some unknown slimepuppy from that dreadful club?"

"Ray couldn't have been following me around the city yesterday. His wound made for some heavy sleeping. And Mahindra wouldn't have substituted a trophy. He'd merely take the statue and be off with her. No wasted words or actions for our friend, Kirkee. But Patel? He'd want to rub our noses in it. Show us up. Prove how clever he is."

He whirled the Jeep around. "I'm going back to see if anyone fitting Patel's description might have been in the club today. You scrunch down and hide. I'll walk."

I stayed silent. This time Brig parked the Jeep in the racetrack parking lot alongside two other vehicles.

He sprinted toward the club, a good mile down the road. I tried to stay calm, but I kept worrying that some night watchman for Mahalaxmi Racetrack would demand to know why an American tourist was pretending to be invisible in the back of a Jeep that shouldn't be parked there anyway.

I began to panic within minutes. I just knew Brig wasn't coming back. Mr. Bombay and his disgusting doorman had challenged Brig as to why he'd returned so fast. After torturing him, they'd forced him into some dark dungeon in the cellar of the Hot Mares strip club. There to stay until Tassels la Tour did a naked grind routine on Bombay's office desk for zero pay.

"Tempe. It's me."

I unwound myself from under the seat for the second time this evening and crawled over the hump. "Well?"

"Yep. Patel. I asked the sound guy if anyone had been by the club today to look around. Told him a jealous club owner desiring Tassels' services had been out checking clubs trying to discover if you'd been hired elsewhere. Mr. Soundman remembered a man matching Seymour's ugly description dropping by around seven. And our techie didn't care when this man said he wanted to look all around the club."

"Just our luck that Patel found the Diva and made the switch."

Brig nodded. "Probably did it right in front of him, since the kid is a cultural nerd. Excellent with tech equipment but wouldn't know a priceless work of art unless it came with wires, batteries, and cables.

"So it *was* Patel. That's just swell. The worst of the lot, as you might say."

Brig slammed his fist on the steering wheel as we headed back to Bombay. "Damn! I'm such a bloody great idiot. I was so busy fretting about Mahindra following me from Claire's that it never occurred to me that Patel had the wit to do the same. I'll wager he'd staked me out all day and night, the sneakin' bastard."

Since Brig had spent the latter part of last night in a trailer making passionate love to one Tempe Walsh, this news did not thrill me. Patel, the clueless, by now had figured out that Brig and I were more than comrades in the Shiva's Diva escapades. A lot more.

Brig seemed to read my mind. "Don't worry about Patel.

He's got the statue now. He won't be concerned with us. Worse the luck."

"What do you mean?"

Brig stopped the car on the side of the road and took my hands in his.

"This is a crazy thing to ask, but how far would you be willing to trust me?"

"Brig? Why? What are you planning?"

"To get the Diva back."

"Ah. I didn't think you were happy about losing her."

"That's why I'm asking about trust. I do promise you that if all goes well, soon Shiva's Diva will be in a place where her blessings will be poured out. Perhaps for the first time in centuries."

I put the trophy back in the bag, then laid my hand over Brig's forearm.

"You want to go after Patel, don't you?"

Brig stayed silent.

I paused to reflect on the situation, then lifted my chin in an attitude of bravado.

"Well, why not? I've been through hell because of that weasel. He's tried to kill us at least once a day. He kidnapped Asha, which does not come under the heading of sporting things to do. I've just spent the last hour in a den of iniquity so . . . so . . . *iniquitous* I need a shower to wash off my disgust. Plus we've been humiliated and bested."

Brig stared at the sky, obviously waiting for me to finish and make a decision.

I inhaled. "Well. I'll be damned if I just get on the next plane back to the States knowing that Seymour Patel has his greasy hands on Shiva's Diva. I say we go after her. And if you know where the goddess can bless instead of curse, then it's time to get her there."

Brig's laughter sailed out into the night over the bay. "Sure you're not Irish on both sides, lass? 'Tis a fine speech ya just made and one I'm approvin' of. Aside from the statue getting to a good home, I've been thinking those same things as concerns Patel. I don't like our goddess locked up with him while he scours the Internet, no doubt looking for a buyer as rotten as he is. I can see it now. Crooked deals dot com. Meantime he keeps kidnapping and knifing folks along the way."

He stared at me. "Tempe, if you're truly game, then I say it's time for a rescue."

I sat up tall in the passenger seat. "I'm game. Believe me. And I won't even ask you about Saraswati's next, and hopefully final, home. But two things."

"Yes?"

"Well, first of all, how do we find Mr. Patel? I doubt the man has a phone, other than cell, much less a permanent address. And secondly, can we get something to eat before we start a long night of burglary, thievery, and whatever else you have planned?"

Brig started the car and put it into gear. "There's an all-night café on the south end of Marine Road. Designed with American tourists in mind. You can even get a good burger there if that's what you want."

"Oh yeah. Maybe a cheeseburger with onion rings. Fries. The works. Followed by chocolate cream pie and some serious coffee with whipped cream and lots of sugar."

When Brig finished laughing he leaned over and kissed me. I responded with enthusiasm and equal pressure. Then I realized we were still driving and I pushed him away.

"This is great fun, but maybe you should concentrate on avoiding the other drivers? So. Any ideas on how we track down Patel?"

"We don't have to. He's listed. And you'll love this, darlin'—he lives with his mother."

"You've got to be kidding."

"No. I tracked down everyone who's shown an interest in the Diva since I first heard about Khan's sinister little auction. I discovered that Seymour Patel maintains a residence with his dear old mum."

"I didn't think he had one."

Brig snickered. "Thought he sprouted out of the ground, did you?"

"Something like that."

"Diner."

"What?"

"We're here. Diner. Food for Tempe. Let me hide the Jeep in the back parking lot. I'll feel safer."

I was still marveling over Patel's choice of housing ten minutes later as I gobbled down a burger, fries, salad, and a banana split. (They were out of chocolate cream pie.) Brig had ordered black coffee.

"It's rather amazing, Brig."

"What? That I'm content to sip a wee bit of caffeine while you devour your fourth or fifth meal of the day? What's *really* amazing, Tempe, is you're able to still do handsprings over Ferris wheels with that kind of stuff in your system. And you don't gain an ounce."

"I'm not talking about you and your coffee. That's just boring. No offense. After all, you have to have a few dents in that armor of dashing hero. No, I'm still thinking about Patel and mommy. Do you think she knows her baby boy is a thug and a killer?"

"She probably hasn't a single clue. Thinks all the trinkets in her flat are got by sonny lad toiling in the textile mills each day."

"Either that or she's Mrs. Fagin and she's the one who trained her little Artful, wait, make that Artless, Dodger in techniques of knife throwing and bagging movie actresses."

We grinned at each other. Brig stood, then graciously helped me up from the cozy booth.

"Ready for a spot of burglary?"

"Sure. Maybe I'll finally learn how to pick locks."

"I'll try and give you a few pointers while I'm engaged in the actual picking. If it comes to that."

"What? No breaking and entering? We're going to walk up to the door in the dead of night and ask Mrs. Patel if Seymour is expecting us in the parlor for tea and cookies?"

Brig smiled at me. "Not exactly. I'm contemplating a bit of a diversion. Nothing fancy. Just setting off a smoke alarm while you yell 'Fire' in as many Indian dialects as you know. Simple, really."

I considered this. Sounded plausible. It also sounded as if Brig had used this same diversion more than once in his career. Whatever that might be. I planned to ask him sometime when I had him in a position where he couldn't switch topics. Lying on his back while I covered him with kisses might work before he ran his hands through my hair, then flipped me to lie underneath him.

I mentally shook myself. This was not the time to be engaging in all-too-vivid visions of lust and passion.

Patel maintained an apartment in a section of town so run-down I wondered whether anyone would even bother to care about impending blazes. Most of the buildings looked as if they burned to the ground on a nightly basis, then were rebuilt the next day. I shuddered. Brig glanced at me and I knew he'd followed my every thought.

"You okay? You don't have to do this, you know."

"No. I want to get the statue back as much as you do, and quite frankly, if you dumped me back at the restaurant to wait, I'd just worry and eat too much, and worry and get mad at you for not letting me help out."

Brig smiled. "I'm glad you said that. It's extremely nice having you with me. And I don't think we'll be in any great danger this time. With all the people scurrying out of Patel's building once we sound the alarm, no one should pay any mind to two extras in the melee."

He frowned. "Although you need to tuck your hair back again. It's a mite too eye-catching. Charmin', lass, but noticeable."

I tilted my nose up in an attitude of superiority. I reached into my purse and pulled out a black beret that neatly covered every bit of the red.

"Lovely," he said. "How do women do that? It's like the clowns in the tiny cars at the circus."

I smiled. "It's a gift given to all women at birth. The ability to pack a myriad of needed articles into purses that won't strain one's shoulder after five minutes."

I gazed up at him and assumed a good O'Brien brogue. "On the subject of hidin', what about you, Mr. Six-Foot-Four? Aren't ya about thinkin' folks will be wonderin' about the big Irish lad wanderin' amongst the little people during this false alarm?"

"We'el, there I might be after exaggeratin' a bit about the ease of the mission. While you're yellin' and hollerin' in the halls, I'll be doin' a bit of that odd B and E you're so fond of. Plan A is sneaking into Patel's place through the back window."

Chapter 33

Brig parked the Jeep across from another ratty tenement. Literally. The rats doubtless paid monthly rent to slumlords and had better apartments than most of the human residents. For a moment I felt sorry for Patel. No one should have to live like this. The fact that over half of Bombay's population did was a sad fact of life.

A few homeless beggars wandered the street in search of shelter for what remained of the night. Other than those achingly miserable people, Brig and I appeared to be the only folks stirring.

The door leading into what passed for a lobby stood open. The latch was broken and bottles and cigarette butts were littered from the door to the stairwell. Posters from old Masala movies graced the walls. I spotted an ad for *Pirate Princess* on the wall nearest the elevator and couldn't help wondering how many times Patel and Mama had seen the DVD.

I whispered to Brig, "Do you think such a thing as a smoke alarm even exists? This place doesn't look like it's exactly up on the latest hardwired equipment."

Brig pointed to an alarm pull. It had been painted bright red and appeared to be new. Next to the alarm pull stood an ancient elevator. A sign in Marathi reading "Out of Order" had been tacked over the Up button. It looked like it had been there since before India won independence from the Brits. Around 1947? Heck if I could remember just now.

Brig headed back outside. "Give me about four minutes,

then hit the alarm and start yelling. Then get yourself back out onto the street and hide behind anything taller than you are."

"Wait. Brig. You're taking the fire escape, right? To get to the window? What makes you think Patel won't use that to run out?"

"He's on the first floor. It'll be much easier to leave by the door, especially with dear ol' Mum in tow."

"You don't think he'll know it's us and grab the statue as he leaves?"

Brig exhaled soundlessly. "It's a chance we've got to take. If he does and you spot him with anything that looks like our goddess, you whistle."

"I can't."

"Why? You afraid they'll spot you and begin the chase?"

I blushed. "It's not that. I don't know how. Never could whistle. I've tried to learn at various times in my life but never got the technique down."

He grinned. "What's that line from the old Bogart and Bacall film about putting lips together and blowing? You must know it, Miss Movie Buff. Anyway, whistling lessons are definitely in the program for later. All that lip pursing. I'm looking forward to it."

He leaned down and gave me a nice sample, then winked. "Meantime, if you see Patel with Shiva's Diva or any package that even looks like her, well . . . let me think for a second. I don't want you to scream. That could attract their attention."

"So what do I do?"

"Sing."

"Sing? Oh. Sure. Okay."

How he figured singing would cause less notice than screaming I couldn't fathom. It wasn't logical and it wasn't sane. But then, breaking into the apartment of a kidnapper and thief might not merit an award for great analysis or sound thinking.

Brig kissed me again and I must admit I clung to him and

extended that "lip pursing" even while keeping an eye out for anyone who might decide to enter the building.

Brig left. I stayed in the filthy lobby and waited four minutes. Not a second more. Then I yanked hard on the alarm and immediately began to scream "Fire!" in Hindi, Marathi, and what I hoped resembled Gujarati. I even yelled out a "Run for your lives!" in English and one "*Dóiteán*!" just for Brig.

It worked just as Brig had predicted. Terrified residents streamed down the stairs and into the lobby. I could hear others scrambling down the fire escape. I said a quick prayer to various gods and goddesses that no one would be trampled in all this.

I hurried out with the first wave of those who'd been in the lobby, then hid behind a sandwich board sign that enticed readers to hit the Kohlbari Bazaar for the best deals in town. I even paused to check out their claim for silk saris at rock-bottom prices and made a mental note to stop by—if I lived through the night.

I hadn't seen Brig come sneaking out from behind the building just yet. I tried not to worry. Perhaps a minute, maybe two, had passed since my latest act of felony. Or misdemeanor. Or whatever penalty the good people of India imposed for sounding a false alarm.

I spotted a sleepy Patel stumbling outside. He wore no shirt and held nothing except his ever-present knife in his hand. Cool. Brig should be able to get inside the apartment. With Brig's talent for finding hidden objects, he'd be in and out with our ivory statue before I finished reading the Kohlbari ads. In my stupidly innocent glee, I almost did a jig worthy of my Irish dancing thief.

Then I spotted the woman huffing and shuffling about three steps behind Seymour Patel. She looked to be in her seventies. Stringy white hair plastered to her skull appeared to be in need of a good shampoo. Her clothes were just as filthy. Sometime in her life she'd gone from being pleasingly plump to obnoxiously obese. Patel's mother. I did not jump lightly to this conclusion. The woman mirrored her ugly son in every feature down to the sour expression on her face. And if that weren't enough to give her away as a very close relation, she carried Shiva's Diva in her left hand.

Not in a bag. Not wrapped. Not even protected from prying eyes under Mama Patel's disgusting, dirty, faded gray sari. Our goddess, exposed for all the world to see. And right now I was the world most interested.

Brig had said to sing if I spied Patel transporting the statue. Well, Mrs. P. Senior, not Seymour Junior, was the one doing the carrying, but it looked like a Patel and it smelled like a Patel, and it had the Diva. So I sang.

I have to stop the action for a moment here because I feel impelled to point out in defense of the upcoming moves that my mother was a child of the sixties. One who'd never quite gotten over her days with the peace, love, and flower children. One who'd kept every vinyl album from every sixties rock, folk, or solo artist from The Beatles on. And played them for her darling daughter Tempe, who learned to love Cat Stevens and the Moody Blues and Jefferson Airplane and the Mamas and the Papas. And Three Dog Night.

Maybe all my references to Three Dog Night this past week had unhinged my brain. Maybe the fact that Mrs. Patel resembled one of the homelier canine breeds (at a guess, bullmastiff) further fomented my imagination. Whatever the catalyst, I started to sing "Mama Told Me Not to Come." The entire chorus.

Eighty faces whirled to gawk at the girl crouching next to the bazaar ad who was blasting out classic rock at three in the morning during a fire drill. Seymour and Mama were two of them. Both faces twisted in rage. Mother was just as pissed as baby boy. Which is why, again in defense of my actions, I did something totally shameful. I tackled a woman over forty years my senior.

For an overweight, elderly female, this dog was tough. As I grabbed the Diva, Mama P. bit my hand, then kicked me in the shin. I screamed and brought her to the ground, almost gagging from the odor of gardenia perfume. Apparently, dousing herself in exotic floral scent was her alternative to bathing in real soap and water.

I wrapped one arm around what appeared to be a waist and flung her on her back. We rolled on the ground for another twenty seconds before I was able to maintain a good grasp on the statue. I jumped up, then dove into the crowd of gaping fans who'd been cheering for one or the other of us. My beret fell to the ground, letting my red hair shine under the street lamps. Crazy American girl gone wild. I scooped up the beret and took off still singing.

I ran in the direction of where we'd parked the Jeep. Brig met me there. Neither of us bothered to open a door. We jumped in, Brig turned the ignition, and we hauled out of this tenement slum neighborhood. We caught glimpses in the rearview mirror of the shirtless and barefoot Seymour Patel running after the Jeep screaming curses. Mama, the wrestling queen, sprinted right next to him.

"You okay?" Brig asked.

"I think so. Some scratches from Mrs. Patel's badly mani-cured nails plus a bite on my arm. Nothing that can't be taken care of with dabs of iodine and a tetanus shot. The woman had more rust than screws on a boat dock. You?"

"I'm fine. But then I didn't just go ten rounds with a re-pulsive, ancient harridan."

I turned red. "I did, didn't I? My gosh. My mom always taught me to respect my elders. A lesson that went sailing across the bay the instant I saw Madam Patel with the Diva."

I paused.

"Yes, Tempe? What is it you're not saying?"

"Well, I did have another teensy incentive for jumping on Her Hideousness. The lone item Seymour carried with him from the nonburning building glistened in the night. Yep. Patel's favorite big bad blade. He flung it at me just before I had the one-on-one with his nasty mater. Then he retrieved it."

Brig turned the wheel of the Jeep and aimed the vehicle back toward Patel's neighborhood. I grabbed his arm.

"Brig! Are you nuts?"

"I'm taking this Jeep and driving it over the stinkin' son of a bitch. That's not nuts. It's a necessity."

"No! Let's just get out of here. We've got the Diva. Let Patel and his mother work out who lost it."

"He deserves killing, ya know. He and the ugly, misbegotten dame who birthed him. Man's probably been reincarnated as a flippin' terrorist at least twenty times and racked up more bad karma than we've put miles on this car. Damn him. Damn all the blighters who take down innocent women and children. They don't deserve to live."

I stayed quiet. I knew Brig was also thinking about his sister and the cowards who'd blown up a hall full of teens to prove a political point. I had a feeling Brig's temper would diminish if I did nothing to spur it on. And while I might secretly agree with the sentiments expressed, I had no desire to carry them out or let Brig take his anger to an uncontrollable level. Finally, Brig quit ranting and simply stared at the road ahead.

I let a moment or two pass, then I began to sing again. Another Three Dog Night classic but one more soothing—"Old Fashioned Love Song."

Brig visibly relaxed after the first verse. "Sorry, lass. I've got the full Irish temper, and you'd best be knowin' it. But you've got a nice way of dealin' with me. Plus one fine voice."

He chuckled. "Your warning song wasn't quite what I expected, but it worked. I knew it was you. I immediately jumped out the window. The sight of you punching out Mama Patel came as a bit of a surprise, but a welcome one. I'm proud of you, Tempe."

I leaned back in the seat and sighed.

"Well, it didn't go quite as planned. Not that anything we've tried has gone as planned. But it worked."

I stood straight up in the Jeep and yelled, "Yes!" then hurriedly sat back down when Brig hit a bump.

I smiled at him. "We got her back. Shiva's Diva. Safe and sound."

He smiled back. "We do. Although it's just for the moment. Just for the moment."

There were several meanings to this statement. The first might be that a furious Patel would not appreciate having the statue ripped from his (or his mother's) grasp within hours of his stealing it.

Secondly, Mahindra might be sleeping peacefully at this hour in his high-rise, but he hadn't called it quits either. And I felt confident we hadn't heard the last from Raymond Decore. Once Ray regained a bit of strength, he'd be back in the hunt. No doubt feeling less than charitable toward anyone involved in keeping Shiva's Diva, including Mr. Decore's ex-employee and her new friend, the handsome Irishman with the temper.

Lastly, one other person had become uppermost in my mind. The other unnamed someone who apparently had some legitimate claim on the goddess. Claire Dharbar.

"Brig?"

"Hmm?"

"We can't go back to our trailers tonight. I mean, everyone knows that's where we're staying now, don't they?"

He nodded. "They do. But I think we'll be fine there for what's left of the night. It's three-thirty now. Even if Patel gathers his minions and comes after us, it's a two-hour drive from this part of Bombay. Jake's got security guards around the shoot now. Patel might think twice before tangling with a contingent of guards who pack large guns and have a lot of incentive to keep the director and actors on this film safe."

"Yeah?"

"Jake's paying a nice price for this little security team. After he saw how easily the thugs kidnapped his lovely Asha, he did not want to leave anything to chance."

"That's good. For all of us."

"Rest a while, Tempe. I'm wide awake. We'll make it back to the lot safely. I promise not to drive like I'm in either Paris, Boston, or Jersey."

I curled up in the passenger seat with the most-wanted statue in India in my lap and slept. I didn't even dream.

"Tempe. Better wake up."

I hit awake before Brig finished "better." I looked around me. We were not at my trailer. Or Brig's. Or Raj's or Asha's or anyone else's at the Vivek Studio lot. We were at the Sea Harbor Hotel where I'd spent my first night on the run with Brig.

The Tempe who'd slept there in a borrowed T-shirt from a man she'd met hours before would've asked a lot of questions as to why we weren't snug and safe at the studio, letting Jake's security guards do their job. But that Tempe had disappeared with the last punch thrown at Patel's mama.

I calmly asked, "What's up? Pursuers? Plan C? Someplace with better beds than the trailer?"

"Well, the last is true but not the others. I'm a bit flummoxed here. While you slept, I had the radio on. The news is full of the murder of an American businessman. An American who'd been staying at the prestigious Taj Mahal Hotel. An American found in an alleyway near a part of town where a certain fire alarm had disrupted the lives of a certain residence. A false alarm, they said."

He didn't need to say more. American businessman. It had to be Raymond Decore.

"Ray's been murdered? Great God Ganesh, how did that happen? That's awful. I can't believe this. But, wait. Why does that mean we're not back at the studio?"

"Because the police are looking for two foreigners spotted near the residence who are wanted for questioning in the matter of setting off that alarm and also for Raymond Decore's untimely death."

"Terrific. I've gone from businesswoman to stripper to film dancer to burglar to wanted killer in the space of one week. So we're back at the Sea Harbor? Sort of where we started. Why?"

Brig helped me from the car. We checked to be sure our

statue hadn't fallen out of her snug niche in my little purse. Saraswati's lute and the snake head stuck out a good two inches, but with a baseball cap we'd found in the back seat of the Jeep, she easily passed for a souvenir bought by an American tourist too cheap to buy a big bag.

Brig patted the Diva. "It occurred to me that, strange as it seems, this hotel is the one place no one seems to have known where we were. At any time."

He kissed me, then drew back and smiled. "Besides, it holds fond memories of the feisty lass who escaped with me after hiding out in a storeroom."

"Hmmm. I remember that particular lass heading straight for the shower and then collapsing. But perhaps my exhausted state kept me sleeping through great moments of rolling around on the floor doing the he-ing, she-ing routine?"

Brig hugged me. "I do love you. You have a way of making the worst moments fun. And no, darlin', we did no he-in' or she-in' that night. Worse the luck. But the sight of you in the sari and the bare feet and the look of determination to survive? Well, it got to me. It did. Still does. And will."

I couldn't answer. The words "I do love you" swirled through my exhausted psyche. They didn't mean anything. I knew this. How many times has a buddy said, "I do love you" when teasing a friend? But I clung to those words. I barely even heard the rest of what, in actuality, revealed much more of Brig's feelings.

I didn't know whether Brig had ever bothered to check out of this hotel. He escorted me and our precious cargo to the same room we'd shared a week ago. I felt just as tired as that night. But this time my attention was riveted to that bed. Then to Brig. It might be four in the morning, but his eyes shone with desire. The same desire was reflected in mine.

Brig locked the door. He tossed my purse bearing the goddess on a desk chair. Seconds later, we were on that one bed. And this time, there was a fair amount of he-in' and she-in' going on.

Chapter 34

Between us we managed about three hours' sleep. I awoke around nine A.M., snuggled next to Brig's solid chest. Shiva's Diva beamed at us from the dresser in the corner. Brig gently kissed me, then pointed to the statue.

"I don't know if I ever told you, but Saraswati is not just the goddess of speech, music, communication, and arts."

"There's more? Blessing or curse?"

He threw me back on the pillows and didn't answer for the next twenty minutes or so. When we came up for air, he continued his lecture as though he'd never stopped.

"She's known for helping out in matters of fertility."

"As in crops in the field?"

"As in babes in the womb."

"Ah." I grabbed my shirt from the chair next to the bed, then sat up in bed and eyed the goddess with new eyes.

"How long must one have the statue before she graces one with kiddies? Is this instantaneous?"

Brig laughed. The light from the window rippled over his chest and glinted in his dark hair. I didn't think he'd need any help from Saraswati in creating a few babes.

"I'm not certain of the rules of that legend, mind you. I believe one has to ask the favor as well. Unlike the other blessings. Or curses."

I smothered him with my pillow. "I hope so. Just think. If Patel gets his hands on the lady again, we could have scores of little Patels running loose in Bombay within the year, all looking exactly like Seymour's mother. Yow!"

Brig tossed the pillow back at me. "Well, that's just more incentive for us to keep the Diva out of his nasty mitts, then, isn't it?"

"Oh, 'tis, Mr. O'Brien. 'Tis. But nasty is too nice a word for the murdering scumbag."

We both sobered immediately. I saw it in his face. We'd been hit with the same thought at the same time. Ray Decore. Not a nice man. I still questioned whether he would have actually shot me, either that day in his hotel room or at the Flora Fountain. I honestly did not think so. Ray had turned into a crook, but I didn't think he'd have escalated to murderer. And even if his thoughts had been edging toward violence, he didn't deserve to end up in an alley in a foreign country with, what? Bullet holes in his back? A knife in his chest? A king cobra cozily curled up on his brow?

"Brig? Did the news say how Ray was killed?"

"Nope. I'm right with you. It might not even have been Patel who did the deed. Mahindra's been damned quiet the last day or so."

"I can't really see him popping up in the middle of the night just to shoot Ray, but then, I'm not well acquainted enough with Kirk Mahindra's business practices to know if that's how he deals with rivals."

Brig nodded. "Much as I'd love to spend the day right here in your arms, talkin' murder and Mahindra, then moving on to more pleasurable topics, there are things to do today that don't involve either talk or lovemaking. Sadly."

"I know." I oozed out of the bed again. "Oh poo."

"Yes?"

"I'm due on the set! Like an hour ago. Phooey. For the big scene where Asha is running from the kidnappers and hitching the ride with the guy who ends up being worse than the ringmaster. The one who takes her to the Yacht Club and tries to seduce her."

"I don't remember that part of the script."

"The guys weren't in it, Brig. Just Asha and the girl dancers. Damn. I hate being irresponsible."

Brig collapsed on the bed in near hysteria. "I don't think getting the Diva back and ducking murderous thugs quite makes you irresponsible. Besides, I called Jake around six and told him you might be delayed because of what we were doing."

I lifted a brow. "I'll bet that entertained him."

Brig grinned. "Only the doings that involved retrieving the statue. I stayed a gentleman. I did not tell him I had a howling, sweaty, back-clawing wench in my bed who'd barely let me alone long enough for me to make that phone call."

"Thanks. Hey, wait! Sweaty? *Moi*? I'll have you know I glow, mister." I smiled. "It's nice to know chivalry is not dead. As if I believe Jake didn't immediately turn to Ms. Kumar and speculate about what activities we were engaging in at six in the morning. Which was doubtless what the pair of them were doing as well."

I headed toward the bathroom to take a quick shower, then turned. "So, what did Jake say? About the shoot?"

"He's working on the smaller scenes this morning. He wants you to lead the dancers down the road behind Asha, so he's holding off filming till late this afternoon."

I paused before I closed the door. "You think it'll be safe for us to go back?"

"Not us, Tempe. You. I'm putting you on the train as soon as you're dressed. It'll be nearly a three-hour trip, but with the crowds you'll be fine. And I don't think the police are interested in you as much as me."

"What are you going to do?"

"See some friends who might have a bit of influence with the local authorities and plead with them to convince the gents at the jail that I'm a lover, not a fighter."

I tossed my shirt back over the chair with the ease of Tassels la Tour and stepped, topless, into the restroom.

"Feel free to give them my number, lad. I'll be more than happy to attest to exactly that fact."

I shall spare everyone the details of the trip on the train to Vivek Studios. A trip that can be summed up in three words.

Long, dirty, and noisy. Oh yeah. Two more. Crowded and unpleasant. By the time I got to the lot, I had no desire to go dancing around a set that consisted of a dirt road where cars came zipping by and not much else.

But, being a responsible person, I let Reena garb me in her latest concept of American dance queen (i.e., cutoff jeans and a red halter top). I went out and I performed the cartwheels, flips, and splits that had somehow become part of every dance scene Jake stuck me in. I whipped off a quadruple pirouette while standing in bare feet on pavement and didn't even flinch, because this particular responsible little actor/dancer had become a very distracted one.

Visions of Brig in, beg pardon, the brig, haunted me. Visions of Brig being rescued from the brig by a Kirk Mahindra who had unofficial grilling styles in mind made me clench my teeth so hard Jake had to ask if I'd been hurt.

He and Asha had pounced on me the instant I stepped out of the cab. The actors had been given an uncharacteristically long lunch break. I suspected Jake was being kind just so he and his intended could get caught up on the activities of the previous night. The first half anyway. I adored both Jake and Asha but I was not going to entertain them by providing details concerning bedding down with Brig O'Brien. An activity I knew damn well Asha craved to learn about in Technicolor and Dolby THX sound.

She had to settle for the other news. "Ray's dead?"

"Oh yeah. Unless he palmed his ID off on some other fiftyish American with gray hair, a physique courtesy the best trainers in New York, and a thigh wound courtesy of whatever leftover weapon from your kidnap rescue got him."

"Well, that pretty much nails it down," Asha said. "Which bum bumped him off?"

I winced. I couldn't be quite as blasé about this as Asha. I actually had known the man. She'd just snuck out of his room, then yelled at him through a door.

Ray and I had boarded a plane in New York less than a week ago. We'd even enjoyed a few hours of nice conversation during the times I'd been awake and he hadn't tried making a pass. Ray had been a friend of Jeremy, my boss. Although Ray had apparently lost his mind and adopted a penchant for criminal behavior, I still hated for the man to have died alone in an alley in a foreign country as his killer stood over him watching as his life oozed away. Well, that might be over-romanticizing both the man and his demise.

His death wasn't a joke. I sent up a silent prayer that Ray would find peace in a better place.

And a cooler one. The Bombay heat combined with rehearsing had me sweaty and thirsty. I inhaled four two-liter-sized bottles of imported French water in less time than it takes to drink one cup of tea. Then I started in on the tea as well. Five cups in all.

It should come as no surprise then, that after finishing the first sequence of steps for the princess-hitching-a-ride scene, including that quadruple pirouette, I might need to use the facilities. I've never been fond of Porta-Potty restrooms, so I hiked a half mile to my own trailer. The one where I'd enjoyed about three hours' sleep two nights ago. The one where I'd enjoyed the other four that same night with Brig.

The one where, this day, like our own Shiva's Diva, I got bagged.

Chapter 35

It was obvious to all parties involved in *l'affaire* Shiva's
Diva that Brig and I had a thing going. I'd been seen with him
in enough situations to allow Kirk Mahindra to figure out that
Brig meant more to me than a chance to meet Jake Roshan,
break into films, and become a Masala movie star. Mahindra had seen sparks flying between Mr. O'Brien and Miss
Walsh long before Miss Walsh admitted they were sparks of
desire and not just the flash of bullets or knives whizzing by.

So Kirkee decided the way to get to Brig was to get me. He
explained this while I sat, hands tied behind my back, in his
luxurious white stretch limo that cruised easily out of Vivek
Studios.

"You must understand, my dear Miss Walsh, that I believe
coming to you is the quickest course of action to take following Patel's wretched deeds of last night. I refer, of course,
to the death of Raymond Decore."

I sighed. "I somehow figured Patel had been the scum
who'd sent Ray to meet his Maker. Didn't seem your style.
Not that I'm really up on your style. But you seem to have
more class than dispatching people in alleys."

Mahindra inclined his head, then patted my knee. I tried
not to visibly shudder. The man might be a gentleman thief
and kidnapper, but he still possessed a quick trigger finger. I
wasn't exactly comfortable riding with him.

Kirk stated, "As well as being beautiful, you are a wise and
perceptive lady. If I had been the one to decide that Ray
Decore did not need to live, I would have sent one of my busi-

ness associates to his hotel room with instructions to increase his morphine dosage. Patel is indeed a pig. But a knife in the stomach in a filthy alley? Tasteless. Low class. Messy. Inept."

Not to mention damn rough on the knifee's guts. I managed to refrain from vocalizing this thought.

Mahindra continued, "I must say, however, that Patel's actions during the Ganesh festival in seizing Miss Kumar then offering up her release in exchange for the Saraswati statue was nothing short of genius. It gave me the idea to do much the same with you. And I have no doubt, having seen you interact with Mr. O'Brien more than once, that he will trip over himself with great speed to rescue you with the goddess in hand."

He stared at me. "One goddess for another. Very fitting."

"Mr. Mahindra, I'm not so sure Brig even has the statue anymore. I believe there are a few other parties involved. People you may not even be aware of. Other buyers."

He waved his hand, brushing off those pesky others. "I know of several interested buyers. But I have taken steps to insure that Mr. O'Brien will be too busy today to notify anyone that he has the statue. He is currently dealing with inspectors at the police station. He has no time to sell the Shiva's Diva, as you call her. Why that name, I must confess, I am still unclear."

"You saw Brig at the station?"

"Wearing handcuffs and looking most unhappy. Indian jails are not pleasant places. Especially for the foreigners. I rather doubt Mr. O'Brien will be so pretty the next time you see him."

"But if he's in jail, how are you supposed to exchange me for her? The statue, that is?"

He glanced at his watch. A Rolex.

"By this time, proof that Mr. O'Brien had nothing to do with Raymond Decore's murder will have been handed to the lead inspector on the case. A good man. I've known him for many years. We were at school together and played on the cricket team."

This did not surprise me in the least. Mom raised me on too many wiseguy movies where the mobster is best buds with the police commissioner. She and I spent many marathon weekends watching Cagney, Bogart, Pacino, and De Niro play nicey-nicey with the feds. But this particular scene I was playing seemed more reminiscent of the Sheriff of Nottingham holding Maid Marian hostage to ensnare Robin Hood than of any gangster flick.

"Let me see if I've got this straight so far. One of your filthy goo—excuse me, *business associates,* arranged for Brig to be arrested. After Brig has had enough time in jail for the thugs to beat the, uh, charm out of him, you'll send in the next wave. The cavalry arrives with proof that Brig busied himself with other activities far, far away during the time Ray met his sad fate. Correct?"

Mahindra brightened as though envisioning the whole scene with sadistic delight.

"Precisely, Miss Walsh. At this moment, so I have been told, Mr. O'Brien is walking to the parking lot to retrieve his impounded vehicle. We assume he will next attempt to drive out to the film site and reunite with the lady he desires. You. Who he believes will be waiting at her trailer to comfort him after his ordeal in prison."

"I take it he's not going to get very far?"

"If Mr. O'Brien would join the modern world and carry a cell phone, it would make my life much easier. But, since he insists on going about without adequate means of communication, I simply have to track him down."

His own cell rang. Beethoven's Fifth. Mahindra answered and listened quietly. A smile flitted across the refined features. He closed the flap of the phone.

"Briggan O'Brien is now heading back to the hotel where he stayed last night."

Diplomatic of him to refrain from mentioning who else stayed with him. Namely, Tempe Walsh, latest victim of a snatch and grab.

"Mr. O'Brien has been informed that you are currently in my company and that if he wishes for that to change, he needs to meet us at the hour of midnight, tonight, at the appointed place with Saraswati."

"I gather Brig agreed to whatever terms your associate laid out?"

"Most definitely. But I am afraid the young man used language ill befitting a gentleman. Most disgraceful. However, once my position had been made clear, he stated he would be more than pleased to deliver the Saraswati statue to me."

"Well. Nice to know someone's plans around here are swimming along so nicely."

He frowned. "I am only sorry you did not heed my advice concerning association with Mr. O'Brien. Tracking him down all week has been a tedious waste of my time, although having the chance to get to know you has made the effort worthwhile. For this, I am most grateful."

Mahindra's phone rang again. I tried to focus on his responses. Partly to see what I could learn about Brig's situation, but also to avoid thinking about Mahindra's last words to me and the soft, caressing tones he'd used to say them. Not to mention the intent behind them.

His discussion over the wireless was conducted in an Indian language I hadn't covered in my course from Louie's Lingo software. Not that anything Kirk said made a difference in the execution of this latest game of Saraswati tag.

Perhaps Brig could figure out a way to fool Mahindra into thinking Brig had given him the statue. Much the same way Patel had tricked us at the strip joint by substituting the horse trophy. We'd kept that trophy in Brig's hotel room. He could wrap it up, stick it in whichever tote bag he had, hand it to Mahindra, grab me, and run like hell.

Mahindra glanced at me and hit the hold button on his phone. "If you are entertaining thoughts that Mr. O'Brien will be able to switch the Saraswati for another statue, you must forget them. My associate will be accompanying the man to his hotel. I doubt O'Brien will find another statue the appropriate height and weight to exchange anywhere in that room. And he cannot leave his hotel. My men will not allow that."

Well. I hadn't actually been thinking, "substitute statue for statue," unless one could call a trophy from a horse race a statue, but Mahindra had honed in on my thoughts far too easily. Then again, the man had practice in all kinds of crooked commerce. My experience dealing with thugs, robbers, kidnappers, and murderers had started only a week ago. My mind wasn't trained in the art of trickery and deception. Two words, however, that might well fit the man I loved. I brightened.

Brig would find a way to rescue me and still hang on to Shiva's Diva. I had confidence. My Riverdale Robin Hood had a gift for chicanery and sneaky behavior. Brig had plenty of other talents, too, but I didn't want to think of those while I sat next to Kirk Mahindra.

I smiled, not wanting Mahindra to see the fear inside me. A fear that diminished a bit more with every thought of Briggan. He'd come up with something. I hoped. If Plan A didn't work (and let's face it, we'd been pretty lousy at Plan A's this week), then he'd hit Plan B. Or C. Or a thug. Whichever came first.

I nodded at Mahindra since I couldn't motion with my hands. Still tied. Like I might, what? Jump out of a limo equipped with child-lock doors and that clipped along at seventy plus, then try to hitch a ride wearing my red halter top and cutoffs?

"Mr. Mahindra? Where exactly is this exchange going to take place?"

A look of near bliss crossed the man's features.

"Symmetry, my lovely Tempe, has been defined as balance and harmony creating beauty. A definition most apropos to tonight's enterprise. At midnight you and I will be at the table where you sat a week ago with Raymond Decore. At Hot Harry's Saloon."

Chapter 36

Getting kidnapped by an Indian criminal had not topped my list of New Year's resolutions this year. But since the activity had made it into my repertoire of life experiences I least wanted to repeat, I was glad the kidnapper of choice was Kirk Mahindra and not Seymour Patel.

Poor Asha had been tucked into a van, bound, gagged, then forced to endure an hour or so crammed into an archway waiting for rescue. Plus she'd had to deal with Patel himself, a man not known for appreciating the niceties of polite society.

Not so Kirkee Mahindra. This kidnapper had driven the kidnappee (i.e., me) around in an air-conditioned limo. Soothing classical music played around me.

Once we were at Mahindra's residence, he had untied the cord around my wrists, then escorted me into his high-rise apartment, the exterior of which was indeed painted gold. During the elevator ride to the twenty-ninth floor, he'd nodded politely to his neighbors and chatted about the price of oil and the new yoga class at the high-rise spa.

He had not hidden me away in a dark room in his flat, then shoved bread and water down my throat before sticking a filthy rag in my mouth to shut me up. Nope. Mahindra had ordered an elderly servant to rustle up some tea and snacks and let me lounge in a den filled with business magazines featuring India's top tycoons. Mahindras graced every cover. Kirkee's distant cousins, who I assumed were the legitimate branch of the family.

A discreet rap on the den door around ten P.M. let me know

the evening's frolic would be starting soon. The same servant entered with several cloths draped over her arm. I thought she planned to bag and gag me. Fine. Bring it on. I could take her down in a heartbeat. Older, fatter, a lot meaner, and with more teeth had tried and been annihilated only last night by Tempe Walsh, girl wrestler.

Then I realized the cloth was a dress. Well, more specifically, it was a sari. Sage green with the choli underpiece in a darker green. Great colors and they fit perfectly. Either Mahindra had a wife or lover my size who'd conveniently offered up the garment for the prisoner, or his personal shopper had spent the afternoon in bazaars with precise instructions as to the American's height, weight, and coloring.

Neither thought was appealing. But I must admit I liked trashing my sweaty jean/halter-top costume and draping myself in something this deliciously beautiful. Reena could take lessons from Mahindra's tailor.

The reason for the change in outfits became clear when Mahindra took me to dinner at the Royal Yacht Club. Hey, might as well show the kidnap victim a good time.

The Yacht Club was situated just north of the Taj Mahal Hotel. The gorgeous Gateway to India structure graced the club with its presence if one looked across the road. The south overlooked the bay. A landscaped garden sat between the bay and the club.

At least a dozen men in seafaring regalia strolled about the garden chatting about an upcoming yacht race. Mahindra introduced me to five political types as his guest from New York. Which I suppose was smarter than saying, "Mr. Sahib So-and-So? Let me introduce Tempe Walsh, kidnap victim and occasional stripper at C.C. Curry's."

Or, "This is Miss Walsh, aka Tassels la Tour. We're having a flaming-hot affair, so don't even think about disturbing us once we're settled in drinking wine and chowing down on samosas."

Or, "Yo! Hey, guys, meet my babe. Don't fall madly in love

with her unless you're into necrophilia. She'll be a corpse by morning."

Once inside, a waiter wearing a naval cadet uniform escorted us to a table overlooking the bay, then immediately brought drinks I hadn't heard Kirk order.

One might be thinking at this venture, why didn't Miss Tempe Walsh flee? Here we were out in the open. British officials sauntered by passing gallantries with my dinner companion and jailer. Any one of these guys would doubtless be more than happy to accompany the American to her own consulate, then tuck a business card into her bag in case she needed further assistance.

In a word? Ha. Even if Mahindra had given me a chance to speak in private with any of these gentlemen, Brig's life was on the line.

Plus, Mahindra did not let me out of his sight. The one time I asked to be excused to powder my nose, the servant who'd brought me tea and the sari came attached to my hip. I thought she'd enter the damn stall until I politely informed her, in Marathi, that if I didn't get a bit of privacy for this activity, I'd shove her ancient little nose into the nearest sink. I did have a modicum of respect left for my elders. I could have said, and meant, toilet. She backed off.

I had no phone on my person. The window in the restroom didn't seem an option. Even if I could squeeze more than one thigh into that crack, I'd land in the drink. And the water wasn't exactly up to the standards of the beaches in the Hamptons. I idly pondered whether parades of plaster-of-paris pachyderms pitched from the Ganesh festival rested peacefully in the bay below.

I had another reason for trying to stay calm during what could end up being my last meal. Mahindra's constant use of his own cell phone. Mahindra kept calling the fellow watching Brig, then receiving calls from same every five grating minutes, so I hoped I'd learn something about Brig's activities. From what I could gather from Mahindra's end of the conversations, Brig had remained quietly in his hotel room like a good little boy. Taking a nap.

Between calls for updates on Mr. O'Brien, Mahindra quizzed me about New York. The cosmopolitan criminal hadn't made it to the Big Apple yet.

I kept him engrossed for thirty minutes with a history of the city, starting with the Native Americans' negotiations with Peter Stuyvesant. Then I updated the lecture to include George Washington's less-subtle transactions with the British from the fort in northern Manhattan.

I tried to remember everything I knew about the 1800s heyday of Irish street gangs and their hostile negotiations with at least five different sections of various other immigrants. I thought Mahindra would enjoy that since he'd scheduled a one-on-one with Mr. O'Brien of the O'Briens from Dublin and Riverdale later this evening.

I finished with a few current events about the attempts of various New York mayors to negotiate with squeegee wipers, jaywalkers, smokers, and unlicensed street vendors.

"We will visit New York someday," Mahindra declared. "Stay at the Four Seasons. I shall show you off when we attend performances of the Metropolitan Opera, and we shall dance at the Rainbow Room."

I grabbed the glass of wine the waiter had just refilled and chugged it down. I did not like the sound of those "we's." I couldn't help but remember Jake's script for *Carnival of Lust* where Asha's character gets taken to the Royal Yacht Club for a slice of royal seduction by a smooth-talking kidnapper.

I quickly asked Mahindra to name his favorite opera, hoping to steer the conversation toward listening to the greats, rather than focusing on waltzing with Tempe at one of the city's famous night spots.

"*Tosca*. By Puccini."

I nearly fell off my chair. I'd just seen *Tosca* a month ago. It's not a pretty story, although the music is gorgeous.

Tosca, a singer, loves Mario, an artist. Mario is hunted by Scarpia, an obsessed villain. Scarpia wants Tosca for himself.

The parallels to Brig, me, and Mahindra were a bit too close. At least Tosca manages to stab Scarpia, but then she and Mario both die. He gets shot by a firing squad. She jumps off a parapet in despair. Ouch.

I changed topics, even if the newest subject might cause some annoyance. "Mr. Mahindra."

"Kirkee, please. Or, since you Americans prefer a less formal name, Kirk."

"Mr. Mahindra. Why are you going to so much trouble to get Shiva's Diva? Aren't there other statues as precious that don't come with a curse? And without all this hassle to acquire them?"

He frowned. "Because it is mine. I had agreed to pay Khan's price. I arrived at the saloon at the proper time. And my prize was stolen in front of my eyes. First, by that idiotic American Decore who could not begin to understand what he attempted to take. Then by a resourceful Irishman who indeed understands how precious is the Saraswati but has no right to the statue. Yet he sneaks off into the night with it. He swaggers and boasts as if Saraswati were his to dispose of as he pleases."

This was not the right question to have asked the man. Mahindra's voice lost that oh-so-civilized tone. His English became too proper. The man was pissed.

"Then! As though it were not insult enough for Mr. O'Brien to run all over Bombay with the statue, enter Seymour Patel. A man lower than the snakes who crawl on the ground. A man who had Saraswati in his grasp for less than a day. A man who lost her because he was so stupid as to allow his hideous old mother to carry the statue. A man too dumb to see he was fleeing a building that had not even the whisper of smoke."

He smiled at me then and lifted his glass in a toast.

"I do not normally hold with the idea of beating up on elder ladies, but in this case, Tempe, I must applaud you."

"I didn't really beat her up. I just tackled her. If she'd simply let go of the Diva, I wouldn't have punched her. Well, that's not true. I might have anyway just because she's guilty of bad parenting by bringing a swine like Patel into the world."

He nodded. "Quite so. And you accomplished your goal. Unfortunately, you then delivered the statue back to Mr. O'Brien. Leading to the present state of affairs."

Kidnapping and ransom had been reduced to a state of affairs. So the deaths of Brig and me at the end of the night would be labeled, what? An unfortunate set of circumstances? That would be the phrase. Rather like Ray's murder in a back alley.

My eyes opened wide. I'd just realized Kirk Mahindra had witnessed my boxing match with Patel's mother. He'd watched Patel leave the building. Which also meant he'd seen Ray Decore enter the alleyway and meet his death. And had done nothing to stop it. Or caused it, then cleverly blamed and framed Patel?

My hand shook as I reached for the *gajar halwa*, the carrot-based dessert sprinkled with pistachio nuts that had just arrived at our table. I love this stuff. I could have it for breakfast, lunch, tea, and dinner. Not too sweet, not too tart. Just right. But this night, Goldilocks could not even taste a morsel. I tried to reason with Kirkee.

"Mr. Mahindra? I suppose my question wasn't so much why you think you hold claim to Shiva's Diva, but *why* you want the statue at all. Doesn't the curse worry you?"

He laughed. "So Briggan O'Brien has convinced you of the validity of the legend. What is it they say of the Irish and their lies? Blarney? That is all that is, Tempe. Tales to frighten the weak or weak-willed into believing that this particular statue has any power to do anything besides fetch a magnificent price."

"Well, they sounded pretty real to me. I think Brig said once that the previous unlawful owner of the Diva became speechless not long after the guy stole her."

He waved his hand in the air with a slight twist to the wrist. "Rumor. All rumor. Designed to raise the price and discourage lesser buyers from entering the bargaining process. But the blessing? Ah, now this I *do* believe. Saraswati is the goddess of communication and speech and music and the arts. She has blessed many who have worshipped her throughout the centuries."

His face darkened slightly, then brightened as he stared at me. "You may not know this, but she is also a goddess of fertility."

"I'd heard."

"Well then, it is pointless to address the why of those of us who would possess her."

Hot damn. The fog lifted. Mahindra had the bucks. He might even have the modicum of culture needed to appreciate the goddess's blessing of artistic gifts. But his real reason, besides the greed associated with wanting a prize no one else had, was a stunner.

Mahindra, bless his loathsome little heart, wanted kids. Little Kirkees. My dinner companion could have been the Indian version of the Godfather, wanting to pass along the family business to heirs and sons of heirs. And considering the way he'd been staring at me, I knew he now wanted to add red hair to the gene pool.

I opened my mouth to tell him that Saraswati is also a refined goddess and a bit selective with her gifts. That she despised violence and warfare and that he might truly be getting the Diva ticked off with such activities as kidnapping and murder. I didn't get the chance.

Beethoven's Fifth rang out again. This time Kirk did not seem pleased with what he heard. He slammed the flap of the phone over the numbers and stood.

"It is time to leave. Tempe, come."

I didn't know what had transpired, but since Mahindra's anger level had risen about five notches, I assumed Briggan O'Brien had just pulled a fast one. Perhaps he'd slipped out of his room while Mahindra's guard patiently paced the halls waiting to escort him to Hot Harry's. If the sneaky Irishman *had* managed to escape, it should be written up in Ripley's. Brig's hotel window was five stories above sea level.

I'm ashamed to admit I wondered, for only a brief second, if Brig would bother to show up at Hot Harry's at midnight. Then I remembered two nights spent in his arms. Earthshaking, back-clawing, sweat-soaking nights.

Mahindra put his hand on my elbow. I shrugged it off, but he entwined his fingers through mine as he steered me toward the exit doors of the Yacht Club, waving greetings to one and all. After the initial disgust of feeling his touch, I barely noticed. I thought of those nights with Brig and I knew. My rescue was already in motion.

Chapter 37

Symmetry. That's what Mahindra had called it. But when I found myself seated at the same table where I'd watched bullets whizzing by and felt the force of one remove an earring, I had a few other words I could've used for Mahindra's choice of venues. All of them were words that would have caused my paternal grandmother to grab the nearest bar of soap and rinse out daughter Tempe's mouth. I shudder.

I touched the new earrings Brig had bought for me. I hadn't taken them off except to sleep or to bathe. I tilted my chin in defiance of the situation. Brig would be here. He would save me.

The tables at Hot Harry's had been turned back to upright positions. Chairs had been neatly placed at those tables. Glass had been swept away and the odor of booze had been replaced with scents of spicy incense. I did spot a candy wrapper on the floor but charitably concluded Hot Harry himself might have dropped it. If indeed Harry existed.

The saloon wasn't exactly back in business, but the cleanup seemed to be in the last stages of completion before Harry started welcoming paying customers again. I squinted. The sail from my earring lay under the table where I'd sat with the Ray Decore less than a week ago.

Mahindra and I had arrived at the saloon at 11:45 P.M. Time enough for Kirk's boys to check all exits, entrances, and storerooms in case Brig and a contingent of gun-toting Irishmen waited to liberate me and make off with the statue. Leaving Mahindra without his prize once again.

Mahindra even remembered the trapdoor leading to the

cellar. He probably still felt the bruises on his butt caused when Brig had flung that door open and toppled him.

Reports from all business associates indicated that no one matching Brig's description crouched behind the bar, hid inside a barrel, lit up a chandelier, or clung to the underside of a table like a tick to a dog.

Mahindra sat in the chair where Ray had been sitting only a week ago. No pineapple sodas or bourbon-filled drinks were on the table tonight. There was no hooded Strider in the corner. No Strider anywhere in sight.

Midnight. Nothing. No big, handsome Irish pirate came breezing through the saloon door holding a statue and screaming, "Unhand my woman, you fiend!" Or even a succinct, sweet, "Tempe, *tar*!" (Come.)

Twelve-thirty. Mahindra began pacing and caressing the gun he'd taken out of his coat pocket. I have no idea what the gun laws are in Bombay, but Mahindra did not seem concerned that he carried a concealed weapon on him the way most men carry a wallet.

One o'clock. Kirk Mahindra's patience dried up. And my hopes and time were pretty much in the trash. I began to imagine something that might explain why Brig O'Brien had failed to show at the appointed time.

Scenario number one. Seymour Patel had been released from jail (bail by Mommy?) and had been waiting for Brig on the ground when he'd slithered down the wall of the Sea Harbor Hotel. Patel had slit Brig's throat and grabbed the Diva.

No. Not realistic. Patel doubtless remained in the pokey making friends with large, bisexual gentlemen as ugly as his mother. Gentlemen who admired him, if you get my drift.

Number two. Brig had managed to get the Diva to whomever he'd intended selling her to all along. He was now working on getting a credit return. "Look, I'll give you this bloody marvelous horse trophy instead. And really, you believe Saraswati will bless you? Ha! Imagine that grace tripled. A woman's life for the statue. A life belonging to my love, a lass as fair as the mist rising above the moor on a moonlit night."

In that scene, Brig was still trying to wrest or charm the statue away from this anonymous buyer. He'd lost his watch and didn't know midnight had come and gone. Simple. Not great, but easy to understand.

Number three. Brig had decided that the fling with the American babe he'd met in a darkened storeroom had been a grand thing, to be sure, but not worth the price of ivory. So he'd snuck out of the hotel, Diva in hand, then boarded Flight 703 to everyone's favorite spot—Pago Pago. With Claire or Asha or that little dancer who'd been winking at him all week from the bottom of the roller coaster.

Number four. I never got to number four. Mahindra stared at me and I knew he could see my thoughts. Every damn one of them. He probably even knew the flight number to Pago Pago and the name of the dancer.

Mahindra took a deep breath. It did not calm him down. He began screaming curses at Brig, Brig's mother, Brig's father (who apparently had not married Brig's mother according to the translation I gleaned), Brig's ancestors and, if he had one, Brig's dog. I caught Hindi versions of snake and altar, followed by fire. Those words spoken in the same phrase worried me.

He finally reverted to English and lowered his volume to announce, "Enough! We have waited an hour for this scoundrel to uphold his end of this ghastly transaction."

Not good. Exit honored guest, babe of my heart, and future mama of Mahindras. Enter ghastly transaction. Bottom end of a deal gone bad.

"Tempe. I am truly sorry. You are a delightful, beautiful, young lady and I had great hopes for us. I foresaw a long future together with the blessings of the goddess. But I cannot break my word. Ever. I can promise you, however, the method of death will be painless."

He couldn't be serious. Even Mahindra had to think twice before killing me. So he had buddies on the Bombay police force. He needed to understand that Americans don't take kindly to having one of their citizens, especially an innocent female tourist type, being (a) shot, (b) stabbed, or (c) poisoned, then left to rot in the corner of a dive like Hot Harry's Saloon.

Ray's death had made the national news of India. Ray's friend headed up a very prestigious law firm. A law firm that doubtless had half of NYPD and Interpol already checking into Ray's murder. No matter how low I might be on the ladder of Tucker, Harrison and Deville, Esquires, nonetheless, my toes did cling to a rung or two.

I tried to explain this to Mahindra. He didn't care. The curse of the Diva had overtaken him in at least one way. His ability to understand clear communication with another human being had diminished. He waved away my words about my job and my boss and the swarms of angry New York cops who would stomp him into the ground once they discovered darling Tempe Walsh hadn't made it back to Manhattan.

Mahindra lifted his gun. I shut up.

He sighed. "I am what you Americans call a crack shot. If you stay still, Miss Walsh, the bullet will enter your skull correctly and you will feel only a twinge. Again, this saddens me to end our relationship."

How he'd reckoned the "only a twinge" bit eluded me. Maybe he'd met his fate the same way in a previous incarnation? It didn't matter. Twinge or no, I was not going gently, quietly, or with a damn brass band into this night.

I tipped my chair back and fell to the floor. I slammed the bottle Mahindra had been so unwise as to leave on the table across the sandaled foot of a goon hovering nearby.

In the middle of getting to my own feet, I heard a noise. I looked up at what had once been a door leading to the roof of Hot Harry's and was treated to the spectacular view of Briggan O'Brien crashing through, screaming Gaelic curses at the top of those magnificent lungs.

He landed directly on top of Mr. Fat Goon (the one I'd

imagined wearing my cute outfit with the conch belt). The goon shouted as Brig hit him in the mouth with a tote bag.

Brig turned to me with, "Tempe, lass, how are you?"

"I'm okay. Nice entrance, by the way. You must show Jake. He could use it in the sequence in the ringmaster's den. You know, where Asha has to swing from the chandelier?"

"Ah. Good. I was hopin' to impress you."

"Well, you did. By the way, what's in the bag you thwapped villain number one with?"

"That would be the entire lot of the sex toys our friendly vendor delivered with the Diva."

"Hmmm. Smart idea."

"Ready to go?"

"I believe so, yes."

"*Tar*, lass!"

Mind you, we hadn't been conducting this reunion on the floor while sipping tea. As soon as Brig landed on Fat Ugly Goon, I began looking for a way to elude Mahindra and his gun. Fortunately, Kirk had remained a bit stunned after witnessing Brig's swashbuckling entrance. So, I stayed on the floor, grabbed the nearest chair by its legs, then thwacked Kirk's elbow from my position underneath. I hit his funny bone right where it hurts the worst. He dropped the gun.

Brig ran to me, bestowed a quick kiss on my lips, then the pair of us turned to see who was doing what. A skinny hooligan, who looked like Stan Laurel to Fat Ugly Goon's Oliver Hardy, fired his gun in the air, then aimed it at Brig. Brig knocked it out of his hand using a swift chop on the wrist, then he punched "Stan" in the nose and turned to see who was the next idiot with a weapon.

That would be Fat Ugly Goon again. He raised his knife and threw it inches from my feet, then smiled at me. Great. Guns had been fired. Knives had been thrown. Hot Harry's had sparkled again with blazing bullets and flashing blades. I reached up to see if the earrings Brig had given me were still in place and unharmed. They were.

Brig yelled, "*Ais!*" (Back.) We were of one accord. Time to leave before Mahindra and company recovered.

Symmetry. It had worked last week, so I vaulted over the counter again, grabbed the top of the chandelier, swung out, and ended up in the storeroom.

This time Brig swung in right beside me. We looked at the barrels that had been broken and strewn around the floor. Not a single barrel remained intact, and we saw nothing we could stand on to help us through that window leading to the alley.

We heard a war cry that chilled my blood, then the sound of glass shattering. I had a feeling Miss April had not survived this current destruction of the bar counter. Mahindra screamed, "Give me the statue and I will let you live!"

Brig began tossing broken barrels in front of the door to the storeroom. Someone, probably Mahindra, was now kicking that door. Since it was made of steel, that wasn't going to help, but I felt sure a few bullets in the keyhole would solve the problem of unlocking it.

That back exit opened. We were trapped. Mahindra had doubtless figured out that he could bust in via the curtain behind the bar counter. And I fully expected at least two of Mahindra's brute suits to be standing in that back door with guns, knives, or forks. I shut my eyes, preferring not to know which weapon or utensil would hit me first.

"Yo! Tempe! Good to see you, girl. We missed you at the shoot after tea."

I opened my eyes. Asha Kumar stood in the doorway. Under her feet squirmed a male last seen this evening in the company of Kirk Mahindra. His eyes were closed and he appeared to be napping. I looked back at Asha. In her right hand she held a familiar-looking gold object. A trophy engraved with one word—"Miscommunication."

Chapter 38

"Asha! Watch out!"

The thug at Asha's feet reached for her ankle. She thwacked him again with the trophy, then nudged him with her foot. He twitched once, then wisely quit moving. Asha grinned at me. I grinned back.

I felt arms surround me and turned to bury my face into Brig's broad chest. We clung to each other until a bullet whizzed over my head. Mahindra had discovered the curtain.

Brig released me, then grabbed my hand. "Time to go. We'll be havin' a fine reunion later. If we live."

We landed in the alley where Brig and I had exchanged names a week ago. This time none of us stopped for pleasantries. Asha took off at a nice clip. Brig and I ran after her toward a familiar vehicle. The Jeep.

"Jake! Bless you, man!"

"Tempe. I'm so glad you are unharmed. We were very worried when Brig called us to say Mahindra had taken you. And right in front of your trailer. I'm so sorry. I thought you were better protected at the studio lots."

I quickly hugged the worried director. Brig interrupted any further discussion. "Asha? Take the wheel, will you? I have to attend to my woman. I haven't seen her all day."

He kissed me thoroughly, then softly whispered, "I thought I'd lost you, lass. And that I couldn't bear. The damn statue is priceless, but you, my love, are irreplaceable."

"Briggan O'Brien, I would gladly go back into the fray just

to hear those words from you again." I kissed him again, then we held each other tightly and wordlessly.

Asha and Jake had wisely refrained from commenting on the action in the back seat. I don't think their silence had been intended as polite noninterference. It was drive-for-your-life time while maintaining focus. Asha dodged, weaved, and knocked down stalls all to get clear of the area near Hot Harry's. Jake watched his sweet beloved drive with a look of horror on his face.

Brig lifted a fold of the now-torn sage green sari and stroked the material. "Cute outfit, luv."

I patted the shreds of the garment that clung to my chest. "Airy" accurately summed up the fashion statement.

"What? This old thing? Latest in victim fashions. Mahindra seemed determined I would not join the murdered Mr. Decore this evening in the cutoffs and halter top Reena squeezed me into earlier. A bit risqué for the Yacht Club and all. No offense to your costumer, Jake."

Jake nodded. "None taken. Anyway, I do believe I've heard somewhere it's considered bad karma to die in a costume from a Masala film set."

Brig ignored this exchange. His mouth set in a thin line. "Yacht Club. Kirk Mahindra took you to the Yacht Club? Dressed in that?"

"He did indeed. Wanted to impress his captive with the food there. I'm sure it's tasty, though I don't remember much of it. I kept wondering if any of the government nabobs I met would have cared to know they were talking to a girl who was in the throes of a kidnapping."

Brig shook his head. "Corrupt maggots. Every one of them. At least if they were on first-name basis with that heathen scum Kirkee."

He drew me toward him again and held me. I did not resist. His voice grew soft. "Damn, Tempe. I truly panicked when Mahindra's boy pounced on me after my little stay at the police station this afternoon and told me he'd nabbed you. I should have wrung his sorry neck on the spot. It's all my fault for leaving you alone."

I beamed at him and said, "Brig. Listen. Neither of us knew Mahindra was poking from the pockets of the police. Or vice versa. Whatever. Or that he'd arrange for you to get arrested for Ray's murder. And I hadn't been alone all day till I went for the bathroom break. I should have stayed on the lot instead of going over to my trailer."

I touched a bruise over Brig's right eye. "Mahindra's pals or your fellow inmates at the jail?"

"The former. The lads at the pokey were a decent lot. Seemed quite intrigued to have the Irish mug in with them. I regaled them with tales of banshees and wee folk and pots of gold under rainbows. I believe I may have promised more than a few I'd be mailin' a leprechaun to Bombay the next time one of the little blighters jumped into my knapsack."

I might have known Brig would have every felon in the jail inviting him to come visit should he, or they, get out anytime soon. He'd probably made good use of his day by taking the names and addresses of every black marketeering fence in India and jotting them in a little black book.

I said as much. He grinned.

"Handheld electronic black book. I may not like the wireless phones, but the palm-size are very nice for addresses plus playing games on long flights. I hate flying. Too boring and no chance to do anything physical."

I snuggled against his chest. My relief about escaping from Mahindra and his minions was so great I didn't even flinch when Asha hit a police van parked on the side of the road. Fortunately, the cop was too busy stopping a brawl in front of a bar to notice the speeding Jeep or the fact that his vehicle just lost a side mirror.

"Asha? Where are we going? And excuse me, but has anyone noticed that Mahindra is about two cars behind us in his limo? He must be upset. He's actually doing the driving instead of Mr. Perfect Chauffeur. Damn. He got to his car really fast."

Brig answered me. "I noticed. Mahindra and two others were out the front door the minute you and I hit the storeroom. He didn't know I'd restaged Robin Hood saving Maid Marian with the help of Little John and Friar Tuck here, but I'm damn sure he knew there'd be a car involved."

Asha turned and stuck her tongue out at Brig. "Friar Tuck? Huh? Just who you calling Friar Tuck?"

"Hush, Asha! It was figurative for the rescue of my lovely Maid Marian here."

"Humph. Well, the good monkette is about to lose the bad Sheriff back in the forest. Fasten your caps, chaps. It's gonna be a bumpy ride."

"Thank you, Margo Channing," I said.

Brig grinned. "This is good. Asha will lose the bloody fiend up around the Churchgate Rail Station. She's a much faster driver. And Kirk's not used to taking the wheel himself. Probably hasn't driven in twenty years. Look. He's already dropped back by another five cars."

Asha again turned and wrinkled her nose at me. I quickly told her to keep that nose and her eyes aimed at the road.

She sighed, "You asked where we were headed. I'm telling you. We're going back to the studio lot."

I almost jumped out of the Jeep. "You're not serious! Hell, Mahindra knows those lots better than I do. He's managed to get in and out of there and knock on the door of every trailer I've been in for the last three days. He's been on the lot more times than Raj Ravi this week!"

Brig reached for me again and pulled me back against his chest. "It's fine. Believe me. Kirk will assume we'll be heading for Jake's or Asha's place. And there's a score of actors staying on the lot tonight plus security guards. Mahindra will find it difficult to get through now, if he even wants to make the attempt. He may figure I ditched the statue since I showed up determined to make the rescue instead of the exchange."

"That reminds me. Where is the Diva? I assume you never had time to make a delivery this afternoon."

Brig reached down on the floor of the back seat. He pulled

out a spanking new tote bag advertising the film to be released this spring by Jake Roshan, starring Asha Kumar and Raj Ravi. *Carnival of Lust.* The silk-screened print on the front showed a nearly unclad Asha crooning to a couple of snakes. Behind her, atop an elephant, perched Raj Ravi. A cast of dancers posed by a fountain. I squinted. In the background stood a Ferris wheel. On the top of the wheel, a redheaded girl balanced on her head. Me.

"Cool! I can't believe you got this picture so fast! Wow. I'm on a tote bag! My mother will love this. She'll order at least a hundred for Christmas presents."

Laughter burst from all three of the other occupants.

"What? You don't believe me? Quit laughing. I'm serious. She will. She's spent her whole life upset I didn't become a Broadway star. This is the closest I'll get. She'll be thrilled. My father'll have a fit, but it's time he knew who I really am and what I *really* want."

Brig hugged me. "Are you ever going to tell your mother what's inside that promo tote bag right now?"

"Shiva's Diva? The goddess who nearly cost her baby's life?" I smiled. "I may give that one some thought. Mom still has every strand of her gorgeous auburn hair. I don't want it to turn gray all at once."

Brig smiled. "So this is what I get to look forward to, is it? A howling, back-clawing, sweaty—oops, sorry—*glowing* redhaired vixen causing trouble even when she's a senior citizen?"

I couldn't speak. Briggan O'Brien had just made a statement that very strongly implied a future together. With me. A long future. The women on both sides of my family don't turn gray until they're in their nineties.

When I felt sure I could use my vocal chords without heading up a full octave, I croaked, "Did you just say look forward to? With me? Is that what you said?"

He didn't get a chance to answer.

Brig sank. His blood soaked the seat. Everywhere.

Chapter 39

"No!" I screamed.

Mind you, a lesser woman might have become hysterical, thrown herself over the body of her fallen lover, cried, cursed, and quite possibly fainted. I did all the above. Except faint. And once I saw that Brig still breathed and that the bullet had only grazed his ear, I flung myself over his body more to protect him, rather than a show of further histrionics on my part.

Apparently, Kirk Mahindra had turned the wheel over to a more experienced driver at some point in the midst of the traffic jam by the clubs. A driver who rivaled Asha in speed. This shift had allowed Kirk to aim a gun out the window of the limo and fire one bullet. One was enough. Mahindra had been right. "Crack shot" nailed his ability with a weapon.

Asha sent the Jeep hauling at speeds over a hundred miles per hour. She drove silently, with intense concentration. Never again would I hassle her about her skill behind a wheel. Jersey girl was about to save our lives.

We made it to the gates of Vivek Productions in under sixty minutes. Somewhere along the road, Asha managed to lose Mahindra. Whether we'd achieved that goal in front of a nightclub, Churchgate Rail Station, or a brothel, I didn't know. It didn't matter. I cradled Brig's bleeding head in my lap and sobbed.

Asha sent the Jeep into the garage with a squeal of brakes and tires rivaling a pit stop at the Grand Prix. She and Jake jumped out.

Asha peered at Brig. "Is he awake? Can he walk?"

I lightly touched Brig's temple. He was still awake but obviously in shock. But in true, stubborn, O'Brien fashion, he'd managed to hang on to the tote bag.

I looked at Jake. "Where to, do you think? Is there an infirmary out here? What if we all carry him?"

Brig waved his hand. "No! *Tá fáilte romhat!*"

Jake and Asha looked at me.

"He said, 'No!' Which I think you got. The second phrase claimed he's fine. Which I think is a lie."

Brig managed to exit the vehicle on his own, then promptly fell to his knees. I tried to grab him before he toppled, but I tripped and tumbled with him to the ground.

Brig howled. "Ow! I've got one lousy nick in the bottom of my damn earlobe! Which I just scraped again. Not to mention some bloody gravel stones just attacked my knees. But we're not looking at a life-threatening wound here. Slap some stinkin' gauze on it. I'll be fine in the mornin'. Oh. It is mornin'. Well, then, later in the mornin'. Perhaps noon."

He exhaled. "Think there'll come a night when any of us can get to bed before four and not worry about hooligans trying to kill us in our sleep?"

Jake whistled through his teeth, then looked at Brig.

"You are a menace. Do you realize that, Briggan O'Brien? I *had* been enjoying six weeks of calm filming before you showed up. The biggest problem I encountered was keeping Asha from flying off to America during one of her costume-fitting . . . uh . . . fits. Then you waltz in with your statue and turn everything topsy-turvy and nearly get everyone, including yourself, killed."

Brig's eyebrows raised. "And the point of that would be?"

Jake shook his head. "I do not know. I believe I had a point when I started talking. It seems to have vanished. Just like Mahindra. Into the night, I sincerely hope."

Asha patted his hand. "Jake. You don't do well when you don't get sleep. Let's help get Brig to Raj's trailer and call it a night. Tempe can patch up the brave hero and we can regroup around noon."

"Raj is gone again?"

She nodded. "His wife made it clear if his butt didn't make it into their house at close of shooting today, Mr. Ravi could spend the next forty years or so at the bottom of a very deep pool. At least that's what he told Jake. I've met Mrs. Ravi. Far too meek and sweet to ever say such a thing. I think Raj had just gotten into that conjugal mood thing."

"Got it. No need to go further. As long as we don't have to worry about Raj turning up before noon, it sounds great. He has a nice trailer."

We took about three steps away from the Jeep before all of us turned as one. I spoke first. "Shiva's Diva."

Brig groaned. "We've left her!"

Asha held up a hand. "I'll get her. After all the trouble we've had, it would just be too anticlimatic, plus damned inconvenient, for some idiot car thief to decide this is the night he's stealing a Jeep and get our statue."

Brig, Jake, and I waited while Asha brought out the tote bag. The four of us then stared at each other. Jake voiced the feeling. "Where are we going to keep her?"

Brig's ear continued to bleed. He appeared in no shape to think, and I was in no shape to think for him.

Asha took over. "I have a great idea for a hiding place. Don't worry. I promise no one will dare try and take her."

Brig sighed. "Keep it secret. Keep it safe."

I stared at him. "Thank you, Gandalf."

"What?"

"*Lord of the Rings*. I watched the marathon on cable in New York, geez, just last week."

"I thought you saw *Butch Cassidy?*" Brig asked.

"Well, I did. Great week. They had the Paul Newman marathon on for two days, then *Rings* for three days. In between they had Gene Kelly *Singin' in the Rain* all night."

Jake beamed. "Did you notice that Debbie Reynolds is minus a shoelace . . .?"

I joined in on him with "in the dance sequence!" We grinned at each other.

"Do you realize she was just nineteen for that one? As dancers go, you're old, Tempe!"

Brig held up his hand. "Stop! Both of you! Damn. I spent three years with Jake watching old movies in the dorm room. Then I get involved in a shoot-out that far outweighs anything Butch Cassidy ever encountered, I meet Tempe Walsh, film buff, and I now get to look forward to another fifty or so?"

Brig quickly turned to Asha. "So, Miss Kumar? Where will the Diva be kept secret and safe?"

She snickered. "The snake cage."

Brig's eyes popped. "What!"

"It's okay. I'll retrieve the goddess at the proper time. I really don't think anyone will dare try and get her out."

"Especially me," Brig sighed.

Asha snorted at him. "Wimp. Sparky and Fluffy wouldn't hurt a fly. A mouse or a rabbit maybe, but never big brave stalwart Irish-Robin-Hood types."

"Fine. You go bond with the serpents. Would you bring the Diva out tomorrow at four? Please."

Brig could walk without assistance from Asha and Jake, but he leaned heavily on my shoulder during the quiet trek to Raj's trailer. This night, we even had a key.

Symmetry. Raj's trailer. In the very early hours of the morning. I did take the time to find some bandages and deal with Brig's ear. He was right. Barely a dent in him and in no way life threatening.

Once my services as nurse ended, the night became a repeat of the last time we'd stayed in Raj's trailer. Brig and I collapsed together onto the bed. I wrapped my arms around the fallen hero and both of us promptly fell asleep.

Chapter 40

Brig and I spent the remainder of the night in peace.

Upon waking, Brig proceeded to demonstrate one did not need the tip of one's ear to engage in pleasurable, strenuous, amorous activities. I could have easily stayed in that trailer moving from one exotic position to another helping him prove that point, but we did have a scene to shoot.

We made it to Jake's covered tent by noon. Asha and Jake looked far worse than Brig and I. I knew Jake needed about nine hours of sleep to function properly, which could account for the shadows under his eyes, but Asha's lips were set and her chin trembled. She sat as far from Jake as the tent allowed.

"Problems?" I inquired. "Other than the usual with kidnappers and murderers and hidden statues, that is. Don't tell me someone managed to sneak in and grab our goddess from the snake cage. Or steal one of the snakes."

Asha growled, "Nope. Sparky and Fluffy are still there and still guarding Saraswati. This is more important. Jake has ix-nayed the scene in front of the carnival tent where the princess rides in on the llama. He thinks it'll spoil the effect of the lovers reuniting. I totally disagree. It's going to really set up the part where they see each other at the cybercafe."

Artistic differences between director and star. They could easily resolve that kind of problem without resorting to bloodshed, which would be a nice switch.

I plopped next to Asha, poured some tea, grabbed three

scones, then dove into what now constituted brunch. I glanced at Jake. "So, llama or not, are we filming today?"

He ignored Asha and nodded at me. "Yes, indeed. I want to try and finish the big dance sequence over by the fountain. With the boys on one side and the girls on the other. Do you know the one I mean?"

Brig and I nodded with Jake. Asha did not nod. She handed Brig a buttered scone.

"Briggan. I've been really patient in not asking this, but I can't stand it anymore. What do you intend to do with the statue? Now that Tempe and I have been kidnapped, Ray is dead, and you're running around with half an ear missing, I personally don't want to keep the Diva. Maybe she really is cursed."

Brig mumbled as he took a bite. "Only for the greedy, Ms. Kumar. Only for the greedy."

"Yeah. Right. Maybe I got greedy? Is that what you're saying? Well, whatever. So? Where's the goddess off to next?"

Brig glanced at the clock hanging on a hook at the back of the food tent. "With any luck, Shiva's Diva will be in the hands of her rightful owner by four this afternoon. So, when you retrieve her, bring her back to the food-service tent."

Asha and Jake immediately began a barrage of "Who? Why didn't you tell us before? Where are you making the exchange? How much?"

I stayed silent. Claire Dharbar. I knew it. I didn't quite understand this "rightful owner" comment, but I assumed the lady had met his price. A twinge of my unreasonable jealousy hit, but I squelched it with another bite of my scone.

Brig glanced around the table. "It's Claire Braganza Dharbar. Tempe met her the other day in Bombay."

Asha and I looked at each other, then Asha crowed, "Knew it! Tempe nailed it the other day. Said it only made sense for her to be the buyer because otherwise why would you go chatting her up at a restaurant?"

I nearly threw my scone at her. "Asha? Care to take a long

slow ride on top of Binky the elephant? I know how much you love the beasts."

Brig winked at me. "A bit of jealousy, now, is it I'm hearin'?"

I tossed my hair back. "Not a lick. I just told Asha that you wouldn't have been rude enough to leave me sitting by myself less than two hours after nearly getting shot by Ray."

Asha glared at me. "*I* said that, Tempe, and you didn't listen!"

I did throw my scone at her. Then I rolled my eyes and hissed, "Isn't it swell how smart you are? And isn't it time you go jump on a llama?"

She just grinned. I rose. Brig did as well. I waved at him to stay put.

"Finish your tea. I need to shower before we start filming today, then I'm off to Reena's to fight over her latest costume in the let's-make-Tempe-look-like-a-rat's-nest design contest. I'll meet back up with everyone on the set."

I was still wearing the ruined, bloody sari from last night's foray into violence at Hot Harry's. I hadn't had a chance to get back to my own trailer and put on some jeans.

Jake smiled for the first time this morning. "If it were not for your memories of what you went through last night, I would tell you to keep wearing the sari. It's perfect for the scene."

Brig looked closely at me. "It's nicely open in the right places too. Shows a lot of skin." His smile dimmed. "I don't like whose closet it was hanging in originally though. So just as well you're changing."

I sighed. "I'm so glad this look meets with the approval of the men present. But excuse me if I feel I need a bit more coverage and a little less smell. Bye-bye all."

I ran all the way back to Raj's trailer and locked the door. It wouldn't deter Brig if he decided to gain entrance, but it gave me a slight illusion of privacy while I considered the issue of Claire.

I stayed in the shower until the hot water ran out, while I

wondered why Brig hadn't given the woman the statue before today. I was certain he had his reasons, but they eluded me right now. He'd be handing over the statue to her at four. Teatime. Great. Super.

I can be classy when I need to. If I ran into Claire Braganza Dharbar, I would outdo Asha in the acting department. Be gracious and charming and nice. Pour tea into china cups for her and spread fresh marmalade over scones and muffins while I tried not to make comparisons between the two of us. Comparisons that would not be pretty. Because by teatime, after dancing through fountains and doing flips off elephants, my hair would have frizzed, my makeup would be nonexistent, and I'd look much as I did after my first run-in at Hot Harry's. Claire, doubtless, would look classy, calm, collected—and smell fresh too.

I dressed in a short black skirt and black tee in case I managed to change out of my slutty Reena design before the grand presentation of the statue.

Today's filming had the girls on one end of the fountain and the boys on the other, so Brig and I were separated. Just as well. I didn't need to listen to Irish charm. I had enough trouble dealing with the *pas de bourees*, elbow twitches, and pelvic grinds they had me performing in a fountain spewing water down steps that were slippery and hard to traverse.

Jake called a halt to all terpsichorean activity at 3:49. As I walked toward the tent for a badly needed break (and the tea and pastries) I saw an old tan four-door sedan drive up near where we'd been filming.

Claire Dharbar exited the vehicle from the driver's side. This surprised me. I had assumed this buyer for Shiva's Diva would have glided up in a Rolls driven by some gorgeous Swedish male named Sven. (Yeah, yeah. Add snide and tacky to my list of bad personality traits.)

But the sight of Ms. Dharbar looking cool and chic in her immaculate linen suit and low-heeled pumps brought back my feelings of inadequacy. She and Brig were of a kind. They didn't have a perspiration gland between them. A hundred degrees out and she seemed as dry as the wine Mahindra had pressed on me at the Yacht Club.

I had to stop this. Claire couldn't help being rich, gorgeous, and perfect. She was obviously wealthy enough to meet whatever price Brig had asked to release Shiva's Diva. She might even be an artist of some kind, perhaps a painter who normally occupied a loft in Soho in lower Manhattan. Saraswati would abundantly bless her and doubtless the fertility bit would kick in so little Claires would soon overrun Bombay.

Fertility.

That called to mind Mahindra and his own desire to leave a legacy. The man must have heard that particular call, because behind Claire's tan sedan three cars suddenly came screeching to a halt. The first two vehicles were as nondescript as Claire's four-door. The last was a stretch limo. White. Out stepped Kirk Mahindra.

Chapter 41

Mahindra grabbed Claire. She did not scream. She did not claw at him. She did nothing. The woman had turned to ice. But the look on her face made me forget any previous asinine jealousy about this woman and Brig. Claire had passed scared and gone directly to terrified.

Next up were Mahindra's associates, who'd been in the nondescript vehicles providing escort for the limo. They had obviously decided to look around for familiar faces, then go after the closest. That would be me.

Five goons headed my way with broad strides at a swift pace. Much as I wanted to help Claire, I needed to do a one-eighty and book it back to the fountain. At least fifty dancers, male and female, were still crowded around the bottom steps, chattering, laughing, and enjoying the break. Talk ceased when they saw me and saw what followed behind me.

I ran, screaming and waving my arms in the air to warn everyone that trouble had arrived with weapons ready.

Asha came charging out of the carnival tent with two snakes wrapped around her neck. Sparky and Fluffy. She didn't seem the least concerned that the serpents were cozily sliding up and down her arms and torso. The *Carnival of Lust* tote bag that held the Diva swung over her shoulder.

Symmetry again. The routine first choreographed at Flora Fountain during Asha's rescue looked like a rehearsal for the real thing. The dancers and I began improvising a lively little number in the water alongside Mahindra's men. Music blared out from two speakers hooked up far above the fountain itself. All fifty of us danced up and down the steps. Men with guns slid and slithered across wet pavement trying to catch us. Well, mostly me. Everyone, including the goons, stayed in rhythm.

One of Mahindra's thugs stopped flailing long enough to chase me up to the top. I grabbed the rope ladder hanging from the fountain and climbed as fast as I was able up to the platform holding the speakers. I took great delight in watching my pursuer lose his footing, crash into a pool of water below, then scream in fury at the six-plus angry male dancers who tackled him.

The Hindi love song between Asha and Raj that had been playing all morning changed. "Holding Out for a Hero," my favorite song from *Footloose,* suddenly came blasting out at top volume behind me.

From the opposite side of the carnival tent, riding Binky the elephant, appeared one Briggan O'Brien.

Brig charged at Mahindra, who still held Claire in a lethal grip. Screaming, "*Araich*!" (Battle?) Brig stood, then executed a gorgeous aerial somersault from Binky's back. He landed at Mahindra's feet, popped up, and knocked the man in the jaw without harming Claire. Neat.

Mahindra released her. He reached into his breast pocket and pulled out a piece of red cloth. Damn. My halter top. I'd had to leave it at Mahindra's penthouse when I'd changed into the sari. I nearly fell off my perch from the nausea that swept over me.

Brig had seen and very definitely recognized the top as belonging to me. His nostrils flared. He smashed Mahindra in the mouth. Blood spurted. Mahindra slapped Brig's newly bandaged ear. Dazed, Brig fell to the ground. Mahindra dropped and rammed his elbow into Brig's rib cage. Brig rolled away but managed to get to his feet again.

He seemed about to deliver a nice punch to Mahindra's face when Mahindra clipped Brig behind the knees. He sank back to the ground. Mahindra kicked Brig in the stomach, then jumped up. His foot drew back for a kick aimed at Brig's head.

Brig saw it coming. He rolled, caught Mahindra's foot, and threw him. Mahindra again hit the ground, face first. He sat up and spat out a wad of dirt. Brig began to push himself back up but didn't get the chance. Mahindra lunged and hit Brig with his shoulder. Right in Brig's sternum, which knocked the wind out of him and toppled him over on his back.

Mahindra loomed above him. He waved my halter top like a matador taunting the bull. Brig snatched it, then executed a perfect kip. He faced Mahindra and his face darkened as he looked at the scrap of clothing.

Mahindra screamed, "She's mine!"

Brig's shoulders relaxed. A slight smile crossed his features. He said only one word. "No."

Brig bent his knees and prepared to leap in the air and bring that leg around with a roundhouse kick. But in midjump he lost his balance. He fell, managing only to knock Mahindra's shoulder. Both men were now on the ground.

Facing them were two king cobras. Sparky and Fluffy.

Mahindra, quick to use any means as an advantage, dove, grabbed the snake nearest him by what I would call its neck, then threw it at Brig.

His aim was bad. The snake ended up a foot away from Brig's foot. But it was now a most unhappy serpent. It coiled into the classic strike pose with its head flat, open, and ready. It looked at Brig, then back at Mahindra.

I didn't know how long the snake would remain still while it debated whom to bite first. It didn't matter. Brig was frozen with fear. And the other snake was slithering to aid its cage-mate.

There was a twenty-foot rope tied securely to the railing of this platform at the top of the fountain. The finale to Mahindra's favorite opera, *Tosca*, suddenly flashed into my mind. Tosca meeting her doom from a parapet in a vain attempt to rescue her lover. I pushed the images away.

I grabbed the rope and wrapped the upper portion around

my wrist, then made a loop around my ankle as well. I placed a foot on top of the railing. I balanced for perhaps a second, then took a deep breath and jumped.

It was a less-than-graceful ride down. I flopped and twisted and made circles in the air, nearly losing my grip. I sailed past a crowd of stunned, wet dancers and thugs, then continued to sail past Brig, Mahindra, and the snakes, nearly hitting Binky the elephant who stared at me with a look of horror on her broad face.

The backswing was a different story. I landed butt first into Mahindra's chest.

He went down. I hit the ground and immediately went into a back somersault, finishing on my stomach. I looked to my left. Sparky. Or Fluffy. On the other side of the snake lay a furious Kirk Mahindra.

Brig screamed, "Tempe!" and leapt into the air. He rolled me as far he could. Then he reached back over and grabbed the snake to throw it away from me.

It landed near Mahindra.

Brig helped me up. We ran toward the safety of Binky, who had patiently waited for her master to return.

Asha yelled, "Sic him, Sparky!"

Sparky coiled. The snake hissed. Loudly. My bones went cold. Then Sparky struck Mahindra in his chest.

Mahindra fell back, then lay on the ground, quivering. Tears of pain and rage streamed down his cheeks.

It was over.

Asha gathered up the frightened snake and began crooning to it. Claire sat on the ground a few feet away, arms wrapped around her shoulders, rocking and sobbing.

I empathized with how terrified she'd been. But I noted, almost with amusement, that the woman still looked immaculate and that not even tears could ruin the perfection of that face. Figured. I, on the other hand, was wet, dirty, and smelled like chlorine and Binky.

Yet I was the one Brig held close. He began bestowing tiny,

wonderful soft kisses all over my face and neck. He finally lifted my chin and stared into my eyes.

" 'Twas a daft, brave thing ya did there, lass. Remind me to show my true appreciation in a more fitting manner at a more private time."

I smiled at him. His own smile suddenly turned into a scowl and a look of horror crossed his face. He thrust me rudely aside and with a cry rivaling Celtic warriors defending their soil—and their women—he leapt into the air. I quickly turned and watched the glorious sight of Brig O'Brien tackling Kirkee Mahindra. For good reason. Kirk was no quitter. From his coat pocket, he'd brought out his gun. It was aimed at my back.

Brig knocked the gun from Mahindra's hand. Holding him by the collar, Brig punched him in the face. Again and again and again. Somehow I knew he was seeing not only Mahindra but also all the thugs who'd kidnapped and stolen and murdered. The goons who'd shot up Hot Harry's. Patel, who'd knifed Ray Decore. And perhaps he was even seeing the Irish terrorists who'd killed his sister so many years ago and gotten away with it.

I screamed, "Brig! Brig! For God's sake, stop! Please. You'll kill him! Stop! He's not worth it."

Brig let Mahindra drop. Mahindra stared at Brig as if making up his mind whether to try and reach for that gun. Finally he let his hand fall, empty, by his side. Brig spat at him and stood, his chest heaving, his breath coming in spurts for at least a minute.

Finally, when the color in his cheeks had returned to normal, he strode back over to me, threw his arms around me, leaned down and whispered, "He chose wisely."

I giggled. "Indiana Jones. *Last Crusade*. Ha! Don't tell me you're not a film buff."

"I do watch the odd movie from time to time, luv."

"I knew it. That rescue bit with the elephant came from *The Lion King*, didn't it?"

Brig said, "Speaking of . . ."

He whistled and Binky trotted over rather like a dog bringing a stick back to its master. Brig led her to Mahindra's resting place, then nudged her knee. The huge elephant lightly lifted one huge foot and placed it on Mahindra's chest. She held it there with just enough pressure to keep Kirk from trying any other tricks, yet without crushing his chest. Brig winked at me.

"She's a pacifist, our Binky."

"Mmmm. A well-trained little darling as well. Who is she, Bambi's twin? Must be. She seems to adore *you*."

Brig gathered me up in his arms again. "We'el now, and who wouldn't?"

He had me there.

I glanced around the set to see how the dancers were faring with the other nonfriendlies from Mahindra's war party. Five goons lay in a heap at the bottom of the fountain. Water oozed up to their necks. They were tied in ropes as neatly as the calves from a rodeo event.

I glanced at the tallest dancer. He stood proudly with his foot resting on one of the thugs in the exact manner Binky still held Mahindra. The dancer was less kind than the elephant. He gave his captive an occasional kick when the man twitched. He smiled when he saw me, waved, then yelled, "Three of us did a curry western last year. Had a real live American lasso champion come and teach us!"

I nodded and shouted back, "He did a good job."

I turned to Brig. "Is it over? Yes? Whatcha think?"

"Let's just ask Mr. Mahindra there. Beg pardon, Kirkee? What's it to be? Got any fight left, you perverted son of a bitch?"

Mahindra opened his mouth to speak. Nothing happened. Not a sound. Not a croak. Silence. Brig turned and smiled at Asha and at me. "Thought so."

"Okay. I'm confused. Wasn't Sparky the snake defanged? Or devenomed? Both? Which is why Mahindra is still alive. Why can't he talk?" I asked.

"Didn't you hear the hiss? Remember the legend? Mahindra's been struck mute. Permanently, I imagine."

Claire had recovered enough to watch this latest drama with much interest. She smiled. She said something to Brig in an Indian language I wasn't familiar with. His eyes grew wide. He nodded.

"What? What did she say?"

"Well, let me explain that these are the first words Claire has spoken in ten years since she had a throat operation that went bad. She said she agreed with my assessment. Mahindra has been cursed. Saraswati had enough of him. She took away his power to speak and blessed Claire with that ability again."

I stared at Claire, then at Brig. "How does she know that?"

He gently took Claire's hand and led her toward me.

"Tempe Walsh, let me reintroduce you to Claire Braganza Dharbar. The rightful heir to Shiva's Diva."

Chapter 42

"I need food. Now."

It wasn't the most gracious thing I could have said after Brig made this introduction. But it was what came out and I meant every word.

No one disagreed. Claire stared at me as if I'd lost my wits, but then, she didn't strike me as a stress-eating type. Asha and Brig nodded.

Brig decided that, cursed or not, he couldn't trust Mahindra. One does not need words to throw a knife or shoot a gun. He yelled at the three rodeo-trained dancers to bring more rope and work their magic on Mahindra.

Brig glanced at me. "You know, now that I think about it, Mahindra may own most of the cops around Bombay, but I'd wager the boys at Interpol are not so easily bribed and would be happy to take possession of the thieving, kidnapping scum. Or maybe I should just let my elephant crush his rotten, speechless neck."

"No. Don't upset Binky. She's been through enough."

The dancers quickly bound Mahindra with the rope. Asha sneered at him, kept well away from the elephant, then giggled. "Guess we don't need to gag him though, do we?"

"Ouch. I guess not."

Mahindra wasn't going anywhere. For a truly tacky coup de grâce, Asha set Sparky the snake down a few feet away from the man.

"Stay, Sparky. Good girl."

I crossed my eyes at her. "It's not a dog, Asha. You really

think she's not going to crawl off in search of a nice mouse somewhere?"

Asha lifted her chin. "She's very well trained. She'll stay. Besides, she's had a very alarming experience and it's her nap time."

"Fine. I can't say it would upset me much if the dear little girl wound herself around Mahindra and kept him company for the rest of the day."

Brig put his arm around me. "No offense to the 'dear girl,' but I'd be a mite more relaxed if Sparky did not accompany us at the table for tea. Nor her buddy. The one now reclinin' around Asha's neck."

Asha smiled and released the second serpent. "Go on, Fluffy. Go with your sister and make friends with the bad man there. Good girl."

Both snakes curled up and stared at Mahindra. They seemed quite content to remain in that position.

Claire spoke then, in Portuguese. Her English skills must have been better than I'd thought, at least as far as her understanding. Translated, she stated that king cobras using that flat-headed strike pose are males, not females. I told Asha. She snorted.

Claire, Asha, Brig, and I walked toward the food-service tent. I gathered tea cups and saucers. Asha headed for a stack of freshly baked Indian desserts. Brig found tea strainers and a small canister of *chai*. Claire sat and let us wait on her. She still seemed to be in shock over all the events of the day. I sympathized.

We sipped and chewed and did not mention anything that had transpired over the last hour until all color had been restored to everyone's cheeks. Asha scanned the tent.

"Anybody have a clue where Jake is? He's usually first in line for tea." She grinned. "Or third, behind Tempe and me."

I thought about this. "Last I saw him he was hanging on to the crane overlooking the fountain. With the zoom camera and the CD player. Come to think of it, he's probably the joker who decided to play tunes from *Footloose* during Brig's gallant rescue atop Binky the brave."

"What's this?" Brig turned to me. "I couldn't hear anything besides the voice in my head telling me to finish it. I was rather intent on climbing onto Binky's back."

I told him about the music changing to "Holding Out for a Hero" during his ride.

He beamed. "Nice. Wish I'd had the wit to hear it. But I was somewhat focused on urging the elephant into the fray. It might have spurred me on."

"I think you were spurred enough."

" 'Twas seeing your garment held in his *lochdah lorgair* hand what did it. The very thought of him touching anything of yours made me crazy."

I inhaled. Then I squinted at Brig. "Criminal dog tracker? Is that what you just called Mahindra?"

He grinned. He leaned over and kissed me. "I did. Trying to stay polite for my Gaelic-speaking lass here."

Asha interrupted. "Will you guys shut up? I want to know why Ms. Dharbar is the rightful heir. Brig? Get on with it."

Brig sat back, inclined his head toward Claire, then took a long sip from his cup. "Let me back up a bit. Okay. Claire speaks only Portuguese and the native language of her village. A very obscure Indian language, I might add. She understands English but can't speak it."

Asha groaned. "Are you about to start one of your long-winded Irish tales?"

"I am hurt. Wounded, you might say. I was going about being direct and getting to the point. But now that you've impugned my integrity in telling the story, I may have to elaborate after all."

I poked Asha under the table with my foot. "You started this, Jersey girl. You ought to know better. Brig. Continue. Or start. Whichever."

"Thank you, luv. Where was I?"

"Nowhere," Asha snorted.

I wrinkled my nose at her. "Will you just let the man talk? Jeez. This is going to take forever."

She sighed. Brig lifted his chin.

"All right, then. Claire's husband, Sachin Dharbar, is another friend from college."

I groaned. "I might have known. By the way, did you ever get anything done at Yale or did you just make international buddies so you'd never have to stay at a hotel?"

Brig kissed me and Asha tried to shush me.

"Now who's interrupting? Let him get on with it."

I did. Happily. Claire was married to a friend of Brig's. Brig could tell any tale he wanted now that he'd spoken those two words. "Claire's husband."

Claire smiled. I translated for Asha's benefit when Claire stated, in Portuguese, "Sachin and I are from the village of Chaul. My maiden name is Braganza."

Asha coughed. "That's nice. Hello? Point?"

Brig tapped Asha. "Hush. We're getting to it. And Braganza is important. Just keep the name in mind. Now, if you and Tempe will let me be, I might finish this before the next Ganesh festival. The pair of you are dangerous together, you know that?"

My turn to motion Asha to be quiet. Brig threw her a quick look and began to speak faster on the very probable chance either of us decided to interrupt again.

"Sachin called me about three weeks ago. He'd gotten word that Shiva's Diva was about to be sold by that slithering Khan. To more than one buyer, including most of the players we've been dealing with all week. Sachin needed my help to get into what started out as an auction among at least a dozen customers."

My turn to call time-out. "Why you?"

"Tempe. I'll explain. Promise. But can I get to the good part of the story?"

"Yeah, fine. Go ahead."

He sighed. "Women. Lord love them, but they're a sore trial to a man, and that's for sure. Well, I got to India about a week before Khan set up the so-called buy at Hot Harry's with Raymond Decore and Mahindra and Patel. Apparently, Khan had whittled the bidding down to those three, which could be why the whip toting Rashee didn't show."

I raised my hand. "Don't throw anything at me, but why couldn't Sachin come himself? I mean, he's like what, two hundred miles tops from here? And you were, where?"

"London. And, darlin', Sachin couldn't make it to the meeting because he'd broken his leg in two places not one week earlier."

"Was this by courtesy of Mahindra or Patel?"

He grinned. "Neither. The man was trying to get his satellite TV set hooked up on his roof and fell off. Nothing sinister about it."

"Should have known it would be something ridiculous since he's one of your friends. Okay. So, you're at the meeting. Ready to buy?"

Brig shook his head. "I was there to observe who else was interested and find out the price. Then, of course, all bloody hell breaks loose and Tempe and I end up with the statue." He smiled at me. "And each other."

I was getting warm again and it wasn't the tea. Asha "Ahem'ed!" and "Yo'd!" and Claire chuckled. I gathered she'd understood that last phrase. Brig winked at them both.

"So Tempe and I go on the run with the statue. Which is where Asha and Jake come in. And I apologize for that."

Asha rolled her eyes. "Get over it, Brig. Other than the night I spent under Patel's watchful evil eye, I've been having a terrific time. And Jake, wherever he is, now has all sorts of ideas for his next flick."

"I appreciate your saying that. I'm just very glad you didn't suffer any harm at his hands. Unlike Ray Decore. Dead in an alley over a piece of ivory. Bloody stupid."

I nodded. "I still don't know whether to tell Jeremy, my boss, that his friend Ray turned rotten during this jaunt to Bombay. Maybe it's best to let it go? Ray's dead. Nothing can be gained by destroying his memory."

"Very charitable of you, Tempe. You're a sweet girl. Anyone ever tell you that?"

"Thanks, I think. Brig. I have a question. Well, I have several, but mainly, why didn't you just hand the statue over to Claire once we had it?"

"She and Sachin were terrified when I told them about the cast of characters who were showing a keen interest in the Diva. None of whom would take no for an answer if the question was 'Can we get our hands on the goddess?' She relied on me to keep the statue safe."

Claire smiled at him as he continued.

"I had to prevent the thugs chasing our goddess from knowing the ultimate destination was Chaul. I couldn't simply deliver Shiva's Diva to Claire and send her back there. The way Mahindra and Patel, even Ray, were following and snatching people and all that, well, they'd've been on Claire, then Sachin in a flash. And it's a tiny village they're from. So we couldn't risk letting them take Saraswati home."

"Why risk it today? With Mahindra chasing us and kidnapping me and the last shoot-out at Hot Harry's?"

"I set things up with Claire early yesterday to come to take the Diva today. Ray was dead. I figured I could handle Patel by letting the cops know he'd killed Ray. I didn't know I'd end up in jail for that same thing. And I thought Mahindra would be chasing us anywhere but here."

Brig grinned. "I forgot to tell you, I waved at Seymour as I was leaving the pokey and he was coming in. I then turned and told a few of my new friends in enforced captivity that the man liked small children as more than a legacy to his name, if you get my drift. I knew there'd be no more interference from Patel."

He frowned. "I really hadn't counted on Mahindra snatching Tempe out here on the lot. Once I learned that Tempe had been kidnapped, I let that idiot pal of Mahindra's stand guard outside my door at the hotel while I snuck out and crawled down with the Diva. I hid it in the Jeep after calling Jake and

Asha to ask them to come help with a rescue. I figured Kirk wouldn't think of looking for the statue in Jake's vehicle."

I lightly caressed his hair. "And he didn't. Mahindra really thought you were being a good little boy and staying put till midnight at the hotel. Sleeping."

He stared at me with a look that melted my insides down to my toes. "He had no idea how true and deep my feelings were, and are, for you, Tempe. His mistake."

I reached for Brig's hand. "Okay. I've got the gist of this. But I still have a question."

"And that would be?"

"You've explained everything except what makes Claire the rightful heir."

Brig smiled. "She's a direct descendent of the Portuguese sculptor who carved the Diva in the first place and added the blessing and the curse five hundred years ago. Christopho Braganza was kin to Catherine of Braganza, who married King Charles the Second of England back in 1661 and presented Bombay to him as part of her dowry."

"Wow," I said.

"Wow," Asha said.

"Well put. Christopho aside, Claire and Sachin have another claim I like even better. They run a school in Chaul. They teach art, music, and acting to kids. Actually, that's mostly what Sachin does. Claire's been teaching sign language to the hearing impaired in the school. So, Shiva's Diva can finally come home and spread the gifts where they need them most."

Claire stood and smiled. In Portuguese she said, "As she did today. I am blessed again by Saraswati herself."

Chapter 43

Brig, Asha, and I stayed at the table for the next five hours. Two men in dark suits who flashed badges and ID at us at least ten times to prove they were indeed from Interpol, and not associates of Patel or Mahindra, took the permanently speechless Kirkee and his soggy male dancer wannabes away. They waited until Asha gathered up Sparky and Fluffy, the guardian snakes. By then, Mahindra seemed grateful to be in international police custody.

Claire hugged everyone, casually slung the tote bag with Shiva's Diva over her arm, then headed for her car. She paused just before leaving and turned to me. In Portuguese she told me to take care of the man. I assumed she meant Brig, which sounded fine to me.

She then said that she and Sachin would come to the States for a visit the first chance they had. She even winked and said they'd throw the Diva into a bag and bring her so we could see her again.

The cast of *Carnival of Lust* left for the day.

Asha, Brig, and I sat drinking more tea, debating whether we wanted to head into Bombay for dinner. Asha rose. "I've had it. This is nuts. I want to know where Jake disappeared to. He's missed all the action."

She shrieked as the man himself wrapped his arms around her and lifted her into the air.

"I'm right here. Sorry I couldn't join you earlier. But I had things to take care of, and I did *not* miss the action, Miss Kumar."

"What things? Where were you? Hell, Jake, you didn't even get to hear the whole explanation about Claire and Shiva's Diva and everything."

"I realize this. Brig will fill me in later."

He sank into a chair and gratefully accepted the cup of tea I handed him. "So? Not to echo Asha, but what happened to you, Mr. Roshan?"

A huge smile spread over his face. "I was standing on the crane lift while all that action Asha spoke of took place on the ground. I watched my sweet fiancée throwing snakes, dancers tapping around Mahindra's men in the fountain, Brig riding in on the elephant. I loved that great bit where Tempe came swinging down on the rope and knocked Mahindra off his feet. Magnificent. I caught every moment of it on film!"

We stared at him. He seemed oblivious to the looks.

"I have a new movie planned."

Asha sighed. "Might have known. After this one wraps and after our wedding, I hope. By the way, I've been thinking about that. I've decided I want to have the ceremony here after all. Mom and Dad need to visit. Perfect way to get them to India."

I nearly fell off my chair, but Jake nodded as if he'd always known this would be her choice. He turned to Brig. "Can you stay? Be my best man?"

Asha interrupted before Brig had a chance to speak. "Tempe's going to be my maid of honor if that makes any difference."

Brig smiled. He reached for my hand. "Well, yes and no. When do you plan to have the wedding?"

Jake thought for a second. "April. Right after *Carnival of Lust* is released." He smiled. "It's far less hot here in India that time of year."

Brig shook his head. "Well, then, Tempe will be Asha's *matron* of honor. Because, if my charm still works on the lass, I plan on her having a status change several months before that."

He knelt down on the ground in front of me. One knee.

"Will you marry me?"

For a moment, I thought Shiva's Diva had gone insane. She'd cursed and blessed me all at once. I was speechless and delirious with joy. When I finally found my voice, I could only utter one word. "Yes."

Brig helped me stand up from the table and held me. And kissed me. And kissed me a bit more.

My skills as a linguist had deserted me. Even when we came up for air, I kept repeating, "Yes. Oh yes!" Then I stared at my newly intended and thought of all the days and nights we'd be sharing until we both were very, very old.

Asha broke the silence since Brig and I were still too busy hugging and gazing into one another's eyes to be coherent about anything.

"You two have just proved something for me. I'd always heard love makes you stupid. I'm now witnessing exactly that."

Jake grabbed her and planted a firm kiss on her mouth. "I seem to remember a certain Miss Kumar and a Mr. Roshan spending no less than thirty minutes crying and hugging and one or the other asking, 'Is it true? We're engaged?' not that many months long ago. Right?"

I interrupted while Jake was keeping Asha quiet but happy. "I, personally, would rather be stupid and be loved than be brilliant, not loved, and lonely, thank you."

Brig nuzzled my neck. "You'll never be those latter two, lass. That I can promise you."

We kissed again, then I drew back for a second.

"Wait. One thing I need to ask. Yes, I love you and will proudly become Tempe O'Brien." I giggled. "That is so cool! Talk about dreams coming true."

Brig grinned at me. "So, what do you need to know?"

"Oh yeah. I almost forgot. Stupidity whacking me again. What exactly do you do for a living, O'Brien? I mean, do I need to fear Interpol coming back and throwing you into the pokey with Mahindra and friends for trafficking in hot merchandise?"

Brig shook his head. "I work for a firm called Restoration. We . . . well . . . we find lost items and things and we . . . well . . . we restore them to their rightful owners. Simple."

"Beg pardon?"

He laughed. "You're going to hit me. *Another* college buddy asked for help about ten years ago. He was searching for paintings that had been stolen from his grandparents during the Holocaust. The few leads he had led to Amsterdam. I trotted on over and I found the blighters. Both the paintings and the neo-Nazi spawn who had them."

I had a feeling there was a lot more to this than Brig paddling around the canals, then popping up with a Rembrandt or two in his pocket. Maybe someday the full story would seep out in polite conversation. Perhaps when my hair finally turned gray from old age and not horror.

"Yes? Go on."

"My buddy became my business partner. Actually, he funds Restoration. People like Claire and Sachin come to us for help in getting back pieces that have been stolen from them. No matter how long ago they were taken, it's still stinking thievery. I dislike people absconding with others' belongings. Hence the name Restoration."

"I guess that clears up a few things. Kind of." I paused. "Wait a second. I do have one other question."

Brig kissed me. "Anything."

"Who exactly is Saint Swithen?"

He assumed his brogue. "Swithen was a foin bishop plyin' his trade in the latter half of the first century, don't ya know. Legend has it, if it rains on Swithen's day in July, then it'll rain for the next forty days. Not a damn thing to do with the affair of Shiva's Diva, but I love his name. And ya know, the sun shone on the bishop's feast day this past July?"

"Where? Here in Bombay? During monsoon season?"

"Nope. Manhattan. I remember that day. July twelfth. The heat wave had broken but no rain. I'd just spied a red-haired beauty in a cream-colored blouse and jade earbobs juggling coffee cups on her way to an elevator in a building on the corner of forty-ninth and seventh."

"What?"

"Aye. Mind now, I didn't know 'twas you. But I did some talkin' with the good bishop and asked his help in arrangin' a meeting in honor of his own blessed day. And he did."

I blinked. "So you're saying Saint Swithen stuck me with you at Hot Harry's just because you made a request?"

"Yes."

I had no response for this other than to ignore him. My new intended who believed in Indian goddesses and first-century weather saints.

Funny. I remembered July twelfth. Two days after my birthday. I'd worn my cream-colored blouse and jade earrings that had been a birthday gift from my aunt Moira, another Irish-born American who adhered to the credo of the little people, rainbows, and all saints canonized before the seventeenth century.

"Got it. So. Any more fables, myths, or great Irish stories I need to know? And what were you doing in my building anyway? Assuming that was even me. I mean I."

"The diamond district is only a few blocks away. And, don't worry, I'll fill you in on the tales of my exploits with Restoration throughout the years. We have time. And don't imagine I'll leave you at home when I'm doing a job. Aside from not being able to be parted from you for more than an hour or so, you'll be an asset in the work."

I didn't ask why he was loitering in the diamond district. I didn't care. My thoughts were focused on the years of listening to Brig telling me about his adventures and making me part of his life.

Asha had not stopped beaming at us. Jake took a more practical stance. "I must ask this of you both. Would you be in my next movie? After all, I had to steal Tempe's passport to keep her here this past week. Do I need to do worse?"

My eyes nearly popped. "You took it? You? Why on earth?"

Jake snickered. He didn't seem the least sorry.

"Brig told me to. He didn't want you to hop aboard the fastest flight back to New York. And after I saw your dancing and those marvelous aerial tricks, I was very glad he convinced me to commit this slight misdemeanor so you would stay. Don't worry. I still have both the passport and your suitcase in my trailer."

I squinched my eyes at Brig. "What was this about not approving of stealing? Huh? What do you call sneaking into my hotel room and snatching my passport? And I thought you were trying to keep me safe?"

Brig didn't seem at all sorry either. "'Twas for a good cause, lass. For sartin. I knew I loved you the second I saw you come sashayin' into Hot Harry's Saloon. I hadn't been plannin' on Mahindra's bullets forcin' ya into me arms, but once you were there, I was determined ta keep ya. Forever and a day. I hoped that the heat generated between us would keep ya here, but just in case? I couldn't have ya hoppin' aboard a jet and out of me life, I swear. I had no idea you'd keep gettin' inta trouble now."

The man was incorrigible. I hoped Saint Swithen would help keep him exactly that way.

Jake continued as though the discussion about stolen passports hadn't just taken place. "I plan on using the footage I shot today, so you're already in the best scenes for the new movie. Yes?"

Brig had started kissing me again. We stopped long enough to turn and stare at Jake. He smiled.

"Tempe, luv? What do you think? Ready to be a star? I can see the posters now. *The Return of Shiva's Diva*, starring Asha Kumar, soon to also be Missus Jake Roshan, plus Briggan and Tempe O'Brien. All newlyweds. A great publicity move. And, of course, introducing Binky the heroic elephant. Jake might even have to bring back Spot the tiger and let both Tempe and Asha sing to her."

Asha brightened. "And Sparky the snake. Don't forget her. And her sister, Fluffy. I mean brother, I guess."

Brig sighed. "I was trying not to remember. If you must, Asha. Just keep them both a good ten yards away from me and I'll remove all elephants from your sight? Deal?"

Jake whooped. "You'll do it, then? Both of you? We can shoot on location at Hot Harry's and at the Taj Mahal Hotel. We'll film at the Flora Fountain. We can add a few scenes in the park with the animals. I'll even let Asha ride the llama if she wants. It will be magnificent."

All eyes turned to me. I rolled my shoulders in a pure dance isolation move. I fluttered my lashes.

"Oh heck. Why not? My mother will go nuts. In a good way. Let's see. First, I get married. That she won't really care about. I mean, she'll adore Brig and be pleased for us."

I paused to curl up solidly within the circle of the adored one's arms. "But the movie? Oh, lads and lassies. She'll be about shoutin', screamin', shriekin' proud, and ya'd best be believin' it. Because after all these many years, and after all the lessons? Finally, her darlin' daughter will be a star."

About the Author

Flo Fitzpatrick is a performer and choreographer, with a BFA in Dance and a Masters degree in Drama. She first attempted to write a novel at the age of eight, but was persuaded not to submit the piece by her brothers, who were skeptical that her characters were traveling across the Atlantic from New York to London—by train. A transplanted Texan, Flo currently lives in New Jersey with her husband, singer/actor Edmound Fitzpatrick, and their two Border Collie wannabes, Lucy and Huckleberry.

Visit Flo's website at www.flofitzpatrick.com.

Say Yes! To Sizzling Romance by
Lori Foster

__Too Much Temptation
0-7582-0431-0   **$6.99**US/**$9.99**CAN

Grace Jenkins feels too awkward and insecure to free the passionate woman inside her. But that hasn't stopped her from dreaming about Noah Harper. Gorgeous, strong and sexy, his rough edge beneath the polish promises no mercy in the bedroom. When Grace learns Noah's engagement has ended in scandal, she shyly offers him her support and her friendship. But Noah's looking for something extra . . .

__Never Too Much
0-7582-0087-0   **$6.99**US/**$9.99**CAN

A confirmed bachelor, Ben Badwin has had his share of women, and he likes them as wild and uninhibited as his desires. Nothing at all like the brash, wholesomely cute woman who just strutted into his diner. But something about Sierra Murphy's independent attitude makes Ben's fantasies run wild. He'd love to dazzle her with his sensual skills . . . to make her want him as badly as he suddenly wants her . . .

__Say No to Joe?
0-8217-7512-X   **$6.99**US/**$9.99**CAN

Joe Winston can have any woman—except the one he really wants. Secretly, Luna Clark may lust after Joe, but she's made it clear that she's too smart to fall for him. He can just keep holding his breath, thank you very much. But now, Luna's inherited two kids who need more than she alone can give in a small town that seems hell-bent on driving them away. She needs someone to help out . . . someone who can't be intimidated . . . someone just like Joe.

__When Bruce Met Cyn
0-8217-7513-8   **$6.99**US/**$9.99**CAN

Compassionate and kind, Bruce Kelly understands that everyone makes mistakes, even if he's never actually done anything but color inside the lines. Nobody's perfect, but Bruce is about to meet a woman who's perfect for him. He's determined to show her that he can be trusted. And if that means proving it by being the absolute gentleman at all times, then so be it. No matter how many cold showers it takes . . .

Available Wherever Books Are Sold!

Visit our website at **www.kensingtonbooks.com**.